THE KEEP

THE SECRET OF SPELLSHADOW MANOR
— 4 —

BELLA FORREST

THE
KEEP

THE SECRET OF
SPELLSHADOW MANOR
4

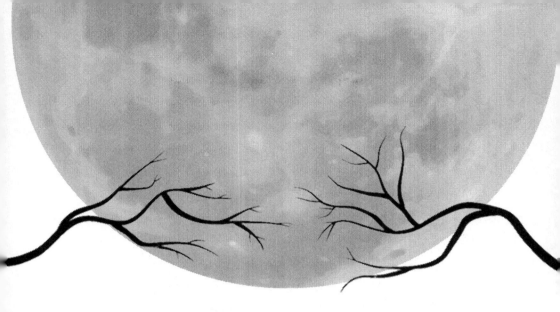

CHAPTER I

A
LEX STARED IN SHOCK AS PROFESSOR LINTZ EMERGED
from the hallway, stepping into the light of the
courtyard. The professor grinned as he caught sight
of his former students, his moustache twitching upward. It was
strange to see him out of his usual professor's robes; he was
now clad in muted, gray attire that looked oddly formal, like a
uniform of some sort, with shiny brass buttons and a high, stiff
collar. An emblem resembling a small castle was emblazoned
on the pocket.

Alex wondered how it was that the professor had come
to be here. They had thought him dead, and seeing him alive
and kicking was a much-needed dose of positivity. Still, Alex
couldn't get one thought out of his mind: *If Lintz was here,
then what did that mean for the state of Spellshadow Manor?* He

was about to ask, when Lintz cut in.

"Welcome, my dear creatures, to Kingstone Keep!" the professor boomed, moving toward the group. He reached out to shake Alex's hand. "Good to see you, boy! Glad you could finally make it. It's such a pleasure to see you all!"

As happy as Lintz seemed, Alex detected a hint of agitation in the old man's eyes. In between welcoming the others and doling out firm handshakes, his gaze flickered toward the moss-covered wall, where the portal to Stillwater had just disappeared.

It seemed the professor shared Alex's anxiety where Alypia was concerned. The portal was gone, but for how long, Alex had no idea; he could only hope the damage done by the golden beasts, forged from the life essence of his pilfered bottles, was enough to keep the vengeful Headmistress at bay—at least for a short while.

"Professor, how can you be here?" Alex asked.

"We thought we lost you!" Natalie added.

"Not lost at all, my dears, simply displaced. With the Head back in charge, it was stay and die or run and live… It is a treat to my old eyes to see you all in one piece, and I will tell you all you want to know in good time, I promise. But, for now, we must be on our way," Lintz insisted, checking an invisible watch on his wrist. "The prisoners will be waking up soon, and I'd like you to have as little contact with them as possible." He urged them away from the courtyard, with its tall, imposing walls, and pushed them toward the shadows of the hallway he had emerged from moments before.

Alex paused in alarm as another figure appeared in the

corridor, blocking their way. Then his lips curved into a smile as he realized who it was. Master Demeter.

"Alex! Well, well, you can lead a horse to water, but you cannot make it swim," Demeter chortled. The others looked toward Alex in bemusement, but Alex had no clue how to describe the unique nature of Master Demeter; he was a person to be experienced, not explained. "It's so lovely to meet you all. I've heard so much—all of it good, worry not."

The auburn-haired man seemed anxious, as if waiting for instruction from Lintz. When Lintz nodded insistently, Demeter gestured toward the corridor with a flamboyant wave of his arms.

"Follow me. You're very welcome at Kingstone Keep, but make sure you wipe your feet. Wouldn't want you traipsing any dirt in," Demeter smirked as he led the others into the keep itself, which looked less than pristine, with its grimy walls and slick floor.

Alex noticed that Demeter was dressed in the same gray uniform that Lintz wore, and wondered about its significance. Demeter's presence here filled Alex with a multitude of questions.

Glancing back, Alex spotted Lintz flitting about the courtyard. From a battered leather bag, Lintz pulled two large, beetle-like clockwork objects and affixed them to the wall. He pressed his palms to the sleek metallic carapaces of the beetles and began to layer his glimmering magic into them. The beetles sparked to life with a ripple of golden light and scuttled along the damp masonry, their clockwork legs moving swiftly. They were beautifully crafted, as all of Lintz's clockwork was, but Alex wasn't sure of their purpose. Every so often, the beetles would stop, their glinting silver antennae twitching, before moving on again in an apparently random fashion. Alex had stalled, mesmerized.

"Alex! You're dopey today," Demeter called. "Hurry up!"

"Sorry," Alex muttered as he ducked into the corridor and joined the others. They were looking at him with a mixture of amusement and confusion.

"Demeter's quite the joker," whispered Jari.

"He is," Alex replied quietly, "though his jokes don't always land."

"Understatement of the century," Jari breathed.

"How do you two know each other?" asked Natalie, gesturing to Demeter.

"He was the teacher I was telling you about. The only one I had at Stillwater," Alex explained, raising his voice.

Demeter nodded. "Indeed, Alex is the first student I've had in a long time. Like a sponge, this one, soaking everything up. Knowledge is next to godliness, after all," he enthused, with an ill-executed wink that looked more like a slow, uncoordinated blink. It made Alex and the others smile in spite of themselves. It was hard not to warm to Demeter.

"Come on! We need to hurry," said Lintz, his chest heaving as he caught up with them, despite the short distance.

His manner definitely more agitated now, Lintz led the group through a series of grim hallways barely lit by the flicker of rusted torches. Behind the narrow grates in the center of the moldering, wooden doors that lined the corridors, Alex was certain he could see the glitter of black, silent eyes, watching them pass by. The rooms appeared to be cells, the doors locked. On more than one occasion, he thought he heard a whisper, or the sound of something scraping the wood from beyond the doorways, and the hairs on the back of his neck prickled in defense. There was a sour, ancient smell to the place; it seemed to loom around them, the scent so thick and overwhelming it was almost tangible. It made Alex uneasy, and he saw the others seemed to share his feelings, as they glanced about anxiously, pinching their noses against the stench.

Feeling the urge to distract himself from the dark labyrinth that surrounded them, Alex moved up to walk beside Lintz.

"How do you know Master Demeter?" he asked.

"Ah, a fine man indeed. It was something of a serendipitous meeting," began Lintz with a sigh. "He's been feeding information back to me from Stillwater since I escaped here from Spellshadow, so I could make sure you were all okay. He's a talented fellow, to say the least, with a useful skillset. He's been most helpful in keeping an eye on all of you. My inside man, if you like—or he was, until he got himself sent back here."

Demeter shrugged. "Once a rebel, always a rebel. My teaching always seems to end with a dismissal," he murmured, though there was a hint of amusement in his voice. "I'm like a monkey, mind you—I always land on my feet."

Although Alex was curious about what had caused the auburn-haired man to be sent back, a hundred other questions whirled inside his head.

"What's with the uniforms?" he asked, pointing at the identical gray clothes the two men wore.

"Guards," said Lintz simply, gesturing toward himself.

"You're *guards* here?"

Lintz nodded. "In a manner of speaking. There haven't been any others wandering these halls for a while, so we thought we'd step up and pretend to be freshly employed sentries—rather successfully, I might add. The other guards pretty much keep themselves permanently occupied in their private quarters, after Demeter…encouraged them to do so. They were crueler than Demeter liked, and we decided it might be easier with just the two of us. Less to worry about." A hint of a wink passed between the two apparent friends. "Demeter was already a guard when I arrived, and he found a way to get me promoted. I was in charge while he had his brief sojourn in Stillwater House though, I'll have you know." He grinned.

"I just gave him a uniform and he ran with it," Demeter chuckled. "It's been the two of us ever since, aside from my short vacation." A half-amused, half-serious look darkened the ex-teacher's face.

"So, this place is a prison?" Alex asked, wanting to confirm his suspicions.

"Precisely. This place is teeming with fearsome mages. The ones who disobey, the ones who are too powerful, the ones who don't abide by the status quo, the ones who run away—they're all here," replied Lintz, gesturing to the walls around them. "All this is ruled by a warden called Caius. Another royal, though this one is a real nasty piece of work—you haven't seen anything until you've witnessed what Caius can do."

"Who is he exactly?" Alex asked.

"He's the uncle of Alypia and the Head of Spellshadow. He

rarely bothers to show his face around here due to a limp in his leg, but one shouldn't underestimate him. A very dangerous man I sincerely hope you never have to meet. I'll endeavor to keep you all hidden from him, until I can get you out." A quiver of fear hovered in Lintz's voice.

If even Lintz is afraid of this man, how much of a monster must this Caius be?

Looking around, his brow furrowed, Alex questioned why there was so little in the way of security, if this place was full of magical prisoners. Lintz had spoken of a small number of other guards tucked away in their private quarters—they must *really* have been keeping themselves to themselves, because Alex and his friends hadn't passed any, and they had been walking for a while. Though there was no mistaking the eyes of the countless individuals peering at them from the locked cells of countless corridors, giving Alex the sense of a large number of inmates… definitely more than would be expected with such minimal security. It didn't make sense to him, unless this Caius figure truly was a force to be reckoned with, so powerful and fearsome that even hardened criminals were afraid of him. The thought unnerved Alex.

"Why are there—"

Lintz raised his finger to his lips, sharply cutting Alex off.

"This isn't the time for questions. I'll explain everything once we're away from listening ears," Lintz hissed.

Alex's heart pounded as the group walked through a broader hallway, with a few doors off to either side. The whisper of threatening voices susurrated around them.

"Why don't you come over here and let me get a closer

look?" a deep voice cackled.

"Fresh meat!" another growled, followed closely by the sound of lips smacking.

"Open the door... I'm innocent... Please open the door... I'm so scared here in the dark," begged a third—somehow more alarming than the other two. This voice was soft and sad, almost feminine, as enticing as the mythological sirens calling sailors to their deaths.

Alex tried to ignore the sounds, hoping the doors were strong enough to hold back whoever—or whatever—lived inside. Turning to his friends, he saw the same fear on their faces as they tried to keep as far away from the doors as possible, their eyes staring dead ahead at the dark depths of Kingstone Keep, hoping their journey would soon end.

Lintz led them for what felt like forever. No matter how quiet they were, it appeared as if the inmates could *smell* them, the group's presence drawing the prisoners to the grates. There was real evil within these walls—Alex could sense it.

He guessed this must be the place Helena said people were "sent to" if they didn't follow the rules. It saddened him to think there were young people in here too, locked up in the darkness, their freedom snatched away, forced to live alongside truly vile individuals who deserved the chains they wore.

Finally, just as Alex thought his nerves couldn't take any more, Lintz stopped them at the edge of a wide, bright common room. The walls were pale and dry, and sunlight shone on the flagstones. It would have been close to pleasant, had it not been eerily empty.

A sudden wave of nausea crashed over Alex, and a

stabbing pain coursed through him. Wincing, he pressed his hand against the stone wall to steady himself, dragging air into his lungs, his vision growing spotty.

What's happening to me? he wanted to scream. Underneath his palm, he felt an intense pulse of power. His anti-magic escaped, unbidden, from between his fingers and snaked into the wall, seeking out the source of the thrumming energy as snowflakes flurried from beneath his skin and drifted to the ground.

Turning back to the group, Alex saw the blood drain from Lintz's face.

"Alex? Oh no, no—" Lintz stuttered. The professor looked toward the walls, which had suddenly begun to glow with a bright red light. The stone crackled, and something almost liquid emerged from within.

It was too late to run. The red fog surged toward the group in undulating waves. Lintz opened his mouth, as if to warn them, but the fog lunged toward him and poured itself down his throat, silencing his words.

Alex watched, horrified, as the fog swarmed around his friends, soaking into their skin, rushing into their eyes, flooding their nostrils and mouths, making their bodies shudder. He didn't know what to do, so he just stood there, holding his breath.

Once the fog had faded away, returning to the stone, Alex glanced at each one of his friends in turn. Their bodies were no longer shaking. Sighing with relief, he hoped the fog had only been some kind of warning.

Then, the screaming began.

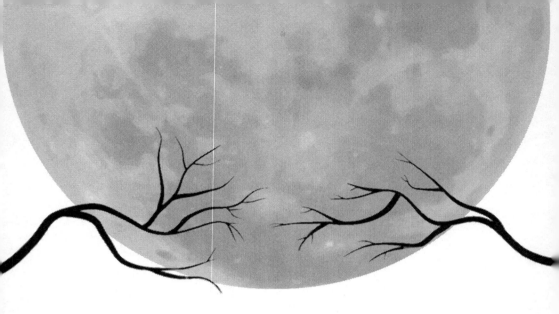

CHAPTER 2

THE WHOLE PRISON ERUPTED IN SHRIEKS THAT MADE the very walls tremble. Alex gaped as the faces of his friends distorted into all manner of terrifying masks, their eyes flashing wildly, like those of spooked horses. They looked like changelings—twisted versions of themselves.

Panicking, Alex moved toward Ellabell, who seemed frozen to the spot, rooted by a paralyzing fear. Hoping to calm her, he reached out to grasp her hand. She whipped toward him and screamed directly in his face, clawing at his neck like a savage animal. When he tried to grab her by the shoulders, she howled, snapping her teeth at him. With the way her eyes darted around, like there were creatures all around her, Alex knew she wasn't seeing him as he was. Whatever it was she saw, fear was driving her to fight back.

Alex skirted Ellabell's frantic blows and retreated to the center of the room, breathing hard. His gaze trailed over to Jari, who was crouched and huddled in a corner, his hands over his ears as he mouthed silent words: *"Go away. Please, go away."*

On the other side of the room, Natalie was staring blankly at one particular section of the common area, tears brimming in her dark eyes, a look of utter despair on her face. She raised a hand in the direction of whatever she was looking at, as if trying to reach out and touch it. Her eyes widened and she let out a harrowing shriek.

On the floor, Aamir was trying to physically fight something off, side-stepping and falling backward beneath the movements of some invisible demon. Lintz wept openly in the center of the room, whispering something that sounded a lot like "Derhin," before collapsing in a heap, where he twisted and turned, as if consumed by fire.

Everywhere Alex looked, his friends and mentors were fending off unseen horrors, and he had never felt so helpless.

The only one who seemed to be mentally battling the illusions was Demeter, who was standing still against the far wall, his fists balled so tightly that his knuckles had turned a stark white.

"This isn't real, this isn't real, this isn't real," Demeter intoned, over and over again.

Alex couldn't watch anymore. Running toward Ellabell again earned him a smack to the face and several keenly placed punches to the body, but he had an idea he hoped would work. He took a vicious scratch to the neck but managed to grab her wrists, feeding his anti-magic up her arms, focusing his mind to find the errant strands of fog that had taken hold inside her, before dissipating each one. Once they had all evaporated, he ran to the others, avoiding their flailing arms and hoping their deafening screams wouldn't implode his eardrums as he fed his anti-magic through their bodies, forcing the wispy strands of red fog away.

The excessive use of anti-magic left him shaky. His weakened state was no surprise, really, considering that he had removed a small piece of his soul during the fight against Alypia. He was mostly running on adrenaline now, but he soldiered on, sweating profusely as his muscles ached and his lungs burned, bringing his friends back to reality one by one. Absorbing the fog made his skin crawl, but it didn't seem to affect him the way it had the others. His Spellbreaker qualities, he assumed, were acting as a buffer, preventing the fog from seeking him out and putting its spell upon him.

After he had dissipated the last of the red strands, Alex sank to the ground, exhausted. The rest of the prison still echoed with screams from the other residents, the sounds burning into Alex's mind.

Lintz was the first to rally the group. "With me!" he insisted, running for one of the doors.

They all followed, Alex falling behind, helped along by Aamir and Ellabell. Lintz hurried them out of the common room and through a door on the far side, entering a smaller, circular room that seemed to be inside a large tower of some sort. Lintz quickly urged them up a set of stairs to another room, above the first.

Stepping through the door to this final sanctuary, Alex noticed how quiet it was—the screaming was almost inaudible here.

Glancing around, he could see everyone was shaken by what had just happened, but he was too weak to offer more than a cursory look of empathy. His body was on the edge of collapse. Aamir helped Alex over to a moth-eaten chaise longue, where he settled him onto the dusty cushions.

"You okay?" Aamir asked, his dark eyebrows furrowing.

"I will be," Alex breathed. "I-I just need a minute."

Ellabell came to his side. "What you did back there—that was incredible… Are you *sure* you're all right?"

"Just need to catch my breath," Alex insisted, but no one looked convinced. The faces staring back at him were pale and uncertain. Even Lintz looked shaken as he settled in an armchair across the room, a plume of dust rising as he sank onto the ancient upholstery.

"What *was* that red fog, anyway?" Natalie asked, turning to the professors.

A regretful expression fell across Lintz's face. "A security measure, put in place by Caius to keep the inmates in order. Magic is woven throughout the keep's walls, and it can spring at any moment, though it's usually in response to something it doesn't like—something it's threatened by," he admitted, turning to Alex. "Sorry I didn't inform you earlier. I didn't know your anti-magic would react in such a way."

"So this is why there aren't many guards on duty," concluded Alex, still trying to regulate his breathing.

"Yup," Lintz replied grimly. "Why have guards when you

can have terrifying, mind-altering magic? Most of the mages could overthrow any guard you threw their way. Caius's evil measures keep everyone in line—there isn't a mage here who isn't afraid of him and his Pandora's box of tricks. They come in all kinds of dark and shocking forms, using methods of torture you couldn't even imagine. Nobody is safe, not even the guards… as you saw."

"It's in the walls? Like barrier magic?" asked Alex.

"It's everywhere in the keep."

The barrier at Spellshadow had been seemingly impenetrable, so it was no surprise to Alex that Kingstone was no different. Still, he wondered at the barrier's strength. Ignoring the gasp of alarm from the others, Alex reached out to touch the wall behind him. He was careful not to let his anti-magic escape from beneath his skin, though he could feel the impulse to retaliate blistering inside him as he pressed his palm against the stone. Whatever the barrier magic was made from, it was far stronger than the barrier around Spellshadow; he could feel it actively pushing against him. He could well believe it would zap back if it didn't like what it felt, and Alex had provoked it in some way.

As if reading Alex's mind, Lintz gestured toward him. "You must have done something it really didn't like, for it to react that intensely. The 'nightmare fog,' as we like to call it, is a rarer evil in Caius's armory—one we try to avoid at all costs."

"I didn't realize I was doing it," Alex said, rubbing at his neck.

"How'd these prisoners get here, anyway?" Jari asked, his hazel eyes wide as he looked from Lintz to Demeter. "They must have done something really nasty to end up in a place like this."

"It varies," Demeter murmured. "Some are the vilest criminals you could ever come across, while some are simply here because they did something the royals and the nobles didn't like. Either way, they all have a death sentence."

Alex frowned. "What do you mean?"

"Every prison sentence is a death sentence here," Lintz explained. "At the end of a sentence, be it three years or a hundred years, Caius comes to remove the prisoner's life essence and bottles it for further use."

"Like at the schools," Aamir said quietly.

"Yes," Lintz replied, "only this essence is matured to such a point that it is the most potent of all the havens—really strong stuff. Here, it is quality over quantity."

"But how could someone be in here for one hundred years? That is ridiculous," stated Natalie, her expression incredulous.

"Well, magic does things to a person," said Demeter. "It can extend the life of a mage long past what would be considered natural in the outside world, especially for very powerful mages. Take Caius, for example—he is known to be several hundred years old, and he's not the only one to reach such lofty years. Some of the essence collected here is extremely old and, as a result, extraordinarily strong."

Alex let the information sink in, his mind racing with questions. He wondered if that meant Caius was alive during the Spellbreaker battles, and what that meant for Alypia and the Head—how old did that make them? His curiosity was in overdrive, but he could also feel the cold, sluggish creep of exhaustion working its way through his bones.

There was one question he felt compelled to get off his chest, however.

"So are the Stillwater students here too? The ones who tried to run?" he asked, remembering Helena's words again.

Demeter gave a heavy-hearted sigh. "They are, but you won't find them in a good state. Despite my best efforts in my time here, I haven't been able to prevent a single one from losing their mind. This place has a terrible effect on the young and hopeful; it steals their souls as well as their sanity. The keep is particularly cruel to those who don't deserve to be here."

"They can't be helped?" Alex pressed.

Demeter shook his head. "Believe me, I've tried. Some seem fine for a while, but then their sanity simply leaves. It can take days, weeks, months, years, but every single one crumbles the same way. It's like a disease—it starts slow, with secret whispers. Then the scrape of nails on the wall. Then their eyes go wild and their howls fill the air, and they become something more animal than human. I can't stop it—they are lost to me, once the madness takes them."

It shook Alex to think there was nothing to be done for those students who had been brought here from Stillwater House, especially as their assistance would have been appreciated, and he could have tried to repay them with true freedom, one day. But, if what Demeter said was true, they were lost for good.

A dread-tinged silence filled the room.

"So, you promised you'd tell us how you both ended up here," Jari said, breaking the tension as he lay on the floor, propping himself up on his elbows.

"Ah, an excellent story. Well, this fine gentleman found me sprawled on my caboose after bounding through an ill-placed portal, following quite the hair-raising journey," chuckled Lintz, nudging Demeter in the arm. "I'd had a rough time after high-tailing it from Spellshadow, once that devilish little weakling returned with his gang of cronies, and that darned other place wasn't much friendlier. I barely got out in one piece!"

Alex assumed "that darned other place" was the mysterious fourth haven, Falleaf House. In his mind, the four havens were connected in a sort of ring, so it made sense that the next one along, the one between here and Spellshadow, should be the undiscovered realm of Falleaf. However, it didn't quite sound like the sanctuary Alex was hoping to find. He wondered whether or not he'd ever get to see what Falleaf had to offer—and whether he even wanted to. Kingstone would have to serve as their escape route for now.

I suppose it's better the devil you know, he mused.

"So after giving him a guard's uniform, I made it so it was just the two of us on duty, so nobody suspected he hadn't always been here. Our job is easy thanks to the barrier magic," the auburn-haired man piped up. "I, on the other hand, was a former teacher at Stillwater, but I got sent here a long time ago for telling one too many Spellbreaker stories to my students… There were complaints."

"Phooey! Your stories are wonderful," insisted Lintz.

"Very kind of you. Alas, fortune favors the ignorant," Demeter quipped. "Then, they have the audacity to waltz back through here, asking after me, wanting me to teach a student again. Naturally, I got on my high hat and said, 'Not a chance,' but then—"

"But I persuaded him otherwise. I had a feeling it was you, Alex, and I asked if Demeter here wouldn't mind keeping an eye on you all, to make sure you were safe." Lintz smiled encouragingly.

"Oh goodness, I was thrilled to be meeting a real-life Spellbreaker—if they'd led with that, I'd have been over there like a bullet, but it was Lintz here who told me what you were and who you were. And I have to say, you met my expectations and then some!" Demeter gushed.

Alex hardly thought himself worthy of that accolade. All he'd done in his lessons with Demeter was encourage the teacher to keep speaking so he wouldn't have to do any actual work.

"Mind you, I made him promise to get you all out if anything bad happened," Lintz added.

"Yes, then I was sent back for not toeing the line," said Demeter, nodding to Lintz. "Alypia thought I was up to my old tricks…"

"Gosh, yes, quite the wrench in the works!"

"Fortunately, you seemed to have that all in your fingers, didn't you, Alex?" said Demeter.

Alex wondered if Demeter's dismissal had something to do with the reason he was being disciplined when Alex had caught sight of him in the windowless study room. He made a mental note to ask him about it later, in private.

"I'm not sure I had it quite in hand, but we got out." Alex shrugged, subtly correcting Demeter's phrasing.

"Ah, speaking of getting out, we need to get you all out of the magical realm as soon as possible," announced Lintz. "It's the only place you'll be safe—"

"And we're going to help," Demeter said.

The group exchanged dubious glances.

"How?" asked Alex, staring at the two men.

Lintz met the eyes of each of his former students. "With a portal to the outside world."

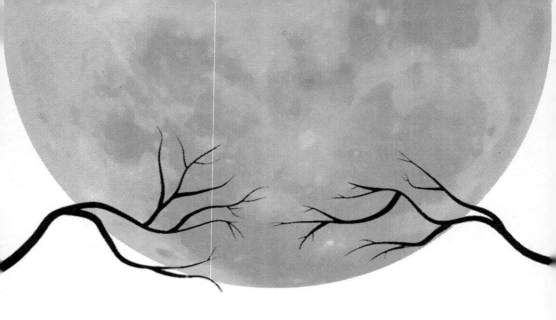

CHAPTER 3

THE IDEA OF CREATING A PORTAL HAD BEEN ON ALEX'S mind for a long time now, but they'd never had the opportunity to put that plan into action—or even figure out where to start.

After a dumbfounded silence, Natalie was the first to speak. "You… know how to build one?"

"A dear friend of mine happened to have a book on the subject, stashed away," Demeter said. "Lintz and I had been studying it in preparation for your arrival."

Lintz twirled his moustache thoughtfully. "It will be a difficult task, as portal-building usually is, made all the more complex by the fact that we're starting from scratch. But with all of you here, we should be able to make it a success. Though, I should warn you that this type of portal requires one of two things—either a great deal of time and energy, or a great deal of essence."

"Is this enough?" Alex asked, holding up the satchel he still wore over his shoulder. Carefully, he lifted the flap to show Lintz the smoky, black glass bottles and their pulsing red contents. Lintz gaped, moving toward the bag for a closer look. The shock on Lintz's face remained as he let his chubby fingers trail across some of the bottles.

"Goodness… Are these from Stillwater?" Lintz asked breathlessly.

"Straight from Alypia's study. Will it work?" Alex asked, more insistently.

Lintz sighed. "It will certainly help… but a portal to the real world takes an enormous amount of essence, given that you are essentially tearing a hole in the fabric of reality. Building one to another magical place is child's play by comparison, as you are using an already established network and simply opening an old wound instead of creating a fresh cut… The quantity of essence in this satchel is not enough. With all your help, I believe it can be built, but it will take six months at the very least." He shook his head, continuing to twist his moustache in contemplation.

Six months. That was out of the question, especially with Alypia at their heels.

"We need to speed up the process. We need more essence," Alex said, glancing at his friends, who stood anxiously around him.

Lintz frowned. "Indeed, but it's not possible to obtain more."

"But you mentioned there was essence here at Kingstone? From the prisoners?" Natalie asked. "If what you said is true, it will be stronger than any we have come across."

"Locating the essence will be no easy task, and Caius is *not* someone to mess with," Lintz said. "The risks are too great."

"The keep is riddled with booby traps and obstacles of all kinds, conjured from the darkest depths of a cruel mind, no doubt to prevent such snooping," Demeter chimed in.

"It's why I would never ask such a thing of you all," Lintz concluded solemnly. "I don't want you getting into needless danger, though I know you attract it like honey does flies," he said with a grimace, half-amused, half-serious.

"But we *have* to get the portal built," Alex pressed, trying to rally his friends to the cause. They looked to Lintz for a reply. "We don't have any other options, Professor."

"There will be no point in building a portal home if there are none of you left to go through it, having been skewered by giant magic spears or fried in a supernatural blaze or eaten alive by golden beasts or something equally vile, which is what would happen if I let you go hunting for the essence in this prison. Caius won't allow you to find it, and I don't want to risk you trying."

"The risk is ours, Professor," Alex replied firmly, "and you can either help us or hinder us. You two know this place better than any of us, and we could really use your help in mapping it out, to stand the best chance of finding the stuff." Alex leveled his gaze at Lintz, then Demeter. He couldn't gauge the latter's feelings, his eyes giving nothing away. "Either way, we have to go looking for it. Am I right?" Crossing his arms, he turned to the others, expecting to hear their agreement. Their collective nod reassured him; this was happening whether Lintz liked it or not.

There was a moment of tense silence as they waited for Lintz's response.

"You know he's right, Lintz," Demeter muttered. "If we don't help, they'll only end up dead, or worse… What other option do we have?"

Lintz groaned. "I see I am outnumbered…"

Alex let out a breath. "Thank you, Professor."

"You won't regret this," Natalie added.

"Oh, but I fear I shall," the professor mumbled. "Well… If we *are* going to look for the essence, we should get more hands on deck. Tomorrow, we can swing by a few old friends of Demeter's before we head into a whole world of danger. They'll be able to help lessen the collateral damage, I hope." There was a note of vexation in the old man's voice.

"There's also Alypia to think of," Aamir said grimly. "We have to keep her at bay until we find the essence and ready the portal."

"There must be something we can do to prevent her from breaking through," Ellabell spoke up, nervously adjusting the spectacles over her nose. "At least for a little while—to buy us more time."

"That's where my beetles come in," Lintz replied, pulling one from his satchel to show the group. "They work like beacons, showing me where a portal is trying to break through, so I can run and close it before it fully opens. The only problem is they won't work forever—they need new magic poured into them after every use. But they should come in handy." He paused. "Now that I think of it, you may have to help me with that little problem too—keeping the portals from opening, and filling my beetles with magic as they deplete. It won't be easy, when combined with the task of mapping out the keep and avoiding Caius's traps. Caius himself is a rare sight at the keep, so hopefully we won't have to meet him along the way. But his traps are most prevalent... and the keep is huge." He grimaced, evidently realizing the enormity of the work that lay ahead.

It worried Alex too, making him wonder whether they had the required power to juggle so many taxing things at once. He wanted to get a closer look at the clockwork beetle, to see how it worked, but as he tried to stand, a wave of nausea crashed over him again, forcing him back down onto the dusty seat.

"We'll have to take it in turns," said Alex, sinking into the chair. "If possible, we work in groups. One group fills the beetles and stops the portals, while the other maps out the keep in search of the essence."

All around the room, he was met with nods and noises of agreement.

"It's settled then. We begin at dawn," Lintz replied. "But for now, you should all rest."

Alex was glad of the instruction. Even if he hadn't been missing a piece of his soul, he knew dealing with the red fog would have taken its toll on him. His body was trying to recover from the fight against Alypia, and every time he did something that drained his energy, he knew he was taking a step back in the healing process. An acute exhaustion trickled through his system, unlike any tiredness Alex had ever known;

it was almost as if the very weight of his body had become too much and was beginning to crush him from the inside.

It's nothing a good sleep won't fix, he told himself, repeating the mantra to prevent fear from creeping in. In truth, he had no idea what kind of pressure he was putting his body under, or what the consequences might be in the long term.

"I need some air," he croaked, his eyes glancing toward the far window.

With Aamir's help, Alex rose and stepped toward it. His burning lungs were desperate for some fresh oxygen, and his eyes longed for the sight of something that wasn't hewn from hefty gray stone. However, as he reached the windowsill, he saw that the landscape beyond was blurred from sight behind a veil of shimmering bronze fog. He could make out vague shapes on the horizon—the hint of trees, perhaps the point of a mountain—but nothing solid. It was all a haze, no doubt intended to keep morale low. How could the prisoners hope, when they had no outside reference to remind them of why they kept living? Without sky and trees and sunshine, the world became very small and very bleak.

Alex tried not to let the disappointing view get to him as he attempted to drag wisps of crisp oxygen into his lungs, filtered through the bronze fog. When he focused all his attention on breathing, needing the pureness of real air, it made him feel suddenly panicky, like he was trying to breathe through a straw filled with cotton wool. If he hadn't been conscious of Aamir's hand upon his arm, he knew he might have allowed the penetrating fear to take hold of him. As it was, Aamir's presence calmed him somewhat, reminding him that he still had his friends to fight for, even if he couldn't see the trees and the sky that might give him renewed hope. Someday, he would look upon the real sky again, the one drifting aimlessly above his hometown, and that would be worth everything.

Across the room, he heard Natalie and Ellabell begin to share all that had happened at Stillwater with the professors in hushed tones, with Jari chiming in where he saw fit. Alex paused, not wanting to disturb their chat, though part of him wanted to go to where they were congregated and encourage them to talk about the illusions they had seen while under the hold of the nightmare fog. No one had seemed eager to discuss it, and Alex didn't want to pry, not when the group's mood had only just returned to some semblance of normalcy. Suddenly, he heard the name "Gaze" mentioned in somber tones and saw Lintz's face fall; it was more sadness than Alex could take.

He turned back around, his attention distracted a moment later by the sound of a splash. Peering curiously over the edge of the windowsill, he saw that there was murky water below, running in a kind of moat around the keep itself, but he couldn't make out the shape of the thing that had made the loud splash. Whatever it was, it was big, the ripples it had made continuing to undulate outward before bumping against the steep, muddy bank. He watched the still moat closely, wondering if the creature might emerge again. For a moment, he thought he saw a vast shadowy form moving beneath the surface, but it disappeared as quickly as it had appeared.

He let his exhausted eyes wash over the hazy fog again, and the blurry shapes of trees behind it, and, beyond that, the possibility of a mountain peeking up on the distant horizon.

He closed his eyes, imagining that the real world lay just beyond those imagined peaks.

He turned again as Lintz and Demeter moved toward the door of the tower, saying their farewells. The professor toyed with his moustache anxiously, his face a picture of grief. Alex understood; it couldn't have been easy to hear the fate of a much-beloved friend. Guard duty called the two older men back into the depths of the keep again, and they had to heed it, checking the prison for any escapees, locking all the doors that needed locking, keeping everything in order.

As soon as they had departed, Alex was suddenly overwhelmed with prickles of irritation, which flared inside him and spread like wildfire, clawing under his skin. He struggled to suppress the annoyance that had emerged so unexpectedly, breathing heavily to try to calm his piqued emotions. It didn't make sense for him to feel something so violently, so quickly. Perhaps it had something to do with the barrier and its crackling, livid magic.

Then claustrophobia washed over him just as suddenly, and his chest felt like it was constricting, his throat tightening. The stabbing pain inside his body came back with a vengeance, pulsing through his nerves like a white-hot blade, and it was as if the walls were closing in on him.

He stood quickly, wanting to escape the room, but his body had other ideas. The pain made his vision go blurry for a moment, his knees buckling as he crumpled to the floor. Natalie reached out to catch him, her reflexes lightning fast, setting him on his feet again. Hurriedly, he scrambled to regain his balance, pushing away from her in an attempt to stop his unruly anti-magic from running through his hands and into her skin. He didn't want his uncontrolled emotions to hurt any of those around him.

"Are you okay, Alex?" she asked, but Alex was looking at the other two now, who were also eyeing him strangely.

He didn't know if he was just being paranoid, his fears fed by the barrier, but suddenly everyone's eyes seemed to be on him and he didn't like the feel of them burning intensely into his flesh, judging him, scrutinizing him, assessing him. He'd had enough.

"No, I'm not," he panted. "I-I have to go. Don't follow me." With that, he rushed from the tower room and headed toward the door of a guard room that lay adjacent to it.

Reaching the guards' quarters, he lay down on one of the makeshift beds and hoped sleep would come quickly, only to sit bolt upright a moment later as he heard the door open. Natalie walked in. She looked concerned, and Alex was paradoxically both annoyed and relieved that she had followed him. At least she had come alone. He wasn't sure he could handle more than one person at a time right now.

She sat on the chair next to him. "What's wrong, Alex? You're acting really strangely."

"I just… haven't been feeling very well," he said.

"It is more than that, I can tell," she pressed, narrowing her dark eyes. "We've been through so much—you can tell me anything, and I will not judge you for it, as you have tried not to judge me when I have strayed off the path a bit."

He exhaled, closing his eyes. "Fine," he grated out. "There's a reason I'm not feeling well. I feel all… twisted up inside, and being in this place isn't helping."

"Why do think you feel this way?" she asked, sounding like a psychiatrist. It irked Alex, despite himself.

"Something happened at Stillwater, and it's making everything worse. It has something to do with the golden beasts I set on Alypia... I used some of my essence, I think," he said, wincing. He hated to say the words aloud. He didn't know why, but he felt a sort of shame about it, as if he had damaged a gift or broken something very precious, and he didn't like the way that felt. Every negative emotion felt heightened by the barrier's persistent presence.

"I thought that may have been the case," Natalie replied in a hushed tone. "I know it made me feel like that... Always on edge, everything feeling terrible, every nerve irritated."

Even if she had known of his sacrifice, she couldn't have warned him of the repercussions. He had acted on impulse, seizing the moment, and now he was dealing with the consequences. Hadn't he said that once, brimming with bravado in the halls of Spellshadow? Hadn't he said that he would deal with the consequences of a missing piece of himself when the time came? Well, the time had come and gone, and it felt agonizing and impossible to deal with. He looked to Natalie with a renewed sense of respect, understanding that after her portal act she had likely gone through much the same as he was.

"How did you get through it?" he asked her quietly, feeling his frayed nerves begin to calm slightly.

She gave him a warm smile. "Friends looking out for me, and plenty of rest."

He managed to return her smile. "Well, that's what friends

do, right? They look out for each other when they do idiotic things."

"I doubt it will be our last time," she chuckled, though it was somewhat strained. It felt to Alex as if there was something else she wanted to say, but whatever it was, she didn't say it.

"Are you all better now?" he asked.

She shrugged. "As strange as it may sound, I think the focus of learning again at Stillwater has had something to do with it. I do not know how I felt before it happened, but I feel closer to the normal I remember than I have in a long while." There it was, a hint of the unspoken thing.

Alex skirted the allusion to missing Stillwater, taking comfort from her latter words instead.

"And it took rest?"

"Rest and not rushing into anything major, or you will only make it worse... though I believe you have already defied that a few times recently." She smirked, picking up a blanket from the pile on the table beside her and handing it to him. "Thanks, by the way, for saving us from those hallucinations—I have not had the chance to say it yet."

"Don't mention it," he muttered. "It's what we do."

She nodded, her mouth set in a grim line. "It is what we do."

As he pulled the blanket around himself, Alex realized he must have been running on the fumes of residual adrenaline and sheer determination all this time, because the exhaustion hit him like a tidal wave.

On the far side of the room, he could hear Natalie clattering around, and she soon returned, clutching a mug in her hands. She crouched on the floor beside him and passed him the steaming beverage. Lifting it to his lips, the familiar prickle of peppermint wafted into his nostrils, and he felt a small smile curve at the corners of his mouth, remembering Gaze and her endless teas. Sipping cautiously, he swallowed the hot liquid, feeling it warm him as it slipped down his throat. There had been an undeniable method to Gaze's tea madness—it worked, and whether it was a peculiar placebo effect or not, it made him feel better.

He was still awake and sipping tea when Ellabell entered the guards' quarters and hovered in the doorway. Alex watched Natalie walk over to where Ellabell stood. For what seemed like a lifetime, they whispered between themselves, glancing in his direction every so often, as if just to add to his gathering anxiety.

So it was an unexpected delight when Ellabell came over to where he lay and sat on the bed beside him, encouraging him to use her lap as a pillow as he curled up to rest. Whatever Natalie had said, Ellabell was wearing a fresh expression of deep worry as she absently stroked his hair, soothing him and willing him to sleep. It felt nice to have her so close, but he didn't like to see concern furrowing her brow, especially when it was there because of him.

"What's up?" he asked sleepily.

She smiled, brushing hair from his eyes. "Never mind me. You have to sleep now, Alex."

"I'm not tired," he lied.

"Sleep."

"Why the frown?" he mumbled, teetering on the edge of slumber.

"I worry for you," she whispered.

He reached for her hand, his eyelids sliding shut. "Why?"

"Oh, Alex, you fool," she breathed. "I worry for you because…"

He didn't hear what she said next, as he found himself drifting off into a deep, dreamless sleep, the sleep of the world-weary.

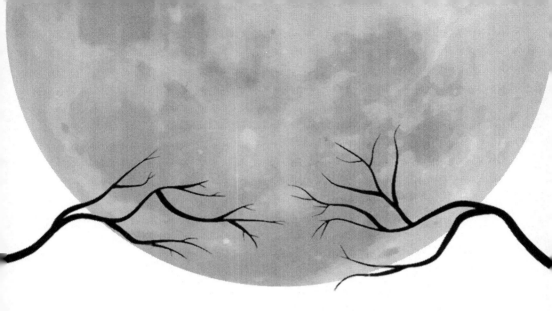

CHAPTER 4

T HE NEXT MORNING, FROM THE MEAGER SUPPLIES
Lintz had stashed away for them in the tower room, the
group ate and drank quickly, talking very little between
bites and sips. The food in their bowls was some sort of thin,
gelatinous porridge, gray in both color and flavor, though the
tea they had to wash it down with made it more palatable. Alex
still felt on edge, but the nourishment perked him up slightly.
A few times, he caught Ellabell looking at him with concern,
but he smiled reassuringly at her, trying to let her know he was
okay. Whether she believed him or not was another story.

After breakfast, Lintz was going to show them the beetles
that would alert them to any opening portals, before Demeter
introduced them to his friends so they could get on with their
mission of locating the keep's stash of essence. In a place full of

necromancers and murderers, Alex couldn't imagine the label "friend" being a wholly accurate one.

The group got to their feet, with Aamir holding out a hand to Alex. Alex shook his head, confident he was recovered enough to walk unaided.

"You sure?" Aamir asked, frowning at Alex.

"I'm fine," he replied, more tersely than he had intended, though Aamir didn't seem to notice.

After the first few minutes of walking, Alex found he could ignore the dull pain in his chest. As long as he kept moving one foot in front of the other, he could pretend he was okay. Slowly, he followed the others, with Lintz leading the way, until they came to the large common room below. A workbench was set up against the far wall, with a few of the beautiful clockwork beetles arranged on top.

"You'll each need to take one of these," Lintz said, passing out smaller variations of the beetles to everyone present.

Alex turned the intricate mechanism in his hands, marveling at the craftsmanship. The beetles themselves were no bigger than the palm of a hand and looked more like scarabs than their larger counterparts. The metal that formed the carapace had been tempered to look multicolored, the hue changing depending on how the light hit it.

"Incredible," Alex murmured.

Lintz grinned. "These are my beetle beacons," he explained. "I've been using them to inform me when a portal is detected. If one senses a portal appearing, it will flash and make a high-pitched siren sound. The lights work like a compass. Allow me to demonstrate."

Lintz ran some of his magic through the mechanism. The scarab lit up, a shrill sound piercing the air. A light shone on each side of its shell, four in total. The alarm sent a shiver through Alex as he wondered what it would be like when the device went off for real, signaling the impending arrival of Alypia. He knew such an event was imminent, and that knowledge filled him with a cold dread.

"Now, you see, all four lights are flashing, but if a real portal had appeared, it would only flash in the direction of where the portal was opening. All you have to do is follow it, and the sound will grow louder the closer you get," Lintz continued.

"And how do we turn it off?" Ellabell asked, covering her ears. The sound was irritating, to say the least.

"You simply press down firmly on the carapace of the beetle," he replied. With his chubby thumb, he pressed down on the multicolored metal shell; there was a small *click*, and the shrill sound came to a grateful end. "So, say the two of you are on beetle duty," he said, gesturing toward Alex and Ellabell. "You would follow the sound and light, reach the destination, and then pull away the portal. If you find yourself on beetle duty, you will need to carry fully charged big beetles with you, and once you have removed the portal, you'll need to replace the used-up beetles with the fresh ones, and bring the depleted ones either to me or whoever is on magic-filling duty. And so the cycle will repeat."

The process seemed simple enough, and Alex was eager to begin their exploration of the keep.

"So, you're sure these friends of yours will be able to help us, Professor?" he asked.

"The two of them have been here for a very long time," Lintz said, pocketing his own beetle beacon. "I daresay they know this place better than even Demeter or I by now."

"They've been allowed out of their cells?" Aamir asked dubiously.

"They're good people, and their doors are always unlocked because they're important... associates... of ours, and so they have as much free rein of the place as we do," Demeter said. "They'll be expecting us shortly. Come on, we must strike while the iron is on fire!"

"I should check on my other beetles—I'll catch up with you folks later," Lintz said, a slight grimace crossing his face. Alex suspected the professor was still peeved at their choice to find the keep's essence against his warnings.

They made their way out of the room, heading through a number of hallways and corridors in a series of turns. Demeter paused in front of two wooden doors that were ajar, situated at the end of a wide hall. He knocked on the first of the two doors.

A willowy older woman emerged, dressed in a tattered, once-violet dress. Her hair was dark gray, falling well past her waist, several sections woven with what looked like strands of colorful silk—though where she would have gotten such a luxury, Alex wasn't sure. She wore dried flowers in a woven band across her forehead and around the back of her hair too, structured into a sort of flower crown that gave her a distinctly earth-mother quality. As the torchlight caught the side of her face, Alex could see that she had once been beautiful. Her high cheekbones gave her a dignified air, and her green eyes glittered with a perpetual irreverence. She flashed an easy smile at them as she stepped out into the corridor. It was bright and welcoming, and Alex felt an instant warmth toward the woman, who seemed pleasant enough—much too pleasant to be in a place like this, surrounded by so much grime and darkness, nowhere near the bounty of nature.

"You must be the little cherubs!" she cried in a crisp, clear voice. "My name is Agatha Spjut, and I am delighted to meet you all. What brings your angelic faces to my door?"

"We need your assistance, Agatha," Demeter explained. "We're going in search of hidden essence, and we need good minds to help us map out the prison, so we don't keep looking over the same old ground."

"How exquisitely adventurous of you all! I love a spot of bravado." She grinned more widely, clapping her hands together. "Delighted to offer my help, dear ones, absolutely delighted! I might look ancient, but this mind is as sharp as any you'll find. Are we roping in old Forcier?"

Lintz nodded. "I was just about to knock."

With that, the professor knocked on the second door down, bringing the arrival of Lintz's second friend, though he didn't make quite the same first impression as the pleasant, hippie-like Agatha. In fact, at first glance he was quite alarming. The skin of his face was paper-thin, a network of blue veins running visibly beneath the pale surface, connecting from pallid lips, across sunken cheeks, and up over a high forehead into a hairline of silvery gray. The man looked startlingly emaciated, his clavicles protruding from beneath a black waistcoat, leading to a thin neck that barely looked capable of holding his head up, like the stick of a lollipop. It didn't seem to bother him, however, as he moved fluidly from the room.

"Vincent, my darling!" cried Agatha, rushing past the others to embrace the strange figure.

"Agatha, dearest. Good day to you all—I was not expecting so many visitors. I am Vincent Forcier. It's a pleasure to make your various acquaintances." The man's voice was soft, bordering on eerie, yet somehow strangely hypnotic. "Did I hear someone mention a spot of bravado?" he asked, his mouth pulled tight in what Alex presumed was meant to be a smile, but the effect was disconcerting on the man's unnaturally pale, almost transparent skin, giving him a slightly manic look.

"We need some help finding the Kingstone essence, and Demeter has told us you'd be willing to help," Alex explained, finding his voice.

"A remarkable task, one that I would be honored to assist with, in any way I can," Vincent replied. "You don't mind if I take the lead?" His impossibly large, black eyes, completely devoid of white, surveyed the group.

"Lead the way," Alex said.

Vincent strode along with assured, knowledgeable footsteps, pointing out rooms to avoid and corridors to keep out of, due to the unsavory characters within. It was like being led by a tour guide, Alex thought wryly.

"It is truly a shame you had to be present for such a thing," Vincent said quietly. "An awful way to begin—you must all have been so frightened. I know it passes, but still, it's a terrible thing."

Alex realized he was talking about the nightmare fog,

though it had taken him a moment to tune in, he was so mesmerized by the lilting, soothing cadence of the words upon his tired and aching soul.

"Were it not for the recollection of feeling a little strange, I might never have known it happened. I trust it is the same for you?" Vincent asked the group.

Natalie nodded, clearly as mesmerized as Alex was. "I can hardly remember it now, and I cannot recall what I saw."

"That is the way of these awful measures Caius has put in place—they last just long enough for us to fear and remember and never want to experience it again. The details don't remain, but the feeling does, am I right?" Vincent asked, his piercing black eyes staring intensely into Natalie's.

"That is exactly right. I could not have put it better myself!" she piped up.

"Even the most powerful among us fear the wrath of Caius," Vincent admitted. "He has an inexhaustible arsenal of tricks, and I'm certain I have experienced a thousand or more in my time here. It's what keeps us compliant. Fear is a potent weapon, when wielded correctly, and Caius is the greatest marksman I know."

There was a bitterness to the unnatural man's words that resonated with Alex, and, looking around, he could see that the rest of the group were just as hooked upon Vincent's every feeling. Where Demeter's presence made Alex feel calm, Vincent's presence had already made him feel a whole spectrum of emotions, in a short span of time.

"What did you do? To land yourselves in prison, I mean," asked Jari eagerly, his gaze flitting between Agatha and

Vincent. It was the question Alex had been too polite to ask.

Vincent smiled his peculiar smile. "Ladies first," he said, gesturing toward Agatha.

She blushed. "Oh, no! You go first, Vincent."

"Very well," he acquiesced with a delicate wave of his hand. Every movement he made seemed deliberate and exquisite, like macabre cabaret. "You wish to know my story?"

The group nodded, and Alex found himself nodding too.

"Well, young ones, I am afraid to say I was placed in here for necromancy. As you no doubt know, necromancy is frowned upon among our kind," he began, his voice like honey.

Unless you're a noble, Alex thought, remembering what the Head had done to Malachi Grey and had been encouraged to do again with Renmark.

"I admit that I moved in shadows, and I was duly punished for it, although I sought discovery of the darkest arts for a pure purpose. My heart was in the right place, as they say. You see, I am not like other necromancers you may come across, though I hope you never meet another—the other necromancers held within these walls are here for good reason. They are cold and cruel and unnatural and should never be permitted to feel daylight upon their faces again, for the acts they have committed," he seethed, his dark eyes flashing. He seemed too disgusted to tell them the actual crimes these other necromancers had been imprisoned for, but the emotion lacing Vincent's voice reinforced the certainty that it was bad beyond words, whatever it was that had led to their incarceration.

"What kind of necromancy did you do?" pressed Jari, his eyes as wide as saucers.

Vincent grinned oddly. "Those are not tales for mortal ears."

Alex felt disappointed he wasn't going to hear the nitty-gritty of what had put the strange man behind bars.

"Shall I take it from here, dear heart?" Agatha asked.

Vincent nodded, his thin neck bobbing with unexpected grace. "The floor is yours, dear lady."

Agatha seemed a little eccentric, but far too nice to be a criminal. Alex couldn't imagine her committing any misdeed worthy of as harsh a punishment as Kingstone.

"Well, cherubs, I was put in this place many moons ago for the petty crime of theft and the somewhat larger crime of trying to kill a royal… though I didn't know he was a royal at the time." She winked. "If I'd known, I'd have tried twice as hard. I'm not even anti-royalist—well, I wasn't before they put me in here. I sure am now!"

"What did you steal?" asked Ellabell shyly, pushing her spectacles back up onto the bridge of her nose.

"Just the question I was hoping for!" Agatha cried with delight. "I stole a diamond as big as a Thunderbird's egg—oh, you should have seen it! It was a beauty. I saw it through a window, and it was in this glass box, just sitting there, sparkling away, calling my name, and I couldn't just walk past it. So, into this great big house I slipped, and I nabbed it, and on the way I ran into some problems, what with alarms and guards and whatnot. That's where the almost-killing part comes into play. But I held that glorious diamond in my hands for a good hour before they could pry it away from me. I can still feel it now, if I close my eyes and wish hard enough." Accentuating the point, she squeezed her eyes shut and rounded her palms, as if she were holding an invisible egg. A smile spread across her face. "It was the most beautiful thing I've ever seen."

"Impressive." Ellabell grinned. Alex could see why; it was hard to imagine this old hippie as a jewel thief, no matter how unsuccessful she'd been.

"Oh, you've no idea how lovely it is to have some young blood wandering freely about the place, with the blooms still freshly in your cheeks and your whole lives ahead of you. Goodness, what I wouldn't give to be your age again. The things I got up to!" She cackled mischievously, and Alex could only imagine what this woman had gotten up to at his age. On second thought, he wasn't sure he wanted to know. "I say that, but I suppose it can't be so lovely if you're in here, can it? It's devastating when they bring those youngsters through from that fancy-pants school. Terribly sad, the way their minds depart for greener pastures, leaving only the wild-eyed husks behind. Is that why you're here? I do hope you don't end up the same way, cherubs. You're such dear things!"

"These ones are more like guests than prisoners," Demeter explained. "They're here purely to make a pit stop while they build a portal home. And, with your assistance, they're going to be able to do it all the swifter," he added in a low voice.

Both of Demeter's friends shared a smile at this news, which made Alex feel even more hopeful as they pressed on, moving deeper and deeper into the keep in search of the essence that would take them home.

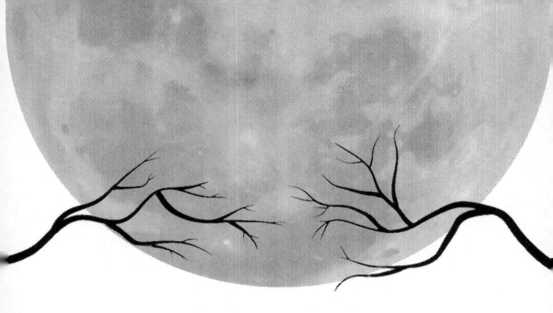

CHAPTER 5

AS THEY WALKED, IT BEGAN TO DAWN ON ALEX THAT the keep was far bigger than he had imagined. Taking a quick look out of one of the nearby windows, he could count at least ten other windows descending beneath, but that was only what his eyes could see. The more they mapped out, the more he realized just how vast this place was.

Passing hallways upon hallways of cells, Alex noticed there was a small vestibule at the end of many of the corridors, and each one had a long, cylindrical contraption attached to the wall. Sometimes it was beside an open window, looking out on the bronze fog; sometimes it was in the center of a solid stretch of masonry. The contraptions themselves were built from pure gold that shone in the torchlight. Alex wondered what purpose they served, thinking that, perhaps, they were some kind of alarm system that alerted the guards when a prisoner escaped. It would certainly explain why they seemed to be at the end of most corridors.

Coming into a space with a dozen or so tunnels stretching out from the central point, they passed another of the large, golden cylinders, clinging to the wall beside a wide, open window that looked out on the many stories below. Alex wanted to pause and take a closer look at the object, but the others had already powered on. He thought about following, but the cylinder called to him. Knowing he would catch up eventually, he placed his beetle beacon down beside the tunnel through which they had passed and walked over to the strange gold object.

The outer shell was embossed with swirling designs, which seemed out of place in the dank misery of the prison. He let his thumb trace over the shapes of flowers and vines. Something sparked against his skin, like an electric shock, and he jerked his hand back. He knew he really shouldn't be going around and touching random things.

Listening closely, he could hear the sound of something whirring within. There were six small screws along the length of the golden exterior, making Alex think it might be made of clockwork. He was desperate to know its purpose. However, he stopped short of prying off the metal to see what lay hidden inside. If it was important, it would undoubtedly be booby trapped.

Perhaps Vincent or Agatha can shed some light on it. He turned back toward the hallways that led off from the inside courtyard, but as he looked at each one, he realized his beetle had gone—leaving him with no idea which one the others had disappeared down. They all looked so similar.

Cursing under his breath, he tried to wrack his brain, hoping it would remember which path his friends had taken. He thought the third hallway seemed the most familiar, so, deciding to chance it, he walked toward it.

As he stepped over the threshold, he saw something twinkling just ahead, tucked into the bottom of either wall. It looked familiar, somehow…

He realized too late that it reminded him of the mechanical triggers that had been used at Stillwater House. A great blast of raw magical energy came rushing out of the darkness toward him. It hit him like a blockade, knocking him off his feet and sending him hurtling backward, away from the third tunnel and through the wide, open window.

"ALEX!" he heard Ellabell's scream as he went soaring over the ledge, catching a glimpse of her and the others appearing in the doorway of the sixth tunnel as he went over.

Six, not three. He cursed himself as solid ground disappeared.

Before he knew it, he was falling, unable to do anything to stop himself. He was aware of only three things: Ellabell's terrified blue eyes looking down from above, the increasing speed of his descent, and the thought of the ground rising up to meet him. The latter contemplation caused his whole body to tense up, in preparation for the impact. As he rushed to meet his fate, he kept his gaze firmly on Ellabell, who grew smaller and smaller in the distance. He realized he wouldn't mind if she was the last thing he saw on this earth, but he was too young to die. There were so many things he hadn't done, and this was going to hurt so much.

He had almost forgotten about the moat, but the cold, icy impact of the water all around him reminded him of it immediately, as he hit the surface with crushing force. It pushed the air out of his lungs, and it felt more like he had slammed into concrete than liquid. He sank beneath the surface, feeling the water close over his face as he descended into the murk. Everything hurt, but the realization dawned on him that he was not, in fact, dead.

Feeling his muscles twinge, he kicked his legs and dragged his arms through the freezing water, pulling himself back up toward the beacon of light that signaled the moat's surface. With a gasp and a splash, he emerged, grateful to be alive, with all of his limbs in apparent working order. He heaved in great gulps of air, and though the cold temperature of the water was biting, he had never been more grateful to feel such an intense chill.

With chattering teeth, he swam toward the muddy bank, climbing it awkwardly as his fingers clawed at the slick surface for purchase. He managed to haul himself onto the grassy lip of the bank, a short distance from where the bronze fog began. He didn't dare to think what might happen if he crossed it, and, though he was curious about whether he could simply pass through it with his anti-magic, he didn't feel like pushing his luck after what had just happened. Sitting on the edge of the bank, gathering his thoughts, his heart racing, he found himself staring out toward the moat.

It was the first time he had seen the moat close up, and the sight disturbed him. The water was a murky black, as far from natural-looking as it was possible to be, so thick and opaque it almost looked like oil. Not to mention the fact that it absolutely stank; he could smell it on his skin already, reeking of all things rotten and festering. The stench made him gag, but since he was drenched in the stuff, he wasn't sure how he was going to evade the smell.

Looking back up toward the window he had fallen from, he saw that Agatha and Ellabell were still peering over.

"Are you okay?" Ellabell yelled, the words barely audible to Alex's ears.

"I think so!" Alex shouted back.

"We're trying to find a rope long enough—Vincent says we can't conjure one in case it sets off the fog!" Ellabell replied. "Hold on, we're ransacking rooms for bedsheets!"

"Quite right—if we set off the barrier, you'll be stuck down there!" Agatha cackled. "Now, don't get too close to the water. You don't want to slip back in!" she added, while Ellabell disappeared from sight.

"Okay… I'm, uh, not exactly going anywhere," Alex called back. He guessed it made sense that they couldn't simply conjure a magical rope. If mages could just dangle magic ropes out and climb down them without repercussion, Caius would have needed to reassess his security measures. Plus, Alex doubted he'd be able to keep hold of a magical one anyway, given the way his anti-magic was prone to attacking magic.

Suddenly, something slithered beneath the dark water, rippling the viscous surface. Alex jumped to his feet and stepped back, seeing the flash of something moving beneath the black water. Whatever was living under there, it was big, and he was almost certain there was more than one. A splash a short distance away confirmed his chilling suspicions.

The next thing he knew, something was lunging toward him from the moat. Alex toppled backward, losing his footing on the wet grass. A huge black creature that looked part snake, part lizard surged from the black liquid, darting toward Alex at alarming speed, its amphibian nostrils flaring. It paused, sniffing the air, seeking something out.

Lying flat in the grass, feeling the blades tickling the back of his neck, Alex kept entirely still, hoping the creature wouldn't see him. It lurched over him, giving him a closer look than he would have liked. Where eyes should have been, there were none—the beast was blind. With water that thick and black, Alex supposed eyesight wouldn't make much difference. The beast's head was horribly oversized, with two strange, three-pronged fronds above where eye sockets would be that twitched as the creature sniffed more insistently. The body was long and sleek, as it had seemed beneath the water, though the black color changed to a lighter, gunmetal gray when it turned its body this way and that. Alex wondered if it was camouflage of some sort—in between the coursing panic that the beast was about to make a meal out of him and the desperation to keep himself still and silent.

The monster curved too close for comfort, the dank scent of swamp and rotting meat making Alex gag as droplets of black water dripped from the slimy body onto his face. But he stayed still, not daring to move.

With a few final snorts, the beast slunk back into the water with a barely audible splash. Whatever it had been sniffing for, Alex guessed he wasn't it.

Though he wanted to run from the moat's edge, he waited a moment longer, just in case the creature decided to rear its ugly head again. Once he was confident it was gone, Alex sat up in the grass, wondering what the thing had been smelling for. Magic, perhaps? It would explain why it had left him alone, he mused, contemplating its presence in the moat. Was it just another deterrent to escape, the fear of climbing down the walls only to meet a grisly end down the throat of a giant amphibian? Alex shuddered to think.

Not wanting to get too close to the water's edge again, he waited patiently for the makeshift rope to be lowered, though he realized with some trepidation that he was going to have to get into the moat again in order to reach the proffered mode of rescue.

As he looked up, he saw that Agatha was still peering out over the window ledge. It was hard to make out at this distance, but there was something odd in the way she was surveying him. Her head was tilted in contemplation, her mouth set in a grim line, but Alex couldn't be sure how much was simply his own imagination as he turned back to watch the surface of the moat, praying no more beasts came out to attack him.

"Alex, we're lowering the rope!" Ellabell called, reappearing at the window. It was a sight he was happy to see, now that he knew it wasn't going to be the last thing he saw. Well, as long as a beast didn't get him on his way out.

Finally, a rope made of countless bedsheets was lowered from the window. It seemed to take forever, and Alex waited with as much patience as he could muster, until the very tip of the last sheet dipped into the murky black water. Taking that as his signal to move, he dove into the icy moat, swimming for the bottom of the rope.

Grasping it tightly, he began to climb up, ever-conscious of the creatures lurking beneath the water below. He just hoped that it would hold, that the knots were tied tight enough, as he pressed on.

A quarter of the way up the rope, the ache of his muscles made itself known again. After so much suffering, he was surprised he'd even made it that far by himself. Staring up toward the window, his arms shaking with the strain of hauling his body up the rope, he realized he wasn't going to make it under his own steam; he needed help, or he was going to fall again.

"Pull me up!" he yelled.

The bedsheets began to move in a jerky motion. It was a nerve-wracking ascent, the fabric straining as he got higher and higher, the knots above his head looking less and less sturdy with every foot he moved away from the moat. At one point, he thought he heard the sound of something ripping, the noise convincing him that he was headed for another nasty fall.

All he could do was cling tight and hope he reached the window ledge before the sheets gave way. It drew nearer, and he could see the relieved faces of his friends as they continued to pull. It was a relief to him too, and he smiled as he came within a few inches of the sill.

This time, the ripping sound was unmistakable as the last bedsheet tore away from the one above it. The relieved faces turned to expressions of panic. Alex felt himself falling again, before an arm shot out, lightning fast, and he reached up to grasp it. Agatha held him firmly, her hand gripped in a vise around his with surprising strength. Glancing down, he saw the sheet fall toward the moat, dancing on the breeze like a ghost. The sight made his stomach turn.

"Pull me up," he rasped, looking up to meet Agatha's green eyes.

"With pleasure," Agatha replied, hauling him up over the window ledge and back into the relative safety of the prison. Alex had never been so happy to feel hard stone beneath his cheek.

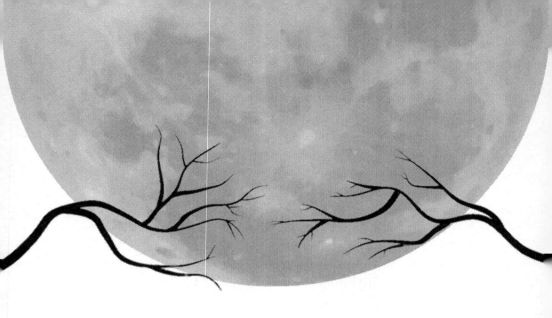

CHAPTER 6

FTER A BRIEF REST AND A MUCH-NEEDED SHOWER,
Alex returned to the fray, against his better judgment.
Over the next few days, they scoured as many floors
as they could, following the roughly sketched map of suitable
hallways that Vincent and Agatha had drawn out for them. It
seemed their rough idea of safe passageways was in need of
updating, as they ended up running into countless traps from
the depths of Caius's box of trickery, ducking swarms of flying
golden arrows and powerful waves of force fields that knocked
the air right out of them. Not to mention the pack of golden
hounds that chased them through at least four floors, their
teeth snapping at their heels. Still, Alex pressed on, reviewing
the rudimentary map that was beginning to take shape and the
crosses upon it that signaled traps. They managed to reach as

far down as a subterranean floor of mildewed, yet-to-be-filled cells, only to be faced with a black swell of bats that triggered the tremble of the ground beneath them, sending them sprinting back the way they had come.

Back in the comfort of the tower room, after a particularly nasty encounter with a jet of toxic gas that had left their throats raw and their eyes running, Alex realized there were just too many unknowns in Kingstone Keep. Glancing down at the map in his hands, he saw that most of the floors were covered in more crosses than there was room for. He hated to admit it, but Lintz had been right—the risk was too great. They needed a better way to track down the essence, instead of blindly scouting the whole prison in search of it.

Lintz had disappeared after the moat incident, claiming there was something he needed to attend to, but Alex knew the professor had every right to say, "I told you so." Still, even given the opportunity, the old man hadn't said any such words. He just seemed relieved that Alex was still in one piece.

Demeter and Vincent had stayed in the tower room to review the notes they had compiled about the keep's layout. Alex almost wanted to tell them not to bother; there was no point in pretending they could find the essence using their current strategies—not before one of them got killed.

"So what do you suggest we do now?" Aamir asked the group sullenly. "We've mapped out this whole place, searched every corridor—well, the ones that haven't tried to murder us. I've yet to stumble across any secret passageways, and Jari has been completely unhelpful."

"What! I take one nap, and now I'm 'unhelpful?'" Jari

snapped, using air quotes.

"You locked me in the guard's toilet, you dunce," Aamir retorted. "I swear, I thought I was going to suffocate."

"I let you out eventually, didn't I?"

"Should we just give up on the idea of going home, then?" Ellabell asked suddenly. Her quiet words brought a hush about the room. Even Jari didn't have a quip for what they all knew to be a hopeless situation. Alex swallowed hard. He wanted to comfort her, to assure everyone that they would find a way out soon. But how could he, when he had no such hope himself?

From the well of despair, an idea slowly began to come to him, materializing in his mind—another way of tracking down the essence. He was certain Caius had the essence, or would keep it close by, as all his royal brethren did.

"We need to think of a way to make Caius *tell* us where the bottles are," Alex announced, breaking the tension.

The others looked at him as if he were mad, but Demeter seemed more optimistic as a thoughtful expression flashed across his eyes.

"If I was given the right opportunity, I might have a way of making Caius talk," he replied cryptically. There was a dark glimmer in the ex-teacher's eyes that intensified Alex's curiosity as to what Demeter's "special skillset" actually was.

"Really?" asked Alex. He could understand the bewildered expression in his friends' eyes; Caius was a dangerous, terrifying mage—the last person they wanted to meet in this dark place. But time was ticking, and Alex didn't know how they would escape before Alypia arrived if they didn't figure out how to glean the essence's location from the one person who knew. He just hoped that, if they did come face-to-face with him, they would all be able to hold their nerve—and escape alive.

Demeter nodded, all eyes now on him. "It would be extremely dangerous, but I think I can make him talk if we can find him... Tracking him down will be tricky, however."

"Can it be done?" Natalie asked.

"There are areas of the prison that Caius visits sometimes, on the few occasions he comes to the keep, so I suppose we could stake out those places and take him by surprise, spring on him when he appears," Demeter suggested.

"Sounds like a lot of waiting around," Jari mumbled, evidently not as impressed by the plan as everyone else.

Demeter nodded. "It would definitely be a lot of waiting around, and the man is unpredictable at best. When I say, 'visits sometimes,' I mean once in a full moon, but I think it's our best option if we wish to catch him."

"It is 'blue moon,' I believe," muttered Natalie.

Demeter frowned. "Is it?"

The refreshed news of Caius's evasiveness came as a blow to Alex's boosted optimism. He was already on edge from the influence of the barrier, Alypia's impending arrival, and the events of the past few days, all these things feeding his anxieties and bristling his nerves, but he knew he had to force down the spike of irritation threatening to rise through him. Balling his fists until his nails pressed into the flesh of his palms, he focused on calming his nerves.

It's just the barrier making me feel this way. I'm the one in control of my emotions, not the barrier. Not even my missing piece of soul.

"Don't be disheartened, Alex Webber," Vincent spoke up. "You have myself and Agatha to assist in your endeavors now, and we have keener eyes than most. Rats always emerge from their hidey-holes, and I know a few spots he likes to frequent."

"Bad news, my friends!" A frazzled Lintz burst through the door of the tower room and threw a bagful of beetles on the table. A dark cloud of anxiety hovered about him, and it only served to reignite Alex's concerns.

"Are you okay, Professor?" Alex asked.

Lintz wiped sweat from his brow. "I'm afraid our time may have just been cut shorter."

"Why, what's the matter?" Jari pressed.

"Well, someone is constantly trying to open a portal to the keep. It's happened twice in the last hour, and I fear if they continue to increase their efforts it will end up taking much of everyone's time, layering more magic into the beetles and fixing them up when they break, which they keep doing. If we keep at it, we'll all end up running around like headless chickens, responding to beacons and making sure the portals have been properly closed. Eventually, someone will make a tiny mistake, and Alypia will get through... I just know it. And my beetles won't last forever. One missed portal, and we're done for."

"We have to find Caius!" Alex said, realizing they needed the Kingstone essence sooner than ever before. He quickly filled in the professor on what they had decided to do where Caius was concerned. Lintz listened intently, but didn't seem pleased by the prospect.

"If Caius wants to stay hidden then there's nothing we can

do," he said.

"We'll find him," Alex insisted, trying to boost his own morale. "Our only hope is to find Caius. We'll quadruple our efforts to smoke him out, even if that means staking out every possible corridor where he might be, every minute of every day. Vincent, you said you know some places he likes to go?"

Vincent looked at Alex, a twinkle of admiration in his eyes. "Indeed. I'll lead you to those spots, if you wish."

"Yes," Alex replied, grateful for the necromancer's presence. "And those who aren't on a shift seeking Caius should help Lintz with portals and beetles, to try to ease some of the strain," he added through gritted teeth, hoping the others wouldn't notice the tension in his body as he spoke. "And in case any of us finds him or herself with a bit of free time in between all this, we brush up on our skills to stay sharp. Okay?"

"Sounds perfectly viable!" Demeter agreed, but not even the teacher's calming presence could soothe another bolt of annoyance that pulsed through Alex, provoked by the barrier magic all around him.

The others were similarly enthusiastic, and they all agreed to take an hour to regroup before setting off with Vincent to begin staking out Caius's usual haunts. The necromancer had informed them he had a personal task to attend to, but he would return for them when the hour was up, to show them the royal's preferred spots. Alex needed the time to gather his thoughts, to try to keep a lid on the strange anger that kept spiking up and overwhelming him.

He stumbled over to the rudimentary kitchen area that had been set up in the corner and made himself a cup of tea.

His friends disbanded, flashing concerned looks in his direction, though he chose to ignore them as best as he could and focus on the practical task before him. Out of the corner of his eye, he saw Aamir and Jari leave the tower completely, while Ellabell and Natalie went off to one side, moving into the most open space in the tower room and taking up sparring stances. Alex could hear the crackle and whoosh of golden magic moving through the air behind him. He was glad they were spending the time to practice for whatever lay ahead, as he'd suggested—but instead of watching their duel, he focused his mind, returning it to a calmer state, slowly breathing in and breathing out.

He could have stayed that way, silently meditating. It was only when he caught sight of Ellabell out of the corner of his eye, sprawling backward onto the hard stone, that he whirled around to see what was going on. A yelp of pain left her lips as she fell. Golden wisps of magic twisted around her, constricting her throat, making her eyes bulge behind her glasses as her body lifted itself back up again, though it didn't seem to be Ellabell who was in control of her body. She rose as if possessed.

Glancing toward Natalie, Alex saw her hands turning quickly in neat, deft movements, manipulating Ellabell like a puppet, as if she held the marionette strings between her fingers and was making Ellabell dance to her bidding.

"Natalie," Ellabell pleaded, her voice raspy as she tried to force words through lips not controlled by her own mind anymore. "Natalie, stop," she repeated, a little louder.

"I did it!" Grinning with delight, Natalie twisted her hands sharply, stopping the spell in an instant. But the suddenness of the spell's removal seemed to come as a surprise to Ellabell, as the bespectacled girl collapsed to the floor.

"Sorry, I got a bit carried away," Natalie said, still smiling. "You're okay, aren't you?"

"Yeah, I'm okay—" Ellabell winced as she tried to stand.

Alex ran over, his fury bristling again, though this time for a more valid reason. He couldn't believe what he had just seen.

"Natalie, what the hell?" he yelled, helping Ellabell up off the ground.

"*What?* You were just saying we need to keep our skills from getting rusty!" she retorted, looking at Alex as if *he* were the crazy one.

"Yes, but you *hurt* Ellabell," he snapped. "We can't afford unnecessary injury!"

Natalie rolled her eyes. "Ellabell is fine. Stop overreacting."

"She could have cracked her head open on the floor—you could have strangled her! You don't realize how strong you are sometimes," he growled, propping Ellabell up on a nearby chair. She seemed fine, and even tried to grasp his hand to get his attention, but Alex's focus was elsewhere.

"If it were anyone else, you would not have a problem," Natalie said, suddenly defensive. "Ellabell can handle herself, you know. She is not a damsel in need of rescuing."

"Don't make this about me, Natalie. You just wanted to try out something dark and dangerous and thought you'd use Ellabell as a guinea pig." Alex was raging now, struggling to keep a lid on his anger. He felt Ellabell tugging on his arm.

"I'm fine, Alex. Honestly, we were just practicing

something Natalie learned at Stillwater. I knew what I was getting into," she said.

Alex didn't dare voice his thoughts on Natalie's magical predilections, worried it would come out of his mouth as a torrent of accusation and irritation. He didn't know what was wrong with him, but he didn't feel like himself with so much anger coursing through his veins. It wasn't him.

Turning back to Natalie, he caught a flash of something in her eyes that unsettled him, as if she were biting her tongue again, longing to say something but preventing herself, much the same as he was. Frowning, he wondered what it was she wanted to say to him, and was about to encourage her to spew whatever venom she wanted his way, when Jari entered the room. He had left with Aamir when the group disbanded twenty minutes earlier, but Aamir was no longer with him.

"Where's Aamir?" Alex asked.

Jari shrugged. "Dunno. I'm not his keeper."

"It's like trying to wrangle slippery eels," Alex said under his breath. "Why didn't you two stay here and work on your magic? We're supposed to be moving out soon, into God knows how much danger—and we don't have time to waste, waiting for people!" As he spoke, his voice rose into a shout and his fists clenched.

In the haze of anger that had settled upon him, he was only vaguely aware that he might be blowing the situation out of proportion. All he could think was that his friends simply weren't taking their situation seriously enough; they seemed frivolous, more than eager to wander off and do as they pleased instead of putting plans into action or coming up with fresh ideas that might help them succeed. That job seemed to perpetually fall upon *his* shoulders, and he was growing tired of bearing its weight. The whole group was in a great deal of danger, and he had enough on his plate without having to chase after everyone and make sure they weren't up to no good. He was sick of playing dad to them. Aamir of all people should have known better—he was older than Alex.

Despite his attempts to smother the feelings roiling inside him, he felt his eyes beginning to burn with white-hot rage.

"Whoa… dude. Your eyes are, like… glowing," Jari said, taking a step back.

Alex turned quickly away from Jari's gaze. The barrier and its influence made him feel more out of control than he had felt since he first learned of his strange heritage, to the point that he wasn't sure he was even governing his own body anymore.

When Aamir appeared a minute later, Alex strode over, cornering his friend.

"Where have you been?" he hissed.

"The bathroom," Aamir replied evenly, his brow furrowed.

Alex moved in close, his face mere inches from Aamir's. "You had better not be up to your old tricks again," he whispered.

Aamir stared at Alex, his expression a mix of surprise and confusion. "No, of course not," he said, lowering his voice. "I was just in the bathroom, as I said. I passed Lintz on the way there—you can ask him."

Alex couldn't decide what to believe as he tried to focus on his friend's face, seeking out any sign of a lie. His mind felt so clouded, and his chest ached dully, jolting sharply every so often and refreshing the pain. Before he knew what he was doing, Alex lunged forward and grasped Aamir roughly by the shoulders.

"If you *ever* betray us again, you'll wish you'd never been born," he growled.

It shocked Alex, and everyone else in the room by the looks on their faces, to hear the words pouring from his mouth. He quickly let go of Aamir, an expression of abject horror on both their faces. It was entirely out of character for Alex, and he didn't know where it had come from or what had prompted him to say it—he felt as if he were watching a twisted version of himself from behind a glass screen, unable to stop his avatar from lashing out.

"The Head has no control over me now. I would never betray you," said Aamir steadily, though his breath hitched, and his expression showed deep distress at Alex's outburst. "Are you feeling okay?" He reached for Alex's shoulder.

Alex wrenched his arm away. "It's just the air," he murmured. "I can't breathe. I'm sorry… I'm so sorry. I'll be back… I'm sorry." He rushed from the room, hoping his friends wouldn't hate him upon his return. He felt like a hypocrite now and loathed the fact that he was wasting valuable time, but he knew he couldn't spend a moment longer in that room, feeling as he did.

As he ran toward an open space, desperate for fresh air upon his face, he knew the outburst had something to do with his torn soul, aggravated by the bristle of the barrier magic. It worried him, and he hoped fervently that he had not done himself irreversible damage.

Bursting through an unknown door, he found himself on a walkway between turrets. Instantly, the pressure of the barrier faded slightly and he moved toward the wall, clinging to it for purchase, thinking he might collapse. He gripped the edge of the slick stone until his head stopped spinning, ignoring the flakes of snow gathering beneath his palms. This time, his anti-magic didn't even try to delve deeper into the barrier; it seemed his defenses had learned their lesson. No red fog came, no demons pounced, no spears hurtled toward his head. The only reaction was the flurries.

Everything seemed to be slipping away from him. No matter how hard he gripped the wall, he couldn't fully regain his hold on reality. Squeezing his eyes shut, he wondered if he might be on the verge of a mental breakdown. Nothing felt right anymore—he didn't recognize himself.

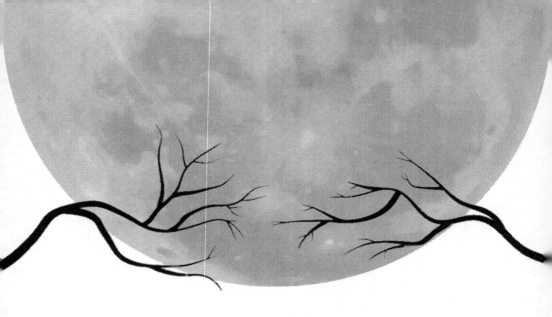

CHAPTER 7

A FTER CALMING HIMSELF AS BEST HE COULD, ALEX made his way toward the tower room to join the others, hoping to get back before Vincent came to collect them. He walked slowly, hoping he was going the right way as he passed identical hallway after identical hallway.

His heart missed a beat as he saw a door ahead of him, slightly ajar. The only people he knew with keys were the guards, and the only guards he knew were Lintz and Demeter, but he couldn't see them anywhere nearby. Taking a deep breath, he skirted the open door, his back pressed to the opposite wall, hoping he could get past it without something emerging from within.

Alex froze at the sound of whispered words. It sounded like his name.

Barely breathing, he listened more closely, wondering if the voice would speak again.

"Alex," it whispered, undeniable this time.

He followed the sound, pushing gently on the wooden door. It swung open with a rusty creak, leading into a dimly lit room strewn with dust-sheeted furniture. Alex stepped in cautiously, realizing afterward what an idiotic thing that was to do in a place like this—just because somewhere looked safe, that didn't mean it was.

Fortunately for him, the figure that greeted him was a familiar one.

"Alex Webber, as I live and breathe." The shadows glinted with the flash of a grin Alex knew would be sardonic.

Elias unfurled from the darkness at the far side of the room, emerging from beneath the pale glow of a torch like a performer sliding into the spotlight. All he needed was a top hat and cane, though Alex wasn't sure a hat would stay on top of his insubstantial head.

Slipping through the air, the shadow-man rose up to his full, wispy height, draping himself casually against the wall, though it seemed as if he was once again having trouble with the shadowed fronds of his being. Alex wondered if the barrier magic was playing havoc with Elias, as Alypia's version had done at Stillwater. This time, he didn't seem to be having issues holding his actual self together, but his whole shape appeared to crackle, fizzing and snapping in places. Even Elias himself seemed startled by it, jolting in surprise every time his body sparked. He was clearer, at least, than he had been at Stillwater, and looked more like his old self.

"I should have known it would be you. Creepy noise, creepy place, creepy shadows—guaranteed to be you," Alex groaned.

Elias cackled deep in the back of his black throat. "Very good, Webber—you're learning. Still not smart enough to avoid following said creepy whisper into an unknown room in the depths of a prison full of criminals... but alas, we must walk before we can run," he teased, his face contorting into what Alex thought was meant to be a frown of displeasure. "Ugh! I'm starting to sound like that halfwit Demeter. If I start spouting half-formed proverbs, feel free to send me back from whence I came—I implore you. I'd rather die a thousand deaths than use fortune cookies as my sole source of inspiration."

Alex hated to admit it, but seeing Elias brought him a sense of relief and more than a hint of amusement. What he hated even more was that he knew Elias could tell.

"How can you be here?" Alex asked, trying to erase the smile from his face.

"I am an exceptional creature. I can go anywhere I please," Elias purred, elegantly brushing misty fingers through starry tendrils, where hair might be found on a physical being.

Alex sighed. It seemed they were back to mystery, though he was used to it by now.

"I think you missed me," Alex taunted.

"You amuse me," Elias said simply, turning his wispy wrists as if flicking away a buzzing insect. "You pass the time between here and eternity. I suspect I'll grow bored of you one of these days." Before Alex could retort, the shadow continued. "Speaking of amusing things—bravo on the exquisite mess you made of Alypia." Elias grinned, the expression as eerie and unnatural as ever upon his shifting, ever-moving face.

The back-handed compliment made Alex uncomfortable. He could take no pleasure in what he had done to her, especially as it didn't seem to be stopping her pursuit of him. All he could derive from the experience was an intensified fear of her volatile retribution. The fact that Elias was taking such delight in it made him all the more nervous. Nothing Elias found joyful was ever something to celebrate.

"I'm not sure it did me any favors," Alex said.

Elias swooped closer, scrutinizing Alex. "If you're worrying about that old hag coming after you, don't just yet. Don't get me wrong—she's beyond peeved, and you should see the state of her face, but she's still a way off from a full recovery. After the havoc you wrought upon her, who wouldn't be?" he murmured, his galactic eyes glinting. "She's a strong mage, but nobody is strong enough to fend off two savage beasties and come away unscathed. Well, nobody but me," he boasted. "I could have taken them on, though I'm not sure I'd have expected such moxie from a kid like you."

Alex wasn't sure how the shadow-man managed it, but every word from Elias's mouth managed to make him feel disgusted and comforted in equal measure.

"Well, you're wrong, because she's already trying to get to me. She's tried to make a portal a few times," Alex said grimly.

"Lintz and his precious creepy-crawlies will hold her a while, you mark my words." Elias's shifting features tightened in a twisted expression of glee. "Those golden creatures were intent on her demise, and they went to town, believe me—the memory of it still brightens my day. I doubt you'd recognize the old girl if you saw her. I'm sure she'll make herself decent before she comes for you—she's not one to head into battle without her mascara on. If somebody is trying to get through, they're doing it on her behalf. Some of her cronies no doubt, trying to curry favor with the boss—first one through wins a prize! I've seen the old witch with my own two eyes, and she is going nowhere just yet."

Alex still found it difficult to stomach the memory of the injuries he had inflicted on Alypia, and the recollection of her blood-curdling screams still rang in his ears from time to time, whenever he allowed himself to dwell too long on what he had done. None of it made him feel particularly good about himself, and he knew he could never share the thrill Elias felt at another person's suffering, no matter what that person had done. It had never been his intention to kill someone, and Elias's words made him realize how close he had come to doing just that. It didn't sit easy with Alex, though it led him to wonder whether he would have to kill somebody, before his time in the magical world came to an end. A shudder ran up his spine.

Thoughts of golden beasts and spilt essence and traumatizing screams made the pain in his chest return with a vengeance, the sudden jolt of it taking his breath away.

Elias's face contorted in a frown. "Can I help?" he asked.

Alex wondered what the shadow-man meant, somewhat perturbed by the borderline compassionate note in Elias's echoing, otherworldly voice.

"With what?"

"With that," Elias replied, resting a shadowy finger on Alex's chest.

Glancing down, Alex's eyes went wide in alarm as he saw a dim silver light glowing beneath his skin. He found himself frozen to the spot, unable to pull away as Elias felt for the damaged pulse of his coiled essence, his wispy fingers sinking disturbingly through Alex's flesh, into his ribcage. Alex could feel the cold chill of the dark mist moving through him, but as soon as Elias touched the broken edge of his soul, everything felt better, like smoothing a cooling ointment on a burn. What surprised him most, however, was the lack of snowflakes where the wispy creature touched him. Whatever Elias was made from, it wasn't an ordinary sort of magic.

"It's good I wasn't wearing my nurse's uniform, or this could have been really uncomfortable," Elias cackled, making Alex laugh despite himself.

Elias removed the fronds of his wispy hands, the raw edge of Alex's essence calming to an almost imperceptible ache. Even breathing felt easier, his chest relaxing, his shoulders loosening.

"Elias?"

"Yes?"

"How did you know Professor Gaze?" Alex asked, remembering that she had mentioned him before she died, telling them that she had adored him once. He presumed she hadn't meant the wispy anomaly before him, giving rise to the question of what Elias had been before he was this. It was a question Alex had been consistently curious about, but to have heard Elias spoken about by someone else made the shadow-man's humanity somehow more possible.

"Ah, that wizened old thing," he said, though, to Alex's surprise, the insult carried no malice. It sounded almost affectionate, though Elias quickly covered it with a languorous flick of his wrist. "A memory from a lifetime ago, no more, from a time when I was both more and less than I am now." He tapped his vaporous foot against the floor, though it made no sound.

"She said she adored you once," Alex murmured. "You must have known her well, at one time?"

"A tragic passing." Elias seemed to nod, the words spoken through gritted, starry teeth, as if he hadn't wanted to say it but could not prevent himself. "A fine mage from a former life."

A vision returned to Alex's mind.

"There was a figure standing in the hallway, in the flashback I had when I picked up Derhin's bottle—that was you," Alex said, realization dawning. "You were a professor at Spellshadow, dressed in robes, and you were watching them laughing. It *was* you, wasn't it?" he pressed, though he was sure of it. The figure had seemed somehow familiar, even then. It had been the same with the portrait on the wall, in one of the Spellshadow corridors—the only portrait with the plaque torn off. The man in the painting had been so familiar, yet Alex hadn't been able to put his finger on why. Now, it made sense.

The stars in Elias's eyes flashed a warning at Alex. "Elias made me, and I am Elias."

"It was you, wasn't it? Just tell me it was you."

"Life comes and life goes. There is no avoiding fate," he replied cryptically, his voice dripping with bitterness.

"What happened to you?"

Elias was more evasive than ever, glancing around, looking anywhere but at Alex. It was clear he didn't wish to dwell on what he had been before, but Alex couldn't drop it. People didn't just end up as wafting shadows, flitting here and there. There had to be a reason Elias was the way he was, and Alex was desperate to know it.

"I thought I was clever... but never mind that," the shadow-man sighed. "You seem to be all in a pickle. I can feel it, buzzing off you—most annoying." He shook out his vaporous body, swatting the air as if ridding himself of a vexatious wasp.

"What do you know of Caius and the Kingstone essence?" Alex asked, knowing he wasn't going to get the answers to Elias's existence just yet, but remembering there were other answers he might be able to coax out of the shadow-man.

"I know that you're barking up the wrong tree, wasting time with the idea of waiting on corners like the sad little vagrants you are. Caius is no fool. He will sense you before you're even close—he'll certainly smell *you*," taunted Elias, wrinkling up the place where his nose should have been. "What is that? Eau de Pond Scum?"

Alex frowned, realizing he still needed to find something to replace his moat-soaked clothes. He had cleaned them as best he could, but Elias was right—the scent still lingered.

"I fell into the moat," he muttered.

Elias roared with laughter. "Didn't get munched by one of the monsters?"

"Evidently not," Alex retorted, wanting to get back to the topic of Caius. "So how would you do it? How would you smoke him out?"

Elias flashed his starry teeth in a gleeful grin. "I never do the chasing, I always let the admirers chase me. Why wait, when you can have the pleasure of making him come to you? Give him a reason, and he will come."

Elias's words suddenly gave Alex an idea, far better than his previous one. In order to smoke out a predator, bait was needed, and the perfect thing was just beginning to take shape in Alex's mind. He would just need to check the logistics with one of Kingstone Keep's long-term occupants first.

He had been planning to thank Elias for the seed of a plan, but the shadow-man had descended into a strange sort of reverie, his impossible eyes glancing at the walls around him. Alex held his tongue as the misty creature spoke again.

"They wanted to send me here, to Kingstone, you know, but that skeleton-faced idiot listened to the weasels who were whispering in his ears, telling him all sorts of tales. He tried to keep me to himself instead... He misjudged me," Elias said. "I would never have allowed my essence to be taken by anyone else, not with the power I had brimming inside me, once upon a time. Now, it is all I can do to keep myself from evaporating back into the ether, but I was a threat to him back then, Alex—I knew things about him and what he could do. I was a force to be reckoned with. I knew things, and he hated me for it. They all hated me for it, and they knew I would have—"

His words were interrupted by the sudden shifting of his unstable face, as it scrunched into an expression of pain, a hiss escaping from between his shadowed lips. Twists of black mist twirled away from him, disappearing into the air with a startling snap.

Alex jerked back in surprise. He had seen Elias make all kinds of dramatic exits, but this was something entirely different; it felt wrong, somehow. Elias simply watched as the strands of himself evaporated into the darkness, his galactic eyes following them with a look of half-hearted regret. Swiftly, his expression changed, as if shaking off a dark thought, and he turned back toward Alex.

"You are in grave danger, Alex. More danger than you know," he said hurriedly, though Alex wasn't sure why. This wasn't exactly new information to him.

He frowned. "I know."

Elias waved his head from side to side in a slow, wispy shake, the vapor of his form trailing sluggishly after each movement.

"There is more to it than you realize—more to it than you can possibly comprehend. There are so many who have been looking for one like you, for such a long time. The thing is, now they've all seen the finish line, they're squabbling to cross it first... They don't understand. They don't get it. It is not their—" He trailed off, his voice snatched sharply from the air. A crackle of bright light burst from within him, shattering the shadows of his being, dispersing them faster than he could put himself back together.

When the blinding light died down, Elias was gone.

"Elias?" Alex whispered, trying to keep the worry out of his voice. He didn't know if Elias could even come back from what he had just witnessed. He had never seen Elias do anything like that before, but it hadn't looked particularly good for the shadow-man.

Fear prickled the hairs on the back of Alex's neck. Given the extent of what had just happened, whatever it was abruptly silencing his shadow-guide, Alex couldn't help but wonder what Elias had been about to say.

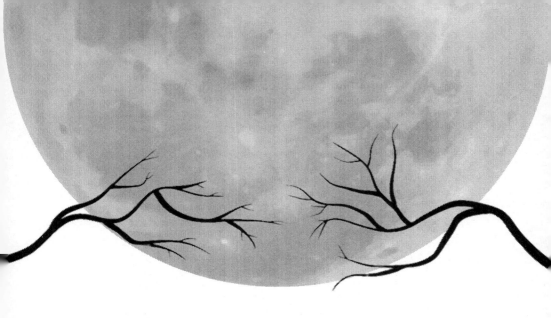

CHAPTER 8

Rushing through the hallways, Alex arrived at the tower, still hoping to catch the others before they left to scope out Caius's favorite spots. His mind was buzzing with the idea Elias had planted there. It was better than any idea he'd had so far, and he was desperate to inform his friends, in the hopes it might bolster their optimism.

The others stood in a group, preparing to leave with Vincent, as Alex burst through the door. Their immediate reaction to him was stiff, given their last exchange, but their apprehension was short-lived, as they saw his excited expression—which he was sure seemed out of place alongside the exhaustion upon his features and the dark circles around his eyes.

"Change of plan! And you're going to like it," Alex

announced. He skidded to a stop in front of Aamir. "But first, I'm sorry for acting like a complete and utter asshole."

"It's okay," Aamir said quietly. "I won't hold your words against you; they were spoken from a place of pain. I, of all people, know what it is like to feel out of control, and the crazy things that can make you do." The shadow of a smile crossed the older boy's lips, and he brought Alex in for a firm hug.

"So, uh, you have good news?" Natalie asked, eyeing him warily but managing to smile.

"We need to come up with a way of luring Caius out of his hiding place," Alex said. "It won't do us any good to wait around, hoping he'll appear—we have to give him a reason to come to us. We have to do something so big, so crazy, that he can't ignore it."

His friends' expressions turned doubtful.

"And what did you have in mind?" Vincent asked, his eerie voice cutting through the nervous silence.

"I hadn't really gotten that far—I'm still thinking about it myself and was hoping you guys might have some ideas."

"An explosion," Jari declared, an evil grin twisting his face.

"It's always explosions with you," Aamir grumbled.

"Explosions aren't easy to ignore," Jari retorted.

"That's true," Alex said, thinking. "But what could we blow up?"

"It will have to be something he will notice, no matter how far away from the keep he is," Natalie mused. "If he's beyond the walls, it needs to be something that will trigger him to return… An alarm or something?"

A lightbulb went off in Alex's head. "Vincent, do you know

what those golden cylinders are, the ones that seem to be stuck on lots of the walls in the keep?"

Vincent smiled. "I do indeed. Good eye, young man. After so long within these walls, I often forget certain sights and sounds that a newcomer would think strange. They are components in a network, running throughout the prison, ensuring Caius's bidding is done. I believe they are modules that guarantee the smooth operation of the barrier magic that keeps us all at heel... Oft times, I have thought of destroying them myself, but the repercussions have rarely seemed worth the effort. You, on the other hand, have more than adequate motivation for such a thing, and I, for one, shall wait in anticipation of the sight and shall do whatever you require of me, to assist in the act. Any action which aggravates the dear warden is music to my old ears."

"Wait, so we can actually bring down the barrier magic?" Alex asked, dumbfounded.

"That enough of a spectacle for you?" Vincent smirked.

"Damn right it is!" Jari answered for him.

"How do we do it?" Ellabell pressed, a look of tentative hope in her blue eyes.

Vincent stretched out his arms, his bony fingers clicking. "It won't be a simple endeavor, and it will require the utmost precision and concentration, but it can be achieved if you are willing to put in the focus, especially with there being so many of you. If we all shoulder a portion of the responsibility, we can have Caius running to us before you know it." He paused. "However, it is not all plain sailing, and I would not advise we remove the barrier in its entirety, given the nature of so many of the miscreants within these walls. But I do believe the same effect can be achieved if we remove a mere portion of the barrier magic. Its failure should trigger enough of an alarm to force Caius's hand, and urge him from his lair."

"And that can be done?" Natalie asked.

Vincent nodded, his large head bobbing on his fragile neck. "The golden cylinders, to my knowledge, work much in the way of a circuit. If we break a section of the circuit, we break a section of the barrier. In addition, the mechanisms within each cylinder are representative of a circuit, so we will be required to investigate more closely the inner workings of a cylinder before we can proceed."

"How so?" Aamir asked.

"Well, we must discover whether the cylinders' circuits need to be halted at the exact same time, in order to break the larger body of circuitry. There are many safeguards such as this in place all over the keep, and if this turns out to be the case, everyone will need to halt the cylinders precisely at the given time, to break that portion of the barrier. If it is not required, the task will be far simpler," he explained.

Alex had a feeling it would be the former. Nothing was ever simple in the magical world. And yet, there was something practical in the explanation that excited Alex; it gave him the same feeling that clockwork gave him—that coding had once given him in the real world—and he was more than ready to examine the mechanisms within the golden cylinders.

"This is gonna be awesome," Jari said with a fist pump.

"I hate to be the party-pooper, but how are we supposed to capture Caius once he's actually here?" Ellabell asked.

Alex swallowed. "Well… If we can get him to come to the connecting hallways where the broken barrier modules will be, and if we bring some bottles of the Stillwater essence…we could use them against him, the way I did with Alypia." He shuddered slightly at the memory. "Combined with the element of surprise, that should give us fairly good odds, especially if we can block the exits—right?"

"It should…" Vincent replied.

"Will this take a long time?" Professor Lintz spoke up for the first time from his spot at the table, where he was still tinkering away with his mechanical beetles.

As if taking the signal from Lintz, Demeter chimed in. "I don't believe it will, though of course it will depend on the nature of the circuitry."

Vincent nodded. "Even if the circuitry turns out to be more complex than expected, the whole endeavor should take a few days, once we get everything in order."

"Jammers will need to be fitted, which I'm sure Lintz can handle, as long as the rest of us shoulder the bulk of the work," Demeter said.

Lintz nodded. "If you're telling me we can have Caius here in a matter of days, with the potential of having the Kingstone essence in hand, then I'm all for it. I will make the best darned jammers you have ever seen, though I will need to get a report from the cylinders, so I know which kind to make. Demeter, would you go with Vincent to investigate and then report back? I just want to get these finished, so there aren't bits falling off them." He sighed wearily.

"Yes, shall we head down now?" Demeter asked. "After all,

there is no time like the future."

"I'll come with you," Alex said. "I want to see what I can do with these cylinders."

"We'll meet up with Agatha too—she'll be thrilled to know what devilish affairs I'm getting us into," Vincent remarked, chuckling softly.

Alex nodded. "Okay. Anyone else want to come look at the cylinders?"

The others shook their heads.

"Ellabell and I will go on Alypia duty and help to keep those portals at bay," said Natalie, and Ellabell nodded her confirmation.

"And Jari and I are going to go on beetle duty, to get them fixed up and fit for use," Aamir added.

"I'll fill you in when I get back," Alex said.

Ellabell grasped his hand. "Make sure you don't go anywhere you're not supposed to by yourself," she warned. "We don't want you hurtling out of any more windows."

"No more falling out of windows."

"Good." She smirked.

Demeter was already heading out of the room, and Alex hurriedly followed him, with Vincent bringing up the rear. As they made their way through the prison, toward Agatha and the first golden cylinder, Alex finally felt as if they were getting somewhere.

Caius, we're coming for you, he thought, unable to stop the smile as it spread across his face.

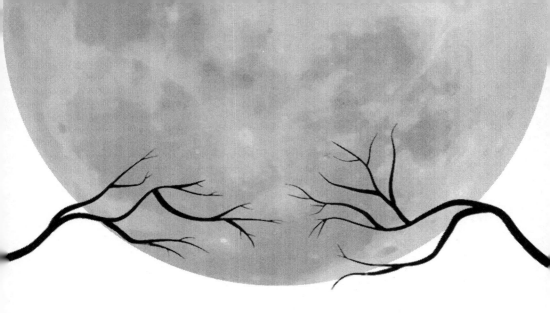

CHAPTER 9

LTHOUGH DEMETER AND VINCENT DIDN'T SAY MUCH
as they wandered down the corridors, Alex could
hardly contain his optimism. If their new plan
worked, they might just manage to stay one step ahead of
the game, evading Alypia before she had the chance to break
through to the keep. It seemed as if she was doubling her
efforts to reconnect the portal from Stillwater, but, as worried
as that made him, Alex refused to feel disheartened. Where
there were options, there was hope.

Turning the corner from one of the inner vestibules, complete with its enticing golden cylinder, they reached the hallway where Agatha and Vincent's cells were, though the necromancer continued past the two half-open doors, moving
away from his own room and heading toward another door a

little way up. He knocked lightly, awaiting the response from within.

"Come in!" cried Agatha.

Alex wasn't sure what this room was, but it sure didn't look like a cell. Beyond the door was a small common room of sorts, though Agatha was the only inhabitant. She had said her farewells to Alex and the others after his near-death experience out of the window, blaming a sudden onset of fatigue, though she seemed rejuvenated now as she greeted Alex, Demeter and Vincent.

A fire burned fiercely in a grate on the far side, with dusty armchairs arranged in front of it. Alex thought it might be something of a fire hazard, but he didn't mention it as he followed Vincent and Demeter inside, choosing to stand while the others sat before the roaring flames. On the back wall, Alex caught a glimpse of gold fixed into the masonry, half-covered by a carved wooden sculpture of a goddess. The sight took him by surprise, making him realize that this must once have been an old guard room or something, not intended for the use of prisoners. It was actually a barrier module, similar to the ones that graced the walls in the various courtyards and vestibules within the prison. Alex wandered toward it, wanting to get a better look.

"Welcome, welcome, to our little prison oasis—tea, my cherubs?" Agatha asked, offering a cup.

"No, thanks." Alex shook his head, not turning in her direction. He felt too hot for tea.

"As you please. What brings you back into my loving arms?" Agatha asked, as she sipped from her own cup.

"Just a notifying errand, Agatha," Vincent explained. "There's a plan afoot to fiddle with the pesky barrier modules and bring dear old Caius into something of an ambush. I thought you'd want to be kept informed of such exciting goings-on."

Alex reached the far wall, moving the carved sculpture aside. The gold glinted as he lifted a hand toward it, wanting to feel the cylinder's smooth, ornate surface. Even at this distance, he could hear the thrum of something mechanical within, and knew he would have to pry the outer shell off somehow to get to what was inside.

Agatha inclined her head in a subtle nod. "I imagine the warden is currently out and about, darting among the shadows at the edge of the forest, no doubt inspired by the darkness. What new, vile methods shall he find with which to torment us next, I wonder? Anything to keep us like soldiers, all in a line, never setting a foot wrong," she murmured.

"So this is a magic barrier module, here?" Alex wanted to double check, scrutinizing the screws that held the top cover in place, wondering how he was going to lift it off.

Vincent eyed the contraption with calm curiosity. "Goodness, in all these years, I had forgotten that thing was even in here. It has become such a part of the furniture," he mused. "Yes, it is, though it's a little bigger than the others, wouldn't you say? How about we take a look at it?"

"I think it needs a screwdriver or something," Alex said, tapping the metal. A spark stung the end of his fingertip, as he had experienced with the first module he had happened upon. He took it as a good sign.

"Agatha, would you be of any use to our new friend? I know you love a good lock-pick," Vincent asked, glancing at her.

She shook her head. "Cripes, no! Don't you remember the last time I gave it a try? Sent me flying halfway across the room!"

"Ah, yes, I knew there was something I forgot to mention about it," the necromancer said, tapping the side of his head. "You don't seem to be having much trouble, mind you," he remarked to Alex, drawing a curious expression from Agatha.

"Thanks for the warning," said Alex, with a note of sarcasm. If he hadn't already had a brief encounter with one of these things, he might have approached it more carefully, had he known it could knock him back. Vincent was right, though—so far it hadn't seemed to affect him much, save for a little electric shock. He frowned, trying to ignore the strange look Agatha was giving him. He wondered if the shock meant there was some sort of shield protecting the module. It made sense, given that it was placed within a prison full of criminals, and yet he couldn't sense any magic coming from the shell itself.

Perhaps it's something underneath?

"Well, we certainly have enough detritus lying around our beloved sitting room. I'm almost certain there will be something of use among the bric-a-brac," the pale man assured Alex as he rose to seek it out.

Sure enough, in the depths of a dusty chest of drawers, Vincent found a screwdriver and brandished it aloft with a whoop of triumph, before bringing it over to where Alex stood. Alex took the tool gratefully, and set to work on the eight screws that held the larger module's cover in place. He made swift work of it, the shell easily coming away to reveal a complex mechanism of gleaming clockwork within. It was truly a work of art, and Alex gasped as he leaned closer, wanting to inspect every cog, every bolt, every delicately placed bit of solder. Sure enough, the whole inner structure glittered with the threat of a protective shield, moving liquidly across the surface. Alex paused, wondering how to get around it.

Carefully, not wanting to set off something terrible, he fed delicate strands of his anti-magic through the glittering shield and let it flow through the mechanisms. As it took hold, he realized he could manipulate sections of the clockwork, making certain pieces stop, and other pieces work backward. However, controlling the entire mechanism was near impossible with the shield in place, making Alex realize they would have to come up with a way of breaking down the shields first, before they could even begin to think about manipulating the clockwork. Looking at the mechanism itself, he could also see that feeding Lintz's jammers into the system wouldn't work; it would help, but they were going to have to overload the mechanisms too, if they wanted to destroy the modules. Simply stopping them wouldn't be enough.

Jari will be pleased, Alex thought. *He'll get his explosions.*

However, they still had the protective shield to contend with. Alex could get around it using thin slivers of anti-magic, but that wouldn't be nearly enough power to overload the system. Just as he was about to lose hope, becoming frustrated with the device, his eye was caught by the sight of something at the very top of the cylinder. Running along the top and bottom edges were two thin golden lines. It was a sight he recognized.

Reaching tentatively toward it, careful to avoid the glimmering shield, Alex paused. He wasn't sure if it was the focus on barrier magic or the blazing fire or the thick walls, trapping the heat in, but the room had grown very hot all of a sudden, making him feel strange. His back was drenched in a cold sweat. Careful not to lose his footing, Alex moved toward the window that stood beside the golden module, to try to get at some of the fog-filtered air drifting feebly in, but he knew he wasn't going to make it. He was going to faint, and it was going to happen any moment.

Awkwardly, he stumbled, reaching out for the nearest thing, which happened to be the top of the golden cylinder. His hands clamped around the edge of it, the sharp metal sides digging into his palms, as his knees buckled beneath him. Managing to keep upright, he leaned forward into the wall, resting his head against it until the woozy feeling went away. He stood there, swaying slightly, his head throbbing, the cold stone soothing against the bare skin of his forehead. It took him a while to notice the flakes of snow that flurried around him, but by then it was too late, and he felt the prickle of a different heat on his skin—the heat of intense eyes on him.

As his own eyes cleared from their hazy, semi-conscious fog, he became aware of a figure lunging in his direction. He moved out of the way just in time to see Agatha hurl herself at the spot where he had been, with a savage, enraged grimace of hatred on her formerly kind face.

"SPELLBREAKER SCUM!" she screamed, her face

contorted in a mask of pure loathing. She rounded on him with lightning speed, clearly intent on doing him real harm.

It shocked Alex to witness the split-second change in Agatha, who had seemed so sweet and nice mere moments before. He ducked as she twisted magic toward him, powerful magic. The next onslaught he managed to bat away, though he could feel the strength of her magic as he made contact with it, swiping it from the air, all the while continuing to duck and dive away from her vicious attacks.

"HOW DARE YOU! HOW *DARE* YOU!" Agatha roared.

It seemed to him as if she were everywhere at once, and he wasn't sure how long he could fend her off, in his current state. Adrenaline had come to his aid again, but it was close to running out.

Suddenly, a spell hit him square in the chest, precisely against the point that had been giving him so much trouble, where the raw edge of his essence still pulsed painfully. The agony was instantaneous, and his body doubled over in an attempt to quash the searing burn of it. She had found his weak spot.

Alex lifted his head to see Demeter stepping quietly up behind Agatha, placing his palms on either side of her head as his lips moved silently, his fingers weaving golden magic into her skull. Agatha froze, and her eyes went blank. Alex watched as Demeter carefully picked her up, carrying her to the largest armchair, where he laid her down.

Fear gripped Alex again as he saw Vincent coming toward him, but the eerie man's face didn't denote any hint of a threat. Rather, there was an expression of sympathy upon his strange, pale face.

"Come with me, dear boy," the necromancer urged, taking Alex gently by the arm as he led him past the still figure draped across the armchair, and out into the hallway. He took him to the vestibule at the top of the corridor, and leaned him against the wall by the open window, encouraging him to catch his breath. "Breathe, breathe. Good, heavy, deep breaths."

"What just happened?" Alex gasped, doing as Vincent said, drawing in breath after breath as evenly as he could. It was becoming increasingly evident that he could not escape the curse of people wanting to kill him. If it wasn't Alypia, it was someone else. And yet, he had never expected such a reaction from one as seemingly sweet and kind as Agatha.

"I apologize for the actions of my friend," Vincent said. "You must understand, it is not easy for those who have lived as long as we have lived—the ghosts grow louder as our years recede into the ether, and Agatha is particularly haunted."

"I don't understand." Alex leaned back, shaking his head.

"Ah, I would not expect you to," Vincent said, his face pulling into a taut, uncomfortable smile. "You are untouched by the hatred that once brewed between our two races."

Alex wasn't sure that was entirely true, having experienced a multitude of hateful tales, but he said nothing to the contrary, allowing Vincent to continue.

"In a war between races, nobody wins," Vincent sighed, "and Agatha lost dearly. As we all did, on all sides. You were guilty only of bringing bad memories back to the forefront of her mind, after countless years of pushing them farther and farther back."

"What happened to her?" Alex asked.

"A particularly grisly battle was fought, and Agatha lost everything. She was not unique in that respect, but her pain is particularly pronounced. As the dust settled, she picked her way through the battlefield, following the crows. Trailing those winged harbingers led her to the bodies of her entire family, the flames of their lives snuffed out by Spellbreakers," he explained. "Agatha never quite recovered. I doubt any of us did—any of those unfortunate souls who lived through it."

Alex watched Vincent cautiously, wondering if the strange man harbored any of the same feelings that Agatha had toward him and his long-dead kind. There was certainly a note of bitterness in the eerie man's voice, but Alex could not be sure where such bitterness was directed.

As if sensing Alex's concern, Vincent smiled reassuringly.

"Fear not, Spellbreaker. I sympathize with your plight. I always have, much like your friend Demeter. Genocide is the foulest plague known to the world, and I offer you my apologies, that you have found yourself alone among us. My words can never make up for the suffering of your people, but I hope they may ease a fraction of your own."

Strangely, they did. Vincent was right—one apology could never make up for what had happened to his people, but it served to remind him that there had been losses and suffering on both sides, not just his own. True, his people had been wiped out in their entirety, save him, but there had been mages and Spellbreakers, no doubt, who had been caught up in a fray they wanted no part of. The peaceful had paid dearly for the arrogance and bigotry of the aggressive. Innocents had fallen on both sides, and, to Alex, there was nothing more tragic.

As his heartrate lowered, and he stopped fearing that Agatha was going to come running up the corridor after him, Alex found himself at something of a loss. Agatha had left his concentration in tatters.

Vincent smiled at him. "The mind needs rest in times of great stress, dear boy, and I feel you are suffering under the worst of it."

"Something like that." If the thought of a vengeful warrior princess forcibly finding a way to make him suffer wasn't stressful, he didn't know what was. He knew it stemmed from the feeling of being endlessly pursued, never being able to fully let his guard down and relax his mind; he wasn't sure he could even remember what it felt like to be at ease.

"Perhaps your mind is in need of a welcome distraction?" Vincent suggested.

Alex nodded. "I'd give anything to divert it, even just for a few minutes. It would really help with… all this."

"In such a case as this, with such a mind as yours teetering on the brink, I would be willing to breach a lifelong pledge never to impart my knowledge to another," the necromancer said. "I will endeavor to distract your mind with a talent of great import, although the task will require a bottle of essence. Demeter has told me you have some in your possession?"

"Why do you need it?" Alex asked tersely, suddenly suspicious of the necromancer's motivations.

"Nothing sinister, I promise—I merely require it as a teaching implement. Think of it as you would a ruler or a piece of chalk," Vincent reassured. "Only if it can be spared, mind you. I'll return it to you immediately after the lesson is over."

"Will you?"

"Will I what?" Vincent raised a silvery gray eyebrow.

"Give it straight back?" Alex asked, seeking confirmation. It felt somehow wrong to trust a necromancer.

"I swear I'll send you back with it, just as it was," he replied with mock solemnity.

No matter how hard he tried, Alex couldn't exactly picture the bottles of essence in the same way he did school chalk and stationery. He was undeniably intrigued by the strange man with the transparent skin, black eyes, and shock of gray hair, and the powers he possessed. Vincent may have been a necromancer who dabbled in a dark and dangerous art, but Demeter seemed to trust him in a way he didn't trust the other imprisoned necromancers. Alex wondered if that meant Vincent was stronger or weaker than the others, or whether he was simply a different sort of individual altogether—a good necromancer, if such a thing existed?

For a moment, Alex's mind dwelled upon the image of Demeter, rendering Agatha immobilized with just his palms. He could see that Demeter and Vincent were two fiercely strong mages whom he could certainly learn a lot from. He knew for sure he had underestimated Demeter, who was not only capable of endless Spellbreaker history lectures and the world's worst dad jokes, but also of a magic far more useful than simple spells and shields. At last, Alex understood what Demeter had meant when he said he had a way of making Caius give them the essence—he could manipulate minds. It was a skill Alex knew could come in very handy when dealing with royals in the near future, including Caius, though he wasn't sure he'd be able to convince Demeter to teach him how.

If only I could do mind control, Alex thought sardonically, *I'd be able to make him teach me.* For now, he'd settle for whatever Vincent had in store to help him.

Alex raced to the tower room where he had left his satchel of bottled essence. Eager to start the lesson—and get it over with quickly, so he could focus again on the modules—he hurried through the labyrinth of hallways, ignoring the beady eyes that watched him through the grates and the steady *drip-drip* of the moldy water falling from the ceiling and hitting the floor in a steady rhythm.

Passing through an intersection of hallways, Alex paused. Down the corridor to the left, which happened to be one of the corridors Vincent had pointed out as one to be avoided at all costs, he spied Natalie. She was pressed close to the wall, talking to someone through a grate in one of the wooden cell doors. Ducking behind the corner, he watched her for a while, unseen, trying to listen to what she was discussing with the person on the other side of the grate. A shiver ran up his spine as he picked up the sound of a low, raspy voice coming from within the cell, but what worried him more was the gleam of excitement he saw in Natalie's dark eyes as she listened intently to what the man was saying.

Creeping closer to get a better look, Alex saw a repulsive, deathly pale face peering through at Natalie, with impossibly black eyes that flashed with malice. Alex guessed this must be one of the necromancers Vincent had been talking about when he had mentioned vile, despicable creatures who could not be trusted. There was a resemblance in the two men's appearances, undoubtedly, but this individual radiated darkness in a way Vincent did not. This man's evil was tangible in the way he sneered, his veins running vividly in a network of sickly black beneath his translucent skin. Alex couldn't understand why Natalie wasn't the least bit alarmed by the necromancer's disdainful smile, and could hardly believe what he was seeing. He knew Natalie enjoyed the powerful side of magic, but this was beyond reckless.

Natalie caught sight of him as he edged closer, and her eyes narrowed in something akin to annoyance. She muttered a swift farewell to her black-eyed acquaintance before turning and walking straight past Alex, practically pushing him out of her way.

"Natalie, stop!" he called.

"I am not in the mood for a lecture, Alex," she said over her shoulder.

"We need to talk about this—" Alex began, grasping for her, but she tore her hand away.

"I am free to do as I please," she snapped. "What is your problem?"

"When you start fraternizing with necromancers, *you* are my problem!" he hissed. He realized they hadn't completely made up since the last argument they'd had, over Ellabell. "Need I remind you what happened last time you got involved with dark magic?"

Her eyes flashed with a look of sudden hurt, and Alex wondered if his words had hit too close to home. For a moment, she was silent, before the hurt transformed into an expression of defensiveness.

"That is rich, coming from you, Alex. How is *your* chest feeling, by the way?"

Natalie kept walking, and Alex struggled to keep up with her brisk pace.

"I don't want to get into another argument with you, Natalie. We don't have *time* to argue. I just want you to stay away from those mages—from people like that!" he said. "You have no idea what they're capable of. And we've already been warned away from them. It's like you go looking for trouble." He shook his head in disbelief, but his words only seemed to aggravate Natalie's defensiveness further.

"That is a little bit hypocritical, is it not?" she remarked tersely, just as they reached the wide, circular common room that led to their quarters in the tower above.

"I was only visiting with Vincent to talk about the barrier modules. You know that! I only spoke with him to help *us*." He knew it was the barrier again, heightening his emotions, making them spike impulsively. Regardless, he didn't think she'd buy it if he tried to explain. He had already overstepped the line.

"We should have never left Stillwater," Natalie said softly. "We had so many opportunities to strengthen ourselves there—the books, the professors, Helena. Now, we have so little. You cannot blame me for trying to learn whatever I can, to improve our chances of survival."

"We had no choice but to leave!" Alex insisted. "Stillwater House was a fantasy, Natalie. It didn't exist—Alypia's offer didn't exist. Surely the fact that she keeps coming for us is proof enough of that?"

Natalie looked at him with quiet disappointment. "As much as you hated Alypia, her offer was genuine—it granted us a security we will never get again. Here, there is only running and hiding and fearing the smallest sound in case it is someone coming for us in the night, to kill us." Natalie shook her head, biting her lip as if holding back tears. "I want to see my family again, Alex. I want to let them know I am okay, and continue protecting myself and others, and if that means learning a few things from a few unsavory characters, then so be it. I will do whatever it takes."

"There's a difference between doing something to survive and doing it because you enjoy it," Alex replied, trying to push down the anger rising through his body.

This time, the look she gave him was one of pure determination. "You think you are a hero, yet you run from true power—you fear it. Heroes fear nothing."

Alex opened his mouth to respond, but he wasn't sure how. In the heat of the moment, he almost wanted to snap that he didn't fear anything, but it would be a lie. Neither did he consider himself a hero. He was just a young person like her, trying to survive, trying to make sense of this crazy world, trying to get home.

His expression must have been simmering though, from the way Natalie was staring at him with a fearful glint in her widened eyes, though perhaps it was just the atmosphere playing tricks on him, making him see and feel things that didn't exist.

Her expression made more sense as he glanced down at himself, seeing the crackle of his anti-magical aura beginning to edge through his skin, trying to defend against the on-slaught of Natalie's words.

He had to get away. Her words had intensified the crawl of rage beneath his skin, and it was overwhelming him. He turned and ran.

"Alex, come back! Don't leave me like this!" she called.

Her voice faded away until he could no longer hear it. He couldn't trust himself around any of them, with the barrier manipulating him the way it was. He wondered if it might also have something to do with Elias's attempt at healing him, the shadow-man's touch simply making things worse in the long-run, after a momentary relief. Alex felt he needed Vincent's lesson more than ever to escape the pressure of it all, if only for a short while. He needed the claustrophobia and the anger and the skin-crawling sensation of the keep to pause. If he didn't catch a break, he sensed he might lose his grip on reality for good. It was already slipping away from him.

He continued on his way to the tower room and reached it quickly. After retrieving two of the black bottles, Alex strode back through the corridors of Kingstone Keep, trying to take the edge off his anger, and soon found himself once again at Vincent's cell.

Inside, it was unexpectedly spacious, with a large window cut into the far wall that made the room seem airy and bright. Vincent sat in a chair in the corner, a book open on his lap.

"Are you all right?" Vincent asked as Alex entered. "You look like you have a thousand demons whispering away in that head of yours, young Spellbreaker."

"There's been a lot to think about, that's all." Alex sighed, trying to push all thoughts of Natalie aside—for the time being, at least. "I'm ready to get on with this."

"Come, sit," Vincent said, gesturing toward the chair opposite. A small fire burned in the grate between the two seats, making Alex anxious. Vincent smiled, gazing down into the warming blaze. "If you begin to feel faint, I shall extinguish its flames. We don't want a repeat of what happened earlier…"

"Thanks," Alex said, taking the offered seat. It seemed as if the necromancer was settling down for a long discussion, and the idea made Alex instantly antsy. He didn't know how Vincent could be so calm when they still had so much to do.

"I feel it's important we get to know one another a fraction better, before I begin to teach you about a side of necromancy I feel comfortable with—spirit lines and how to walk along them."

"You said it's a talent of…great import, right?" Alex asked, the formal phrasing feeling strange coming from his own mouth.

"Most certainly. Spirit lines can reveal deep-seated fears and secrets. If you know a person's past, you know their vulnerabilities. Such a skill may be of use in your fight against the royals," Vincent said with a wave of his long fingers. "Now, trust is the key to success, and if you do not trust, doors will not open. I hope you feel able to trust me, by the end of this session. I realize you must have your concerns; I wouldn't think you sound of mind if you didn't."

"I'm still not sure what to make of you," Alex replied bluntly.

"Good, we are off to an excellent start. Honesty from the outset—wonderful." Vincent clasped his hands together in apparent delight. "Now, allow me to paint you a picture. As I mentioned before, I am a sympathizer with your kind. I have always been so. You see, I was there on the last day of the Spellbreakers, when the earth was drenched in a ravenous silver that turned many mages into dust... I saw and I understood the painful price, and Leander Wyvern's revenge. There are many within these walls who were there, though they do not all share my sentiments. I sought equality where they sought bloodshed. I do not think either side won."

Alex wasn't sure Vincent looked old enough to have been alive in 1908, but that was the mystery of the necromancer—he could have told Alex he was any age, and Alex would have believed it. The man's eerie skin and blacker-than-black eyes made him seem infinite, as if he might go on forever, never changing. Alex wondered if it was a trait of necromancers, to look this way, prompting him to wonder why the veins beneath Vincent's translucent flesh were the same color as the veins beneath his own flesh, only clearer—whereas the man behind the grate, the one Natalie had been speaking with, had been covered in tangled webs of deep, poisonous black.

"Does necromancy turn your blood black?" he asked, intrigued.

Vincent tilted his head, gazing curiously at Alex. "What makes you ask such a question?"

"I think I saw another necromancer, in one of the cells, but the veins beneath his skin were dark, not at all like yours," he replied, hoping it wasn't a rude question. How was he to know whether or not it was polite to ask a necromancer about his strange appearance?

Vincent nodded. "While I am indeed a necromancer, I do not share in the wicked delights others find in it. I do not perform the ungodly—I seek only to help, following the light, trying not to stray too far into the darkness. It is the darkness that blackens the blood," he explained. "My joy is in tracing spirit lines and focusing upon them, utilizing but not seeking to control the phantoms within. Keeping to the light, I do not poison my body with dark magic, though I have had to compromise on the eyes." He smiled wryly, gesturing languidly in the direction of the onyx pools that stared, unblinking, in Alex's direction.

It intrigued Alex, as he listened to the explanation, wondering what Vincent was going to teach him and how on earth he was going to invert such powerful magic. Natalie's voice played on a loop in his head, taunting him, reminding him not to fear power, but to embrace it. It was easier said than done.

"Did you bring the bottle I requested?" Vincent asked.

Alex nodded, retrieving the two bottles from his pockets and placing them on the small, square table that sat between them, the surface devoid of anything homey—no trinkets, no saucers, not even a book or two.

"Very good," said Vincent. "I thought it best we had these for you to practice on. I would not like to let you loose on some poor soul, not having tried it out first. I know my magic doesn't work as your magic does, but I'm sure we'll find a solution—you seem a bright sort."

Alex felt calmer, knowing the bottles were only to practice on, though he hoped he wouldn't make a mess of it and accidentally destroy something. Especially with the barrier's influence, he wasn't sure how his anti-magic might play out under new pressures.

"Do you think I'll be able to do it?" he asked.

Vincent shrugged, the bones of his shoulders poking through his shirt at sharp angles. "I am ever the optimist. Now, pick up one of the bottles," he instructed.

Alex did as he was told, the solemn face of a young man rushing into his mind as his fingers closed around a bottle marked "S. Epstein." Slowly, he forced his mind away from the image, returning to the room, focusing as hard as he could on Vincent.

"Very good—promising control," said Vincent with a smile, though Alex wasn't aware he was doing anything profound. "Now, necromancy can also be performed on yourself, but we are beginning with somebody else, in case things go awry."

Alex nodded, eager to begin. The memories of S. Epstein were growing more insistent, banging on the barrier he had put up in his mind to keep them out.

"First, you must focus on the path of someone's spirit line. Then, you can follow it back as far as you are able. Though, I should warn you, it gets harder the farther back you go. The spiritual memory is filtered through generation after generation, growing weaker with each stage, if you will, like taping too many times over a cassette," he explained.

Alex looked at him blankly.

"A cassette?" Still nothing. Vincent shook his head in mock despair.

"Never mind—you understand my meaning?"

"I think so," he replied.

"Superb. So, a spirit line is precisely as described: it is the line of somebody's spirit." He grinned, long teeth pushing against the thin flesh of his lips.

Alex frowned. "How do I find it?"

"I will instruct you as best I can, though your instincts may have to do some of the work, tailoring it to your particular style of magic," Vincent began, smiling as reassuringly as his strange face permitted. "And, please, don't worry if you don't succeed on your first attempt. Necromancy takes practice, but is invaluable once mastered. First, close your eyes and focus on the image in your mind, surging forth from the vial in your hand."

Alex obeyed, allowing S. Epstein back into his mind. He found himself floating above a familiar piazza, the sun baking the sandstone as the heady scent of roses filled the air. Against the far wall, the stern-faced young man stood beside a young woman, talking secretively beneath the tensed bow of a cupid-like cherub carved into the stone above their heads. It was easy to get lost in these visions, and Alex felt lighter in the false world of another's former life, his troubles fading away as he soared above the square, observing the couple, unseen. It was only the sound of Vincent's voice, piercing the scene, that brought his focus back to where it ought to be.

"You must seek out a pulse within the vision. Delve deeper

into the essence, transcending the layers, and you should find it within," he instructed.

It sounded like a vague sort of command, but Alex found it far easier to follow than expected, once his mind had made sense of it. It was like staring into a moving stream to try to see the shapes of fish and pebbles beneath. Focusing beyond the bright lights and vivid colors of Stillwater House, he moved through the layers of S. Epstein's surface memories, reaching deeper and deeper toward something else, pulsing acutely in the center of it all. A glowing heart of silvery white light. This had to be it, Alex thought, as he awaited further instruction from the godlike voice of Vincent, bellowing to him from all around.

"Now, follow the light as if it is a pathway, going back as far as you wish to go. It should stretch out ahead of you once you focus your mind upon it," he explained, moments later.

Alex concentrated on the glowing light, realizing he no longer possessed a body as he glanced down with invisible eyes. He could see and he could hear, but he was not an entity as such, merely a concealed observer in the life of another. It did not perturb him as much as he thought it might have, and he diverted his attention back to the task at hand. No sooner had he poured all of his attention toward it than the light began to spill out, running in a shimmering line into the darkness of a distant gray horizon.

Following Epstein's spirit was a slightly harder skill to master, however, and Alex struggled to walk the silvery line. It was not a case of simply putting one foot in front of the other, as he had no feet to move. Reaching within himself, he drew upon the strength of his anti-magic, gathering it into one core point of focus and sending it out toward the silvery line of Epstein's spirit. As if magnetized, the ripple of his anti-magic stretched ahead, pulling him along behind. The place where his mouth normally was curved into a smile as the first fresh visions began to come to him; he had mastered the skill with a degree of success he had not anticipated.

"It is up to you where you wish to go," Vincent boomed in his head. "Direct your energy and dive into the spirit line at any interval you please."

He did so, though the exertion was titanic as he dragged himself along the gleaming spirit line of S. Epstein. It became easier, the more used to the sensation he got, but he could feel his energy straining to achieve his desires. In these visions, Alex felt different from the omnipresent figure he'd been in the surface memories. As he delved deeper into this young man's past, he realized he *was* the person whose spirit he was piggy-backing upon. The view was limited, his eyes seeing only what Epstein had seen. It was the same as he moved gradually backward, inhabiting the souls of Epstein's parents and grandparents and great-grandparents, going as far back as he was able.

He saw days filled with laughter and days filled with tears, first kisses and last kisses, triumphs and failures, all in one sweeping observation of Epstein's spirit. In one vision, seeing the black clothes and rainy skies of a funeral, he almost felt as if he were trespassing, stealing a precious moment from within the pulsing red soul of S. Epstein. He wasn't sure how comfortable that made him feel, and yet he couldn't stop himself from experiencing it through the stranger's eyes, watching it and living it as if it were him. It was deeply sad and deeply moving, and he found he could not leave.

There was something oddly addictive about escaping into the body of another, seeing their life instead of his own, especially considering the pressures that awaited him in his own existence. Here, there was no Alypia, no portal, no stress, no time constraints, no imposing barrier magic overpowering his emotions. Here, there was only what he wanted to see, and he felt this was exactly what his mind needed.

Pulling away from the funeral, he stretched farther and farther back along the line. It was like flicking through the pages of a painstakingly made family tree, with some images less clear, getting fuzzier and fuzzier the farther back he went. Eventually, the visions became nothing but grainy tableaux; he could still hear things that were being said, but he could no longer see any of the actors playing out the scene.

"When you're ready, return as carefully as you can, recoiling slowly," instructed Vincent.

As Alex returned to the cell, which seemed so ordinary now, a ripple of concern flowed through him. He worried that performing such a feat might have used up some of his essence, as other powerful spells did, but he realized, as he clutched his chest, that the spirit line he was following had acted like a buffer, keeping his own essence safe. It was almost as if the spirit line was a power source all its own.

"Why are you really teaching me this?" Alex asked suddenly, gripping the bottle in his hand. He wasn't sure if Vincent's motives were as altruistic as he'd made out.

Vincent picked at a thread on his armchair. "I felt…

compelled to instruct you in the ways of spirit lines. There was an inkling within me that it may be of some use to you—a compulsion… as I said," he explained, a tightness in his usually crisp voice.

Alex frowned, eyeing the necromancer with curiosity. If there was more to the story, Vincent didn't seem particularly forthcoming, his stern expression preventing Alex from inquiring further. Still, Alex couldn't quite suppress the sense that there was more to it than met the eye.

As Alex placed the bottle back on the table, he realized how relaxed his mind still felt, how much joy the fleeting escapism had given him, within the lines and lives of others. Though, the attraction he felt to it also scared him slightly, making him think he might have to keep his spiritual endeavors to a minimum for fear of the dark places they might lead. After all, there was a reason necromancy was frowned upon, no matter how pleasant it might feel.

Deciding to take a brief pause, Vincent offered Alex something to eat and drink, to help replenish his energy. Alex took the food eagerly, quickly wolfing down a snack of soft white bread, tangy cheese, and sweet figs. He had to wonder where Vincent had gotten such things—perhaps he and Agatha had their own means of pilfering better items, seeing as they had free rein of the place. Alex just wished Lintz and Demeter would nick food from the same place, so they didn't have to eat another bowlful of insipid gray gruel. The drink was a tall glass of something fizzy. As it touched his lips, he realized it was the same stuff Alypia had offered him, in her glass-roofed office. The taste brought bad memories with it, but he gulped it down nonetheless; his spiritual adventures had left him parched.

"How did I do?" Alex asked, swallowing the last of the cheese.

Vincent grinned. "Better than expected, for a beginner."

The five-minute interval had given Alex a chance to think about the potential of these newfound skills, and how he might use them for his own means. It was encouraging, and Alex realized it was probably worth every moment of time he spent away from the task of breaking down the barrier magic. An idea had come to him while he was biting into a plump fig, though the thought of actually trying it out made him nervous. His own spirit beckoned, whispering to him the possible secrets of his hidden lineage.

"Do you think I could try my own spirit line?" he wondered aloud.

"Do you feel up to the challenge? You look a touch pale." A strange expression crossed Vincent's pale face, but Alex would not be deterred, not when such a huge opportunity was orbiting within his grasp.

"I'll be okay—the food helped, and we'll end the lesson straight afterward," he said.

Vincent raised a silver eyebrow. "You're certain?"

"Yes," he replied, though he had to wonder if this was the whole point of Vincent teaching him how to trace spirit lines, to encourage him to try it on himself and learn more of his secret past, as a secondary observer. Who was to say that, while Alex was in someone else's memories, Vincent wasn't rooting around in his? Trusting a necromancer only went so far. Still, he was desperate to try his own spirit line.

"Very well, then. Let's begin." Vincent spoke softly, gesturing for Alex to close his eyes, as he had done before. "Seek out the pulse of your own spirit, deep within the heart of your inner core, beyond the realms of solid flesh."

Alex searched through the darkness, reaching through the blockades of his conscious mind, pushing deeper into the very epicenter of himself, feeling his physical self fall away as he sought out the glow of his own spirit line. It burned brightly, though it surprised him to see that his was the same color as the mages'.

See, we are not so different after all.

"Now, follow it," whispered Vincent, somewhere in the air around him.

Gathering his anti-magic, he poured it toward the burning heart of his spirit, watching in delight as a silver stream flowed away into the distance, mapping out the history of his existence. Alex wasn't interested in the near past; he had lived those days and moments, and he did not need to see them again. However, he paused awhile on a memory of his mother. It wasn't something he could pass up, seeing her again, even if it was just in memory.

In the vision, she was sitting, curled up on the sofa with a tartan blanket draped across her legs, laughing at a terrible gameshow answer on the television. There was a mug of steaming hot chocolate on the coffee table, a mountain of marshmallows bobbing on the surface—too many to melt, just the way she liked it. The memory stung him with a bittersweet barb. He must have been sitting in the armchair opposite, because his view of her was perfect. It was a simple, domestic scene between the two of them, no doubt identical to a million others he could find in his library of remembrances, but it was everything Alex had wanted and needed to see. He didn't even remember it, or how old he must have been, but it didn't matter; it was enough just to see her, to refresh the picture he held of her within his mind.

It was tricky to pull away from her. He knew he could have spent a week there, watching only her, but the draw of his past soon overcame his desire to linger in the realm of his old life.

Moving farther back, things began to speed up, like a fast-forwarded version of *This is Your Life*, until there was no more of him to see. Reaching the edges of the next person in his spiritual timeline, he came to a standstill, pressing the metaphorical pause button. However, the images that rushed into his mind were foggy, swirling around his vision like a black mist. He wondered if it was just this small section of memory that was distorted, but, as he pushed farther and farther back, the visions grew even worse; they were barely discernible, as if someone had tied a blindfold around his eyes, blocking the images from sight.

Frustrated, he flitted back to the gleaming spool of recent times and childhood memories, just to check that it wasn't him losing strength, causing the images to blur. To his utter vexation, the images of his own life were crystal clear, but as soon as he moved back along the line, to delve into the ancestry of his father and beyond, everything went dark. It was like a curtain being dragged across the scenes that were playing out, keeping him from seeing. The shapes and images weren't discernible at all, but he could feel things and hear muffled words and conversations—he just couldn't see them or touch anything, in the way that he had been able to in his own, personal memories.

Trying to push away his annoyance, he honed in on the emotions he was vicariously feeling, through the person whose life he was viewing, and the sounds that rushed all around him, drowning his senses in a cacophony of noise. Without warning, grief and fear shot through him like a lightning bolt, driven by the experiences of someone else and a scene he couldn't see. It coursed through every cell with an intensity he had never felt before. His body was in shock, his anti-magic faltering in defense against the pain, until the sensation was so overwhelming it drove Alex to pull away from the hidden memory.

He tore back into reality, his chest heaving, tears pouring from his eyes. Inside his ribcage, his heart thundered against the bone so hard he felt it might explode. Once again, the adventure had taken a vast amount of energy from him, but he was relieved to feel that it had not touched the edge of his essence, even though he felt utterly broken. It had taken nothing important, but this excursion had drained him as physically as it had emotionally.

"You must be careful!" said Vincent, worry furrowing his veined brow. "Rushing from a spirit line as fast as you did is never advisable. It takes time to unpick your consciousness from the spirit world—do you feel well? Do you feel strange? Are you in one piece, do you think? Is there any chance you may have left a piece of yourself behind?"

Alex couldn't deal with the bombardment of questions while his mind was still reeling, and it was everything he could do not to yell at Vincent. The memory he had dwelled upon had made him feel exhausted and bitter, opening him up to a world of accumulated pain and torment within his own past, so intense he didn't even need to see the faces of those who had suffered through it to feel the agony and persecution they had felt. It lingered inside him, haunting him. He wasn't sure what he had expected, but he could never have anticipated the wave of pure terror and searing pain that had coursed through him, leaking through from some unseen point in his ancestry.

I shouldn't have delved into my own past. I should have just followed Epstein and left this room while I still felt rested and calm.

A panic attack began to claw through Alex's body, but Vincent was quick to step in, trying to calm Alex by helping him up and moving him over to the window at the far side of the room. The stale air washed over Alex's face, soothing the livid red of his flushed cheeks. Moments later, as Alex leaned heavily against the sill, Vincent began to speak of other matters, probably in an attempt to distract Alex from the panic that threatened to tip him over the edge.

"Caius often disappears into a forest that lies just beyond this fog," the necromancer said, pointing toward the blurry shape of trees. "It seems to be his favorite spot. I often see the vague silhouette of him, darting about out there."

To Alex's surprise, Vincent's tactic worked. The light outside was growing dim, making Alex wonder just how long he had been in Vincent's cell, dabbling in the spirit world. The idea that he had wasted a great chunk of time made him feel suddenly guilty, but this new information about the forest was somehow managing to shift his focus from his inner turmoil.

"Why does he go there?" Alex asked quietly, his voice thick with emotion.

"Who can say? He never brings anything out and he never takes anything in, though there have been rumors from time to time of him stealing away the odd prisoner to torture, to punish and play with at his leisure. No doubt a test subject for his latest batch of horrors," Vincent mused. "He's not the worst of them, mind you—the royals. His brother holds that title, more monster than man." He shuddered, the movement causing the darkest veins in his head to pulsate in a somewhat nauseating fashion. Alex could barely look at them, though it was harder still to look away.

"His brother?"

Vincent nodded. "The king, Julius. If I had not experienced his cruelty for myself, I would think his vile reputation was nothing but exaggerated hearsay. He makes Caius's box of tricks look like a parcel of kittens."

The more Alex learned about the royals, the more he grew to detest them. Although, it seemed that those in charge of the havens had split off into their own factions. Alypia and the Head were one team, albeit a dysfunctional one, while Kingstone and, presumably, the haven he had not yet had the pleasure of visiting, Falleaf House, were laws unto themselves, quite separate from the closer sibling bond, however tense, of Alypia and her brother.

Glancing uncertainly at Vincent, Alex couldn't help but again wonder *why* Vincent wanted to show him these skills or help him by imparting all this knowledge. What did Vincent get out of it? It was all of very real interest to Alex, but he wasn't sure how Vincent could know so much, unless he was guilty of snooping in royal spirit lines. It seemed like a crime that could definitely get a person locked up.

No matter how much Alex wanted to believe Vincent's motives were purely altruistic, the whole thing reeked somehow of Elias. He supposed Elias must have run out of books, and was now bringing people.

The only thing Alex knew for certain was that, as traumatic as the experience he'd just had was, it had left him with an unshakeable urge to know more about his own spirit line. It overpowered all other concerns—even the initial reason he had agreed to this lesson, which was to calm himself. He couldn't stop now. Finally, he was embracing power. He smiled wryly, knowing with a bitter twinge that Natalie would be proud of this step in his personal growth. When he got back, he knew there would be apologies to make and forgiveness to seek, but now was not the time to dwell on that; he had visions to see, answers to find.

"I'd like to try just once more before we finish," he said to Vincent. He wanted to master this skill as well as he could, while he had the chance.

Vincent seemed dubious, but replied, "What is it you need my help with?"

"Is it possible to focus the lines of my own spirit to get a better image of the memories and lives around me?"

Vincent thought for a moment, taking his time, tapping a long, pale finger against the edge of his sharp chin.

"There is a chance," he said, finally, "though the way you

manipulate and travel through spirit lines is different from the way the rest of us do it. It is not something I am entirely familiar with, though I may be able to instruct you. I hope I can, but I can give you no assurances of its success."

"I'll take those odds," Alex replied.

"I must warn you—there is one caveat to spiritual travel."

"What's that?"

"You can only move within the timeline of those who share your magical credentials," the necromancer explained.

Alex frowned. "What do you mean?"

"If you have a non-magical parent, for example, you won't be able to follow their history or move along their spirit line. You will only be able to see them if they appear in the timeline of your magical side, viewed in a memory, only as your ancestor saw them," he elaborated.

The understanding of it saddened Alex; he would have liked to explore his mother's side a little, but he knew that wasn't going to be possible now, unless there was a magical side to her she hadn't told him about. Somehow, he doubted it. If she were magical, surely there would have been a way her magic could have cured her sickness, and as far as he knew she was still sick.

"Shall we begin?" asked Vincent.

Alex nodded, closing his eyes.

Seeking out the glowing heart of his spirit once more, Alex began the increasingly familiar journey down his spirit line, watching the memories of his life whizz past in a blur, taking him backward through his childhood—vacations, school plays, finger-painted porcupines, picnics in the park, hugs from his grandparents, his mother running after him, smiling with the naivety of her remaining youth. He could see they were rapidly approaching the place his memories ended.

"Now, focus on the bridge between your life and the life before," Vincent instructed, his voice echoing in Alex's ears.

Alex did as he was told, gathering his energy and pouring it into the place where his childhood met the adulthood of someone else, like gluing bits of film together to make a whole reel. Suddenly, his eyes were not his own. He had made the jump successfully, the image before him blazing back in crystal-clear Technicolor. It felt odd at first, slipping into the body of a person from his own history, but it became more comfortable as he moved through the man's memories, getting a feel for them.

It took a while for him to realize he was witnessing the moment his father first laid eyes on his mother. He could feel his father's anxiety feeding into his own emotions, followed by the instant flash of love his father had felt for the girl standing behind the café counter, pouring coffee from a jug. The sight of his mother, so much younger than he had ever known her, broke Alex's heart. As he watched his father approach the counter, he saw his mother turn and flash her most dazzling smile at him. Yet Alex could feel no joy for the young soon-to-be couple, not when he was privy to the end of the story, flipping to the last page before he had read the whole book. She had been so happy once—he knew she had—so what had gone wrong?

What happened to you? Where did you go? he asked his father silently.

With a jerk, the vision shifted.

Before Alex's eyes, flashes of his parents' life together blended in and out, kaleidoscopic to behold. It was hard to keep up, but the visions filled him with bittersweet joy as they played out in front of him. He saw his mother in a way he had never seen her before, so much younger and healthier, without as many worry lines upon her face.

He couldn't deny there was a strangeness to it, and he made sure to skip quickly over any romantic moments that came along, but there was a pleasantness to the rest of the memories—to wander with her on warm, sunlit walks and to hear her laugh again, the sound ringing comfortingly in his ears. His mother had always loved to laugh, and it was heart-warming to see that she had once been deeply in love. Her affection glimmered in her eyes each time she looked at Alexei. She had truly adored his father.

The images slowed for a moment upon the sight of his mother holding up a plastic, pen-like object with two tiny displays that showed pink double lines. She looked scared but excited, and Alex wished he could see his father's expression, but he could only feel the emotion his father had felt. It echoed his mother's—there was fear and excitement bristling within.

"I'm pregnant," she whispered. "We're having a baby."

"I can't wait," he heard his father reply, his voice choked with emotion.

Alex moved swiftly on, leaving them to their moment in the bathroom, not wanting to intrude upon it, even though he had technically been present at the scene anyway.

In the next image, Alex realized they were in the house

he had grown up in, though there were subtle differences. The walls were the same color, but the carpet was different, with a garish pattern Alex was sure hadn't been popular since the seventies, and there were paintings and pictures on the walls that he had never seen before. Many of them were of Alex's mother and Alexei, grinning into a camera, posing against beautiful backdrops of glistening lakes and bright forests. There was one of his mother standing beside a giant redwood that towered over her like a skyscraper. It seemed somehow familiar in Alex's mind, but he could not place where he'd seen the picture before. In the shoebox under the bed, perhaps? He wasn't certain. He realized his mother must have taken the pictures down when his father went away, wherever it was he had gone.

A feeling of sudden panic shivered through him, not one of his own emotions, as the visions shifted onto a street. Alex recognized it as Main Street in his town, with most of the shops unchanged, even now. He smiled with invisible lips—not a lot ever changed in Middledale, Iowa.

Alex could sense that his father was behaving strangely, his mood shifting rapidly, his eyes constantly looking over his shoulder as he walked beside Alex's mother, though Alex couldn't see anything untoward in the direction his father kept glancing. It was as if Alexei were trying to find a face in the crowd. To Alex, there was nothing but plain old Main Street, with the grocery store, the clothing boutiques, and the antique shops he had only ever seen old people go into, the displays unchanged since the 1940s. Cars beeped their horns and people wandered up and down the sidewalk, minding their own business. Nothing seemed out of place. But perhaps that was the problem. There was definitely something worrying Alexei, and that, in turn, worried Alex.

In every vision afterwards, Alexei's mood felt tense, his eyes perpetually looking all around, scanning the horizon, flinching at the smallest sound. Even Alex's mother seemed concerned by her partner's behavior, always asking if he was all right, always getting the same response.

"Just tired, my love," he replied.

To Alex, Alexei still seemed happy, still brimming with love for the beautiful mother of his unborn child. It didn't feel as if his father was planning to up and leave, in the way that Alex had always thought he had. There was no hatred, no animosity, no lack of love—but there was a permeating chill of dread running in Alexei's veins.

What had he been so afraid of? It didn't add up to Alex—they seemed so happy.

With another jerk, the vision jolted forward.

Alex's mother and father were walking through Middledale Park in the early evening, the sun heavy in the deepening azure sky, casting a bronze glow upon the world below as it sank. It was a balmy evening, signaling the arrival of a baking hot summer. As they wandered, his mother turned to Alexei with a mischievous grin.

"Feel like some ice cream? I think the little kidney bean is after some mint chocolate chip," she said, contentment clear in her soft voice.

Alexei nodded. "Whatever the kidney bean wants," he replied, leaving Alex frustrated that he couldn't see his father's expressions. It made him feel strange, to hear himself referred to as "the kidney bean"—somewhere between happy and sad. "You want me to go?"

Alex's mother shook her head. "No, it's okay. My treat." She grinned, bounding off toward the ice cream truck parked beside the children's play area. There were still a few kids scrambling over the brightly colored, somewhat rusted jungle gym, and Alex watched as his mother paused for a moment, watching them with a wide smile upon her face, gently rubbing her stomach. She wasn't visibly pregnant yet, her belly still mostly flat, but Alex knew he was in there, and he knew what she was thinking. She was picturing a bright future for herself, her child, and the love of her life.

Alexei turned, wandering toward the edge of the lake that gleamed in the center of the park, the murky water looking oddly tempting in the close heat of the evening. Where Alexei went, Alex had to follow. Stepping as near as he dared to the lake's edge, Alexei looked down into the shifting surface, giving Alex his first proper sight of his father, in the flesh. The reflection was wobbly, small waves distorting the image, but it was definitely the same man Alex half-remembered from the grainy photograph he had found in the shoebox beneath his mother's bed—the one that had made her cry such painful tears. Alexei was handsome and youthful, bearing a strong resemblance to Alex himself, making him wonder how his mother could bear to look at him, when the similarity was so clear.

Suddenly, Alexei looked up.

There was a man standing on the opposite side of the lake, watching Alex's father intently, a smirk upon his face. Alex didn't recognize the man, nor did he have the chance to get a better look. Alexei broke into a sprint, running away from the lake and his dearest love, who was standing obliviously beside the ice cream truck, ordering a cone of mint chocolate chip.

Alex wanted to scream at his father to turn back, but he had no control over his father's actions—he could only watch and wish things were different.

It took a while for Alex's focus to move away from his mother, but once he understood he could not go back to her, Alex realized his father was running down a familiar route. He ran across the main road that skirted the town, ducking into the dark, cool shade of the forest that ran alongside the highway, then moving down toward the train tracks and the railway bridge that crossed the ravine. It was the spot Alex had liked to run to when he was a kid, eagerly awaiting the arrival of a train so he could watch it clatter across the rails above him, the sound of it thundering in his ears, the vibrations shaking his whole body.

Alexei climbed past the place between the wooden beams where Alex had liked to hide, clambering up onto the train tracks themselves, not pausing for a moment as he took off across the bridge. Alex could hear the sound of footsteps behind his father. Alexei flashed a look back over his shoulder for any oncoming trains. Instead of a train, Alex saw the same man from across the lake, gaining ground, chasing his father down with a determined, cruel look upon his unkempt face.

The man was impossibly fast, and Alex realized with a sinking feeling that the pursuer was now too close to his father. He was almost within arm's reach.

Alexei turned back, Alex's vision following, just in time to see a shadow swoop from the darkness beneath the tracks and cut straight through the body of Alexei's would-be attacker. For the briefest moment, Alex felt a wave of relief, but it was not to last. Seconds later, he felt his father's body buckle. Alexei froze, turning back to see his pursuer evaporate into a black mist, blown away on the wind, disappearing into nothing.

In the shifting shadows below, Alex could see the flash of teeth and the ripple of a vaporous form. It was unmistakable—a sight Alex had come to associate with relief, now filling him with horror.

Something caught Alexei's eye in the tree-line on the right-hand side of the tracks, distracting Alex for a moment. A hooded figure stood between the mossy trunks, smiling coldly from beneath the overhanging branches. Alex was certain he knew who that was too, making him wonder if the two had been in cahoots all along. He wanted to watch the figure for longer, to try to get a clearer image of the mostly shrouded face, but Alexei's focus had turned to the sluggish river trickling away at the bottom of the ravine, far below where he stood.

The shadow swooped again. Alex looked down at his father's hands, only to see that they were beginning to disappear into the same dark mist. Alex guessed, with a heavy heart, that what had happened to the pursuer was now happening to his father, as everything went black.

He wanted to travel back to the park, to see what his mother had done, but he couldn't. It was no longer in his father's timeline. His father was dead. Alex didn't need to see a funeral or a headstone; he understood what the abrupt, black ending meant. But he realized, with a pang of heartache, that his mother did not. The thought of her being oblivious to the truth frustrated him more than he thought possible, as he imagined her turning with two ice cream cones in her hands, only to find her lover gone, never to be heard from again. Worst of all, he knew she would have agonized over it, wondering if it was something she had done that made her love leave without a word. Alex couldn't even begin to imagine how that must have felt, but he found he now had a greater understanding of her tears whenever he had brought his father up in conversation. She must have thought he had up and left her pregnant self, since there was no body to find, and she would never know why he had run or where he had gone.

Slowly, he unfurled from the vision, feeling utterly overwhelmed and vengeful toward the evil, shadowy sprite who was responsible for all this mess—the creature who had killed his father. He wanted answers. He wanted to know why. He wanted to know everything.

"Are you well?" Vincent asked, reminding Alex that he was still in the room.

Alex turned to the eerie necromancer. "I will be," he said quietly. "Thank you for all you have shown me. It's time for me to leave."

"Certainly, young Spellbreaker. We have much work to be getting on with," Vincent said, though there was a flash in his black eyes that made Alex wonder how much the necromancer really knew of what he had just seen. There wasn't time to ask now.

"Of course," said Alex. He stood, almost in a trance, and

hurried from the room.

He ran toward the doorway, up to one of the small turrets he had passed days before, and pounded the stairs to the summit. Bursting out into the cold evening air, Alex stepped up to the very edge of the wall and screamed at the top of his lungs.

"ELIAS!" His voice echoed until he had no air left, his chest burning. "Elias, come out and face me, you coward!" he yelled, hot tears prickling his eyes. "Face me! Face what you did! Come out and admit your crime, you monster!" He slammed a fist into the wall, feeling it crackle against his skin as he screamed and screamed, the tears running down his cheeks.

Nothing made sense. Why had Elias bothered to help him, when the shadow-man had been keeping such a vile secret to himself all this time?

As his screams echoed into the ether, Alex became aware of a shadow loitering at the very edge of the steps behind him.

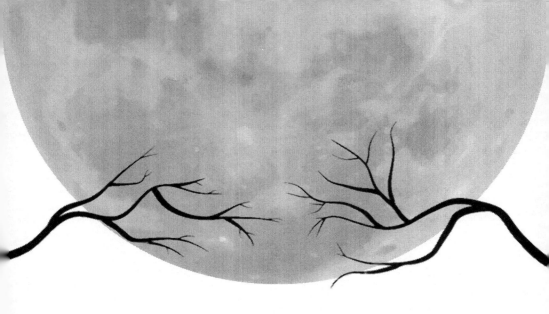

CHAPTER 10

SIREN MAVE STOOD AT THE ENTRANCE TO THE TURRET.
An initial shock rippled through Alex, seeing the toady woman standing there, her cheeks ablaze with liberally applied blush. But his gaze quickly moved elsewhere, driven by frustration. He didn't want to see Siren Mave; he wanted to see Elias.

"Oh dear, Alex Webber, what a state you've gotten yourself into," she murmured quietly, her voice not unkind. Cautiously, she approached.

"You?" he snapped. "What are you doing here?"

"I go where am I needed, Alex," she replied simply.

He glowered in her direction. "How can you even be here?"

"I go where I please," she said, making Alex remember her

appearance at Stillwater too.

"It's not you I want to see… Where is he?" Alex growled, completely beside himself. This wasn't what he wanted—Siren Mave was no good. He wanted the shadow-man, and nothing else would suffice.

"You know I'm not going to tell you that, not with you like this," she said firmly, adjusting her horn-rimmed spectacles. "Let's try some breathing, see if we can't get you to calm down." There was a slightly patronizing note in her voice that set Alex's nerves on edge.

He shook his head. "I don't need to calm down, I need to see *him*. If you stand in my way, I will take you down too," he hissed.

Siren Mave sighed like a henpecked mother. "You won't, Alex, and as much as I'd love to see you try, I don't think you'd come out of it too well," she said, amused. "You really do need to calm down—getting worked up like this will do nobody any favors, least of all yourself."

He glared at her, wishing she would go away and disappear into the hallways of the keep, as she had done in all the other hallways in all the other havens. Why was it that the one time he least wanted to see her, there she was? He thought about saying so, but held his tongue, reserving his venom for Elias.

"I don't have time for this. I need to see Elias, now!" he yelled, growing more impatient by the second.

"How about we begin with you telling me what has caused all this?" she said, gesturing at Alex, a mass of beaded bracelets jangling heavily on her wrist. She mimicked the state he was in by puffing out her rouged cheeks, making herself look somewhat ridiculous. "I'm not going anywhere, Alex, so you may as well speak to me. I can be of help to you, but it's a two-way street," she added, with a note of frustration in her voice.

Alex wondered what on earth she had to be frustrated about. She wasn't the one who had just found out his father was dead, and learned that the creature who killed him was the very same creature that had been his constant guide throughout all of the madness that had become his life.

"Why should I tell you anything?" he spat.

"Because I'm the only one who can understand," she replied, staring intently at him through the thick lenses of her glasses, her eyes almost bug-like.

Alex scoffed. "You can't understand what I'm going through."

"You won't know if you don't try. Are you a quitter, Alex Webber? You never seemed like a quitter to me—definitely not one to shy away from a challenge," she said.

"Do you even know who I'm looking for?" he asked bitterly, realizing he had never heard her mention the shadow-man before, though she had seemed to know whom he meant when he asked where Elias was. Were they in cahoots too? It didn't sit well with Alex; none of it did.

Siren Mave laughed sarcastically. "The things I know about that shadowy pest—I could tell you stories that would make your toes curl and tales that would split your sides with laughter. Do I look dumb to you?" she asked, raising a drawn-on eyebrow. "Mm, perhaps you should not answer that in your current, heated state. Let's not get into flinging childish insults—that's more Elias's style. In short, yes, I know who you are seeking, though I would like you to explain why. Think of me as a reluctant mediator." She smiled, her thick lipstick cracking slightly.

"He killed my father," Alex whispered, pushing away tears.

"You have seen it with your own eyes?" she asked curiously.

He nodded. "I have."

"Pesky necromancers, always meddling," she muttered. "I presume it *was* the necromancer who showed you?"

"I'm glad he taught me how," Alex said defensively.

"Yes, as well you might be, but it has brought a whole lot of trouble my way," she sighed. "Always fixing everyone else's mess."

"It's good to see you haven't lost your compassionate side," Alex said mockingly, feeling angry at the stout, toady woman before him, who was making little attempt at empathy for his loss.

She stared down her nose at Alex. "Kindly remove yourself from your high horse, Alex. It doesn't suit you," she remarked curtly. "You see, the thing about necromancy, especially the way you see the spirit world, is you only get a snippet of the whole story. You make assumptions and fill in the gaps of what you don't see, and you know what happens when you assume, don't you?"

Alex frowned. "What?"

"It makes an ass out of you and me," she quipped. "So, let's agree not to assume anything, yes?"

"I don't think witnessing a murder is an assumption," he said tightly.

She sighed. "Okay, you're clearly not in a cooperative

mood, so how about you just listen for a while? You might learn that everything is not always as it seems," she said, an unexpected touch of sadness in her voice.

It was a lesson Alex was already more than familiar with. Nothing was ever as it seemed, Elias included. He did not need a lecture on perception.

But he shrugged anyway. "I'm all ears."

"Things didn't happen exactly as you believe they did," she began.

"How do you know?" Alex cut in, wondering what the relationship was between Siren Mave and Elias.

"Elias and I are not so dissimilar, as much as I hate to admit it—we are branches of the same tree, if you'll excuse my flowery language," she explained. "Our purpose here is the same."

Alex tilted his head. "Purpose?"

She nodded. "At the time of your father's death, we were both entrusted with the protection of the last Spellbreaker. He and I are… guardians of sorts, for lack of a better word. Mm, I wish I could think of a better word," she muttered. "Anyway, Elias came into this 'business,' if you like, voluntarily. I, however, was drawn out of the void by the royals, when the imbalance was created in our world and they didn't know how to fix what had been done, with the mists of the Great Evil coming for their kind. Silly name, if you ask me—not very original," she remarked. "Still, they created me from the void. Like I said, always fixing other people's problems."

Alex took a moment to let Siren Mave's words sink in. If what she was saying was true, then she had been aware of Elias for a long while. Perhaps she already knew Elias had been visiting him on the sly, feeding him information. What intrigued him more, however, was the idea of her being created by the royals—she seemed real enough, but did that mean she wasn't flesh and bone, like he was? He had to wonder what she was forged from, if not the usual materials.

"How did Elias become what you are?" he asked, trying to understand.

She gave him a withering look. "He is not what I am. Do I look like a formless wisp to you? No, we serve the same purpose, but he created himself, as a guardian, to avoid a worse fate. Some might say it was a bold move; I would say it was… Well, it's not for young ears like yours. The thing is, something must have happened during the metamorphosis, meaning he did not come out as solid as he might have liked. He's come to love it, mind you—I know he finds a sick sort of pleasure in his mistiness, always sneaking in shadows and slipping from place to place, snooping where he's not welcome. I lost count of the times I used to catch him hiding in Esmerelda's chambers and had to shoo him out," she said, her face puckering in distaste. "I digress—Elias was new to it all, still learning the ropes of seeking out hope for mage-kind, when the news came that a Spellbreaker had been sensed. It had been a long time since there was a confirmed sighting of one of you, and it was big news."

"Looks like you didn't do a very good job of keeping my father safe," he remarked drily.

"Are we assuming things again?" she challenged.

"Just making an observation."

"We were doing a perfectly good job, I'll have you know, but I will admit—and I am not prone to doing so—we made a slight error in judgment. We thought we were safe, and we weren't," she explained, her tone regretful. "There were other mages who sought to capture and use the last Spellbreaker for their own purposes, driven by personal vengeance and hatred."

Alex thought of the hooded figure with the twisted mouth he had seen in the trees, and wondered if the Head had been behind the plan that saw his father evaporated into a black mist. Perhaps Elias had been working as a double agent the whole time, with Siren Mave believing him to be on her side, when in reality he had been working to kill Alexei.

"It forced our hand when we saw that someone had started to trail your father—someone working for an underground organization of mages, disgruntled with the king and his rule. It was Elias's job to watch your father, that day in the park. I told him to summon me if anything happened, but he didn't—I think he was trying to prove his worth. I hadn't been the most supportive of mentors, and I think it got to him—again, that is my fault. Enjoy these admissions of failure, as I will not be repeating them," she remarked. "Ultimately, he failed, but I promise you he was trying to save your father."

Alex shook his head vehemently. "You expect me to believe that?"

"You should—it's the truth. Elias tried to attack your father's assailant, but the attack was too strong, and it ended up killing your father too. Think of it as magical shrapnel, which unfortunately took your father's life. Had it been normal magic, your father would have lived, but the magic we use is different… It is stronger, more volatile, more unpredictable, especially when wielded by novice hands," she said sadly. "It was a tragic accident, and we admit our responsibility."

"I don't see Elias admitting to it," said Alex sharply, gesturing around at the otherwise empty turret. "It makes no difference, really—my mother was left without her partner, believing he had just up and left without a word."

She fingered the beads of a bracelet. "About that… We didn't know about you."

"It seems you didn't know a lot of things." Alex flashed her a look of resentment.

For the first time, Siren Mave looked genuinely apologetic. "I'm sorry we left your mother alone. We didn't realize she was pregnant—she wasn't showing, and she hadn't told anyone other than your father, so we figured that was it… no more Spellbreakers. It didn't occur to us to try to explain to her what had happened to him. It was a can of worms we didn't want to open. We don't believe he knew what he was, and your mother certainly didn't know anything about the magical world. So we went back to the royals with our tails between our legs, believing our jobs to be over. We had nothing to protect, nobody to guard. It was a real blow… We had been searching for him for years and years, trying to follow snippets of information about Leander Wyvern's non-magical mistress and their progeny, following leads, usually ending up at dead ends. He was the end of the road," she sighed.

"So I *am* a descendant of Leander Wyvern?" Alex asked. He had hoped and believed he might be.

"You are." She nodded, a look of relief on her face.

"What happened when you went back, after what Elias had done?" he pressed. He felt no less angry at Elias, but he was willing to hear the whole story before he made any further judgment.

She smiled wryly. "As punishment for losing the last hope of balance in the magical world—quite the crime, I'm sure you'll agree—I was made to do menial labor around the havens. Elias being Elias, he decided to make himself scarce, using his shadowy form to his advantage, shirking off his share of the punishment, disappearing into thin air. I wasn't pleased, I can assure you," she grumbled. "I presumed he'd gone for good until I saw him again recently, speaking with you. I think he's trying to make amends for what he did—trying not to make the same mistake again."

Alex wasn't sure which part enraged him more—that she was defending Elias, trying to make what he had done seem less awful than it was, or that she had known all of this and had chosen to say nothing, for so long. He said as much, venom dripping from his words.

"Why didn't you say anything to me, after all this time? Do you have any idea the heartache and pain you could have saved, if you had both just been honest? Are you that inhuman?" he snapped, his eyes burning. "Not once have you lifted a finger to help me! Isn't that your job?" He gripped his fists into a tight ball, trying to push away the sparks of his aura that burned at the edges of his skin.

"That's not entirely true, is it?" Siren Mave replied, her voice calm.

"Fine, that *creature* has helped me, but *you*—you have

done nothing."

She shook her head sadly. "I have tried, Alex. Not every kind of aid is one you can see," she said softly. "I have been there for you. I tried to get you out."

He frowned. "What?"

"I tried to get you out," she repeated. "It took me a while to realize what you were, initially, but once I understood, I *did* try to help. I bent the rules, and I tried to intervene… I am not supposed to use my magic to manipulate anyone, as it can be very dangerous, but that is exactly what I did, for you. I got in Aamir's head and maneuvered him into letting you go."

Alex looked at her in wide-eyed shock. "Why would you do that?" he gasped, realizing with a pang of sorrow that it had been Siren Mave's offer and not the Head's or Aamir's. It had been the real deal. For a moment, he truly had been so close to going home. It physically stung as the wound tore open afresh.

"It's my duty to protect you and help you, and I wanted you to see your mother again. I wanted you to go home, so you could explain to her where you had been—that you had not abandoned her. It was supposed to be a gift, the chance to put her mind your own at ease, refreshing your soul and your motivation," said Siren Mave, fidgeting with the glass beads of her many bracelets. Alex felt as if there was more Siren Mave wanted to say, but she did not say it, her lips pressed firmly together, preventing further words from slipping out.

"Surely, life would have been easier if you had just spoken to me? I don't understand why you and Elias seem so eager to skirt around everything all the time. It's like I can't get a straight answer from either of you!" he sniped, absorbing the information she had just imparted, though it was painful to accept.

She shook her head. "It's not that simple. Believe me, I'd rather be straight with you than have to tiptoe around everything all the time. I'm not exactly built for tiptoeing," she quipped.

"It's easy—you open your mouth and speak," he remarked coldly.

"We are governed by rules of our own, Alex. It is not in our jurisdiction to directly intervene, and I would not be speaking to you now had my hand not been forced by the progression of recent events. We can only answer to what you already know, or if the right question is asked. It's intensely frustrating, for both parties, believe me, but we can't give you any new information, theoretically," she explained.

Alex wanted to scream at the cryptic nature of it all; it didn't make sense to him, and he couldn't wrap his head around it. He was tired of the games—he didn't have time for riddles. Still, he managed to force his mind to concentrate for a moment, trying to consider what Siren Mave had said, and trying to think of what the right questions might be to get the answers that he wanted.

His brow furrowed in thought. "What is your purpose, as a guardian?"

"We are supposed to seek out hope for the magical race."

"What does that even *mean*? You say these things and they don't *mean* anything!" Alex cried, exasperated. "Why am I so valuable to them? What is it that the royals *want* from me?"

"You are vital to their existence," she replied, with the same maddeningly cryptic tone.

Alex's cheeks were purple with frustration. "I am vital to their existence? How?"

"There is something within you that they lack," she said, clarifying nothing.

Alex wanted to scream, and shake the toady woman until she told him something in plain terms that he could wrap his head around. Infuriated, but knowing he wasn't going to get anything clearer from the over-painted lips of Siren Mave, he switched his train of inquiry, trying to fill in some other gaps.

"And my father didn't know that he was a Spellbreaker?"

Siren Mave shook her head. "He didn't know—he didn't know why he was being followed and chased. He was scared, and Elias misjudged the situation."

"And when he died, what did you think?"

"When he died, as I say, we thought that was it. No more."

"So, you can't believe my surprise when I saw you," whispered Elias, appearing sheepishly from the gathering darkness.

Alex wasn't sure he could control his rage, seeing the shadow-man shift into sight. Whatever the reasoning, Elias had still killed his father, and he wasn't sure there was anything that could be said to make him forgive that.

"What did I tell you?" snapped Siren Mave.

Elias lifted his misty shoulders, playing coy. "I couldn't just watch."

"You could, but you had to slink into the spotlight, didn't you? I have this handled, Elias—your presence is neither required nor wanted," she said frostily.

"I don't 'slink,' I sashay," he remarked sourly. "It only felt right that I come and defend myself."

Siren Mave raised an eyebrow. "Says the creature that wouldn't know what the decent thing was if it came up and smacked him in his wispy head."

"If you're going to call me a creature, at least include the 'exceptional' part—I thought we were pals," he purred.

Siren Mave rolled her eyes. "How about *vexatious* creature?"

He flicked a wispy wrist. "Better... It brings me such joy to know I get under your skin."

Alex listened to their back-and-forth in silence, wondering if they even knew he was still there. Glancing between the two of them, he thought about what his next move might be, but found he no longer had the patience to confront his shadowy acquaintance. Siren Mave had told him all he needed to know on that score, and to ask Elias would only bring forth a barrage of smart remarks, vague comments, and backhanded compliments. It wasn't something he particularly felt like suffering through. There were too many other things whizzing about in his overwrought brain.

"If you two are finished, I'd like to go now. I have pressing matters to attend to, and I've wasted more than enough time on the both of you," he said, cutting Elias off mid-insult. The shadow-man was in the middle of a rude remark involving a toad, in response to Siren Mave calling him an idiotic, self-centered ghoul.

They looked at him in surprise.

"No, don't go!" said Elias hurriedly. "We have a lot to talk about, Webber."

Alex shook his head. "I'm done talking. I have more important things to do right now. Seeing as neither of you would stand in the way if Alypia wanted to tear out my insides, I need to go and make sure she doesn't."

"See what you've done!" snarled Elias, rounding on Siren Mave, teeth flashing. "Alex, I was trying to protect him, you have to believe me," he pleaded suddenly, turning back to Alex.

"I can't forgive what you did, Elias. Not today, not tomorrow, probably never," Alex replied heavily, turning to leave. His father was dead and his mother had been left alone, wondering what happened to the love of her life, because of what that shadow creature did—and worse, kept secret.

He was done with questions. He just wanted to be left alone with his thoughts, and the memories of what he had seen. He had no energy left to give.

Walking back down the stone steps, into the main body of the keep, he didn't know if he'd ever see either of them again, and, with sudden realization, he knew he was absolutely fine with that. His world would be much quieter without them.

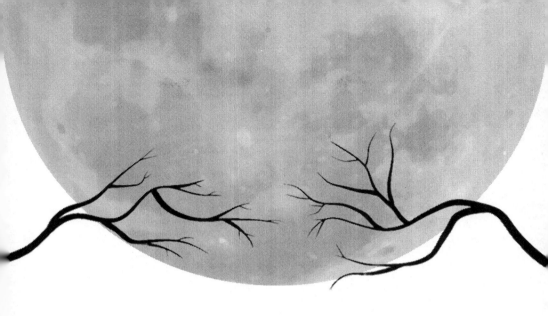

CHAPTER 11

FEELING UTTERLY DISORIENTED, ALEX WALKED BACK toward the tower room, his head down, hoping his two mysterious "guardians" wouldn't think about following him.

Stepping through the door of the tower room, he was met with a wave of tension from his four friends and remembered his and Natalie's angry exchange. It seemed as if it belonged to another time entirely. A very different Alex had re-entered the tower, though he was determined that they should resolve their differences as best as possible before he began to tell them all about the barrier magic. With everything else going on, he didn't want to lose a friendship.

Before he could reach Natalie, however, Jari popped up from his makeshift bed and punched Alex hard in the arm.

"You had us worried, man! I've nearly worn my eyeballs out searching for you—look at them!" he cried, pulling his lids open in a gruesome fashion and pushing his eye as close to Alex as he dared.

Alex grimaced at the sight, turning his face away. "Just what I needed to see—the inner workings of your eyeballs."

"Just showing you the damage you've done," Jari retorted. "We've been busy filling beetles with magic and pulling down portals. *You* were supposed to be working on those module things. Where have you been hiding?"

Alex sighed. "It's a long story."

"Hey, we've been given time—we're in a prison." Jari chuckled to himself.

"I see Demeter has been rubbing off on you," Alex remarked.

Jari nodded. "That guy is hilarious! I'm getting some of my best material from him. Seriously." He paused for dramatic effect. "He's like a mushroom."

Alex shook his head. "Don't do it."

"What do you mean?" A grin spread across Jari's face.

"Don't do it," Alex repeated, though he was unable to keep the smirk off his face.

"No, seriously, he's like a mushroom," the blond-haired boy said, his eyes glinting mischievously.

"Don't say it, Jari," Aamir warned.

"Because he's a fun guy!" Jari cackled.

Alex groaned and flashed a look at Aamir. "He said it."

Aamir deadpanned. "He went there."

"Dad joke central, population Jari," Ellabell quipped.

Alex was surprised to see Natalie breaking a smile too. She walked over to where they stood.

"I am French, and even *I* know that was terrible," she announced.

Alex smiled wearily at his friend, and she smiled back, making him realize that much of their former animosity had already been dispelled in the wake of Alex's disappearance and the group's shared concern for his welfare.

"Natalie, can I talk to you for a minute?" he asked.

She nodded. "I was about to ask the same thing."

They walked over to the corner and sat down, conscious of the rest of the group watching them. Jari seemed particularly interested, hanging from one of the windowsills to get a better vantage point for his apparent prying.

"Hey, no eavesdropping!" Alex shouted.

Jari grinned. "I have dropped zero eaves, thank you very much!"

"Jari!" Natalie turned, giving Jari the kind of withering look he seemed to garner from a lot of women.

"Fine—spoilsports," he muttered, dropping back down off the sill and retreating to fetch a snack.

Alex turned back to Natalie. "I just wanted to—"

"I would like to say sorry, for the things I said," she said, cutting him off. "We are friends, and I should not have spoken to you like that. It was unfair. You were only looking out for me. In truth, you caught me out and I was defensive."

"I shouldn't have attacked you either," Alex replied. "I was just worried. I should've dealt with it in a better way, and I'm sorry if I came off like a jerk."

"I was the jerk," insisted Natalie.

"Shall we agree you were both jerks?" Jari's voice wafted over.

Alex rolled his eyes. "Friends?"

"Friends," she agreed, as they shook tentative hands.

"You two sorted out your squabble?" Jari asked, grinning.

Alex sighed. "Yes, as a matter of fact."

"So, where have you been?" Aamir asked.

For a moment, Alex thought about telling them everything, the whole complex tale, but there were much more urgent matters to contend with. If they were going to get Caius to tell them where the essence was, they needed to move fast. There was no more time to waste. He would have to put aside his grief and his confusion for the time being.

"I figured out how to break down the barrier magic," he said, choosing the simpler route, before diving into a brief explanation of what they would have to do in order to bring it down. As far as he could tell, as soon as he removed each of the protective shields, they would be able to fit the jammers and then overload the mechanisms, forcing the whole structure to explode and bringing down their chosen section of the barrier magic.

"That was the definition of a *short* story," Jari said. "Here I was, gearing myself up for an epic tale, and you give me *that*? Disappointing, Webber. I've had burps that lasted longer."

Alex laughed tightly. "Sorry for the letdown."

"Leave him be, Jari, you wind-up merchant," Aamir chastised. "This is exciting news."

"I thought so," replied Alex. "I'm hoping to start on the

shields tonight, but I might need your help in case any of Caius's curses decide to jump out and take us by surprise."

Ellabell nodded excitedly. "Absolutely! I can't think of a better way to spend an evening."

"It'll give us a chance to get some practice in, to flex our magical muscles before we bring the sucker down!" Jari chirped.

"Does anyone know where Lintz and Demeter are?" Alex asked, knowing the teachers' power might be useful.

"I believe Demeter is with Agatha, tending to her. She was taken ill earlier, and he is keeping an eye on her until she feels better. Lintz is with them too, but he's working away on the circuit jammers," Aamir replied. "Shall I get them?"

Alex shook his head, recalling the image of Agatha rushing toward him. "Better leave them where they're most needed. We'll be okay, the five of us. It might sap a lot of my strength to break so many barriers in one evening, but I'll need you all to be at your peak when the time comes to overload the cylinders—it's going to take a lot of effort, but it'll be worth it if we can get Caius to take the bait," Alex said.

"Together, we are strong," Natalie stated.

"After so many setbacks, I feel good about this. It's our time," Aamir said, though Alex wished he hadn't spoken quite so confidently. It made him fear some sort of jinx being placed upon their plan.

"Caius will take the bait. We just need to make sure it looks juicy enough for him to bite," Jari said, grinning wolfishly.

With that, the group moved from the warmth and comfort of the tower room and headed back down the steps. As they came to the first vestibule area, Alex stopped and moved toward the cylinder that clung to the wall. Using the screwdriver he had taken from Vincent's sitting room, he unscrewed the detailed golden shell and placed it carefully on the floor, knowing that all of the covers would have to be replaced once the mechanism shields were down and the jammers had been fitted, so the modules themselves didn't draw too much attention when Caius came to investigate. If the warden saw the deliberately broken mechanisms, Alex knew he might suspect an ambush before they even had the chance to strike, and disappear back from whence he came. With the covers back on, looking like nothing had happened, Alex knew Caius would have to come closer, for a better look.

Jari gave a low whistle over Alex's shoulder as the inner clockwork was revealed. "She's a beauty!"

"Isn't she?" Alex said, glad to hear that someone else appreciated the intricate handiwork as much as he did.

Ellabell stepped up beside Alex. "This must regulate the flow of the barrier magic, keeping it working without the need for a mage. Once the magic has been poured inside, much like Lintz's beetles, the system does the rest, holding the barrier magic in place, where it wants it. Very clever," she said, taking a closer look, the golden shimmer reflected in her blue eyes.

"I imagine it must monitor the fog outside too, as part of the system," Natalie added.

"Yeah, it sounds like it's constantly in use—like it's funneling the barrier magic, directing it this way and that, stopping it from escaping into the atmosphere," Alex replied, watching the delicate cogs whir incessantly and move the metal arms and pumps that kept the magic flowing as it should, filtering it and sending it back out into the walls in an endless stream.

Ellabell squinted at the mechanism. "Do you think they're in any specific order?"

"What do you mean?" Alex asked.

"Well, if this is, for example, number one, do you think the next one down is number two, and so on and so forth?" she said. "If there were some way of knowing what order they were in, we could make sure we were breaking the right ones, to take down one specific section."

Aamir nodded. "If we could break, say, one to nine, one for each of us, then that would only take down that section of barrier."

"But how can we know which is which?" Natalie cut in, her brow furrowed in deep thought.

Alex bent down and picked the golden cover back up, running his thumb along the carved detailing that coiled along the metal shell. Exotic flowers ran into twisting vines, and thorns protruded from long stems. He was hoping for some inspiration as he let his eyes follow the beautiful design. To his disappointment, it seemed to be solely decorative. Turning it around, he saw that not even the inside had any distinguishing features; it was simply smooth, blank metal. Frowning, he lifted it toward the glow of torchlight, hoping something might jump out at him as he took a final look.

Something did. At the bottom right of the gold cover was a small etching of a swallow, its wings stretched out as if in flight, and upon each wing was a number. On the left wing, the number one; on the right wing, the number six. This was module number sixteen.

"Guys, I think I've cracked it," he said, grinning.

"How?" Jari asked, peering once more over Alex's shoulder.

Alex pointed to the swallow. "This is module number sixteen. So, if we take down our nine modules, we should be able to make a decent dent in the barrier magic. It'll certainly give old Caius enough to worry about."

"Are we going to blow them up now?" Jari wondered, excitement in his eyes.

"Not tonight—we need to wait for the jammers," Alex replied. "Tonight, I'm going to break all the shields and put the covers back on, so nobody suspects they've been tampered with. Then, we can return tomorrow with the jammers Lintz has made. Once they're fitted, it should stop any further flow of barrier magic, so we'll only have to deal with what is already in the walls. When the time is right and a signal is given, we will each have to overload the modules at the same time, to break the system and hopefully bring down the section we want to bring down," he explained, as much for his own benefit as the others'.

Natalie nodded. "We should check each number as we go along, to make sure we are exploding them in sequence."

"Exactly," Alex replied.

Jari grinned delightedly. "I must say, dude, I'm thrilled you decided we should go with explosions."

"It wasn't exactly a choice," said Alex, a reluctant smile pulling at his own lips.

"And this is the protective shield, to keep out prying hands?" Ellabell asked, pointing toward the golden shield that rippled across the stunning clockwork.

Alex nodded. "I believe so. If you look at the top and bottom of the cylinder, you'll see why."

They peered closer as Alex gestured toward the two golden lines that thrummed at either end of the cylinder, holding the shield in place.

"It's like the Head's golden lines," Aamir said solemnly, a visible shudder running through him. Indeed, they were very much like the golden lines at Spellshadow Manor, simply in miniature. Alex didn't know if it would make the consequences any less perilous, however; smaller didn't always mean safer.

"Exactly the same, which means there'll probably be a little kickback when I remove it," Alex replied grimly. "I suggest we brace ourselves for golden beasts, rushing blockades, and who knows what else," he warned as he moved his hands closer to the top of the cylinder.

"What if it sets off the red fog?" Natalie asked, her tone anxious.

Alex frowned. "I'll be here to get rid of it, if it gets into your systems." He grimaced; it wasn't exactly a pleasant thought, and he could see the displeasure reflected in the faces of his friends.

"Let's just keep all our extremities crossed that it doesn't come to that," Jari muttered.

The others stepped back a short distance, giving Alex space to work. He conjured twisting strands of black and silver beneath his hands, forging a small, solid blade of rippling anti-magic that he could physically hold. Feeling the cold sturdiness of the handle in his palm, he lifted the blade to the shimmering line and felt the resistance as he tried to slice through the energy. For a brief moment, he thought it wasn't going to work, but as he pressed harder with the silver blade, the shield shattered with a loud snap. The broken shield flew toward Alex's eyes in a million tiny shards of light that solidified as they rushed through the air, forcing him to duck quickly out of the way, covering his eyes with his forearm. Some of the splinters bit into his skin, hailing down on his face and bare arms like a thousand drops of pure ice, and he could feel the trickle of something unexpectedly warm running down the side of his head. He didn't dare remove his arm from over his eyes, for fear of what the shards might do, but without his sight he was helpless to fend off the vicious hail.

Natalie, Aamir, and Jari swiped away the slivers of light, sending the shards crashing against the wall, where they evaporated into puffs of golden dust. Ellabell ran to Alex, sending up a shield around them, keeping out the rest of the hail. She held him tightly, even though his anti-magic was resisting the presence of her magical shield, causing flurries of snow to fall all around them. She didn't seem to mind, holding him until the worst of it was over.

"You can come out now, lovebirds!" Jari quipped.

Flashing Alex a bashful smile, Ellabell removed the shield and stepped back, giving Alex space to stand. Her expression shifted to one of concern as she moved closer to him again, removing a tissue from her pocket and reaching up to touch the side of Alex's head. All across his forehead and cheeks, tiny cuts had appeared, thin rivulets of blood meandering down his skin. It stung as she pressed the tissue firmly against his face.

"Is everyone okay?" Natalie asked.

Alex nodded, taking the tissue from Ellabell's delicate fingers. "A few scratches. I'll live." He squeezed Ellabell's hand tightly. "I think we were lucky—that felt like an old one. I don't think it's been tended to in a while," he said, turning back toward the cylinder. He just hoped the rest were as ancient.

"And hey, no red fog!" Jari whooped.

Alex was more than grateful for its absence. He wondered if the shield's trickery was supposed to be deterrent enough, a way of keeping out unwanted hands without ruining the flow of the magic through the mechanism. Carefully, Alex replaced the cover and screwed two of the screws loosely back in place, to hold it on. He knew it would give them easier access to the mechanism the following day, when they had the chance to get the jammers from Lintz.

One down, eight to go, he thought wryly as they set off down the corridor.

Glancing at the cover of the next cylinder, he was pleased to see the number seventeen etched onto the back of a frog in mid-hop. It meant they were at least in sequence. Deftly, he unscrewed the cover and placed it on the floor, conjuring his knife again so that he might cut the golden line at the top. As he pressed it to the gleaming energy, he felt the familiar pushback of magical resistance, but the blade cut through it easily, as if it were butter. He frowned, unsure whether that meant this one was even older.

Instantly, the room swirled with a maelstrom of golden light, whipping up his hair and blasting in his face. Within the twisting tornado of energy, horrifying faces emerged. They were haggard and harpy-like women, their cheeks sunken, their features witchy and pointed. A blood-chilling cackle rose up from their vile throats, and they swooped down, their talon-like fingernails curved and ready to claw at their victims. It wasn't like the red fog; Alex could see these monsters with his own eyes. They spun around the room, howling and cackling, trying to snatch at Alex's face every time they brushed near. One caught Natalie square on the cheek, a livid gash appearing, but they were tricky creatures, managing to evade the twisting streams of magic and anti-magic blasted in their direction.

In a rush of inspiration, Alex ran toward the bottom of the maelstrom and reached for it with his anti-magic. Pulling tightly with his palms and feeling the strain in his muscles, he drew the spinning light back into itself. The harpies howled in displeasure as they were dragged backward, compressed and contorted into the orb of twisting magic collecting in Alex's palms. As soon as everything had been sucked into the same place, the glowing ball of light proving a little rambunctious as it struggled to escape Alex's grasp, he pressed his hands together, feeling the force of the energy between his palms, and urged his anti-magic into the center of it, disintegrating it from the inside out. With a blinding flash and a satisfying crack, the orb evaporated into the ether.

Everyone was breathless and sweating.

"Good job," Aamir gasped, clutching his ribs.

"I'm so out of shape," Jari sighed, collapsing against the far wall.

"No time to rest," Alex said, his chest heaving. "We have

seven more to get done. The sooner we do this, the sooner we find the essence and go home."

It did the trick, encouraging everyone to stand up. Although their tiredness was beginning to show, morale was still high, and Alex knew their chances were good as long as that optimism remained. He replaced the cover of module seventeen, and rallied his friends behind him as they moved on toward number eighteen.

It was going to be a long night, after all.

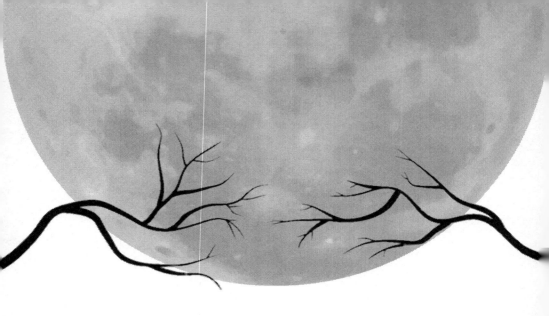

CHAPTER 12

T HEY RETURNED TO THE TOWER ROOM JUST BEFORE dawn, completely exhausted. The night had been filled with all manner of monsters and mayhem, and though their bodies were shattered, their hearts were filled with the joy of success. All the protective shields had been removed from the cylinders, meaning all they had to do now was fit the jammers and overload the systems.

There had been giant golden snakes with poisonous fangs, fierce blockades of pure energy that sent them flying back against the wall, blasts of fire that surged up from the flag-stones, a wall of flying golden arrows that had nearly caught everyone off guard, a bristling mist that had rendered them temporarily blind, a hooded reaper wielding a scythe with ter-rifying skill, and a few more hags on brooms swooping down to claw at their faces. Alex had been a little disappointed by the last one, wondering if Caius had simply run out of grim ideas and had to repeat one.

Either way, it had been a very long night, and they were ready to sleep. Twice in the night, the girls' scarab devices had gone off, only to stop abruptly, leaving them to hope that Lintz or Demeter was seeing to the intrusion, in the middle of jammer-building and tending to Agatha. Alypia's continued absence in the keep gave them confidence that it had been dealt with, but with the threat of the royal's arrival perpetually looming over them, the group was spurred on to get the job done. The girls' screeching scarabs led Jari and Aamir to realize that their devices had run out of juice, and were in need of fixing, though it would have to wait until morning, when they could seek out Lintz. Alex had forgotten to replace his own beacon after losing it on that first day exploring the keep, and he hoped Professor Lintz wouldn't be too disappointed in him if he asked for another.

The group settled in for a few fitful hours of sleep. When he awoke, Alex checked himself for wounds in the full light of day, and found he had scabs on his shoulder and forearm where the tip of the reaper's scythe had gotten him. And he wasn't the only one. They all looked as if they had traveled through a warzone.

Ellabell had a bruise or ten from the blockade that had sent her hurtling into the wall, and the beginnings of a black eye where a broom had collided with her face. Natalie had the livid cut on her cheek, and another just above her eyebrow, where an arrow had skimmed past her. There was one on her arm too, where she had ducked too late to evade the scythe. Jari was covered in a crosshatch of cuts, having borne the brunt of the wall of arrows, as well as the wrath of the flying hags. Aamir was the only one who seemed to have emerged visibly unscathed, though he had narrowly missed having his arm bitten off by the fanged serpent. He'd lost his shirt sleeve as proof, but the actual arm beneath it was unharmed save for a small burn where the poison fang had touched him for the briefest moment.

Lintz and Demeter entered the room, chatting jovially. Words died on their lips as they took in the sight of the walking wounded, their faces morphing into expressions of pure shock.

"Oh my..." Demeter began.

"Goodness me, what happened to you?" Lintz cried, rushing to their aid.

Alex raised his hands. "We're fine, Professor. It looks worse than it is. We just spent the night breaking down the module shields, so we can fit the jammers and overload the systems," he explained, wincing as he tried to move his twisted shoulder.

Lintz frowned. "Why didn't you come and get us?"

"You were busy," Alex said, nodding toward the cluster of metallic objects the professor cradled in his plump arms. It looked as if Alex and his friends weren't the only ones who'd had a busy night. He flashed a knowing look toward Demeter too, knowing the cause of the sickness that had kept the ex-teacher at Agatha's bedside, tending to her tortured mind.

"Still, we'd have come with you if we'd known you were going on such a dangerous errand!" Lintz insisted.

"Honestly, Professor, we're fine," Aamir interjected. "A few scratches and bruises, nothing we can't handle. It needed to be done, and it needed to be done quickly. Now we can move on with today's tasks."

"Well, you look in no state to bring down the barriers today," Lintz remarked sternly.

Alex straightened in his chair. "It can't wait any longer. Are those the jammers?" he asked, looking at the cluster of devices Lintz had lain on the tabletop. They were small and neat, crafted from solid bronze and shaped like miniature crabs, though the shells had been tempered to shine a brighter red color.

"Yes, these are the jammers," Lintz replied reluctantly.

"Then let's blow this thing sky-high!" Jari announced, flashing the professor a grin.

"I suppose there's no point in trying to dissuade this stubborn lot," Demeter said.

Lintz sighed, shaking his head. "Give me your beetle beacons, then, please."

They passed him their devices.

"Ours are out of juice," Aamir said, gesturing toward himself and Jari.

"I was wondering when they might begin to fail... I'll do what I can with them. Come, I suppose we must go and fit the jammers, if you will not be dissuaded," Lintz mumbled, scooping the jammers off the table and tipping them carefully into the front pocket of his satchel.

Alert and nervous for what was to come, the group went down the stairs and followed the familiar route to the first vestibule, where module sixteen lay against the wall, waiting for someone to blow it up.

Alex froze as he saw Agatha coming toward them, heading up the hallway from the opposite direction. Vincent walked beside her, and it was only as she neared that Alex realized he had nothing to fear from her anymore. Her eyes were misty, and she wore a contented smile upon her face as she twirled a long, gray tendril of hair around her fingers in an oddly girlish manner. She paused when she came close to where Alex stood, her eyes narrowing for a moment, as if she were trying to remember something from long ago. Unable to grasp the memory, she waved in greeting instead, no hint of attack in her body language.

"Hello, you beautiful creatures!" she cried, in her melodic voice. "So wonderful to see you all. Goodness, you're getting quite the shiner," she remarked, reaching up to touch the bruise on Ellabell's face. "Excellent day for a rebellion, if I say so myself." She chuckled warmly.

"Good morning, Agatha," the group chorused politely.

Alex gave Demeter a questioning look. He wasn't sure how Demeter had roped the Spellbreaker-hating woman into helping, but it looked as if he had. His mind trailed back to the glowing strands pouring from Demeter's hands into the skull of the usually mellow mage, and wondered if that was how he'd gotten her to change her mind. Whatever Demeter had done, Alex thought she seemed happy enough. She appeared unharmed by the act, but still, something didn't sit quite right in his mind. Alex pushed the negative thoughts away, trying to convince himself that mind control couldn't be all that bad if it could be used for good too, and if nobody was any the wiser, and nobody got hurt, was it really such an immoral thing?

"She's come around to the idea of you," whispered Demeter with a knowing smile, half-confirming Alex's suspicions.

The auburn-haired man volunteered to be the first. He stepped up to the golden cylinder and removed the cover, pulling the two loose screws away.

"I suppose we must have a screw loose too, doing this," Demeter chuckled, surprising everyone.

Alex smiled tensely. "I think we probably do."

Lintz stepped up and pointed toward the clockwork, adopting his most teacher-like tone as he instructed the others.

"So, I shall walk along with you and fit the jammers into the system. Once a short period of time has passed, all you will have to do is surge a vast amount of power into the mechanism. The system will already be jammed, but the jammer doesn't stop the barrier magic completely—it simply halts the flow, preventing more from taking its place. Blowing the mechanism itself will blow the barrier magic, hopefully resulting in a section of it being brought down completely," he explained, twisting the corners of his moustache with anxious fingers. "You will wait for my signal, which will be the appearance of a golden orb in the space behind you. Okay?"

Everyone nodded, and Alex could feel a tremor of nervous anticipation course through his body. It had all become very real. In the planning of it, there had been a detachment in which they could feel confident of their success, but now, faced with the stark truth of it, Alex didn't feel quite as gung-ho about the whole thing. The imminent threat of the warden coming for them sent a shiver of fear up his spine; the evasive man was powerful, and Alex just hoped they would be strong enough to take him down, when it came to it. They had plotted as best as they could, but Alex knew there were no assurances of success in this. Glancing at the others, he saw his fear mirrored on their faces. They were about to step into a relative unknown. As soon as they broke the barrier down, there would be no turning back.

Lintz stepped toward the clockwork and lifted one crab-shaped jammer out of his bag, pressing the metal crustacean up against a connecting section of cogs and pulleys. Sparking into life, the bronze crab snapped its claws and grasped two nodes that stuck out at the top of the mechanism, clinging fast. The jammer-crabs might have looked small and weak, but they were surprisingly strong. Immediately, the clockwork began to struggle, the cogs stalling, the pulleys straining.

"Mechanism successfully jammed," Lintz said, visibly unable to contain his pride in the miniature crustaceans. "Shall we move on?" he encouraged, though there was a tightness in his voice that belied his true fears. The group did just that, following Lintz as they left Demeter behind.

Natalie took the second module, with Aamir, Jari, Ellabell, Vincent, and Agatha taking the ones that followed. At each stop, another jammer was fitted, the claws snapping triumphantly into place. Alex took the penultimate module, and Lintz carried on to the final one in their chosen section.

Glancing around, Alex thought it was strange to be in such isolation in the midst of a collaborative task. The vestibule in which he stood was oddly silent, with nothing but the steady rumble of the day-to-day prison life filling the quietude. It made things all the more unsettling as he waited, head turned over his shoulder, in anticipation of Lintz's signal. He tried to imagine his friends, lined up along the hallways, wondering if they were feeling as nervous as he was. There was excitement, too, that the plan was finally coming together, but it was all tinged with a streak of terror. If Caius took the bait, Alex knew they could have the essence in their hands by dinnertime, but he also knew there was a good chance they could be dead. Alex had to cling to the hope that it would be the former. If he allowed himself to think of Caius overcoming them, he knew he might just lose his nerve.

They had strength, they had power, they would hopefully have the element of surprise, but that didn't mean anything in the realm of Kingstone Keep. Alex knew Caius could scupper it at any stage.

Behind him, a floating golden orb brightened into view, coming to rest in the center of the room. Alex's heart began to pound harder. Taking it as his indication to move, he turned toward the clockwork mechanism and rested his hands on top of the cylinder. Glancing down, he saw that they were shaking slightly, as he conjured a vast ball of raw energy, feeling the swell and surge of it beneath his hands. Focusing, he pressed the anti-magic into the module's mechanics, feeling it come up against the resistance of the jammer Lintz had fitted. Using that as a point against which to brace his anti-magic, he let the pressure build and build, using all his strength to push it harder against the jammer, feeling it grow to an extraordinary force beneath his hands. He was giving it everything, and still the mechanism wasn't giving way. He could feel a trickle of sweat on his brow as he surged more and more anti-magic into the system, willing it to overload. Finally, with an enormous explosion that sent him sprawling backward, the mechanism relented, the whole thing breaking apart, releasing the hold it had on the barrier magic.

Alex scrambled to his feet, hearing the echo of explosions down the hallway. Rushing toward the mechanism, which was still searing hot from the blast, he picked up the golden cover from the floor and hurriedly fixed it back into place, burning his hands slightly as he tried to make it look the way it had before. Stepping back, he was pleased to see that it looked as if nothing had happened, save for the rush of red fog that was escaping upward, out of the keep.

His pulse was racing, and he could feel the sweat on his brow go cold as he braced for Caius's arrival. The barrier was down; they couldn't bring it back now.

For the first time, out of the window that stood beside the module, Alex could see out into the world, the bronze fog clearing to reveal the landscape beyond. He peered out over the ledge, soaking it all in, feeling the rush of cool, fresh air on his skin, trying to calm his nerves. In the near distance, a fair stretch from the moat, a lush, dark green forest ran as far as the eye could see, leading to the faint shadow of mountains behind, which rose up to meet the darkening sky. Closer still, nestled in the shade of the forest, where the trees separated to forge a rudimentary path, Alex could see a gatehouse, perfectly formed and almost quaint to behold. It stood a fair distance from the wide moat that surrounded the keep. It was just far enough away from the prison, Alex thought, which, to his mind, looked like a promising place for a warden to visit.

He wondered if that was where Caius would come from.

Breaking into a sprint, he ran to meet the others. Everyone seemed on edge, chattering anxiously, but their modules were suitably exploded, the covers replaced. It had already been a few minutes, and still Caius had not come.

"Any sign?" Alex asked, as Lintz, Vincent, and Agatha came up the corridor.

Lintz shook his head. "Nothing as yet, but it may take a short while."

Alex didn't want to wait any longer. He knew Caius need-ed to appear before they all lost momentum; they were ready for him *now*. There was no time to lose, and Alex felt the fa-miliar bristle of annoyance ripple through him, mixing with his anxiety.

"It worked, right?" he pressed.

Demeter nodded. "It worked perfectly."

"Then where is he?" Alex stared out the nearby window, scrutinizing the gatehouse in the distance.

As a frustrated sigh emerged from Alex's lips, the ground shook beneath their feet, beginning as a small tremor, then de-scending into a full-blown, wall-shattering, earth-trembling quake. Shouts of fear erupted from the prisoners nearby. Alex grasped the wall, trying to stay on his feet. A deafening roar filled his ears, and he turned to the others, fear pulsing in his veins. If this was Caius making his entrance, Alex had never expected the warden to make such a violent arrival.

Demeter and Vincent were trying to say something, their mouths wide, but Alex couldn't hear them above the din.

"WHAT?" Alex screamed.

This time, he realized what the two men were saying: *Run! Hide! Get out of here!*

Alex didn't even have a chance to grab the Stillwater essence Ellabell had hidden a few feet further up the corridor in preparation. All he could do was dive toward the nearest door. He saw Ellabell and Natalie throw themselves into a cell just ahead, with Aamir and Jari following suit through another door at the top of the hall. Vincent and Agatha sprinted past him with surprising speed.

Alex broke the lock to the cell with a twist of his anti-magic and jumped inside, slamming the door behind him. He peered through the grate. Demeter and Lintz whispered hurriedly in the corner, brushing down the fronts of their gray uniforms and sweeping their hair back, their faces pale pictures of abject fear.

The ground continued to shake, and Alex felt as if the whole keep might crumble and collapse on top of them. Clusters of dust and debris dropped from the ancient ceiling, chunks of rock falling away from the walls.

This wasn't right. They had known Caius would come, and so the reaction of Vincent, Demeter, and Lintz didn't make sense. They were truly, wholeheartedly terrified of what was coming, and Alex had no idea why.

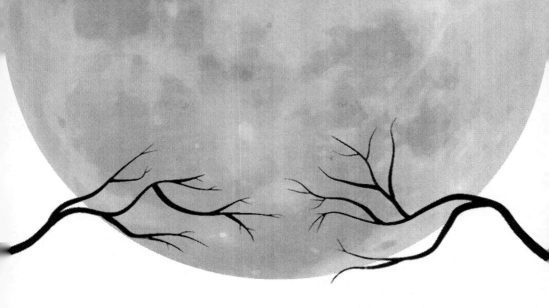

CHAPTER 13

THE EARTHQUAKE CEASED AS SUDDENLY AS IT HAD begun, although the suffering cries of the inmates still echoed through the Keep. Alex glanced behind him, unnerved. He could feel the burn of eyes, watching him. Turning slowly, he peered into the darkness. With a startled gasp, he saw a hunched figure, crouched down in one corner of the cell. The beady eyes of an ugly, sagging face followed him, a rotten-toothed smile stretching across the pale skin of the frightening troglodyte. The limbs of the prisoner stuck out at unnatural angles, the hair limp and greasy.

Piercing the unpleasant tension, the man began to laugh hysterically, the sound jarring amid the shouting. Alex wanted to shut him up, but he didn't dare get close. He had no idea what the prisoner was in here for, and he didn't think it wise to go toe-to-toe with a murderer.

The sound of heavy footsteps on the flagstones outside distracted Alex's attention, though he was careful to keep one eye on the manically laughing man.

"What do I have to do to find someone who has at least bathed in the last fortnight?" a sharp voice bellowed from the end of the hallway just beyond Alex's line of vision. The prison went silent, the only sound the cackling of Alex's cellmate.

Lintz and Demeter stood at attention outside Alex's cell, and though they must have known he was in there, they didn't as much as flash a glance in his direction. It made Alex all the more nervous. Hadn't it been the plan all along to fight Caius?

"King Julius, an unexpected pleasure," said Demeter, his voice trembling as he bowed low.

Alex's heart rose into his throat as he realized why they were so afraid. It wasn't Caius after all. It was far worse than that—it was his brother. Hadn't Vincent said that Julius made the warden's box of tricks look like a parcel of kittens? Alex shuddered, wondering how they had managed to summon the even crueler brother. He had the sinking feeling they had missed something in the mechanisms—an alarm of some sort, perhaps, that had somehow caught the attention of the king instead. It was likely the reason removing the shield hadn't provoked the red fog.

Alex held his breath as King Julius came into view. His harsh, regal features were framed by royal white hair. There was a cruelness around his mouth, the smile he gave Demeter and Lintz devoid of any pleasantry. His eyes were a piercing, pure gold that shone with amused malice, and his skin lacked any wrinkles, despite his age. Alex supposed the king sipped from the same youth serum as Alypia. Julius's stride was tall and proud, and he wore a cream-colored suit that resembled military dress, with black epaulettes, a high collar, and several medals dangling from his chest.

Julius cracked his fingers. His golden eyes rolled in annoyance, and Alex felt his entire body tense as he waited to see what Julius was about to do. The man behind Alex was still laughing hysterically, the sound cutting straight through Alex like a scythe. It was impossible to block out, and it seemed the king shared his irritation.

"Open this cell," Julius demanded, turning toward where Alex was staring out. Alex ducked into the corner of the room, pressing back against the wall.

"Nothing in there but two petty thieves, Your Highness," said Lintz quickly, stumbling over his words.

Julius eyed Lintz sharply. "Open this cell, or you shall receive the punishment yourself."

Lintz glanced between the cell and the king, his mouth agape. Demeter hurried forward and made a show of opening the already broken lock, pulling the door toward him and gesturing for Julius to step inside.

"After you, Your Highness."

"At least one of you has his wits about him," Julius snarled.

Alex pressed himself farther back into the corner of the cell as Julius entered, using the door as extra shelter. The king stepped toward the laughing man, who continued in his mania. Whatever had happened to the guy while he had been at Kingstone Keep, it had removed all of his senses. Any functioning person could see that Julius was incredibly dangerous, and incredibly unpredictable.

"You! Shut your mouth. You are in the presence of a king," Julius snapped, but it did nothing to shut the laughing man up. "You dare defy me, you vile wretch? You dare to laugh in my face?" Julius asked calmly. Then he smacked the poor man hard across the face. It silenced his laughter for a split second, but then the cackling sound rose from the prisoner's throat once more, even more manic than before.

This time, there was no reprieve. Gripping the laughing man by the neck, Julius pressed his hand against the man's face and unleashed a wave of bright bronze magic that crackled through the air like a lightning storm. It poured down the man's throat, crawled through his skin. The prisoner's laughter turned to a heart-rending scream, and he clawed at his own flesh, trying to rake off the magic that oozed through him, burning everything up. Alex could see it slithering under the man's skin, dissolving his insides.

Alex wanted to turn away, but he was frozen to the spot.

The screaming and clawing seemed to go on forever, but finally, the prisoner made a gurgling sound and collapsed in a heap, the life gone from his eyes. His skin sagged inward, leaving him in a ghastly puddle, as if there was nothing left within to hold up the fleshy outer husk.

Julius turned sharply, a delighted look upon his cold face. His gold eyes connected with Alex's, and Alex didn't know whether to turn away or keep looking. The king stepped closer, until he and Alex were almost nose-to-nose.

"And I don't want to hear so much as a whimper from

you," the king whispered with a smirk. He turned and stepped out of the dank cell. Alex thought his lungs might explode, he had been holding his breath for so long. Pressing his ear to the grate, not daring to move back around, he listened to what Julius had to say to Lintz and Demeter.

"That laugh! I couldn't have borne it a moment longer. A waste of perfectly good essence—but you two should know by now, I don't have patience for disobedience. Speaking of which, what has occurred here?" the king asked, threat dripping from his words.

"Your Highness, I believe there has been a fault with the barrier," explained Demeter, his voice surprisingly calm.

"Well, clearly. That doesn't take a genius to see. Have any prisoners escaped?"

"Not to our knowledge, Your Highness. We have everything under control now," Demeter replied.

"Where's that delinquent brother of mine?" Julius asked.

"Not here, Your Highness."

Julius gave an irritated sigh. "Another observant remark, guard. Well done," he mocked. "Have you seen him? Is he *aware* that his prison is in utter disarray? Is the old goat even still breathing?"

An anxious silence stretched between Julius and the guards. Alex desperately wanted one of them to speak, in case they ended up like his cellmate.

"Speak up! Or would you rather I make you speak?" Julius demanded coldly.

Lintz was the one to respond. "I believe he has gone on some errands, and will shortly return. He is aware of the mishap, and… yes, I believe he is still breathing."

"That's a shame." Julius laughed spitefully. "I'm presuming this 'mishap,' as you call it, happened because he's too incompetent to perform basic maintenance. Please inform my dear brother that, if this happens again, and if matters do not improve, I will return. And I will not be so forgiving next time. Show him my new friend Floppy if he needs some extra encouragement," he sneered, giving a sharp, jarring snort. "I trust you're capable of passing on a simple message, yes?"

"Yes, Your Highness," Demeter replied.

"You might also mention that I need him to start shouldering his share of responsibility when it comes to essence. Too long these prisoners have gotten away with the bare minimum, and I won't see it continue. Is that clear?" the king added icily.

It made Alex furious to hear Julius alluding to more essence-extraction, especially after displaying such a blasé attitude toward the murder of the laughing prisoner. Alex could tell Julius was exactly the sort of person who would waste essence, only to insist upon someone else extracting more for him moments later. He didn't seem to be the kind of king who worried much about the fate of his subjects, or troubled himself with the dirty work. With that in mind, Alex couldn't help but wonder if the king's request had something to do with the lack of magical children being born, increasing the royal need for essence. It certainly sounded like it.

"Clear as crystal, Your Highness," Lintz replied.

"And one other thing," he added sharply. "I've been hearing rumors I don't much like the sound of. By all accounts, my dear daughter is having some sort of squabble with my brother, though she refuses to tell me what it's about, and while I have very little interest in her petty feuds, I want to see it resolved… and quickly. They can kill one another if they so please, but it is tedious and inconvenient to find replacements to extract essence. You can tell Caius that he is to make peace with my daughter at the earliest possible opportunity. This has gone on long enough… It's unseemly for royals to act this way. Do you understand what I say?"

"Perfectly," said Demeter. "Message received, and will be duly passed on, Your Highness."

Alex smiled wryly—it seemed very few royals were fond of their brothers.

"Excellent. Well, that was somewhat rejuvenating. I shall be returning now, but if I hear that you haven't passed on my messages, or if I am forced to return, you shall receive the same punishment as my brother. I can't abide slack staff," Julius remarked. "I suppose you'll be wanting me to put this barrier back up before I go?" the king sighed.

At the unmistakable crackle of the king's magic, Alex took his chances and peered around the cell door. Bronze light flowed wildly and effortlessly from the man's deft hands as he pressed his palms against the wall. A spider web of luminescent power branched through the masonry, rushing into the nearest golden cylinder. With an almost imperceptible whir of clockwork, the module burst back into life. Alex wasn't sure how Julius had done it, what with how the mechanisms had exploded so violently—yet the king had managed the impossible. Julius's magic had pieced everything back together in moments, leaving the clockwork clunking louder than before, and Alex knew what that meant.

"Well, I'd love to say it was a pleasure, but it wasn't," Julius sneered. "I hope we don't meet again, more for your sakes than mine."

A moment later, Alex heard the steady beat of footsteps retreating, and the heavy exhale of Lintz and Demeter as the king disappeared from sight. They rushed into Alex's cell.

"Are you okay?" Demeter asked rapidly.

"I'm fine," he lied. He was far from fine, though it wasn't a physical injury that wounded him. It was the knowledge that, after coming so close, and expending so much effort, they were back to square one again. They had no essence, no portal, the continued threat of Alypia, and the fresh threat of Julius.

The barrier was back up, and with its rise their hopes had fallen down.

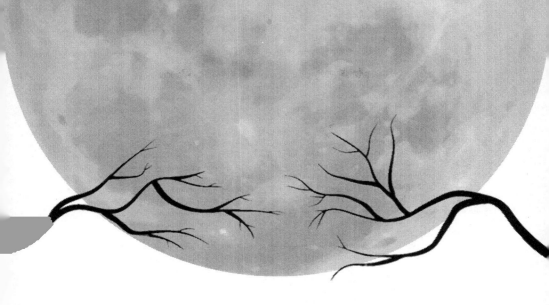

CHAPTER 14

BACK IN THE TOWER ROOM, THE MOOD WAS DESPONDENT. Alex had returned the satchel of Stillwater essence and filled in the others on what had happened after the earthquake, though Natalie and Ellabell had heard much of it from their hiding spot. To his relief, nobody seemed harmed by the day's events, having shared their hiding spots with more amenable criminals than Alex, but there was an air of utter physical and emotional exhaustion in the room.

When the beetle beacons stacked on the table began to trill, Alex wanted to pick them all up and dash them against the wall. He didn't need to be reminded of the predicament they were in.

"I'll go," said Lintz solemnly, taking one of the beacons and silencing the rest. Alex watched him leave the tower room, hating Alypia for causing so much chaos. For a moment, he almost forgot his guilt for what he had done to her.

"So… where do we go from here?" muttered Aamir, resting his head back against the wall. It was barely a question. There was no energy in his voice.

"Well, we can't risk luring Caius out again," Alex said, recalling Julius's threat. It wasn't something he wanted to chance. "And going back to staking out parts of the keep he likes to visit seems more futile than ever. I… I'm fresh out of ideas." He exhaled, closing his eyes.

It wasn't just their own problems playing on his mind, either. After hearing what Julius had said in the hallway, Alex was beginning to feel less and less comfortable about returning to the real world, while so many others suffered at the hands of royals. If Julius's intent to extract more essence was put into action, it meant more death, more loss of innocent lives, more suffering, and Alex just wished he could do more to help those they would be leaving behind. He wished he could give them the same glimmer of hope that he felt within him… or that he had felt before Julius had come and snuffed it out.

"We could try to… build the portal home without the Kingstone essence," suggested Jari halfheartedly. Of course, that just wasn't an option, given their timeframe. It was clear from the ever-increasing pile of clockwork bits and pieces that Lintz's beetles were beginning to fail, and the scarab-like devices were running out of juice too. It was only a matter of time before the devices stopped working altogether, and they all found themselves in an even more dangerous situation than they were already in.

Alex wondered if they were thinking about it all wrong, if they should try to come up with a way that they could kill two birds with one stone… seek their own freedom and give hope to the students who remained in the other havens. It seemed like a vast, impossible task, and yet Alex couldn't shake the idea. He knew there had to be a way, but he just couldn't quite see it. His mind was so full of fog and pain and grief and disappointment, and it clouded his judgment. It was hard to see anything clearly. He still hadn't found the space in which to grieve for his dead father, because he knew that still had to wait until they had found their sanctuary.

Overwhelmed and exhausted, Alex got to his feet and headed for the door.

"I'm going to go for a short walk… clear my head, hopefully come up with a plan," he said, briefly turning back to the others. They nodded, understanding the need.

Natalie was already fast asleep, curled up against the wall, and Jari wasn't far off. It was only Aamir and Ellabell who seemed to be battling sleep.

Alex headed down the stairs, but he looked over his shoulder at the sound of feet pounding on the flagstones behind him.

"I thought I'd come and see how you were. I hope you don't mind," said Ellabell shyly. It was all he could do not to wrap his arms around her there and then. Having her near, after so much trauma, was like the first sip of water given to a desperately thirsty man.

"Ellabell," he whispered as she neared.

"It sounds like the dumbest question, but are you okay?"

she asked, holding his face in her hands and tilting his chin down, making him look in her eyes. "You don't seem okay."

He shook his head, lost for words.

"Is it the barrier?" she asked softly.

He shrugged. "Partly."

"Is it Alypia? Or the portal home?"

He smiled bitterly. "It's everything, and yet so much more."

"What do you mean?" she asked, stroking the side of his head.

"It's nothing. We're all suffering. I shouldn't have said anything… I'm fine," he sighed, his throat tight with raw emotion.

She took his hand in hers, squeezing it tightly. "You're hurting, and you have as much right as anyone to talk about it. I'm here to listen," she reassured him. "If something is troubling you, you can tell me."

"Sorry I haven't been myself lately," Alex replied quietly after a moment's silence, unable to meet her gaze. He didn't want her to see him like this, all over the place.

"Did something happen, something you're not telling us?" she pressed, her voice still laced with concern.

He shook his head again, unable to put it into words.

"Let's just sit out here for a while," Ellabell said, tugging at his wrist.

He nodded, trying to force a smile upon his lips. "That sounds nice."

Gripping her hand, he followed her up to a narrow pew fastened to the far wall, just beneath the sill of a long, narrow window that looked like it might once have served as a hole for archers to fire their arrows from. Outside, the sky was invisible, smothered in the bronze fog that served as a reminder of just how trapped they were. He sighed, turning away from it.

He could see that Ellabell was wracked with concern for him, her eyes scanning his face for signs of anything that might be useful in telling her what had happened to him. He would have told her himself, but, for the moment, words failed him. Fatigue sapped whatever was left of his strength, leaving him slumped and silent on the bench's varnished surface, wishing he had something articulate to say to the pretty girl before him who was watching him with such compassion in her sparkling blue eyes. He wanted to reach out for her and pull her into a tight embrace, to let them both know that the world wasn't crumbling away around them, that there was still hope within it. But he couldn't raise his arms to the task. All he could do was sit and stare, a blank expression upon his face, his mind battered by the day's onslaught of events. It was a lot to take in, and he wasn't sure he'd ever absorb it all.

"What happened?" she asked gently, after a lengthy spell of absolute silence. "Aside from the obvious."

For a brief moment, he thought about putting on a brave face and pretending he was okay, coming up with something about it just being the same thing everyone else was upset about, or saying he had just been affected by the barrier's influence or the reparation of his soul. But looking at her, the girl who was gazing back with such trust in her eyes, he knew he had to come out with it instead of keeping it hidden within. Secrets only served to eat away at the hope inside him, and he wasn't willing to suffer its rotting influence again. So, he let the truth flow.

He told her what had happened with Elias, though it now seemed like a lifetime since he had experienced it—he shared every word, letting it all pour from his mouth until there was nothing left. Every detail, every moment, every pain, every face within the story he had to tell. He told her what Elias had done to his father, and how Siren Mave had come to defend the shadow-man's actions, giving Alex a long-winded tale of guardians and accidents and good intentions. Lastly, he told her of the devastation his mother must have felt, never knowing what had happened, and the pain she had suffered in the years afterwards... the pain they had both suffered, not knowing.

"It hurts, Ellabell... It hurts so much," he said through gritted teeth, holding his chest as if his heart might shatter at any moment. "I never knew him, and I keep thinking about all the times I judged him so harshly for leaving her. I used to think about what I'd say to him if I ever saw him again, and it was never going to be anything nice. All that time wasted on anger, when he hadn't done anything wrong. He died, loving my mother, loving me. I felt it, in his heart... He loved us so much," he gasped, the grief overwhelming.

She edged toward him a little self-consciously, holding out her arms. He moved into them, closing his eyes as he felt her wrap her arms tightly around him. Through the fabric of his t-shirt, he could feel the skin of his shoulder dampening beneath her tears, shed for him.

"It's okay," he whispered.

She shook her head, gripping him tighter. "No, it's not. I can't imagine... I'm sorry, Alex. I'm so sorry for your loss."

They held each other for a long while, separating slowly. Ellabell brushed the tears from her eyes and Alex brushed the tears from his, realizing how fiercely he adored the girl in front of him. It was not the right time to tell her—she would think it was just his grief talking. But he knew he would tell her one day soon. He had to, in case there came a day when he might lose her too.

"I don't think you should take any more advice from that shadowy creature," said Ellabell, looking up at him with anxious eyes. "I know he's useful and he helps you where none of us can, but I don't trust him. I didn't before, but now I feel as if he's only capable of creating suffering, delighting in his secrets and in tormenting you. It's all a game to him, and I don't want to see you lose."

Alex could see that her warning was kindly meant. Worry furrowed her brow as she spoke, her hand gripping his, her expression earnest. There was truth in what she said; he knew that. The problem was, Elias was addictive. Alex hung on to every word the shadow-man said, hoping for a morsel to be thrown in his direction. When he was at a loss and feeling as if all hope was gone, as he was now, Elias was like a beacon of promise, of fresh ideas, of inspiration. He could see that now, and even after promising himself he'd never see his shadow-guide again, not after Elias's unforgivable act, he wasn't sure of the strength in his resolve, should he come face-to-face with his shadowy acquaintance again. It was a truth Ellabell knew too; he could see it on her face. It pained him to see it there, that expression of saddened insight, though he couldn't argue against it.

"Can you honestly, in your heart of hearts, tell me you could forgive what he did?" she asked, her voice soft and reassuring.

He shrugged wearily. "He told me it was an accident. I'm not sure how forgivable it is, knowing that," he replied uncertainly, his stance already starting to waver. It annoyed him that he was even entertaining the notion of eventual forgiveness, or that he was trying to defend Elias, even with the tiniest justification. It was not something Elias deserved—he knew that, and yet he couldn't stop the words coming out of his mouth. On Ellabell's face, he saw a reflection of his own doubt.

"Just think about it—how likely is it that anything Elias does is an accident?" she countered.

Alex nodded. "I know."

"I know why you feel as if you need him, and I can understand the appeal. Believe me, I can. Sometimes I wish I had my own spirit guide showing me the way. But you're growing in strength day by day, on your own. You're becoming a force to be reckoned with, and you're doing it by yourself," she encouraged. "With every setback, you get up and you fight again, and you face these battles stronger than you were before. I think Elias has seen that, and I have a feeling he'll try to manipulate you, making you think you need him more than you really do, especially now that you know something he was trying to keep secret from you. He has lost your trust, and I just worry about the lengths he will go to, to get you back, if he thinks there is even the slightest chance." She smiled sadly, like a loved one trying to persuade an addict to get back on the wagon.

"You don't think Elias is capable of feeling remorse?" Alex

asked, genuinely interested to hear her reply.

She shook her head. "I don't think Elias is capable of feeling, period."

"Maybe you're right," he muttered.

She sighed. "Don't think I'm trying to manipulate you or smear him—I don't know him like you know him. I can only go by what I have seen and heard. All I want is for you to do whatever makes you feel better, and my worry is that Elias is only going to make you feel worse. Every time you see him, he tears you down, giving you just enough to keep you coming back." She shrugged. "I don't know, maybe I'm wrong."

"That's the trouble—you're not wrong. It would be easier if you were."

As they spoke of Elias, the keep pressed in upon Alex, worse than it had done since before Vincent's lesson, until the claustrophobia he felt was almost all-consuming. In his veins, he felt a raw, violent need to do something drastic, to get up and fight as Ellabell had said, and make a last-ditch attempt at seeking out the old warden whose elusiveness had only caused them more pain. It was not a half-baked desire or whim, but an intense physical need that, if not met, made him worry for the consequences to his sanity. He knew he couldn't stay a moment longer, doing nothing, without actually losing his mind. He didn't want to stake out hallways and drift around in the hopes of stumbling across Caius—he wanted to go after Caius directly, and scope out the warden for himself, to figure out whether he truly could take the information he wanted by force.

A thought came to him. *The gatehouse.* He remembered

the sight of the little building nestled at the forest's edge, seen for a moment while the barrier was down. He recalled thinking it was the perfect place for someone to hide out. The only problem was, how to get there? There was only one way he could think of, and it made him want to try something he hadn't dared to try before. Now, feeling desperately that it was all or nothing, it seemed like a risk worth taking. If he didn't at least attempt it, he knew Ellabell may as well go in search of a straitjacket now, because he would need it. Hadn't Demeter said that the keep could turn the young and hopeful mad?

"What's going on in there?" she asked, tapping lightly on the side of his head.

A hesitant smile played upon his lips. "What do you know about magical travel?"

"Which kind?" she replied, raising a curious eyebrow.

"I'm talking full-on *Star Trek* teleportation."

She laughed. "I would never have taken you for a Trekkie."

"There's a lot you don't know about me," he said, grinning despite the day he'd had. She had that effect on him.

"Well, I wouldn't advise trying it indoors or in an enclosed space, as a beginner, in case you end up taking a chunk of building with you—stone and stuff. Even for someone more advanced, it's pretty hard to extricate the human body from a room when traveling, by all accounts."

"I'm not sure I'd like to see those accounts." Alex shuddered.

"They're pretty grim," she agreed, grimacing.

"Would an open space with a stone floor work?"

She nodded. "You've got a better chance, for sure. From

what I read, walls seem to be the main problem."

"Come on," he said, grasping her hand and leading her toward the turret where he had left Siren Mave and Elias not so long ago.

"Where are we going?" she asked, dragged along half-willingly.

He flashed a look back. "I need to get out," he called to her. "I need to go after Caius. I need to see first-hand what it is we're dealing with, see if I can spot a weakness or a way to get to him."

"I'm not sure that's a good idea," said Ellabell anxiously.

"What choice do we have?" he asked.

"He's too powerful!"

"It's a risk I'm willing to take—I won't strike alone, I promise. I may do some stupid things now and again, but I'm not that reckless. I just want to see him for myself and gather as much intel as I can, so I can see if there's a way we can get to him. Call it reconnaissance. Besides, I can always teleport back if I get into trouble," he said, trying to convince himself that it was true.

They mounted the steps to the turret, and he was relieved to see that his mysterious guardians had left no trace they had ever been there.

Ellabell glanced over the edge of the turret. "How are you going to get past the barrier? I'm not having you plummeting to your death again, Alex."

"It shouldn't affect me if I'm careful," he replied. "And I have an idea that means I won't end up eaten by the moat monsters."

"Won't you set off something horrible?"

He shook his head. "I'm pretty sure I've got the hang of this barrier magic, so I don't annoy it and make it retaliate against me."

Ellabell pushed her spectacles up to the bridge of her nose in a nervous tic. "Pretty sure?"

"Ninety-nine percent…"

"You better not, Alex Webber. If I have to deal with nightmare demons, I *won't* be happy."

Smiling, Alex began to conjure ribbons of silvery black beneath his fingers, feeling the familiar ripple of them under his skin as he concentrated on what he wanted them to do. He was tired, and they came more slowly than usual, but gradually he had enough to play with.

"Do you think it'll work?" Ellabell asked, distracting him.

"Hopefully—you definitely think this is out in the open enough?"

There was a note of panic in her voice. "I hope so."

It had begun to drizzle, the cold rain falling through the mass of bronze, foggy clouds that moved above them. He raised his face to it; it made a nice change from the stiff, filtered air. It soothed the weary contours of his skin.

Feeling refreshed, he returned to the task at hand, conjuring layer upon layer of icy anti-magic between his palms, focusing on what he needed to do to get his body from A to B. His sights were set on where he knew the gatehouse to be, having seen it gleaming in the near distance for just a moment, when the fog had dispersed earlier. As ever, it was the well of pent-up emotion that seemed to fuel his skills, revealing them. His frustration was spilling over, thanks to the day he had just had, and he was more than happy to use it for something productive, rather than wallowing in the intense misery of it.

Slowly, he reached up to feel for the barrier of magic again, knowing as he touched the edge of it that he needed to get away as soon as humanly possible, to clear the fog in his mind and ease the vise around his chest. Around him, the barrier thrummed more insistently, letting him know he needed to push beyond it. He hoped fervently that, if he was careful and didn't feed his anti-magic directly into the wall, there wouldn't be any dire consequences for those within the keep.

Now for the traveling part. A memory of seeing the Head twist into existence, in the cemetery beside the entrance to the tombs at Spellshadow, crept into Alex's mind. Thinking about it, he realized the technique looked somewhat similar to the travel method Natalie had wanted to try in the Spellshadow gardens, when the barrier had prevented her from moving from one point to another. A true teleport. He wondered silently if he was capable of it, coming to the brazen conclusion that if the Head could do it, then so could he.

He climbed up onto the actual wall of the turret, teetering slightly. Ellabell reached up a hand to steady him, but he refused it.

"You should probably stand over there, just in case," he said reluctantly, gesturing toward the far side of the turret.

She nodded. "Good point. Just… stay safe, and please come back, okay?"

"I promise, on both counts." He smiled, returning to what he was doing as she moved over to the opposite edge of the turret.

Trying and failing to remember the passage in the travel book, Alex decided to wing it, folding his energy inwards and feeling the thrum of the barrier as it tried to fight him. Moving his anti-magic as smoothly as possible through the barrier, he focused his mind on the edge of the forest, beyond the moat with its unsettling splashes, and as close to the gatehouse as possible. It was the only spot he could think about.

Suddenly, he felt everything fall away, air rushing all around him, making him worry that he had, in fact, just hurled himself to his death. Seconds later, his body snapped back into reality as he landed in a heavy heap at the edge of the woods. Instantly, he felt clearer and calmer, the air fresher, the barrier gone, the pressure easing off. As he looked back at the vast stone behemoth of Kingstone Keep, he thought he could see the blurry silhouette of Ellabell waving from the turret's edge, beneath the fog the building was encased in.

The gatehouse lay a short way before him, the windows dimmed. It didn't look like anyone was home.

CHAPTER 15

ALEX RAN ACROSS THE RAIN-JEWELED GRASS TOWARD
the gatehouse nestled at the edge of the forest, the
trees dripping water from their sodden leaves with
a steady *tap-tap*. He slowed as he reached the building, the
windows staring dimly out toward the keep like dead eyes.
Peering over the lip of the outer sill, he cupped a hand to the
pane and looked inside, making sure there was nobody within.
As far as he could see, not a soul resided in the house beyond.

Above him, the sky was a velvety black, patterned here and
there with the fluffy swell of slow-moving rainclouds. Behind
them, the stars peeped out. He had forgotten how much he
loved the sight of real, tangible things, and not just fog and
stone.

The darkness of this unknown place made him feel

nervous, knowing anyone could be hiding in the shadows and he'd never know they were there. Steeling himself, he moved around to the front door of the gatehouse and let himself in, closing the door quietly behind him, in case he disturbed any stealthy sleepers within the building. To his relief, it was empty, though that didn't exactly fill him with confidence. Still not quite feeling comfortable, he decided to put up shields in the windows as an extra precaution. Plus, it meant he could turn the lights on and not fear discovery.

Running anti-magic from his hands, he pressed the rectangles of the dark shields to the window frames and left them there, buzzing quietly, as he moved toward the lanterns hanging from the walls and lit them one by one. Once illuminated, he began to investigate, hoping nobody would catch sight of him from the keep with his extra precautions in place.

Looking around, it was clear to Alex that somebody had been here recently, and that somebody came here often. There were empty cups and stale crusts of bread scattered on dirty plates, with a pile of dishes in the small sink fitted to the wall at one side of the main room. It was oddly domestic, which didn't seem to fit with the vision of Caius he had in his mind, but he supposed even a tyrant had to eat at some point.

Alex moved toward a desk at the back of the room. Snooping through the papers strewn across the workspace, he spied a stack of envelopes, some torn open, some still licked shut, as well as a map, flattened out on the surface of the desk. Intrigued, Alex leaned over to observe it more closely, seeing with some surprise that it appeared to be a map of the local area—a drawing of the keep, neatly labeled, then the mountains he had seen from the prison a long way behind, and various other little settlements dotting the forests and rivers that seemed to crisscross through the landscape. It was the first time he had seen a layout of one of the magical realms, and it was almost comforting to examine it, all drawn out clearly before him. It made it seem more real, somehow.

Knowing it might be important, but not wanting to take the map in case it raised an intruder alarm, Alex riffled through the various drawers until he found a suitably scrappy, insignificant-looking piece of paper. Spreading it out on the desk, he picked up a pen and made a quick sketch of the map before slipping the ragged copy into his pocket.

Alex turned back to the rest of the papers stacked on the desk, and a flash of color caught his eye. A curling letter "A" was imprinted in a circle of blood-red wax on the back of a cream envelope.

A royal seal, perhaps? Alex thought, taking a closer look. Something childlike in him desperately wanted to open the letter, but it hadn't yet been opened by its recipient, and he was fearful of retribution if it were discovered that a trespasser had gotten a sneak peek.

Reluctantly, he left the letter where it was, instead searching the gatehouse to make sure there wasn't any essence hidden in the small, inconsequential rooms that branched from the main one. He tapped books and pulled on torch brackets, checking for hidden chambers, but there were none. In fact, there was nothing particularly interesting at all, to Alex's supreme disappointment—just a few cloaks, some food items, and a lot of books. And most of them had to do with ornithology and geography, nothing that particularly grasped Alex's waning attention. He didn't want to read about bald eagles and common sparrows; he wanted books with a bit more excitement between their pages.

Checking another set of cupboards for any sign of hidden essence, Alex realized he already felt lighter, a sense of calm and relief flooding his body, now that he was beyond the influence of the keep's barrier. His mind was clearer, and there was no fog or pain clouding it; there was only himself and his sanity, restored to him.

He wondered wistfully if he could just stay away from the prison forever. Part of him thought it might be better that way, to give the others the chance to move forward without his outbursts exacerbating their problems, though the other part of him knew he couldn't just give up now. The truth was, playing the hero was starting to take its toll on him. His chest still ached from the missing piece of soul, and his shoulders still sagged beneath the weight of what the future might bring, with so much uncertainty now ahead. It wasn't a role he'd ever pictured himself in, and he could only hope he was doing a good enough job of keeping those dear to him safe.

Each day, his hatred for the royals burned brighter, and he knew it was not just the barrier making him feel a heightened sense of anger. It grew with every atrocity he heard of, with every named bottle of essence he touched that had once been a person, now used as an object instead of respected as an individual. It grew with each day he was kept away from his ailing mother and his friends were kept away from their families. It grew with each revelation of the royals' dark and twisted ways, and the lengths they would go to make others suffer for their benefit. It grew with the knowledge that their king had essentially ordered yet another mass death warrant.

Glancing through the shielded windows toward the keep, Alex's mind turned back to his friends, back to those mages who weren't hateful and terrible, but had stood by his side through all of this, and continued to stand there, despite the hopelessness they all felt.

Checking that he had left everything exactly where he had found it and quickly removing the shields from the windows, Alex slipped out of the gatehouse, back into the night. He knew Caius wasn't here, and probably wasn't likely to come near the keep after Julius's visit. It had been something of a fool's errand, and yet it had given him another idea, one that might just get them back on track. He needed to be more powerful; he needed to have the tools to take on Caius, if they did come face-to-face. Ellabell was right: Caius was too powerful for Alex to take on alone. But Alex knew that, with some help, he could try to match the old warden, at least enough to get him to part with information on the essence. That was all he needed—a way in. A way of eking the knowledge out of Caius's brain. And he knew just the person he would have to ask.

He paused for a moment, looking up at the sky overhead. The rain had stopped and the clouds had cleared, revealing the twinkling lights of a billion stars, burning brightly, so far away that many of them would already be dead by the time their light reached his eyes. In the star-scape, he could pick out the familiar shape of Orion. He wondered if his mother was looking up at the same moon and the same stars, thinking about him as he was thinking about her. It warmed him, his eyes taking in the silvery gleam of the moon, praying that its light would be the one that guided him back to her one day, granting him safe passage, like a lighthouse in a treacherous storm.

Focusing his anti-magic in the same way he had on the journey in, he folded his energy inwards, feeling himself falling away as he envisioned the turret, feeding that into his mind as his destination. There was a whoosh of air around him, everything strange and rapid, before his body reappeared with a sharp crack. The return journey was a bumpier one, as he barely managed to land on the very far side of the turret, overshooting the center by a fair way, smacking hard into the wall, and almost going over the edge. Had it not been for Ellabell's swift reflexes, her hand quickly reaching out to pull him back, he'd almost certainly have met a nasty death. It was higher here, and he knew he might not have been as lucky as last time.

"In one piece?" she said, a relieved expression on her face.

He nodded, checking himself. "I think so, though I might need a fresh pair of boxers," he joked, flushing as he realized it might not be the kind of joke she'd find funny. The sound of raucous laughter pealing from her throat allayed his fears instantly.

"Any run-ins?" she asked, recovering from her chuckling.

"Nobody home," he replied.

"Did you find anything?"

He shook his head. "Not much, but I'm going back out there as soon as I can."

"If you think that's the right thing to do?" she said, her tone anxious.

"I do... Come here," he murmured, holding out his hands to her.

Tentatively, she moved toward him, relaxing against him as he enveloped her in his arms. Each time they embraced, it felt easier, more natural, their mutual self-consciousness dissipating with practice. Beneath the dim moonlight that filtered in through the fog, he clutched her tightly, kissing her soft hair as she tucked her head beneath his chin.

"Thank you for being here," he whispered.

Now that she was in his life, he couldn't picture it without her, nor could he envision a time before her. Despite the misery of it all, there she was, a beacon of promise in the mire of his strange existence. He felt her hold on him tighten, her arms wrapping around him just that little bit tighter.

"I wouldn't be anywhere else," she breathed against his shoulder.

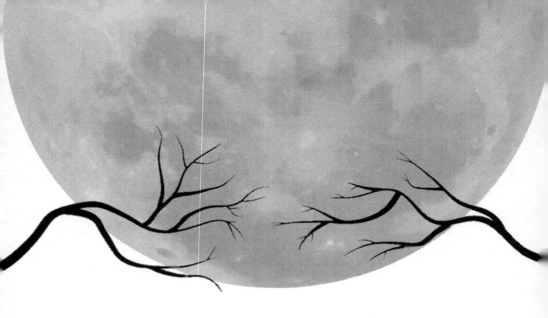

CHAPTER 16

A LEX PARTED WAYS WITH ELLABELL AFTER RETURNING to the tower room, his mind set on finding Demeter. The auburn-haired man was not among those who had sought a sleepy refuge in their communal room. Wearily, Alex walked along the hallways toward the outside courtyard where they had first emerged from Stillwater House, hoping to find the ex-teacher there.

To his utmost relief, he saw the familiar figure of Demeter staring up at the blank wall, his hands on his hips, talking quietly to himself.

"Demeter?" Alex said quietly.

Demeter jumped, turning sharply. "Alex! I nearly jumped out of my bones!"

"Sorry, I didn't mean to frighten you."

"Shouldn't you be asleep?" Demeter asked, a look of concern furrowing his brow.

Alex shrugged. "I couldn't sleep… not yet. There's something I wanted to ask you."

"I won't teach you," the auburn-haired man said, before Alex could say a word.

Alex frowned. "You don't even know I was going to ask you to."

"I know you were going to ask me to, Alex. I'm good at reading people," he replied.

"You *have* to teach me," Alex pressed.

Demeter turned back to the wall. "It isn't something that *should* be taught. I wouldn't feel right, teaching you how to do what I can do."

"If you're worried about me delving into dark magic, I already have some idea of how to manipulate life magic—I'm guessing it's a short leap from that to manipulating the mind," Alex said. "I'm the only one who can get beyond the barrier, and seeing as we don't have many other options right now, I have to make sure I'm equipped to face Caius and get the information we need—I need to be able to do exactly what you were planning to do to him, if we caught him."

Demeter raised an eyebrow. "You can get beyond the barrier?"

Alex nodded.

"How do you know you can?"

"Because I just tried it," Alex replied brazenly.

Demeter frowned. "That seems like a very reckless thing to do. What if you'd met Caius? What if he did something awful to you, and none of us were any the wiser?"

"I had to try it," said Alex quietly. "I had to keep our hope alive. Next time, with your help, I won't be in such a vulnerable position," he added, placing emphasis on the last sentence.

Demeter sighed uncomfortably. "You can't manipulate me, you know," he said, half-amused.

"I don't want to manipulate you—I want you to teach me." Alex grinned, knowing he was getting to Demeter.

"Why would you want to learn something like this? It's not something I'm entirely proud of, believe it or not. It's not something anyone should be proud of," he murmured.

Alex looked Demeter dead in the eye. "Because I need the best weapons possible."

Demeter scrutinized his former student. Alex felt as if the man were sizing him up. After a lengthy pause, it seemed as if Demeter had come to a decision.

"Fine," he said, his voice dripping with reluctance, "but first, you get a full night's sleep. No compromises. That's the deal. Take it or leave it."

Alex smiled. "Deal."

"Don't make me regret this."

Alex slept more deeply than he had since he was kid, his whole body shutting down into rest mode, needing it, savoring every moment. There were no dreams, no nightmares, just pure, unadulterated slumber. Even the fear of Alypia and Julius could not pierce the oblivion into which he fell.

As soon as he awoke, he jumped straight out of bed and rushed to find Demeter, gulping down a meager breakfast and dressing quickly, but the ex-teacher was already waiting for him in the open expanse of the common room.

"I had a feeling you'd be rising early this morning," Demeter sighed.

"I'm eager to learn," Alex replied, smiling. "The sooner I master this, the sooner I can track the warden down."

Demeter grimaced. "Well, let's not get behind ourselves, shall we? We're going to need a more open space than this; it's too enclosed here, and there are too many prying eyes."

They set off toward one of the larger turret rooms, where it was quiet and they would have more room to work. Alex wasn't sure why they would need space for mind control, but he figured Demeter was the expert.

As they walked, Alex's curiosity got the better of him. It was rare that he had time alone with either of the professors, to ask questions, and now seemed like the perfect opportunity to delve a little into the life of Demeter.

"Why does everyone always calm down so much around you?" he asked. "Is it because of what you can do?"

Demeter shrugged. "There is a degree of sharing emotional states that comes with the skills I have. I am empathic, and I can affect those around me by radiating certain feelings. Sometimes I do it without even realizing," he explained, with a look of amused surprise on his face. "I didn't realize I'd been doing it around you all, but I see now that I must have been.

It's a habit of mine—I like people to feel at ease."

"It's cool."

"It can be," Demeter remarked, his reluctance still evident.

Reaching the turret room, Alex was bursting with anticipation. The place where they had arrived, however, was not the most inspiring of classrooms. The windowless room was devoid of any furniture, save for two crisscrossed benches in the center, thrown in haphazardly to be stored, by the looks of it. Dark splotches stained the stone floor, the walls, and even the ceiling.

"You're *sure* you want to learn this?" Demeter asked, moving around the perimeter to light four torches that hung in rusted brackets.

Alex nodded. "Absolutely."

"Very well. Come and stand in the center of the room," Demeter instructed.

Alex did as he was told, his eyes mesmerized by the torches' dancing flames as Demeter moved to stand opposite him. No natural light filtered into the space. It almost felt like a room used for human sacrifice, or something equally ritualistic and dark. Patiently, trying not to let his nerves show, Alex waited for his next instruction.

"I'm going to teach you the basics and instruct you as to how such magic might be inverted, to fit your particular skillset—I have some experience with Spellbreaker anti-magic, as you know," Demeter explained, his voice taking on a teacher-like tone.

Alex nodded.

"First, I want you to place your palms on either side of my

head, and then I want you to close your eyes."

Alex followed the commands, tentatively placing his palms flat against the sides of Demeter's head. It felt strange to be so close to his former teacher, but he shrugged off the bizarreness, focusing instead on Demeter's next direction.

"I want you to, carefully, send your anti-magic into my mind. Once you're in there, you need to seek out the glow of an emotion—any emotion, pick one. When you have, let me know. I should still be able to direct you, even when you're inside my head." He smiled, although it seemed forced. "Ready?"

"Here goes nothing," Alex murmured.

Nervously, Alex wove the silvery black strands of his anti-magic beneath his hands and fed them slowly into Demeter's skull. It was a peculiar sensation, like opening up a secret journal. It felt similar to following a spirit line—the sight that met him was certainly the same, floating through an endless blackness, though there were countless glimmering lights sparkling in the air all around him instead of one big one in the center. Alex wondered if they were the emotions Demeter had been speaking of, pulsing in the darkness of the former teacher's mind.

"Now, it will be easier with me, as I am permitting you inside my head—this would not be so easy on someone who doesn't want you to see their thoughts." Demeter's voice came from somewhere in the room, disconnected from the person beneath Alex's hands. "Have you found an emotion? It should glow dully, like a small bulb, flashing slightly. You should be able to feel it, if you can't visualize it."

"I can see several," said Alex confidently.

"You can?" Demeter sounded surprised.

"Like lots of stars, pulsing in your mind," Alex explained.

"Impressive—not many people can see them, only feel them," said Demeter, the astonishment still clear in his voice. "So, now you need to pick one. Choose whichever one burns brightest and let your anti-magic flow into it—this should create something that resembles a ribbon. Grasp the ribbon, and focus your thoughts upon it, manipulating it to make me feel and do something different than what I might do of my own free will. Think of me like a puppet," he instructed, his tone tinged with amusement.

Alex did so, concentrating hard as he reached for a particularly bright orb of light that flashed over his invisible head. Carefully, he fed his anti-magic into the glow, watching as a ribbon of pure energy poured out toward him. Touching the edge of the ribbon, he knew instantly the emotion he had picked. A sudden wave of sadness coursed through him. It was frustrating not to be able to see the thoughts that came with the feeling, but the emotion was strong, wherever it had come from.

Holding the glowing strand tightly, Alex pushed his own thoughts into it, flowing his energy along the line into the glowing center of the orb, augmenting the feeling projected through him. Steadily, the sadness gave way to a feeling of bubbling elation. Alex, on instinct, began to feed false memories and thoughts into the strand, alongside the pure waves of emotion, wanting to take away the sad sensation. He did not stop until there wasn't a trace of the grief left.

Demeter had gone silent.

"Demeter, you there?"

There was no response.

Worried, Alex slowly coiled the strand of emotion back up, returning it to its former state, and removed himself from the starry mind of his former teacher, extricating himself with care. As Alex opened his eyes and took his hands away, he saw that Demeter was staring at him with tears in his eyes and a smile upon his lips, his shoulders shaking slightly.

"Are you okay?" Alex asked, panicked.

For a moment, Demeter said and did nothing, his body seemingly frozen to the spot. Alex didn't know what to do to help, whether to shake him or nudge him or go and find someone who might be able to assist. And so, he waited. Gradually, the auburn-haired man came out of the trance he appeared to be in, thawing like ice.

"I wasn't expecting your strength," he gasped, shaking off the last of it. "I could fight off most of your anti-magic collateral, but then you started feeding in new thoughts and visions, and my mind didn't know what was going on. I think you gave me a Spellbreaker-induced brain freeze." He laughed, but Alex could see a glint of fear in the man's eyes.

"I'm so sorry—I didn't know what I was doing," Alex said, feeling awful.

Demeter shook his head. "No, don't apologize. I should have prepared for it. Your instincts are faultless. There aren't many who would have started by feeding in new memories to manipulate the mind, changing the one already there. I wonder if…" He trailed off, apparently thinking better of whatever he was about to say.

"You wonder if what?"

Demeter flashed an uncertain look at Alex. "Well, I was just… I thought perhaps it might have something to do with who you are. I mean, you're incredibly strong—strong enough to take me by surprise, and there aren't many who can do that, believe me."

"You mean my heritage?" Alex asked.

"Well, yes… I wondered if… Do you happen to know anything about your forefathers?" Demeter asked shyly, clearly trying to hold back the academic excitement in his voice.

Alex nodded. "Some."

"Oh, really? That's excellent news! I might be able to help—do you have a name at all? There aren't many Spellbreaker families I don't know about, and I could probably give you some information on them if you know their surname—or their House name, as it was referred to back then." He beamed, visibly thrilled at the prospect of hearing about Alex's ancestors.

Alex smiled. "I know who they are already. You might want to sit down or something—I hear he's a pretty big deal," he said wryly.

Demeter frowned. "Who is it?"

"My several times great-grandfather was Leander of the House of Wyvern," Alex said quietly, awaiting Demeter's reaction.

The ex-teacher did not disappoint. "No! This is a joke, isn't it? Somebody's put you up to this? Have they? No—you're telling the truth? I can't tell. Are you playing a trick?" he gasped, his eyes as wide as saucers.

"It's not a lie or a trick. Leander Wyvern was my ancestor,"

Alex repeated, marveling at the way it sounded, out in the open air. With it came a whole world of family he had never known, and though none of them were still living, he felt their presence around him, crowding the room, bringing him a strange sense of peace as he thought of them. Throughout his life, it had been just him and his mom, with a few beautiful years with his grandparents—it felt odd to know there were so many more, whom he might have known had it not been for the powers that be. In his heart, he felt the familiar prickle of hatred, another layer of loss.

"Well, good heavens! I wish I'd known sooner—I've read more stories about Leander Wyvern than you've had hot meals. I could have told you some," Demeter enthused. "Oh, what a turn up for the books! Honestly, I can't believe it. This is wonderful! Of all the Spellbreakers, it makes sense it would be his progeny that made it. That man was a walking, talking legend, in every sense of the word!"

Alex smiled. "I haven't heard too much about him, honestly, except that he was a bit of a Casanova."

"A bit! Goodness, there are stories about that man… which are much too inappropriate for your ears. But there are other stories, too! There is a myth that he once drank the whole Russian army under the table and ended up wrestling a bear and a pack of wolves with his bare hands. Others speak of him riding into battle on the back of the most beautiful Thunderbird imaginable. Her name was Tempest, with blue and silver feathers giving way to a tail of purest gold and white, able to spew ice from her beak and fly quicker than the wind. A gust from her vast wings would frost the grass on their arrival, freezing the air, letting everyone know he was coming. He was quite the showman in his day! Always liked to make an entrance."

Alex's ears pricked up. So his ancestor had ridden a mythical creature, like the ones in all the friezes and frescos he'd seen, depicting the battles fought long ago. He tried to visualize it, Leander sitting astride a great winged beast, but he knew no imagining could do it justice. The legendary warrior must have been a fearsome sight, swooping into battle on the back of Tempest.

"He was well-loved, you know—not just among his own kind. By all accounts, it was hard not to admire the man, even if you were on the opposing side," Demeter added wistfully. "Anyway, enough of my tales. We should get back to your lesson. Time waits for no teaching. Now that I know what to expect, we can really see what you're made of," he said, much to Alex's disappointment. He could have listened to stories of Leander Wyvern all day, and he wondered why Demeter had not told these stories instead, when they'd had the chance back at Stillwater House. "If I had known about your past before, I would have made that the focus of our lessons," said the ex-teacher, apparently reading Alex's mind.

"Why *did* you get sent back here?" he asked, recalling that they had never quite gotten to the core of why Demeter had been dismissed from Stillwater the second time. "It can't be because you were telling me Spellbreaker stories—that's why she rehired you in the first place, right? To do just that?"

Demeter smiled bitterly. "Alypia sent me back because I wasn't telling *her* the stories she wanted to hear."

"What do you mean?" Alex asked, though he could have guessed.

"She enlisted me to report to her regarding your skills and anything secret or useful you might have accidentally said during our lessons. Needless to say, I didn't cooperate—I refused to say a word about what we discussed in our sessions, though I don't think you ever said anything incriminating. I figured it was none of her business." He winked, clearly delighted he'd managed to get the upper hand, even though it had resulted in his return to Kingstone Keep.

"Sorry if I got you into any trouble," Alex said.

"Nonsense! Loose mouths sink ships, and I wasn't willing to give her a smidgen of insight into you, or anything you were capable of—though I knew you were strong, even then," he said, grinning.

Alex smiled. "Will you tell me some more stories after, if we have time?"

"It would be my absolute pleasure," Demeter promised, though his expression grew concerned. "What is it you plan to do after this? How are you planning to seek out Caius?"

"There's a gatehouse, just on the edge of the forest. I saw it after the barrier went down. I'm going to wait for him there, and if he doesn't come, I'm going to leave him a note he can't ignore, to lure him to us," Alex explained.

Demeter nodded, a grim look on his face. "Very well. I don't like it, but I understand why you must do it. It just doesn't seem right that so much should rest on the shoulders of one so young."

"I feel older than I am," Alex admitted.

"Still… it doesn't seem fair," murmured Demeter.

No, thought Alex, *it isn't.* He thought again of the plight of all those students in the other havens, and the fate that lay ahead of them. Alex hadn't lost sight of their doom, and he hoped that, with the Kingstone essence in his hands, he might be able to help them too. If he could build one portal with the powerful essence, then why not two, three, four? Why not get everyone out? He knew it would likely be an improbable task that needed some refining, but the raw thought was in his mind, and he refused to simply forget about it. He wouldn't allow Julius to win—not now, not ever.

Moving back into position, they went over additional ways of manipulating thought and emotion. Alex picked up the skills quickly. It was easy to feel his way around someone else's mind with the tendrils of his anti-magic; they moved fluidly, flitting from emotion to emotion until he was competently handling a number of glowing ribbons at once, manipulating each of them with a focused concentration that, while tricky, was nowhere near as draining as the spirit-line magic Vincent had taught him. It was easier to influence emotions than to watch another's memories, unable to do anything to change them. Here, he had the control. Here, he could change things as he pleased. Even when Demeter tried to push back against him, he managed to force his way through, keeping hold of the ribbons, manipulating Demeter's mind until the ex-teacher no longer wished to fight back. It was only then that he decided to remove himself from Demeter's head, realizing he may have gone a fraction too far, stepping into decidedly shady territory. Putting everything back carefully, he recoiled from Demeter's brain and hoped the auburn-haired mage wouldn't feel too violated by what he had done. It was progress, after all.

Alex could see on Demeter's face, as he shook off another bout of brain freeze, that the ex-teacher wished he had never taught Alex how to do it. Alex was clearly a natural, with great instincts and an ever-increasing aptitude for the darker side of anti-magic.

Mages' minds are simple things, Alex thought to himself a little smugly. With this string to his bow, there would be no more waiting for answers. Now, his enemies would bend to his will.

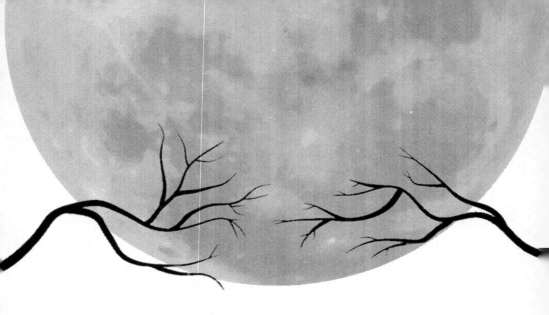

CHAPTER 17

RETURNING TO THE TOWER ROOM AFTER A SUCCESSFUL mind control session, Alex was surprised to see Natalie sitting alone at the table, fixing a leg back onto one of Lintz's battered beetles. In his hand, Alex held the note that he intended to leave at Caius's gatehouse if the evasive warden chose once more to elude him. The missive was freshly inked by his own hand, dripping with enough intrigue to, hopefully, bring the warden in search of them. He had been wanting to ask Ellabell to come up to the turret with him before he left, to make sure his re-entry didn't send him hurtling over the edge of the battlement, but it appeared she was elsewhere.

"Ellabell not with you?" he asked, trying to sound nonchalant.

Natalie shook her head. "No. She went down to the

courtyard with Aamir this morning, to see if they could help Lintz out. They haven't come back yet."

Just then, as if summoned by the mention of his name, Aamir entered with Jari in tow. Ellabell wasn't with them. Alex kept expecting her to follow, peering through the doorway behind them. But she didn't. Worry shivered up his spine.

I'm sure it's nothing. I'm sure she's just taking care of a portal or something, he told himself, trying not to show his immediate concern.

"Have you seen Ellabell?" Alex asked Aamir.

The older boy shook his head. "No, haven't seen her since this morning."

"You missing her already?" Jari grinned, the smile fading as it became clear this wasn't a laughing matter.

"When did you last see her?" Alex pressed.

Aamir frowned. "I saw her maybe three hours ago—we went down to the courtyard to see Lintz, just after you left to meet with Demeter. He didn't need our help, but then Jari showed up, so the two of us stayed down there a while longer, keeping the portals away," he recounted. "Ellabell didn't want to wait around. She said she was coming here, to help Natalie fix beetles. Did she not come back?" Aamir asked Natalie. Alex greatly appreciated Aamir's seriousness; he was sincerely beginning to freak out.

"No, it has just been me all morning. She did not return," Natalie replied solemnly. Genuine alarm glinted in her dark brown eyes.

"So, let me get this straight in my head. When did she leave you?" Alex asked, turning to Aamir.

"Perhaps nine o'clock, maybe a bit earlier," Aamir replied, running an anxious hand through his hair.

Glancing at the clock on the wall, Alex saw that it was just past midday. By Natalie and Aamir's account, they had all left the tower room around eight-thirty, nine o'clock that morning, meaning she had been AWOL for a good three hours. It didn't seem like a long time, but, within the walls of the keep, Alex knew it was long enough for something bad to happen.

Fraught with anxiety, Alex paced the room, trying to come up with a reasonable explanation. It wasn't like her to go off on her own, and seeing his own worries reflected in the eyes of his friends, he knew his fear was justified. They already had enough to worry about, and now Ellabell had gone missing in a labyrinthine prison full of psychopaths, necromancers, murderers, and who knew what else. Granted, they weren't all criminals, but there were enough nut jobs to scare him.

In the pit of his stomach, he felt with sinking certainty that she had been taken, though for what reason and by whom, he didn't know. He wondered if Caius was punishing them for trying to break his precious barrier and bringing his brother's wrath down upon him.

It didn't bear thinking about.

"We need to find her," said Alex, his voice raw with emotion.

"We will search every nook and cranny of this place until she's safe," Aamir promised, resting a reassuring hand on Alex's shoulder.

"We should get going." Alex said, and they moved toward the door.

The four of them set off at a sprint, running through the dripping hallways of the keep, calling out Ellabell's name as they ran. As they made their way through, combing every crevice for a sign of her, the prisoners shouted vile things from their cells.

"The demons have sucked out her soul—you'll never find her now," a raspy voice whispered from behind a grate where black eyes twinkled menacingly.

"Poor little girlie, lost in the labyrinth," another cackled.

"Such beautiful curls. I wonder if she can see without her glasses," a third voice taunted. That one incited Alex's wrath. He moved to the door, a ball of liquid anti-magic swirling in his palm, ready to exact justice upon the voice within. Furtive eyes watched him from the darkness of the cell beyond as he raised his arm, prepared to hurl the ball of bristling energy at the unseen creature.

Suddenly, he felt a hand close around his wrist, holding him back. Turning his head sharply to shout at the person who would prevent him from silencing the vile specimen in the shadows, his rage died on his lips. Vincent stood beside him, a troubled expression on his usually serene face. Beneath the necromancer's translucent skin, the blue veins shifted like ink in water.

"I heard shouting. Is something wrong?" he asked, letting go of Alex's wrist as the ball of anti-magic evaporated.

Alex exhaled. "It's Ellabell—she's gone missing. Nobody has seen her since this morning, and I know it sounds presumptuous, but I think someone may have taken her. I can feel it."

Vincent looked worried for a moment. "Not presumptuous at all, young Spellbreaker—very shrewd, in fact. This place is not for wandering, and nor should we ever ignore an odd feeling. Let us not forget, our bodies are more in tune with the world than we think; we simply choose to drown out the connection. If it is telling you she isn't safe, then I trust your instinct. In fact, I believe I may have seen two figures disappearing beyond the barrier not too long ago. Their forms were shifting in the distance... I did think it a little strange," he said grimly.

"Who was it?"

"That, I can't say. I couldn't make them out clearly through the fog, I'm afraid. If I'd had the gift of foresight I might have looked closer," Vincent said, his long fingers tapping together with apprehension. "Alas, I did not, though I recall thinking it might be Caius and a prisoner he fancied torturing in person—it has been known to happen on very, very rare occasions, and Caius does so love the forest."

"Caius," Alex hissed, the word burning like poison in his mouth.

It was the confirmation he needed. Hearing what Vincent had seen, Alex was convinced Ellabell wasn't in Kingstone Keep anymore, and that the one who had spirited her away was none other than the elusive Caius.

It has to be punishment for what we tried to do, he told himself bitterly.

Fury pulsated within him. He would track the warden down, retrieve Ellabell in one piece, and find the information he needed about the essence—and once he had those things safely in his grasp, he would kill Caius. The thought of murdering someone made his gut twist, but he refused to make the same mistake he had made with Alypia and leave another royal to pursue him.

"Don't be reckless, Alex," warned Vincent.

"I have to go," he replied.

By the time Vincent opened his mouth to say more, Alex was already gone. Running to the turret where he had held Ellabell beneath foggy moonlight, he knew what he had to do. There wasn't time to turn around and tell the others. If he lingered any longer, seeking approval, it left more time for Ellabell to be hurt by the vicious man who had taken her. After all, Caius was known for his love of torturous spells and his joy in others' suffering, and if the warden shared even a sliver of his brother's cruelty, Alex didn't want her anywhere near him. Alex was the only one who could get past the barrier and out into the forest, where she had gone, and it didn't make sense for him to waste more time they didn't have.

Alex coiled the strands of his anti-magic into his body, folding his solid form in on itself, and disappeared with a snap. As the world fell away and the sky rushed around him, he forced his mind to focus on the edge of the forest, pushing back the racket of a million racing thoughts. With a thud, he landed in front of the gatehouse.

I really need to get better at landing, he thought absently, brushing the dirt from his trousers.

Sprinting toward the windows of the gatehouse, he pressed his face up to the glass, checking for any sign of Ellabell in the room beyond. To his frustration, it was empty, but his keen eyes noticed that the map was missing from the desk. Inspired, he reached for his roughly sketched copy of the map, still crumpled at the bottom of his trouser pocket, and scanned it.

There was an indistinct track that led through the dense forest, toward a settlement just below the mountains. Alex figured it was as good a place to start as any.

He ran, following the overgrown path through the woods, snagging his feet on the coiled roots, shivering at the soft caress of creeping vines against his neck. It was a dry day, but the sky above was overcast, not a single patch of blue to be seen in the endless gray. To his left and right, he heard the crack of twigs and the rustle of unseen creatures in the undergrowth, startling him every time. He pushed away his fear, focusing only on what lay ahead, hoping he would find Ellabell before something horrible happened to her. With each step, his rage at Caius burned more fiercely.

The forest came to an abrupt halt. Ahead, the crumbling skeleton of an ancient settlement stood beneath the shadow of the great mountain that rose up behind, a towering tombstone to a ghost town. Black clouds swirled around the summit as the air shuddered with thunder, followed by spidery bolts of lightning that dashed the mountainside, flaring for a moment before fading to nothing. It was too far up for Alex to see the damage it had done, but the storm didn't seem to be going anywhere anytime soon, lingering gloomily upon the peaks.

Nature had begun to reclaim the derelict buildings and broken sidewalks, flowers pushing up through the cracks in the cement and crawling across the decaying masonry. Walking through the deserted town, scattering rubble with every step,

Alex glanced over the peeling names of storefronts and street signs leading to neighborhoods that no longer existed. He saw the name "Thunder Road" painted on a signpost that pointed toward the mountain. It reminded him of an old song his mother used to listen to while she danced around the kitchen, and he smiled with bittersweet remembrance, the memory urging him forward.

Passing what looked like an old tavern, Alex could make out lettering that spelled "The Feather and the Sword."

Good name for an English pub, he thought as he approached it. Stepping carefully over the rotten floorboards at the entrance, he found himself in a damp, moldering room with a bar at one end that had all but fallen away, and a few festering chairs and tables that he imagined would disintegrate if sat on. A great tear in the ceiling revealed the floor above, but the stairs up there looked as if they had given in to dereliction a long time ago.

Where are you, Ellabell?

He returned to the street. As he scoured the tumbledown houses in the wreckage of a town, he came to wonder what this place used to be, and how it had found its way into the magical realm that held Kingstone Keep in its palm. There was something decidedly ordinary about it. It did not look or feel like it belonged to the magical world, yet here it was.

Who lived here? Normal people? Spellbreakers, perhaps? He wasn't sure. He couldn't get a sense of what this place had once been from the ruins, and yet his mind flitted toward his own kind, picturing them walking among a living version of this place.

A movement up ahead snatched his attention, his eyes snapping toward it. At the very end of the street was a building, marginally less derelict than the rest. It looked like it had once been a town hall, and it was still mostly in one piece. The cracked white walls gleamed as a sliver of sunlight pierced the dense cloud for a moment, making Alex wonder if that was all he'd seen—the flash of the sun's glare against the few remaining windowpanes.

Not wanting to chance it, he made a beeline for the grand building. Walking with purpose, he strode toward it, realizing that if someone was watching from within, there was no point in hiding. The windows on the upper floor remained vacant, staring out at him as he approached. Reaching the steps leading up to the battered front door, he paused a moment to glance in at the broken windows of the lower floor, checking for any evidence that Ellabell had been there. The interior was dim, a musty smell wafting toward him from the holes in the shattered pane, but he couldn't make out much. A desk. Some chairs. Empty bookshelves. A rug, furry with decades of mold.

No Ellabell.

He'd have to go in, but something about the old building creeped him out. It looked like the kind of house adults warned children to stay away from, though he could see how it might once have been beautiful. A lick of paint, some new windows, a sash or something hanging from the balcony above, and it'd be good as new.

Alex jumped as a voice pierced the air above him. Instinctively, he ducked, not quite knowing how it would help him.

"Admiring the view?" the voice called from the balcony.

How he hadn't seen the man standing there or heard his cane on the floor, Alex didn't know, but he sensed trickery at work—some kind of illusion or camouflage. The man was certainly pale enough to match the façade. Alex felt bile rise up his throat as he examined the figure more closely. The man was old, his hair white, though not the kind of white brought on by old age. It was a particular kind of white, one Alex instantly recognized. Keen golden eyes glanced down from their vantage point, clearly scrutinizing Alex, trying to assess the threat he presented.

Caius, at long last.

"You needn't be afraid. I'm no danger to you," the man said, the softness in his clear, almost musical voice taking Alex by surprise. "I believe you must be looking for the girl, yes?"

Mention of Ellabell brought Alex back to his senses, and he braced himself, trying to prepare for the fight ahead. Above him, the man he knew to be Caius had disappeared from the balcony, but he could hear the scuffle of feet within the town hall, growing gradually closer. Caius was almost upon him. Alex raised his hands, ready to battle to the death.

Only, the fight did not come.

"Put your hands down, my boy. There's no fight in this old dog." Caius smiled, the expression utterly confusing to Alex, who had been expecting something far more dramatic. "Come on in. You'll see I mean you no harm."

Tentatively, his hands still raised, Alex followed Caius as he limped into the town hall's foyer and up the remnants of a grand stairwell, which had what looked like brass pineapples sticking up at the bottom of each curving banister. Old paintings hung on the walls, but they were so rotten, the canvases so moth-eaten, that Alex couldn't make out many of the images upon them. He thought he saw the mountain in one, a flash of lightning jolting down in a jagged scar across the paintwork, though it could just as easily have been a tear. Still, it left him pondering whether the storm ever went away, and what mad feat of weather kept it there—perhaps it was the magic of the realm, drawing it in, keeping it brewing.

At the top of the stairs, Caius led Alex across the landing toward a room at the front of the building, where he must have accessed the balcony, Alex realized. Inside, there was a study of sorts, a fire roaring in the grate to keep out the mountain chill. Curled up beside the flames was Ellabell, fast asleep on a thick, clean rug, smothered in intricately woven blankets with various vivid patterns that reminded Alex of Native American textiles he'd seen when he was younger. As far as he could tell, she looked unharmed, her slumber a peaceful one.

Alex's heart felt as if it were about to burst with relief. There she was, seemingly safe and sound. He wanted to run over to her and check that she was okay, but Caius's voice distracted him.

"Don't wake the poor girl. She's had a tough time," he said, sitting in one of the armchairs that stood a short distance away from the fire and the sleeping Ellabell. Caius set his cane against the chair, and Alex noticed that the cane's silver top seemed to be in the shape of a falcon's head. "May I offer you a drink?"

Alex raised an eyebrow, still wary of this stranger. "Why

should I trust you?" he muttered, musing upon those very words. Why was he still standing here? Why hadn't he lifted his hands and made the first move? Why had Caius let him approach? There were so many questions, and only one who could answer them.

"Come now, let's not get off on the wrong foot," said Caius softly, gesturing toward the armchair opposite him. "Join me by the fire—we'll talk, we'll drink tea, and then we'll see if you still want to blow my head off."

Alex hesitated.

"Please, if you're thinking of trying to fight me, I would strongly advise you not to. It would be futile, for you and for me," he said calmly. "You see, your anger is misplaced... I am not the kidnapper you are looking for."

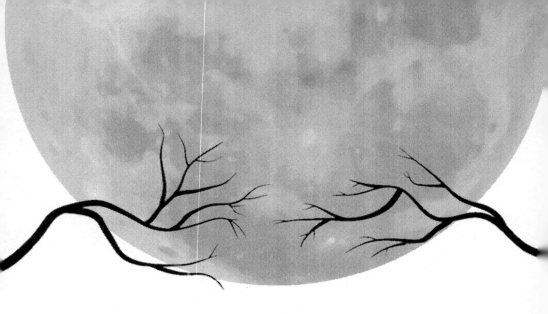

CHAPTER 18

THE OLD MAN WAS A MYSTERY, A MILLION MILES AWAY from the villainous monster Alex had been expecting, the polar opposite of his cruel brother. Although Caius greatly resembled King Julius, there was a welcoming quality to him that reminded Alex of his grandfather, and as much as he tried to stir up thoughts of combat and gaining the upper hand, the warden was one step ahead, warning him against it with his gentle gaze.

"What do you mean, you're not the kidnapper I'm after?" Alex asked, still not taking the seat opposite the old man.

"Exactly as I say—I am not the kidnapper you are looking for," he replied, matter-of-factly. From an elegant crystal decanter, he poured two glasses of blood-red liquid. Alex eyed them cautiously. "It's not poison, I promise. I thought you could use something to warm you up." Caius smiled, a natural expression of warmth washing over his wrinkled face.

Alex frowned. "I thought you said we'd drink tea."

"And indeed we shall—this is more medicinal than flavorsome, sadly," he explained, pushing the glinting crystal glass across the small table between the two armchairs. "Come, sit. It'll do you no good hovering over there like a baffled hornet. You have questions. I am happy to answer them, but only if there is civility between the two of us. I can understand your hesitation, and even your wrath, but I assure you, you have nothing to fear from me—undoubtedly you believe otherwise, but I swear it upon whatever you'd like me to swear upon. I am the architect of my own reputation. I know how I appear on paper; I have written the pages myself, tearing a few from my brother's book, but you will find me quite surprising if you take the time to sit and talk, like two ordinary beings." He gestured once more to the chair opposite him.

This time, Alex obliged, though he felt a little strange, sitting across from a known sadist with Ellabell a short distance away, breathing softly beneath the blankets, the glow of orange flames dancing upon her peaceful face. It was a deep sleep she was under, that much was clear.

"What have you done to her?" he asked, flashing an accusatory look at Caius.

"A small spell to make her sleep, no more."

The admission made Alex bristle. He wanted to snatch her up and take her back to the keep as quickly as he could, and yet something kept him in his place, his curiosity piqued.

"Before you jump to conclusions, let me explain that it was

for her own benefit. I am not the heartless fiend you have no doubt been informed I am," he sighed. "I found her barely conscious at the foot of the mountain, frozen to the bone, shivering so much she almost cracked her teeth, they were chattering that hard. I did what I had to and brought her back here as quickly as possible, to get her temperature back up. I fed her, warmed her, and wove a little spell to help her sleep, to let her forget the nightmares that kept her from drifting off."

Alex frowned. "Nightmares?"

"She kept murmuring something about being too afraid to sleep, but she had clearly been through a traumatic time and needed to rest. I simply helped calm her mind so she could do so," he explained with a cursory nod.

We have all been through a traumatic time, Alex thought bitterly, though he didn't speak the words as Caius continued.

"I have no idea how she came to be there, at the bottom of the mountain path, but I made sure she was safe. You have my word on that."

"Why should I believe a single thing you say? I've heard about you—I know the stories. I can't trust anything that comes out of your mouth," Alex remarked coldly, glancing down at the sleeping figure in the blankets, wondering what had happened to her. It had seemed unlikely it was anyone other than Caius who had snatched her, considering what they had tried to do to his prison, but now he wasn't so sure. Caius was convincing, Alex had to give him that.

Caius smiled sadly. "As I say, I am the architect of my own reputation—I have been forced to make it so. I am not the character I have created, but I have to make everyone believe

I am. As I say, most of it is stolen from my brother's playbook, though I could never be as utterly heartless as he. That man is a true monster, whereas I am simply the illusion of one," he said. "Do you truly believe I could keep that place in order if they did not fear me?"

Alex shrugged. "I suppose not... but they aren't all criminals. Why keep them there if they haven't done anything wrong?"

"No, you are right—they aren't all criminals, but *many* of them are, and the ones who are, are not the kinds of people you want out in the world. In order to control the worst of them, I have to control them all. I am made to abide by the rules of those above me as much as anyone else is. And no, it isn't right and it isn't fair, but I have to oversee it consistently, or the true crooks would crucify me. You aren't stupid, my boy; I can see a sharp mind in that head of yours. Those with evil in their hearts would seek to overthrow me if they saw the man you see before you now," he explained. "My reputation is fierce, and it keeps everyone safe. I rule from afar to keep the balance from tipping."

Alex scrutinized the old man, with his flowing white hair and shrewd golden eyes, and wondered how much he could trust what came from Caius's lips. Alex didn't exactly have a good track record with royals, and he wasn't sure this encounter would be any different, though there was something sincere about the old man that was impossible to ignore.

"I think I'll hold onto my disbelief for now. Your extended family and I haven't exactly seen eye-to-eye in the past, and I haven't decided where you fit into all of this," Alex said evenly, meaning every word. "I even had the pleasure of coming face-to-face, or rather nose-to-nose, with your brother. I believe he is every word of what you say he is, and he seems less than happy with you."

Caius frowned. "You met Julius?"

Alex nodded. "We were trying to lure you out of hiding. We broke down a section of your barrier, and he appeared... He left a stern warning for you."

"A warning, was it?"

"I think the gist of it was, if he has to come to the keep again, there will be dire consequences," Alex explained. "He said he wants you to begin extracting more essence, too," he added, wanting to gauge Caius's reaction.

The old man was thoughtful for a moment. "He's been wanting that for years. If he wants more, he can come and get it himself. Once upon a time, I feared him like you would fear the most crippling of nightmares, but at my age, there is little left he can do to me that he has not already done," the warden said, a faraway look in his eyes.

"Is this some kind of show, to prove to me you're not like the royals I have met before—Alypia, her brother, and her father?" Alex asked.

"A fair question, though I honestly believe you will not find me quite as unpalatable as the royals you have already encountered." Caius smiled wryly. "Alypia was never a favorite of mine, though I think you judge her brother a little too harshly. I would not tar him with the same brush as Alypia and Julius."

Alex begged to differ, but said nothing, not wanting to break the warden's train of thought. Caius rested a thoughtful finger on his chin.

"Yes, he might have been passable had he not followed Alypia around like a little puppy, clinging all the harder the more she beat him. I am not like them, and I am certainly no reflection of my brother—I do not seek out conflict as they do, but avoid it where I can. Nor do I rule out of pleasure; I rule out of necessity. I am the warden of Kingstone so that somebody worse is not. In fact, you would probably find my sentiments more in line with your own, especially where the Crown own is concerned." He chuckled softly to himself, though there was a hint of bitterness behind the laughter.

"I can't imagine we share any of the same values," Alex retorted.

"Though I am technically a royal, I am no royalist. A few times in my long history I have betrayed the Crown, but they can't simply lock you away, not when you're the brother of the king." He smirked, a flash of something strange glinting across his golden eyes. "And my dear brother did so hate that small disclaimer."

Alex gaped. "*You* betrayed the Crown?"

Caius nodded. "Ah, that got your attention," he teased, a smile lifting the corners of his thin lips. "I did it on more than one occasion—we had differing opinions, shall we say, the Crown and I. And when I say the Crown, I mean my brother Julius. My father's opinions, rest his soul, were probably just as unpopular as my own, but he wasn't there when war came and my brother sat on the throne. And so, my views were my undoing, especially considering my relation to the top dog, but I think you would appreciate the stance I took."

The last few words and the knowing expression upon Caius's face took Alex slightly aback, making him wonder how much the warden had known about him before his arrival at this place. It worried him as much as it intrigued him, but he knew Caius could have done away with him already, if that were what he wanted. So far, Alex thought, Caius didn't look as if he had any such intention.

"Why would I appreciate anything you've done?" Alex asked.

"Because of what you are," Caius said simply, pouring two cups of tea and passing one to Alex, who took it automatically, too distracted by Caius's words to do otherwise.

"And what is that?" Alex asked.

Caius smiled. "The last of your kind. The last Spellbreaker."

So Caius knew quite a bit about him, then. Alex's heart beat a little faster.

"Who told you that? Was it Alypia? Did you see something?" he muttered, knowing his flimsy cover was blown.

Caius shook his head. "Nothing so mundane," he replied. "I was firm friends with many of your kind, back in the day… I could never forget the sensation and scent of being near one of you, like being too close to lightning in a thunderstorm." A wistful look glazed his golden eyes for a brief moment, his thoughts visibly distracted.

Alex was stunned by the revelation. "You were friends with Spellbreakers?"

"It's how I know what to look for," Caius explained, making Alex feel instantly less self-conscious about his potential "scent." A wave of nostalgia seemed to ripple across Caius's face. "They were glorious times, the times I spent among your kind. My great love was one of yours—the truest, purest love I have ever known. My dearest Guinevere. In all the time since and all the time before, I could never replicate it. If I had a thousand years more, I would never find it again. That girl was as rare as the very love we shared," he said, his eyes growing misty. "I haven't thought about her in a long while… much too painful. Anyway, that is how I came to know and love your kind. Guinevere showed me peace, and the loss of her only caused my support of the Spellbreakers to grow. I was almost glad of it when they sent me here, to take care of this place."

"Let me guess—strike one?" Alex asked, unexpectedly moved by the old man's speech. For a moment, it seemed as if Caius had almost forgotten Alex was there with him, his mind lost in a bygone world with long-gone players.

Caius nodded. "Strike one indeed. Though, as I said, the king isn't really in the habit of punishing other royals—or rather, he isn't allowed. Even kings have to follow rules," he said with a knowing smile. "He simply exiles them to a place where the others can forget they ever existed, and pops in every now and again, throwing his weight around to remind everyone who is in charge. Not to mention the little alarms he has hidden around the place, to alert him if I should slip up. Undoubtedly, that is what happened when you tried to break down my barrier magic." He gave a conspiratorial wink.

"You're not mad?" Alex asked, slightly confused.

Caius shrugged. "I have little time for bearing grudges. As long as nobody dangerous escaped, I have nothing to be angry about. The barrier is back up, and everyone is safe."

The old man's nonchalance surprised Alex, and his revelation about Julius's means of ridding himself of errant royals
made Alex think of the Head, no doubt exiled to Spellshadow
to be kept out of the way, where he couldn't be an embarrassment to anyone with his hybrid abnormalities. A place where
everyone could just forget he ever existed. Had he not hated
the Head, Alex knew he might have felt sorry for the hooded
creature.

"So, the Head at Spellshadow Manor, he was an exile too?"
Alex asked.

Caius frowned for a second before understanding shifted his features into a grim smile. "You mean Virgil—our little
mixed disgrace? I was wondering if you might have learned
his secret. Spellbreakers have always had a knack for seeking
one another out, though I suppose he doesn't exactly count,"
he mused, tapping the side of his cup thoughtfully. "Yes, I suppose that must have been why they sent him to oversee a haven.
Like me, an abomination—all of us, outcasts, though Alypia
would no doubt argue she was still in favor." He grinned.

Alex couldn't help it—he was warming to this man with
the easy grin and the frankly extraordinary revelations. He
also couldn't help but find it strange to hear the Head referred
to by anything other than "the Head." To give him a name hu-
manized him somehow, making him seem less of a monster
and more of an actual, tangible human being.

Virgil. Virgil. Virgil. Alex let the name roll around in his
mind a few times, but no matter how many times he envisioned it, it still felt wrong.

"That girl, honestly," Caius sighed, shaking his head.

"Alypia has always been like her father. They are two vile peas in an equally vile pod, though I doubt she will ever reach the same lofty climes of cruelty as him. Ever since she was little, she would copy her father's ways, punishing her brother and lording her power over everyone else, torturing the serving staff and such. I could never keep her in check. Who knows, perhaps I looked less frightening back then?" He laughed, pulling his cheeks back a little to smooth out the wrinkles. "Though I doubt she'd listen to me now, either."

It was hard to imagine what Caius would have looked like when he was younger; he looked like the kind of man who had always been old, though he must have had youth on his side at one point.

"I imagine that's probably why she hasn't ceased her little breakthrough attempts. She thinks she can make me do as she pleases, but I'm afraid she is in for a rude awakening," Caius remarked, surprising Alex.

"Wait, you already knew we were in Kingstone?"

Caius shrugged casually. "I told you, I don't like to get involved—as long as nobody escapes and nobody begins to suspect I'm not what I say I am, I'm happy. Plus, no one can accuse me of not doing my job if I do it just well enough. Well, nobody but my brother, but as long as he gets to say his piece and do some suitably terrible things, it'll keep him away for a while… Fear is a powerful tool. Never forget that," he said with grim sincerity. "Though I wonder now what I should do with you… seeing as you've spoiled my rule of 'nobody escapes.'" The joke worried Alex for a second before he realized it wasn't coldly meant. Alex had to remember this wasn't Julius he was speaking to.

Suddenly, a horrible thought came to him.

"Does Julius know about me?" he asked, the fear of such a thing dawning on him.

The old man shook his head slowly. "If he did, you wouldn't be here now," he insisted, and Alex did not doubt the truth in those words. "If Alypia and Virgil know what you are, I presume they intend to tie a little bow around you and give you to him as a gift. If you have escaped her clutches, as it appears you have, I would imagine the shame is currently keeping her from telling her father. He can't abide failures. Either that, or she is still intent on serving you up on a silver platter. My money is on the latter, or perhaps a mixture of the two," he mused.

Alex shuddered at the thought of being handed over like a piece of meat to that awful man. "I think I'd rather have neither."

"And who could blame you! It's far better you put as much distance between yourself and her as possible." The old man smiled wearily.

He seemed jaded by the system that manipulated them all, and Alex could understand why, especially given Caius's age and the injury that seemed to plague him. His was gait labored and his figure stooped, forcing him to lean heavily against the silver-topped cane whenever he was required to stand and walk. Without the stoop and the cane, Alex wondered if Caius might have stood as tall and proud as Julius. As it was, the old man seemed to be a victim of time, and the ache of old wounds; he definitely wasn't sipping from any youth serum.

Alex figured it would be rude to guess his age, but he knew the old man must be far older than he appeared, given what Alex knew about mages and how their magic extended their lives. Remembering the mention of Caius being several hundred years old, Alex assumed the man was in the realm of ancient. He realized that also meant Julius must be too, though that particular royal must certainly be in possession of some potent youth serum, now that Alex pictured the two old brothers side by side.

Another thought sprang to his mind. "What you said before… That means you were around during the great battles, right?"

Caius nodded slowly. "I was."

"Did you get to meet any of the Spellbreaker warriors, when you found your great love?" he pressed, not knowing if it was too sensitive a subject for the old man.

"I did. She moved in impressive circles, my beloved Guinevere." Caius smiled sadly. "Love is the most precious of things, my boy… Never forget that. They write a million stories, a million poems, a million songs about it, and they do so for a reason. They do it to replicate a secret feeling that so few get to hold onto forever, and it can only be shattered by death, if the feeling is true. If you find it, don't let it go," he said, his mind evidently distracted, though his knowing glance toward Ellabell, still sleeping soundly, made Alex's cheeks flush with sudden heat.

"So you met some of them? The Spellbreakers?" Alex asked quickly, wanting to change the subject.

"Would you like to hear some tales of the most fearsome

of them all—the great Leander Wyvern?" Caius asked, an amused smile upon his face.

Alex nodded. "I would."

"The tales I could tell of that man," Caius chuckled, making Alex wonder what all these stories were that kept being deemed too inappropriate for his ears. After all, he wasn't twelve. "But we'll start with the one concerning you, shall we?"

Alex's eyes went wide. "You know that story?"

"Know it? My boy, I was there."

"You were there?" Alex whispered, barely able to contain his emotion.

Caius smiled with compassion. "I played a small part in the survival of his child, and so, I suppose... the survival of you."

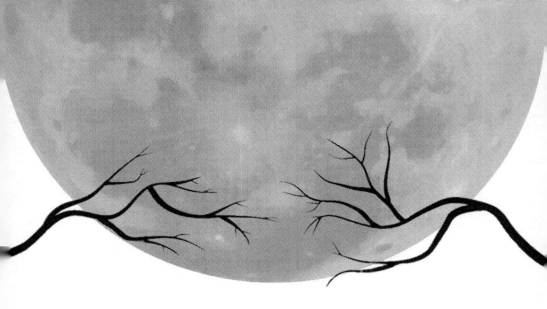

CHAPTER 19

"**B**EFORE ALL OF THIS EXISTED THE WAY IT DOES now," Caius began, gesturing around, "I met Leander at many underground gatherings, where sympathizers would meet in secret with the Spellbreakers, to show our support and to come up with ways of foiling my brother's plans. We shared information and tried to devise a way of healing the rift between our two races, to fight for equality, the way my father had fought for such a thing. But I think we all knew it was too wide a conflict to traverse, even then." He sighed wearily, a haunted expression lingering for a moment.

"But it was at one of these that I met Leander, and he was aware I stood with them as a Spellbreaker sympathizer and avid supporter. Being who I am, that was something of a rarity, and it intrigued Leander. His curiosity led to a friendship, which prevailed even though my brother forced me to fight on the opposite side, utterly against my will. I ran onto the fields I was pushed onto, went through the motions, conjured shields and tried not to die… It was my duty to be seen, but I only took wounds; I did not give them." He smiled wryly, gesturing to the injured leg stretched out stiffly in front of him. "In all the wars, I don't believe I killed a single Spellbreaker."

"You were wounded?" Alex asked solemnly.

Caius nodded. "A particularly nasty bone-shattering spell caught me in the knee. It hasn't been the same since. But it was nothing compared to what others suffered."

Alex could see the strain on Caius's face as he gathered his memories. A thousand ghosts shifted behind the old man's golden eyes, clearly troubling him even now, after so many years. Alex almost felt bad about wanting to know more, staying silent until Caius was ready to speak again. He sipped tea from the china cup still clutched in his hands. It tasted of lemon, ginger, and cloves, the combination filling his nostrils with a rich, heavily spiced scent as the liquid trickled down the back of his throat, now less than lukewarm.

Visibly rallying himself, Caius continued. "A short while before that harrowing final day upon the Fields of Sorrow… Do you know of them?"

Alex nodded. "I do."

"Good… Where was I? Ah, yes, a few weeks prior to that awful day, a letter from Leander arrived at my door, requesting that I help hide the woman he loved… A non-magical woman, from an ordinary town not too far from where I was staying. I can still remember her—one of the most beautiful creatures I'd ever seen, excluding my beloved, of course. The kind of woman you'd do anything for. At the time, I was a sucker for love. I had a secret love of my own, after all. Leander and I had a lot in common. He was willing to do whatever it took for the cause." He paused again, with a heavy sigh. "I agreed to help, naturally, and squirrelled the woman away, somewhere she'd be safe, somewhere they'd never find her. As a royal, I could get her places other mages could not. I never revealed the secret of her whereabouts, nor did I tell a soul about the baby, though they tried their very best to get me to spill my guts, my dear brother and his cronies." He grinned, but there was sadness in it. Alex realized it must be hard, to live so long, to know so much, and to lose so many.

"Strike two?" Alex asked.

Caius nodded. "Strike two, certainly. They didn't even know about the boy's existence until much later, and I only found out a few decades ago that they had finally gotten close to tracking down the descendants of that child… and now *you* are here." He leveled his gaze at Alex. "In truth, I never thought I'd see one like you again. It is an honor to meet you. Though, as you already know, you are not entirely unique in this world. There is perhaps one story sadder than the one written by your ancestors."

The only person Alex thought Caius could be talking about was the Head. Though he understood the Head's existence was somewhat spurned, he could not imagine anyone feeling sympathy for the skeletal creature. And yet there was a note of benevolence in Caius's voice.

"Virgil?" Alex asked, the name still strange on his tongue.

"A strange fish indeed, that one," said Caius, neither confirming nor denying the story was about him. "You see, Leander was always lauded as an errant Lothario, with countless women on his arm, but I truly believe he only had two loves over the span of his life—two that truly mattered to him. I know for certain he loved the non-magical woman who gave your ancestor life, but there was another too—the pang of a first love, that haunted him down the years. There is no escaping first love, you know. It is like a weed; no matter how you cut it away, it always returns, coiling around your heart." He winked, causing Alex to shift uncomfortably once more, unable to glance down at the girl beneath the blankets. "Leander was no different. When he was younger, still a teenager, he met a young woman while vacationing in the ordinary, non-magical world. They met purely by chance, a true Romeo and Juliet story, and it led to a summer romance that never really went away. Unfortunately for Leander, the girl he fell for was none other than Venus, my brother's wife." He raised an eyebrow, letting the ties connect in Alex's mind.

"A mage?" Alex murmured, though the thought didn't seem all that strange to him. After all, Ellabell was a mage.

Caius nodded. "And not just any mage, but one betrothed to my brother. They loved a good betrothal, my mother and father, the old king and queen."

Alex wanted to ask if he'd been betrothed too, but Caius moved quickly on before he could open his mouth to inquire.

"They met again during wartime. Venus saw him from a distance, swooping into battle on the back of his fearsome

Thunderbird, and went in search of him that night. Under cover of darkness, she snuck into the Spellbreaker encampment... and that is how the world ended up with my dear hybrid nephew, Virgil."

Alex couldn't wrap his head around what he was hearing. He had presumed the Head was probably the result of a tryst between a random Spellbreaker and a random mage, or even the end-product of an unknown, mystery mutation, but hearing the truth in Caius's story made his brain hurt. Leander Wyvern was the Head's father. Alex's ancestor was the Head's father... which meant Alex and Virgil were related in some strange, distant way. He wasn't sure whether to be horrified or baffled. At that moment, he was both.

"I can't imagine anyone was very happy," was about all he could muster as he tried to take it all in, working out the complex ties that bound everyone together.

Caius shook his head. "Something of an understatement," he chuckled, but again the smile did not reach his eyes. "Julius already despised Spellbreakers with every fiber of his being, and was naturally furious, calling her every name under the sun, threatening to have her torn apart by kelpies. I stepped in, for Leander and for my sister-in-law. I managed to persuade my brother not to execute Venus for treason—and he would have done so, believe me. There are a thousand different ways to torture a person, and Julius knows every single one of them. He was always a violent, spoiled child, and that volatility only grew as he did." He pressed his lips together, as if remembering cruel memories.

"I had to save Venus's life. I fed him lies about what

Leander had done, terrible lies I am almost too ashamed to admit, calling it a kidnapping instead of the love affair it actually was, so that Julius might take pity on his wife instead of punishing her. It was a long shot, given that my brother is not prone to pity of any kind. Fortunately, Venus is a woman of exquisite beauty and sharp mind, and he did not wish to give up the most precious jewel in his crown if he didn't have to."

"So the plan worked?" Alex murmured.

"It did indeed. Our woven lies tricked Julius just enough to shift the blame—a small mercy, but I knew I had to do it to save not only Venus's life, but the life of her unborn child. Her only crime was falling in love with a Spellbreaker... I understood that feeling more than she knew, and though she has never thanked me for what I did, I know she was grateful," Caius explained. "Nobody ever thought a baby would result from it, least of all her. Until then, it had been unheard of. I had certainly never heard of it happening, but when poor Virgil arrived, everybody knew he was different. It was obvious from the moment he was born. I thought Julius was going to drown him the moment he set eyes on the creature."

It angered Alex that he felt a small twinge of empathy toward the hooded being who had brought him nothing but misery since the moment he set foot in Spellshadow Manor. Surely, a bad past didn't make up for being a bad person, but Alex couldn't even be certain of that. The Head had done bad things, but perhaps he was only the result of an upbringing of hate and derision that had molded him into the cold being he was today—a creature that sought only to better his standing in a family that didn't seem to want him, by doing their bidding as best as he could. Alex knew it didn't absolve the Head, but it certainly put a few things into perspective.

"Did Virgil know who his father was?" Alex asked, feeling utterly overwhelmed by the news he was hearing.

Caius shrugged. "I don't believe so. As far as I know, it was a foul family secret, kept between only those who needed to know. Julius made sure he had the final word, mind you." The old man's voice was tight with anger. "When Leander was put up on the scaffold after being ambushed on the field of battle, it was Julius who chained him up, wanting to be the last thing Leander saw as he died beneath the magic of the firing squad. Julius told me that as he was fixing the chains in place on Leander's wrists, he whispered that he would wipe any remnant of Leander from the face of the earth. That's when Leander broke free from his chains and clawed at my brother's neck, leaving deep scars. Did you notice that my brother was wearing a high collar?"

Alex recalled the cream-colored military suit with the black epaulettes, realizing that the collar had indeed been a high one, hiding most of Julius's neck from sight. He nodded.

Caius smiled. "Well, that's why. Julius managed to fight Leander off using a horrid spell that slowly flays flesh off bone, but the damage had been done. My brother threatened the life of Leander's progeny, though we can never know if Leander knew of Virgil's existence. After all, until then, it had been an impossibility."

"But did Julius even know about Leander's non-magical mistress?" Alex asked.

"The only thing we can presume is that it was this threat,

regardless of which way it was understood by Leander, that made the warrior release the Great Evil upon the mages," Caius said. "Julius's total lack of remorse was the final straw, and the cruel sentiments against Spellbreakers among the mages. Leander wanted to punish Julius for the terrible things he had done, and for the total genocide he had wrought. He wanted to punish all mages for not standing up and refusing to abide by my brother's whims and prejudices. Julius had rendered your race as close to extinct as it was possible to be, with one sole beacon left, bearing the torch for the Spellbreaker race. Leander couldn't allow that to go unpunished, and though his chosen weapon was extreme, it was desperation that spurred your ancestor on—desperation and hatred for my brother, who stood before him and watched him die in the most painful way possible. I ask you, young Spellbreaker, what would you have done differently, in his shoes? I know I would have done precisely the same."

Alex wasn't sure he could answer that. He tried to force down the rage he felt spiking up inside him, realizing who stood in that place now—in the place of that unborn child, with the weight of so much loss and destruction on their shoulders. The torch had been passed down the line, generation to generation, until it had fallen to his father.

Now, he understood, *that beacon is me.*

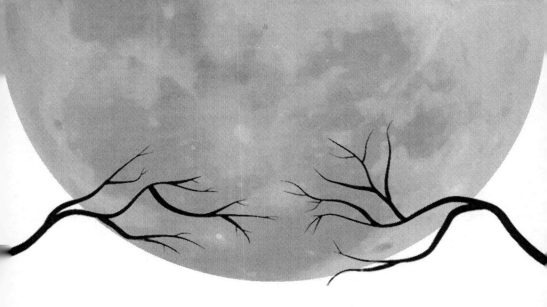

CHAPTER 20

ALEX WAS AS MESMERIZED AS HE WAS APPALLED, TO hear such a tale from someone who had lived through it. It was the kind of story he had never expected to uncover, with Elias gone from his life and all literature on the Spellbreakers beyond his reach, if such books even existed. To hear it from someone who had stood in the center of two warring factions, able to tell it from Leander's perspective and from Julius's, made it feel like so much more than a story remembered from years ago. Fed through the vessel of Caius, every aspect seemed more tangible, more real, even the parts he already knew.

"A fair amount to take in, I know. You must forgive me—I do ramble on when given the opportunity. A solitary life is a lonely life, and I pounce on company when it arises." Caius chuckled, draining the rest of the tea from his cup. For the first time, Alex noticed the blue pattern that snaked across the smooth porcelain, showing winged beasts and drooping willow trees.

His own teacup remained half-full and stone-cold. There had been too much excitement and intrigue to find a moment to finish his tea, though he realized suddenly that his throat had become arid, as if he had hardly dared to gulp throughout Caius's telling of the tale. Reluctantly, he drank what was left in his cup, letting it soothe his dry throat, though it had lost its flavor and its warmth.

Even after everything he had been told, Alex still had questions, though he wasn't sure how happy Caius would be about answering them. There were a few points along the way that had piqued Alex's interest, and he just hoped the old man's generosity would extend a little further.

"That's quite a story," Alex murmured. "Forgive me for asking, but what happened to your great love?"

He instantly regretted the question, as an expression of grief washed over the old man's face, making him seem suddenly even more ancient, if such a thing was possible. Caius sighed heavily, running a hand through his flowing white locks. Deep down, Alex realized he already knew the answer, and he wanted to take the question back—but words, like arrows, could never be returned.

"Like all the others, my Guinevere perished. My brother ensured that she didn't live—another punishment for my so-called crimes. You see now, there isn't much more he can do to hurt me," Caius whispered miserably, staring into the licking flames of the fire. "I keep her close to my heart, though," he said, turning back to Alex.

From his shirt pocket, Caius retrieved a pocket watch. The silver oval glinted in the firelight, and Alex saw that it was engraved with tiny vines that swirled across the metal. When Caius pushed on a minuscule button, the pocket watch popped open, revealing a clock face on one side, ticking slowly, and a portrait on the other. The woman depicted in the image was beautiful, with large, almond-shaped eyes and flowing dark hair, though Alex couldn't tell the color of anything from the sepia tone of the picture.

"She's lovely," Alex said, though it didn't really do the woman justice.

"Smart too, the smartest woman I ever knew, and funny too. I never knew a sense of humor like hers," Caius remarked wistfully, snapping the watch shut and returning it to his shirt pocket.

That description reminded Alex of someone, though he refused to look at her in case Caius picked up on it. Instead, he asked another question, to sate his curiosity.

"How come Julius didn't follow through on his threat with Leander's children? With Virgil?"

"A few reasons," Caius explained. "With the Great Evil released, Julius was convinced by his advisors to let the boy live, in case he proved useful in combatting it. Julius had no qualms about putting Virgil in harm's way, but nobody could confirm whether or not a hybrid could carry out the necessary spell, designed to put an end to the Great Evil, and nobody has been able to confirm it since. In previous attempts, it looked as if

Virgil wasn't quite Spellbreaker enough to make it work, but who can say whether he was made to try hard enough—royals don't punish royals, after all."

Alex frowned. "What do you mean 'carry out the necessary spell?'"

"Ah… I wasn't sure we'd get around to this," Caius said reluctantly, a flash of sorrow in his golden eyes.

"Get around to what?"

"Well, the Great Evil is currently being kept at bay with the life essence of mages, to feed the hungry entity Leander released," Caius explained. "However, magic is fading from this world, and more and more noble families, not to mention regular magical families, are having children with no magical ability whatsoever. I would imagine that is why Julius decided to come down and demand further essence from my haven."

It was something Alex was already vaguely aware of, after hearing it mentioned by Alypia, but Caius seemed as if he was about to elaborate, and Alex was eager to hear what the old man had to say. So far, he had proven to be the greatest well of knowledge Alex had come across.

"The only way to stop the threat of the Great Evil and the ongoing deaths of young mages—and, I suppose, my prisoners—once and for all, is to find a Spellbreaker and have him perform the counter-spell to the one Leander released that day," he said grimly, giving Alex an apologetic look. "They thought they had found him, a while back, but it came to nothing."

Alex knew Caius was talking about his father, and the memory was a painful one, dragging back up all those feelings from the pit of his stomach. The image of his mother heading to the ice cream truck. The strange man across the lake, staring. The panicked heartbeat as his father ran. The swoop of a shadow, and the darkness as his father's life evaporated on the wind.

"Do you know what happened to him?" Alex asked, testing Caius.

Caius nodded slowly. "A shadow creature, supposedly a royal-sent guardian, attempted to defend the Spellbreaker from an assailant who had been sent by an underground group of mages. They no doubt planned to use or dispose of him as they pleased, but the shadow creature wound up killing both assailant and Spellbreaker, his new powers too strong and too unpredictable," he said, holding no secrets back. "Interestingly, I discovered later that the shadow guardian, or what have you, had once been a potential link in the magical chain, one who might have been able to take on the Great Evil due to his extraordinary strength. But something went awry somewhere along the line. The man disappeared, and the shadow emerged, not quite properly formed one way or the other. With him, two hopes were dashed. Three, I suppose," he added, casting a sorrowful glance in Alex's direction. For that acknowledgement of his loss, Alex was grateful.

"And then there was me," he muttered wryly.

"Quite the surprise—nobody knew about you, not a soul, until you walked into the grounds of Spellshadow Manor, entirely by accident," Caius chuckled, but there was remorse in the sound. A remorse Alex shared, though he knew, given the chance again, he probably wouldn't have done anything differently.

Well, perhaps I would have left a note, he thought sadly.

Alex sighed. "How do you know so much?"

"There are perks to being a royal—even an embarrassment to the family like me." He grinned, flashing a hefty jeweled ring on his pinky finger that Alex hadn't noticed before. The stone set in the center was a peculiar mix of black and red that reminded Alex somehow of the squat, toady woman who still made him seethe. Was Caius getting all of his information through Siren Mave? It seemed like the only viable answer, what with her ability to move easily between havens, gathering intel.

A thought sprang to his mind as he realized the opportunity that stood before him. If he was the answer to solving the threat of the Great Evil, and granting freedom to all the students of Stillwater House and Spellshadow Manor, not to mention his friends, then he would accept his fate. There would be no more essence torn from unwilling victims, only liberation and a hopeful future for them all.

"I'll do it. I'll do the counter-spell. You speak to whoever needs to be spoken to about getting this thing arranged, and I will do it," he said enthusiastically, a smile spreading across his face. The solution was right there, in the palms of his hands.

Caius smiled sadly, causing Alex's to fade. "There is a proviso… The price of the counter-spell is the same as the one Leander paid."

Alex crumpled. "My life?" he whispered.

"It is a rare, dark spell that requires a life to conjure. No half-measures, no alternatives, no ways around it," Caius said wearily, evidently hating that he was the bearer of bad news.

Alex's blood ran cold as understanding dawned. The people who had warned him of others wanting to "use" him for their own purposes—*that* was what they meant. They meant others using his life to stop the Great Evil, not caring what it meant for him. As long as everyone else survived, what did he matter? The thought made him furious, but it also brought with it a grim realization. He remembered the words Helena had whispered to him as they parted ways before the portal to Kingstone: *"Today the few, tomorrow the many."* That day, he had saved his friends, but the rest...

Did Helena know? he wondered. Was it just expected of him that he would give his life for the lives of everyone else? If that was the case, he knew he might end up disappointing a lot of people. If he was being honest with himself, he knew he wasn't ready for that kind of sacrifice.

He was just a young man, not a martyr.

A dozen thoughts raced at once, struggling to be heard in the cacophony of his overwrought mind. In the midst of it, he couldn't help wondering whether the Head *could* do the spell but, as Caius suggested, had simply not been forced to try hard enough. If Virgil had never been pushed to actually give it his all, how could they know he wasn't capable? It was an option Alex clung to, though he realized with a sinking feeling that he needed to speak with Elias. He really didn't want to, but he knew the shadow-man might be the only person who could shed more light on whether or not the Head was still a potential counter-spell candidate. Much to Alex's annoyance, the shadowy guide had once again become the only glimmer of hope in a sea of overwhelming darkness. A way out.

Alex looked up at Caius, swallowing. "If you were me, would you do it?"

The old man shook his head. "You have your whole life ahead of you. Too many lives are being stolen far too soon. Although it is ultimately your choice, do not allow yourself to be swayed by the words and pleas of others. It is your life, and they have no right to ask," he said firmly, his steady gaze reassuring.

"What even is it?" Alex asked.

"What?"

"The Great Evil—everybody keeps talking about it, telling me how terrible it is, but I've got no idea what the damn thing even is, or how you're keeping it from doing these terrible things it apparently does. You say you sate its hunger with essence, or whatever, but what is it? Is it a monster, a demon, or what?"

Caius smiled oddly. "I promise I will show you, when we return to the keep."

"You will?" The offer took Alex by surprise.

"I will. Now, I have talked for quite long enough. It's your turn. First of all, what is it you're planning to do with my dear niece?" he asked. "She seems insistent on coming through my walls to retrieve what I imagine she believes to be her stolen property." He smirked, displeasure for the woman evident on his face.

Alex scrutinized Caius closely, hoping his hope wouldn't be crushed, as it had been so many times before. He believed Caius to be the most trustworthy royal he had come across so far, with perhaps the exception of Helena, and so, taking a deep breath, he told Caius of the plan to build a portal using the essence.

"I suppose her persistence makes more sense now," Alex quipped bitterly, gesturing toward himself. "Why be mad about stolen essence when the key to your survival has slipped through your fingers? It isn't the essence she wants back—she wants me. She wants to tie that bow around me and hand-deliver me like a fruit basket."

"She has always been stubborn," Caius mused. "Anyway, we have undoubtedly tarried too long. I'd better be getting the two of you back before your people start to worry. I'll show you what the Great Evil is, too, once we're back inside the keep."

The Great Evil is right there at Kingstone Keep? Alex thought with alarm, worrying for his friends while trying to imagine how that could be true. He wondered if this might be the time to ask Caius about the Kingstone essence, but he decided to wait until they were back in the keep itself, where he might have a better chance of getting the old man to lead him directly to its hiding place.

Outside the windows of the study, rain pounded. Thunder rumbled overhead, then cracked loudly somewhere nearby, followed by the bright flash of lightning. The sound made Alex jump, reminding him of humid summer evenings when the sky would darken and the air would smell metallic, the atmosphere tense, in need of a thunderstorm's sweet relief to quench the thirst of the baked earth below.

Alex nodded. "I think that would be best, thank you."

"Very well—how are your travel skills? Do you think you can reach that far?" he asked.

Alex shrugged. "I'll try."

"Wonderful. I can take Ellabell with me," Caius suggested.

Alex paused anxiously, glancing down at the girl sleeping soundly beside the fire.

Caius frowned. "You still don't trust me?"

"No, no, it's not that. I'm just… a little protective of her, I guess. I'm worried that if I take my eyes off her for a second, she'll disappear again." The admission made his cheeks feel hot.

"I understand that," the old man said, his voice laced with a heartrending sadness. It made Alex wonder how he could be so insensitive, realizing Caius had probably done exactly that—taken his eyes off the woman he adored for a second and then never seen her again. "I will take good care of her. I will treat her as precious cargo, and deliver her safely to the tower," Caius promised, a knowing smile upon his lips.

With that, they parted company, making their separate ways back toward the stagnant fog of the keep.

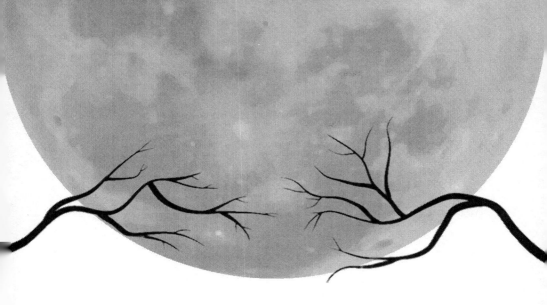

CHAPTER 21

AFTER DROPPING ELLABELL SAFELY ON THE BENCH outside the tower, Alex hurried after Caius as he limped toward the nearest tunnel, his cane echoing against the stone floor. Alex wondered where the Great Evil could possibly be kept within the prison. After all, they had mapped Kingstone almost in its entirety. Surely, they would have known if they had stumbled upon something as supposedly harrowing as the Great Evil. Amid all the strangeness Alex had witnessed in his time within the magical world, it remained the biggest mystery.

Alex followed Caius through the familiar hallways, surprised by the lack of noise and movement from within the cells they passed. Where usually Alex would have expected insults thrown his way and the slam of bodies pounding against the door in protest, everything was still. Gradually, the surrounding sights became less and less recognizable, the damp, dripping hallways growing narrower the farther they traveled into the keep. Torches still flickered, but the shadows were more oppressive in the belly of the prison. Caius plucked one of the torches from a bracket, the flame bobbing as the old man limped down the hallway.

Alex ducked as the ceiling dipped, stooping low, though the slick stone overhead still grazed his hair with decades of slime. The narrow halls and low roof didn't seem to bother Caius, who just hurried on ahead, not slowing his pace for a moment. Even the bats Alex and the others had encountered in their previous explorations remained still and silent, dangling as harmlessly as seed pods as they passed through the subterranean level of empty cells, venturing farther into the keep than Alex and his friends had managed to reach.

The floor below was identical to the one filled with bats, the cells still vacant. Caius turned suddenly to enter one of the empty cells. When Alex didn't immediately follow, Caius stuck his hand out the door and gestured for him to come forward. Alex entered the cell to find the usual amenities—a broken toilet, a sink, and a dusty cot draped in rotten bedsheets. It looked the part, but it was clear this cell wasn't intended for an occupant. Caius moved the bed, revealing a staircase leading down into the floor beneath. The warden stood patiently to one side, as if waiting for Alex to descend first, and so Alex did.

It occurred to him, as he edged down the stairs, that even if he and his friends had continued mapping the keep, they never would have found this staircase.

Glancing back at the entrance above him, swallowed up by the darkness, Alex realized he may have just made a colossal error in following Caius and leaving Ellabell behind. If Caius wanted to keep *him* as a bargaining chip, this would be the perfect ruse, luring him down into the dark, oppressive heart of the keep, where no one could hear him shout for help.

If Alex thought the normal hallways were eerily quiet, it was nothing compared to the deathly silence that lingered down in the catacombs, interrupted only by the occasional click of Caius's cane. The permeating stillness made Alex's skin crawl. He began to feel sick as he descended farther and farther into the prison.

At long last, they arrived at the end of the staircase. Caius moved past Alex, lighting torches to illuminate the way head. As the glow crept forward, Alex saw that he stood at the head of a long, cave-like passageway hewn into the rock foundations of the keep, with an imposing wooden door at the end. Other, smaller doors veered off from the passageway, but it was the large, looming door that drew Alex's attention. They walked toward it, the thud of Caius's cane echoing loudly around them.

Caius opened it, the hinges straining, and led Alex into the unknown. Alex gasped, gazing around at the enormity of the vast, dimly lit room that met him. It only grew larger as Caius set his torch in a bracket, the light spreading out across the walls. The ceiling disappeared above him, too high to be seen by the naked eye. A great, gaping cavern covered the center of the enormous chamber, falling away into the earth, the pit seemingly bottomless. On a shelf of stone jutting above the abyss, a golden bird perched, beating gleaming metallic wings in a steady rhythm, its sharp beak poised toward the impossibly deep crater. The scent of fear and something distinctly sour stung Alex's nostrils.

Getting as close to the edge as he dared, Alex peered down into the maddening darkness. There was nothing to stop him from falling in, no fence or wall, and he could feel the magnetic draw of whatever lay in wait at the pit's center. Beneath his feet, the ground trembled.

"What is this place?" Alex asked, staring down into the shadows.

"This is how the Great Evil is sated," Caius replied calmly.

Alex drew back from the edge. "What is it?"

"Do you recall hearing about a silver mist?"

Alex nodded. "The one that swallowed up the life magic of the mages, on that final day?" he replied, remembering the tale.

"Well, *that* is the Great Evil," Caius said matter-of-factly.

Alex frowned. "A mist?" It didn't seem all that frightening to him.

"Much more than a mist, Alex—it is a ravenous, deadly plague that needs to be fed in order to keep it below the earth, away from where it could do great harm," Caius replied, a haunted expression in his golden eyes.

"I thought it would be a giant monster or something," Alex said. "A mist" just didn't have the same ring to it as "a giant monster." He tried to picture a cloud with eyes and fangs coming toward him. No matter how he envisioned it, the image was a comical one.

"If it were a monster, it could be fought off," Caius said. "How, pray tell, do you fight a miasma that can move freely, shifting and flowing, getting in the smallest of gaps, undeterred by weapons and combat?"

Understanding emerged in Alex's mind. "I suppose you can't."

"Precisely."

"So how do you keep it down there?" Alex asked, starting to feel uneasy at the thought of the hungry, deadly mist.

"We bring the essence of whomever we have taken it from, prisoner or student, to life. I trust you are familiar with the golden creatures that spring from life essence?" he remarked. Alex nodded sheepishly. "Well, we bring those creatures into being and we pour them into the pit, where they fight off the Great Evil, holding it back, keeping it at bay. It is done as often as necessary, sometimes requiring many bottles, sometimes just a few, depending on the state and strength of the miasma. The golden bird you see up there works as a beacon, telling the overseer of a haven—in this case, me—when the Great Evil requires 'feeding.'" Caius sighed, glancing up at the golden bird, whose wings flapped slowly.

Alex wondered what the bird did when the Great Evil was in need of sating, knowing he'd like to see it, yet fearing what it meant. He realized with a sense of awe that Caius and the others must be braver than they appeared, to stand and hold their nerve while they fed golden creatures to a mysterious evil that would kill them if it ever escaped. Plus, who was to say the amount they were feeding it would be enough? What if, one day, they misjudged the quantity and the evil got free—what would the mages do then? Alex presumed they'd have protocols in place, but still, it seemed pretty concerning to him. He wasn't sure he'd like to be in their position.

Caius leveled his gaze at Alex, a strange look in his golden eyes. "It is a rigmarole that will continue until there is no essence left in the world, one way or another."

"So this happens at the other havens too?" Alex asked. "There are only four now, right?"

"Yes, and the existing four havens are arranged in a ring— it's why you can only move from one haven to another in sequence," Caius said. "It is a network, designed to concentrate the spread of essence into one particular place. If you were to look at it from above, you would see the havens as four points on a compass, with all the essence basically flowing into the center of the ring. It is why these four stayed standing, when the other five fell—they succeeded in trapping the Great Evil because they formed a circle, and ensnared the Great Evil in the center."

Alex couldn't tell if this whole display was an attempt to get him to sympathize with the cause, to come around to the idea of giving up his own life in order to save the population of mages from future annihilation—either when no more mage babies were born with magical powers, and all their sources had run out, or when somebody slipped up and the Great Evil eventually broke free. If that was the case, Alex had to commend Caius for his forward-thinking. The only issue was, Alex still wasn't eager to give up his life at all, and he didn't think that was ever likely to change. For now, his mind was set on finding an alternative solution to the problem. He couldn't stop thinking about the Head, and the role he might be able to play in such a loophole, if he could somehow be persuaded.

And by "persuaded," Alex meant "forced."

It seemed greedy, after already being so thoroughly spoiled with information, but Alex knew he had to ask another favor of Caius. It had been the whole purpose of finding Caius, after all, to seek out the Kingstone essence, but he had managed to get somewhat sidetracked by the surprise of meeting the old man, and discovering he was not the demon he had been made out to be. Now, however, there was no excuse. The man was right there, and far more affable than the monster Alex had been prepared to take on.

"Caius, I was wondering if I might ask something of you," he said shyly.

"It depends what you're going to ask." Caius smiled.

"I was just wondering if there was any chance you could give me some essence taken from the prisoners here—just a bagful, perhaps," he said tentatively. "The thing is, without it, and with Alypia and everything, we'd never be able to escape in time. With some essence, we could do it; we could make the portal home and get out of your hair."

The old man scrutinized Alex, his incisive golden eyes making Alex feel uncomfortable. A silence stretched between the duo until, finally, Caius spoke.

"While I fervently believe the five of you should escape the magical realm as quickly as you are able, I won't give you the essence... but there is a reason I will not," he said evenly. "I don't believe the essence here will be of any use to you. It isn't like other essence you may have come across. It is too strong, and I would not feel right handing it over to you in case something awful happened to you. It is too great a risk, I'm afraid. I know you will be disappointed, and I admire your pluck in asking, but I won't be persuaded." He gave Alex a sympathetic smile.

His words struck a blow to Alex. This had been his one final hope. He believed Caius when he said he wouldn't be swayed, and Alex didn't yet know how strong his newly discovered mind control skills would be against someone as ancient and strong as Caius. In truth, he was almost certain he wouldn't stand a chance of forcing Caius to give him the information he wanted. But if they were to have any hope of returning home, they needed that essence, no matter what Caius said about its strength. The old man was probably being overly cautious.

If it's so strong, maybe it will get the job done even quicker, Alex reasoned. Without it, they would be stuck here, and Alypia would break through—and who knew what she would do to them all? No, despite the dangers, the essence was the only way.

Alex waited until the old man turned his back to retrieve his torch from the bracket on the wall, and stepped toward him, moving his palms toward his temples. Swiftly, he fed his anti-magic into Caius's mind, the way Demeter had taught him, but he came up against a sudden blockade. Everything felt wrong and shaky, a scarlet fog shivering in front of Alex's eyes as he entered the head of the ancient royal. Fear rippled through him, driven by the strange barrier Caius had quickly created. Alex recoiled, ripping away the strands of silvery black.

The warden whirled around, tutting under his breath. For the very first time, Alex saw something frightening in Caius's golden eyes, the voice that came from his pursed lips unnervingly steady and calm, as if forced to be so.

"Don't ever presume to try such things on me, my boy. I am far more powerful than you know, and I would not wish you to find yourself on the receiving end of an accidental retaliation," he warned, his voice low. "I have been generous to you, have I not?"

"You have… I-I'm sorry."

"And yet you seek to take from me, even after I have told you the reason I cannot give you the essence you want," he murmured, a distinctly disheartened note in his throaty voice. "I cannot abide thieves."

Alex cleared his throat. "I didn't mean—"

"I despise liars more," Caius remarked, cutting Alex off. "I told you I would not give you the essence because it could be harmful toward you and your friends, and I ask you to respect that. Do not steal from me, do not lie to me, and we will get along just fine, this misdemeanor forgotten. I am a fair man—I can forgive a first offense. But I won't forgive a second. Is that clear?"

"I understand. I… did something desperate, and I'm sorry," he said quietly.

"Well, I guess it shows you've got gumption, and I do admire fighting spirit." The old man smiled broadly, all animosity vanishing from his wrinkled face. Even so, Alex was under no illusions; he had overstepped a boundary he should not over-step again if he valued his life.

"Do you think there might be another way to build a por-tal home?" Alex asked, trying to push away the spike of fear. "Could you help us at all?"

Caius frowned thoughtfully. "If you can wait six months, I can build one for you."

Alex shook his head. "That's too long." Alypia would un-doubtedly break through before then, and Julius might even come back and discover them. It wasn't a chance he wanted to take, under any circumstances. There had to be another way.

The answer came to him suddenly, as he realized he had been looking at the problem all wrong. Like the havens set in a ring when viewed from above, Alex saw the bigger picture as he stepped back from it. There *was* another way, and though it wasn't going to be easy, it might just give them the opportunity he had been looking for, to gain their freedom and save the other students in the process.

Alex looked up at Caius. "If we were to let Alypia through instead of keeping her out, would you be willing to help us trap her here, and keep control of her and Kingstone while we took over Stillwater House and Spellshadow Manor?" he asked, the words tumbling out of his mouth.

A wide smile spread across Caius's face. "I think that's a fine plan!" he cried gleefully. "Though you must promise me you will build a portal home, at your earliest opportunity."

"I swear on my life we will, but there are a few things I think we might have to take care of first." He grinned, sudden-ly eager to return to his friends to see what they thought of the idea. "I'd like to get back and see how Ellabell's doing, and propose this plan to the others."

Caius nodded regally. "The door is open," he said, his expression growing serious. "Keep tight hold of her, Alex, if you believe it to be more than a passing affection."

"I will," Alex replied. "And I will see you again soon, to fill you in on the plan and what part we need you to play."

"Certainly, though I will endeavor to be around, to keep an eye on things and ensure you don't set off any more of my traps by accident," he said sternly, with no room for negotiation. Alex just hoped the warden's presence would be a help and not a hindrance.

Taking his cue, Alex left the cavernous room and its disconcerting epicenter, hurrying through the tunnels and hallways, hoping he could remember the way back to his friends and the girl he had left asleep on the bench by the window.

As he ran, he was troubled by what he had seen and felt, wondering how dangerous the Great Evil actually was. It wasn't something he ever wanted to find out, though he couldn't help his imagination running wild. He envisioned wave upon wave, almost liquid in texture, surging up from the cavernous mouth of the pit like a geyser, spilling out over the edges in search of mages, intent on feeding itself. It would snake through the realms, unperturbed by barriers and walls, seeking out the taste of life essence to sate its hunger. In his mind, he saw the devastation it would wreak upon the land, the lives it would snuff out, neither pausing nor caring as it stole the life from man, woman, and child. Would it care? Would it stop and select its victims? The fact that Alex couldn't be certain was disturbing enough. The more he thought about it, the more he knew it wasn't something he ever wanted to see unleashed.

For it to remain below the ground, however, meant the continued theft of essence from many more innocent victims. It was hard to pinpoint which was the worse deal, the ideas that had seemed so black and white becoming grayer by the second. All Alex knew was that the pit and its grumbling evil would haunt him long after he had left it.

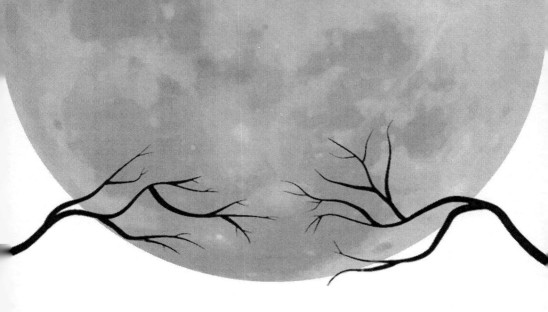

CHAPTER 22

THE BENCH WHERE ALEX HAD LEFT ELLABELL WAS empty.

Rushing toward the tower room, he hoped that was where he'd find her, safely back where nobody could harm her. He burst into the room, and was met by the startled stares of his friends, though Demeter and Lintz were noticeably absent. His gaze settled upon Ellabell, who was propped up on cushions in the corner, looking a little woozy, rubbing her eyes as she glanced toward him with a smile.

Alex jolted forward to join Ellabell, but Jari stood in his path.

"Where did you zip off to?" he asked, narrowing his eyes. "One minute you were running around like a headless chicken, the next you were gone."

Alex nodded toward Ellabell. "I was finding her. Someone had taken her beyond the keep—I would have come to get you, but I didn't want to waste time."

"But Aamir and I found her, outside on the bench," Natalie said, a bemused expression on her face.

Alex shook his head. "She was on the bench because Caius put here there."

"Caius!" Jari yelped. "You *found* him?"

"More than that—I spoke with him," Alex replied. "He didn't take Ellabell."

Aamir frowned. "*What?*"

"He's not what we thought he was. But I'll get to that in a minute," Alex said. "Ellabell, can you remember anything? Do you know who took you?"

Ellabell looked at him with bewilderment. "I can't remember anything much… just the feeling of being cold, perhaps, and a sensation of flying, maybe," she replied slowly. "Everything was black for so long, like I was in a deep darkness. There was a man after the darkness, but I don't think he was the one who took me. He was old… kind and soft-spoken. He gave me something to drink, I think, and then I was asleep. Next thing I know, I'm waking up in the tower room again, though I can't say I know how I got here."

"That man was Caius, and he didn't take you," Alex said firmly. What Ellabell said piqued his suspicions as to who might have taken her, and that thought filled him with a sudden, vengeful anger. He felt his eyes burning as he considered the very short list of culprits in his head. A list of just one.

"Alex," Aamir murmured, pointing toward Alex's body. "I

think you need to calm down."

Looking down, Alex saw that silvery sparks of his energy were bristling through his skin, glittering in a swirling mist about him. Glancing around, he could see that his friends were worried, perhaps wondering what he might do. The way the strands moved, unbidden, through his body was a visible sign of his strength, and the potential lack of control that came with it. It was troubling even for him, as he realized it had happened without his say-so, behaving under its own volition.

"I'm calm. Just… passionate," he said quickly, pushing the light away.

"So let me get this straight. You were with *Caius* all this time?" Jari asked, a suspicious note in his voice.

Alex nodded. "His terrible reputation is just so that he can keep control without actually having to hurt anyone," he explained. "The guy is decent. A little strange, but his values are in the right place. He's promised to help us trap Alypia here."

"You trust this man?" Aamir asked, with a raised eyebrow.

"Honestly, I do. Believe me, nobody is more surprised than I am to hear those words coming out of my mouth," Alex admitted. It had been a strange day. "His story is a long one, but if you'd heard it, you would too. He's the warden here so somebody worse is not, and he seems to hate the royals, particularly his brother, almost as much as I do."

The others were still looking at him as if he were crazy.

"You realize you sound like a total kook, right?" Jari quipped.

Alex chuckled softly. "I can see how it looks, but there's logic in what he does. He knows not everyone here is an actual criminal, but in order to protect the prisoners from those who would do real harm, he has to treat everyone the same. Think about it—do you think the real, pure evil criminals here wouldn't jump at the chance to overthrow Caius and run amok in this place if they didn't fear him? He uses their fear to his advantage. It's a powerful tool, after all, and so far it has worked. It's actually brilliant."

"Wow, you're such a fanboy," Jari sniggered.

"I'm just trying to make you understand why I think we can, and should, trust this guy," Alex sighed. "I know I sound insane, but I believe we can rely on this man to help us, and that's a luxury we can't afford to turn away from."

"If he's the man who saved me, then I trust him too," Ellabell said quietly.

Just then, Demeter walked into the room with Lintz bumbling in behind, clutching a large collection of clockwork beetles. The professor threw them abruptly onto the table, sinking into one of the chairs with a loud, tense sigh of frustration. Along the far wall, Demeter paced. For good measure, Lintz flicked the nearest beetle, wincing as his finger made contact with the hard metal.

"It's the bad news bears," Jari announced as the group gathered around the table to hear what Lintz had to say. Whatever it was, it was evident that Jari was right—Lintz's thunderous face hinted at no good news.

"Kindly keep your remarks to yourself, Petra, unless you have something useful to say," Lintz muttered.

"Sorry, Professor."

"What's wrong?" Alex asked.

Lintz sighed. "It's all no good, I'm afraid. My beetles are all done for—a portal began to come through while Demeter and I were in the courtyard, and not a single one of them noticed it. It was lucky we were nearby to see it. I'm not sure how much more I can patch them up… They'd almost be better off as scrap metal. I'm not sure we can rely on them anymore, but how we're supposed to keep an eye out for all of Alypia's portals, goodness only knows. I wouldn't be surprised if she slipped through any day now."

Alex pressed his hands on the table. "Then we let her."

The group turned to look at him in unison, their mouths open wide in surprise.

"I beg your pardon?" Lintz spluttered.

"We let her come through," he repeated. "I think we've been looking at this all wrong. It was something that came to me when I was with Caius—"

Lintz and Demeter froze. "You *met* Caius?" they chorused.

"Turns out he's not a bad guy," Jari chimed in.

"Though the jury here is still out," Aamir added.

"*Not* a bad guy?" Lintz looked entirely confused.

"I spent some time with him after I went in search of Ellabell. He saved her… He's on our side, and he hates the royals. The violence is an act, to keep control over the prison as non-invasively as possible," Alex explained rapidly. "But this idea that I had, while I was with him—we *let* Alypia come through, and when she comes looking for me, which she inevitably will, we ambush her. Then, we trap her here at Kingstone and steal her portal."

"Why would we want to do that?" Natalie asked.

"It's killing two birds with one stone," Alex replied. "You know what Julius said. The royals are going to keep extracting more and more essence, and I doubt any of us want to stand by and leave innocent victims to their fate, right?"

The others nodded solemnly. He could see it had been playing on their minds too.

"If we do this, with Alypia out of the way, we can go back through to Stillwater House, rally Helena to our cause, and ensure that more people don't have to die. We can't just leave the havens in the hands of cruel royals, Caius being the exception. Even if the situation weren't so dire with the other students, we'd still need to move ourselves to a place with better resources—there's no essence here we can use to get home," he explained.

Demeter frowned. "No essence? That's a lie."

"I didn't say there isn't any essence, I said there's no essence we can use. Caius told me that the stuff here is too strong, and I believe him. He wants us to succeed—I would still be out there looking for it if I thought we stood a chance of using it," Alex replied firmly.

"So we'd all go back to Stillwater?" Ellabell asked, anxiously pushing her spectacles back up to the bridge of her freckled nose.

Alex nodded. "We'll have a better chance of survival if we seize that power back and ensure that good people are in charge of the havens, instead of the current figureheads. With time and numbers and knowledge at our disposal, it would give us a chance to cook up something that might give everyone else their freedom too. We can do more, save more, deal the upper echelons a real blow. Who knows if we'll have that chance again?" he said, adrenaline coursing through him.

"Wait, so you don't want us to go home?" Aamir questioned, bemusement flashing in his eyes.

"No, no, I do—but we can postpone it a short while, to help the other havens," Alex said.

The older boy nodded. "I guess we should… It only seems fair. Why should we get the chance, if they don't?"

"Right. And once we're in Stillwater, we can make our way around to Spellshadow Manor and infiltrate that haven too, with greater numbers than we have now," Alex ventured, looking around. "From Spellshadow, we can figure out a way of breaking down the barrier, so that every single Spellshadow student can simply walk out of that place, or we could try to build another portal home with the extra essence we'll have access to, if we have to. Point is, it gives us more options, and, right now, that's what we need."

"And Helena? You mean, I might get to see her again?" Jari gushed.

"If we did this, we'd definitely need her," Alex said.

"Don't you dare put my darling in harm's way," Jari warned, a stern expression on his face.

"Of course not." Alex smirked. "I just mean that, if we manage to get her to help, it'll be easier to trap our hooded friend and lock him up, out of the way, so we can take control of Spellshadow too."

"But surely the Head knows she's in cahoots with us?" Ellabell remarked.

Alex shrugged. "We can get Helena to pretend she's been

brainwashed by her mother or something—some kind of nonsense that's crazy enough to sound believable. Then we'll have her masquerade as Virgil's ally, or we can use her intel to find a way to capture him. She does have a whole school at her disposal, after all, and if Alypia isn't there to stop anyone going into areas they're not supposed to, then we'll have an even wider scope of knowledge. Like I say, that part will come after we're through the portal." He paused, noting a few bemused expressions. "What?"

"Who is Virgil?" Natalie asked.

Alex smiled. "It's the Head's real name."

"No way!" Jari guffawed. "Virgil, huh? Virgil, Virgil, Virgil… I don't see it. I always thought of him as more of a Norman."

"It takes some getting used to," Alex muttered, realizing it was the first time he had used the name without flinching.

"So, how do you propose we do this, seeing as this is the best plan we have right now?" Aamir asked.

"We run with it," Alex replied. "It's essential that we trap Alypia here without raising any alarms, which we hopefully won't with Caius's help. Think of her as the guard dog, who will bark and bite and sound the alarm if given the chance, but if we can safely trap her here, and Caius can keep her restrained, it will be like a putting a muzzle on her. If she can't spill the beans to the upper ranks, we'll be able to take control of the havens without worrying about an army of royal soldiers descending upon us."

Ellabell frowned. "You don't think they'll find out?"

"I mean, they probably will, but hopefully everyone who

wants to leave will have left by then, and we'll be long gone,"
he replied with a shrug. He realized it meant those in charge
might turn to other, non-royal mages for essence, but there
was a plot running alongside this one in his head that he could
not stop thinking about. His mind trailed for a moment toward the counter-spell, and how he might work it to his advantage without having to sacrifice his own life.

"It seems like a big risk," Natalie murmured.

"In a lot of ways, it is, but if we can get out before Julius
and his cronies realize we've all disappeared, he won't have
time to waste on rounding us all up again—he'll have to
think of finding his essence some other place," he said. "Who
knows, maybe I'll be able to come up with a solution by then,"
he added, his mind resting more insistently on the notion of
the counter-spell. He knew it could save more lives than any
scheme they could come up with—he just had to figure out a
way to channel it through another.

Demeter glanced curiously at Alex. "And you truly believe
Caius can be relied upon to keep Alypia here, without telling
his brother what we're up to?"

"I truly believe he hates his brother even more than we
do," Alex replied, recalling what Julius had done to the love
of Caius's life. The others didn't need to know such a private
truth, but it made Alex sure of where he could place his trust.

"I suppose that makes sense," Demeter said, after a short
silence.

"You believe him too?" Aamir asked, turning to the
professor.

Lintz shrugged. "He let Alex go, he helped Ellabell, and

they're both still alive. Why would he bother protecting them if it was a lie? A damned shame about the essence, though—I wonder if we could still use it, even if it is a little on the strong side? It might even speed things along."

"That's exactly what I thought. I thought maybe he was just being over-cautious in case we set off a trap or something, but he was insistent," Alex replied. "I think we might have to forget about the essence here, Professor."

"It's also a real shame we couldn't get you all home from here, though your alternate plan isn't half bad. It's so risky it might just work," Lintz said, a proud grin emerging from beneath his wilted moustache. "I always knew you'd be a bright spark—all of you, in fact. Who knew such a ragtag bunch could cause so much chaos for the magical elite?" He chuckled.

"What else did Caius tell you?" Natalie asked. There was a strange look in her eyes, as if she knew Alex was holding back. After so long, it seemed the pair of them had grown accustomed to each other's quirks.

"Yeah, what else did he say? You were gone ages—you must have had quite the chit-chat," Jari piped up, resting his chin on his hands with his elbows propped up on the table and blinking dramatically at Alex.

Alex shrugged, smiling sadly. "There was one other, tiny thing."

"Go on," Jari encouraged, his eyes bright.

"If you don't want to tell us, you don't have to," Ellabell countered, punching Jari in the arm.

"What? I can't be curious?"

"You know what they say about curiosity," Demeter said.

Jari grinned mischievously. "No, what do they say?"

"It killed the cat," Demeter replied. A look of sheer disappointment crossed Jari's face.

"What was it, Alex?" Natalie pressed, brushing away Jari's silliness.

Alex looked across the table at his friends' faces, all watching him in anticipation. He hadn't been sure he was going to tell them about what he'd learned from Caius, about his "purpose," but if he couldn't tell them, then whom could he tell? They would support him whatever he chose to do, and he was fairly certain not one of them would expect him to go through with something so awful. He knew them well enough to know that.

"He mentioned something about a counter-spell that can be done to fix what my ancestor Leander did in 1908. Turns out I have the power to stop the Great Evil—the reason these havens even exist, the reason you all got snatched, the reason so many young mages are losing their lives," he explained quietly, trying not to allow a feeling of guilt into his heart as he spoke. He took a deep breath. "But I would have to sacrifice myself in order to do it."

There was an audible gasp from the congregated group. Steadily, it gave way to an uncomfortable silence and the shuffle of people shifting in their chairs. He could see nobody knew what to say, and he knew why; it was a tricky predicament.

"You can't be serious?" Ellabell spoke, breaking the silence. "Tell me you're not thinking about doing such a stupid thing?"

Alex shrugged, putting on a brave face. "Not really. I mean, I'll do it if I have to. If we can't save the havens, if we can't build a portal home or find a way through Spellshadow's barrier, or if it seems as if too many lives will be at stake if I don't, I'll offer myself as a bargaining chip for Julius, so that you all can go free, at least," he said, though he had no real intention of doing the spell, not if there was another way. The others sat in stunned silence.

"We would never let that happen, Alex," said Aamir.

Alex shrugged. "Hopefully, it won't have to come to it."

Since he had heard about the counter-spell, he had wondered if he could force Virgil to do the spell instead, perhaps using his newfound mind-control skills. But the idea was still a sapling in his mind, and until he had a more solid plan of action, he wasn't ready to tell the others. More than that, he wasn't sure what they'd make of its ethicality—even he wasn't sure of that. Nor did he want them to know about his decided lack of enthusiasm when it came to martyrdom, but he knew he could at least give them a sliver of hope that there was a chance of saving everyone. There was, after all—he just prayed it sat with someone other than him.

"So what do we do now?" asked Natalie.

Alex turned to Lintz. "We take every beetle you have left, Professor, and we let that evil witch come through. When those sirens scream, we ignore them. No more waiting, no more contemplating. This is our chance to strike, and strike hard," he said. "When she comes for me, we'll be ready."

Lintz frowned. "I'm not sure we can overcome her power, Alex."

"If we can rope Vincent and Agatha in again, we'll have a fighting chance," Alex assured him. "She might expect the five of us to try something, but she won't be expecting another four."

This seemed to cheer Lintz. "I hadn't thought of it that way… You know, I think we might just manage this."

"That's the spirit, Professor!" Alex cried.

For the first time in a long while, he too thought luck was on their side.

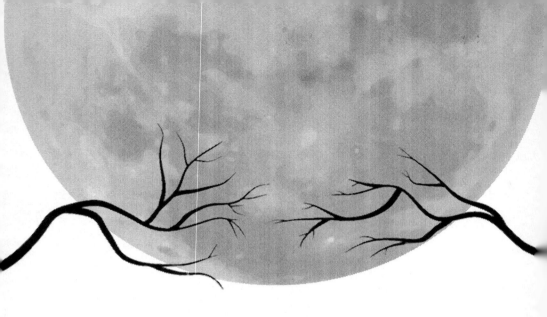

CHAPTER 23

T HE GROUP WERE EATING BOWLS OF THIN SOUP WHEN the shrill sound of Alypia's imminent arrival, emanating from the large pile of beetle beacons that lay on the table, brought their tense meal to an abrupt halt. Alex's heart pounded, fear and exhilaration surging through his body on a tidal wave of adrenaline.

They were out of time. It was happening now.

"Let's go!" Alex roared, rallying the troops. In his out-stretched hand, he held a beetle beacon, brandishing it before him to seek out the portal's location. As they grew closer, the beeping intensified, becoming more insistent with every step. They were headed for the courtyard.

As a unit, the group sprinted toward their respective start-ing positions, parting ways at the long hallway that led to the courtyard. Agatha was the only one who had not joined them, with Vincent apologizing for her absence, citing a relapse. That being the case, Alex had been almost glad she wasn't with them. As much as he liked her, he didn't want to have to worry about her attacking him mid-plan.

Everyone but Alex remained in the lobby area at the top of the corridor, moving into vacant cells and pressing back against the wall, so they could not be seen from the courtyard itself.

"Good luck!" Natalie, who was closest, whispered.

"You too," he whispered back, before making his lonely way toward the courtyard's entrance.

Whirling vividly in the center of the far stone wall, in the exact spot where Helena had pushed him through on the day of their Kingstone arrival, a portal was beginning to appear. It was no bigger than a hockey puck, but it was getting larger by the minute, expanding with each swirl of sizzling white energy.

The portal swirled wider and wider. Alex's hands felt hot and sticky. He stood at the entrance of the open courtyard as the bright light of the gateway stretched and gaped.

Eventually, the swirling light faded away, leaving behind the mirror-like surface of a fully forged portal. Alex inhaled sharply, readying himself. He could see a room beyond the gateway. Blood rushed in his ears as a figure emerged from the glimmering light.

It did not surprise him to see that Alypia had brought a retinue, though there were not as many guards as he might have expected. What did surprise him, however, was the state of her appearance. With the time that had passed, he had expected her to be her usual, formidably beautiful self—or mostly back to normal, at any rate—but it seemed she was still in a bad way, the exquisite mask of her face not yet recovered. Parts of her skin were porcelain-smooth, plump and youthful, while other sections were sagging and covered in liver spots, revealing fractions of her true age.

She stepped across the threshold, her feet touching down on the flagstones. Her pale eyes flashed with fury as soon as she saw Alex standing there, her face twisting up into a sour expression. Her mouth opened as if to speak, but Alex never get to hear what she was about to say.

A blast surged from the walls, knocking Alex backward and sending Alypia tumbling to the ground. The same crackling, red haze they had encountered on the first day swelled from the stone, rippling toward them. Alex scrambled to his feet as the sentient fog poured down the throats of Alypia and the two unfortunate guards who had come through behind her, searing through their eyes. Alex glanced around, trying to figure out what had caused the explosion, but he couldn't see anything nearby that might have sparked the fuse. He guessed it must have been Alypia herself, or the appearance of the portal. It made sense—the barrier reacted because it didn't like the being coming through, just as Caius did not like her.

Alex looked toward the entrance of the courtyard, willing Caius to appear, but it seemed the old warden had forgone his previous promise to hang around, and wasn't about to pop up and save the day. Panicked, Alex looked beyond the entrance and saw that his friends were running pell-mell at the top of the corridor, the fog seeking them out. He sprinted toward them, abandoning the dazed guards and Alypia, who seemed to be out cold on the floor, her body jerking violently as the red fog took over her mind and body. He left them to the haze, rushing instead to his friends, trying to stand between them and the fog—but it simply ran through him as if he weren't even there, dodging his strands of anti-magic.

There was nowhere to run, to escape the fog. The others dashed away from Alex as he tried to reach for them. He called out to them, urging them to fight it off. In running from him, they permitted the fog the time it needed to swallow them up, taking hold... but the screams never came. Instead of night-mares, they were seized by paranoia. Alex could see it on their faces as their eyes flew wide, glancing in all directions, fidget-ing with hands and fingers and the fabric of their clothes, mut-tering about conspiracies.

"They're going to get us!" Ellabell muttered, biting her lip until it bled.

"No, Ellabell, they're not—it's all in your head," Alex said.

"They're going to take him," Jari added, with an anxious nod.

Alex shook his head. "Nobody is going to take anyone."

"They're going to steal him away—he isn't safe." Aamir chewed the sides of his nails, tearing the skin away with his teeth.

Natalie nodded, the whites of her eyes showing like those of a spooked horse. "We have to protect him—it is the only way. They will come."

"Nobody is coming!" Alex shouted, though it seemed to fall on deaf ears.

"They are already here," Lintz whispered, picking up a beetle and hurling it against the stone wall, shattering it into a hundred clockwork pieces.

Only Demeter and Vincent struggled against the paranoia, though Alex wasn't sure either of them was winning this time, as the necromancer let out an inhuman howl and high-tailed it out of the room, disappearing down the nearest hallway. Demeter remained, battling the demons. A muscle spasmed in Demeter's cheek as he bit down, evidently trying any tactic to try to push the fog's influence away.

Suddenly, their collective gaze settled upon him.

"He will try to hand himself over to *them*. He will offer himself on a plate to the royals—he doesn't realize the sacrifice," Aamir spoke solemnly.

"And they *will* sacrifice him!" Jari cried, his voice tense with worry.

"Hide him—don't let the royals get him," Ellabell insisted, a trickle of blood meandering down her chin.

"Keep him safe. Lock him away," Natalie agreed.

As a unit, Lintz and the quartet approached Alex slowly, skirting around him as if he were a wild animal that had escaped from its cage, forcing him to edge backward toward the farthest part of the tower. Demeter joined them, having apparently lost his battle with the mist. Their eyes glowered toward him, both concerned and menacing at once.

Alex raised his hands. "Guys, it's me! I'm not in any danger. There's nobody coming to get me," he fibbed, wanting to calm them down. "I'm already safe, remember? We have a plan— we're supposed to be getting Alypia. She's just over there, look.

Come on, guys, come back to me. Fight it—it's just the barrier playing tricks with you. You can fight this, I know you can," he pleaded, but it made no difference.

He stepped forward, toward Jari, who was the closest to him. The blond-haired boy pulled away from Alex's hands just in time, preventing Alex from reaching his head and restoring his mental faculties. The action seemed to trigger something, as the group darted toward Alex and seized him roughly, shoving him toward one of the open cell doors. Before he could conjure anything, they had shunted him into the cell and slammed the door behind him. A moment later, Alex heard the jangle of keys as Demeter locked him in for good.

Alex lunged for the handle, but it was no good—it wouldn't open. Peering through the grate, he watched his friends drag a table in front of the door, and banged hard on the wood as they came near.

"LET ME OUT!" he yelled.

Alex pressed his palms against the door and fed his anti-magic toward the lock, but the barrier seemed as if it was already sensitive to attack, and his attempts at breaking free only served to strengthen the fog, causing a second wave to surge from the walls. He removed his hands as quickly as he could, but it wasn't quick enough. More red fog rolled from the masonry, pouring straight through him, not affecting him in the same way as his friends, though he felt a familiar spike of anger as it traveled through his body, aggravating his emotions, heightening them. The glistening fog rushed out, through the door, layering more paranoia into his friends' minds. He could do nothing but watch through the bars as their bodies shook and their eyes glowed, the fog taking over entirely. The spasming ceased, and it was then Alex heard the screams he had been expecting.

"LET ME OUT!" he shouted again.

"It's for your own good! There are monsters, Alex!" He could hear Ellabell's muffled voice through the thick wood. She was just on the other side, crouching by the floor. "They want to devour you, they want to put you on an altar and rip out your heart, but we won't let them—you'll be safe in there!"

"Ellabell, please, it's not real—let me out of here and I will *help* you!" Alex begged.

"That's what they told me you'd say," she said quietly. "They want me to let you out so they can have you for their own. I won't do it. I'll keep you safe."

"ELLABELL! Let me out!"

"Don't do it, Ellabell. It's what the demons want!" Jari's voice joined the conversation. "Come on, we need to chase them away."

"Don't go!" Alex yelled.

"I'm sorry… It's for your own good," she whispered, barely audible through the door.

Alex could only watch as they disappeared from sight, darting down branching hallways. Then they were all gone, leaving the hall beyond in silence. Alex banged louder on the door in the futile hope that they might return, but as the minutes ticked past and his fist grew swollen with bruising, he realized they really weren't coming back. His friends were out there, running through the prison, and he worried about where they would end up. He tried the lock again—presuming the red fog could do no worse damage—but was met by a scuttling sound that rushed toward the mechanism, followed by a sharp electric shock that surged up his arm, jolting his hand away from the door. There was something keeping watch over it, preventing his anti-magic from working on the lock.

Casting a wide-eyed glance down, he saw a beetle, its antenna poised to shock him again. He didn't know what Lintz had done to it, but it was making any chance of escape even more difficult. His friends were wandering through a dangerous place, and Alypia could overcome the fog and come for him at any moment. It didn't seem like Caius was going to show up, either. He *had* to find a way out.

There was no window, and the room was too small and confined for teleportation; he didn't want to end up splattered against the ground, his legs in one place, his torso in another.

With dawning realization, Alex knew there was only one person who could get him out of this scrape quickly.

"Person" isn't quite right, Alex thought grimly, hating that necessity had brought him to the conclusion it had. Gritting his teeth, he closed his eyes and spoke the name, resenting the sound as it escaped his lips.

"Elias," he whispered.

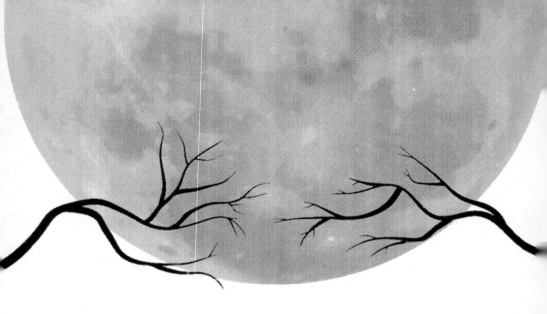

CHAPTER 24

THE RAFTERS ABOVE ALEX'S HEAD WERE SWATHED IN shadow, and his eyes lingered upon the darkness there as he waited for the vaporous troublemaker to arrive. It was bad enough that Alex had been forced to call him, but to have to wait as well... Alex's patience was already growing thin.

"Elias?" he said sharply.

At the second request, the shadows shifted, taking shape as a familiar figure poured from the ceiling. With a soft whisper of air, Elias landed on all fours, taking the crackling form of his feline self.

"You rang?" Elias purred, fangs flashing as he brushed up against the stone wall, scratching a misty itch.

"You took your time," Alex remarked bitterly, although he

was a little surprised that the shadow-man had actually come when called. "Feeling sheepish, are we?"

Elias smirked, despite his form. "Not quite—I'd say more catty. Careful of my tongue. It's sharp today."

"If I hear a single note I don't like on that sharp tongue of yours, or a flash of any cattiness whatsoever, I will not repeat this," Alex warned, gesturing between them.

A strange look shifted across Elias's feline face. With a whoosh, he swirled upward into his semi-human form, still crackling from the effects of the barrier magic, as if tuning in to a distant television station. The stars moved in his eyes, flowing over the shadowy lids, trickling down to meet the galaxies that fluctuated in kaleidoscopic patterns across his features. Alex imagined he saw a sun exploding in a burst of glittering silver light just above the darkness where Elias's heart ought to have been.

"No cattiness of any sort," Elias said, with unexpected solemnity. "Though I must say, I wasn't expecting to hear your dulcet tones beckoning me so soon, not after the way you flounced—sorry, departed—our company the other day. Understandable, certainly, and I was pleasantly surprised to hear your call. As you well know, I'm not normally one for doing as I'm told, but I can make an exception for you." His vaporous hand twisted as he gestured toward Alex, and though he hadn't quite lost all his usual sardonic humor, Alex could see the shadow-man was making attempts to tone it down.

A true challenge for you, Alex thought wryly.

"I wouldn't have called if I weren't desperate," Alex retorted.

"Ouch." Elias feigned a wince, clasping his misty hands to his cavernous chest.

Alex raised an eyebrow. "You can go, if you want."

"Can I?" Elias taunted, a knowing smile stretching the shifting shadows around his mouth. Alex realized they were at something of an impasse; he couldn't just let Elias leave without opening the door, and yet he didn't want to seem as if he truly needed him.

"There's a beetle stopping me from unlocking the door. I need to get out so I can deal with Alypia, and find my friends," he said, not meeting Elias's gaze. "I would like *you* to unlock it."

"I would like a castle of my own, a supermodel wife, a mountain of cash—perhaps an actual body that doesn't keep trying to escape. But sadly we don't always get the things we would like," Elias replied. "I'm afraid it's a no can do—these were not made for unpicking locks." He flapped his vaporous hands at Alex.

It became clear that neither he nor Elias was going anywhere, and nothing was more frustrating. If Alex had known his former guide couldn't do anything, he would never have called him down from his dark bower. Now, not only was Alex locked away, unable to help friends who might be in a world of danger, but he had to endure Elias's sarcastic company.

"You really can't do anything?" Alex asked. If Elias could be of no help, he could do nothing but wait.

Elias lifted the peaks of his shadowy shoulders in a half-hearted shrug. "It would appear not. Looks like it's just the two of us." He grinned, humming a familiar tune that seemed to echo in the peculiarity of whatever served as his throat. Alex had to wonder if this was exactly what the shadow-man wanted—a private audience.

"No humming." Alex glared.

"How about a song? We could duet."

"No singing, no humming—you're distracting me!" Alex snapped, trying to think of what other options he had.

Elias raised his hazy palms. "Temper, temper! My apologies, Webber. I was only suggesting amusing pastimes to make the time tick by all the quicker." A smirk undermined his apology. "Though you always did have trouble with focus."

"One more word, and I swear I'll blow you out of this cell." Alex jabbed a finger in the direction of the shadow-guide's wispy mouth.

"I'd like to see you try," Elias muttered.

"What was that?"

"Nothing—not a word, not a peep."

"Good," Alex grumbled. "Seeing as I'm not getting rid of you anytime soon, I do have a couple of questions."

"Ooh, I love a Q and A, don't you?" Elias purred.

Alex rolled his eyes. "Can we keep the sass to a minimum?"

"Never." Elias grinned.

Alex sighed. "Well, I met with Caius, and he shed some light on why these royals seem to want me," he said, watching Elias's face for any hint of guilt or panic. "It seems I can be of some use to them, thanks to the blood running through my veins."

"Well, the anti-magic," Elias quipped.

Alex frowned. "Is that what you wanted all along, for me

to learn about my 'purpose' without you having to get your hands dirty?"

Elias exhaled, all pretense dissipating. "I couldn't tell you," he replied, a hint of sadness in his voice. "Many times, I thought about damning the consequences, but that hasn't exactly worked in my favor up to now. Whenever I try to tell the full truth, well, let's just say someone shuts my trap for me. I only get a few strikes and then... well, I'm out. Gone. Done. I'm just about down to my last one, if memory serves." Finally, the shadow-man had the decency to look sheepish.

Alex thought of what had happened to Elias in the cell, when he had disappeared in a snap of light. As Siren Mave had said, it seemed that his "guardians" could only tell him the answers when the right questions were asked.

"So it's up to me to perform the counter-spell?" Alex asked.

Elias said nothing, refusing to lift his black, star-spangled eyes in Alex's direction. It infuriated Alex to see the shadowy creature still so reticent, even now, when just about all of the secrets Alex could imagine were out on the table.

"Can Virgil do it?" Alex pressed, the name still sounding utterly alien.

Elias sniggered. "Name doesn't fit him, does it?"

"Can he do it?" Alex repeated. "Can he do the spell and rid the magical world of the Great Evil? If there's a chance it doesn't have to be me, I'd like to hear about it," Alex snapped, losing his already tested patience.

Elias lifted his wispy chin, finally looking Alex in the eye. Alex had forgotten how intense the galactic stare could be, when directed entirely at him. Still, he refused to sever the connection. At long last, he felt as if he were about to get a straight answer. Elias sighed, as if a weight had been lifted from his weightless shoulders, making Alex believe he must be asking the right questions, finally.

"In theory, our wizened friend Virgil should be able to do it, though I should warn you that all his previous attempts have failed, and he hasn't tried it again for several decades. Not that that means much—I think he deliberately threw his endeavors, wanting to make it look like he wasn't capable. A pretty cowardly move, considering most of the royals think he's utterly useless, particularly his apparent step-father. But at least he got to keep his life. Saying that, there is always the slim chance that he was telling the truth and he just can't do it, even if he gave it proper gusto. Looking at him, I wouldn't rule it out." He smirked.

"Could he be made to do it again?"

"You'd be better off getting a giraffe to try," Elias quipped. "Nothing will get that wormy creature to do it again, aside from a king's command, but that won't come again anytime soon. It's probably why he's so intent on handing you over like a bicycle on Christmas morning. The last attempt was something of a drama, and I don't think anyone is ready to repeat that fiasco. I think the wails could be heard from here—in fact, if you listen hard enough, I think you can still hear them... Simple answer: he won't do it again unless somebody makes him." This made Alex curious, seeing as that was exactly what he wanted to do.

"Wait, so how do you know *I* can do the counter-spell?" Alex asked, expecting a suitably vague answer. Instead, Elias came straight out with it.

"I'm sorry to say it, but you've got the stuff, kiddo," he replied, glancing down at his non-existent feet. "It's like an aura around you—I can see it, feel it, sense it. You're lit up like a big silver Christmas tree. With our friend Virgil, it's not so clear. He's like one of those tiny plastic trees made out of tinsel that just look sad, stuffed on a shelf and forgotten about. The energy is weaker, diluted in some way, probably by his magical side."

Alex wondered where Elias's obsession with Christmas-based metaphor had sprung from, but there was no time to joke about it. There were too many questions Alex needed answered, and he still had to think of a way out of the cell. Time, his arch-nemesis, was once more against him.

"Why isn't my Spellbreaker side diluted by my non-magical side?" Alex countered.

"Doesn't work that way. Supernatural energy paired with non-magical ordinariness is complementary, and the supernatural overtakes the ordinary side, using it as a vessel through which to flow. When supernatural energy is paired with supernatural energy, it creates a conflict, and one side has to prevail or the host would implode. In little Virgil's case, the magic side seems stronger," Elias explained. "It's why it was thought to be impossible before he arrived and trounced everyone's painstakingly crafted theories, because the two sides fought on a cellular level too, meaning conception wasn't possible until Virgie Virge came along—he is a true mystery. It's just a shame he's so intolerably dull."

"So are there others like me?" Alex wondered aloud.

Elias sighed. "Afraid not, though I understand the desire to have another stand in your place, when the consequences are what they are. Believe me, we've looked high and low. If there was anyone else, I wouldn't have spent the last eighteen years dangling like a streamer from shadowy corners, keeping out of the way."

"Is this what you wanted all along, then? To feed me little bits and pieces, make me think I was becoming something, building me up to a strength where I might be capable of doing the counter-spell, just so you could then try to coax me into it? Is that what all of this has been for—just a setup for my eventual demise?" Alex asked coldly, trying to stop the bristle of anti-magic that threatened to push through his skin. "Naturally, you couldn't just tell me why you wanted me to do all of these things, so you let others do it for you, watching and waiting until you could strike and get me to do it... thinking you could appeal to my compassionate side, no doubt."

With something akin to regret, Elias spoke. "The curse that was placed on Siren and me, though 'gag order' is a better term, worked like Aamir's golden band. Neither of us could say anything directly—you had to find out your heritage and purpose on your own, to prove your worthiness," he said quietly, his voice echoing strangely around him. "We didn't make the rules, but we had to follow them. We followed them to the letter with your father, in that we weren't allowed to influence anything directly, to help. But, as a result, he learned nothing and discovered nothing about himself. As far as he knew, he was ordinary. If we'd been able to equip him... Well, things may not have happened as they did." In the wispy dark of his throat, he made a strange gulping sound. "So, over the years we discovered ways we could bend the rules a bit, to make things easier if another Spellbreaker ever came along... and you did. Here you are," he whispered, a palpable sorrow in his voice. It was almost worse than the sarcasm.

"I guess I'm asking the right questions now?" Alex said wryly.

"Finally," Elias replied, though the humor sounded forced.

"What were you going to say before you disappeared in a flash of light? You said, 'It is not their—' or something. Then you disappeared—what were you going to say?" Alex asked, hoping the question was precise enough to garner a clear answer.

"I was going to say, it is not their battle. They were all squabbling over who gets you, not realizing that it isn't even their fight or their choice. I mean, they could force you, but it might end up with the same results as Virgil's feeble attempts. In the end, it is your battle, not theirs."

"Can you *make* me do it?" Alex asked, trying to keep the trepidation out of his voice.

Elias shook his shifting head. "Even now, I'm not allowed to influence you one way or the other, as much as I would like to," he jested. "So far, I haven't come up with a way of getting you to do it, and I have been wracking my brains for a *long* time. No, in all seriousness, the decision *has* to be yours."

A sudden, horrifying thought came to Alex's mind. Perhaps Elias hadn't thought of a way around the no-influence clause, but Alex could think of someone who might have figured out an emotional loophole. He wondered if that was why Siren Mave had made Aamir offer to return him to the real world, to be reunited with his mother. With a pang of bitterness, he realized there could well have been a darker, less altruistic side to the offer. If it had happened, if he had accepted the offer before Jari and Natalie had burst in, would the trip home simply have served as a sweetener, to persuade him to accept his "purpose" and give his life for the cause? A reminder of what he was fighting for, to make him feel so overwhelmed with guilt for all those who couldn't go home—a chance to say goodbye before he gave up his life? With a sinking feeling, he understood it was a grave likelihood.

"Now that you know all of this, of course, the gag has loosened a little—it's frankly liberating. I should have roped a necromancer in years ago." Elias chuckled, apparently missing the confounded expression on Alex's face. "This isn't something I signed up for willingly, by the way—my hand was forced a long time ago. I didn't see the noose closing around my neck until it was too late. You should always keep your eye on the unworthy snakes slithering around you." His shadowy lips curled into a grimace, his black eyes taking on an even more distant look. Shaking out his wispy limbs, he snapped back to the moment. "I suppose what I'm trying to say is, I have had to live with that decision, and you have to be sure you can live with your decision too. Or die with it." He chuckled again, his teeth flashing.

"I still haven't heard an apology," Alex said bluntly.

The shadow-man froze. "I thought we had—"

"You thought I'd forgotten you killed my father?" Alex growled. "Or perhaps you just thought I'd forgiven it? It's been a long time since you were human, hasn't it? Maybe you've forgotten what it's like to be human, to feel the way humans do, to hurt the way humans do," he spat.

A flash of rage glinted in the abyss of Elias's eyes. "I have forgotten nothing."

"Have you forgotten what you did to them—what you did to my father, my mother?" Alex pressed, feeling anger return to him, though he wasn't sure it had anything to do with the barrier magic this time.

"I'm sorry," Elias said simply.

"You think 'sorry' covers it?"

Elias fidgeted with his wispy fingers. "You think me cold and unfeeling, but my intentions that day were good. I never intended for your father to get hurt. I attacked the man hunting him, and the level of collateral damage was worse than I expected—I hadn't had to use my abilities for a long time, and the control I had over my power was not what it should have been. I was too strong, and it not only caused an innocent man to lose his life, but it caused an innocent woman unimaginable pain. You think me callous, but while I may not have a physical heart anymore, her tears and suffering made me feel as if I did. It broke for her, and it haunts me still. I am sorry your father got caught in the crossfire of my incompetence," he said, with a greater solemnity than Alex had ever heard from the shadow-man.

The admission affected Alex more intensely than he thought anything Elias said ever could. It was hard to hear, and as much as Alex would have liked to call Elias out for crying crocodile tears, the apologetic revelation sounded undeniably genuine. It wasn't like Elias to feign emotion where he didn't have to, and sorrow was emanating from the shadow-guide, the stars glittering more brightly in his galactic eyes, prickling the tear ducts of Alex's own eyes.

"You want my forgiveness?" Alex asked.

Elias lifted his vaporous shoulders in a shrug. "I could not begin to expect it."

"I can promise a certain level of forgiveness for what you have done, or tolerance of you at the very least, if you will find a way to free me from this room," Alex vowed. "I know you said you couldn't, but you're powerful, Elias. You must have something up those wispy things you call sleeves."

Elias's face shifted into a frown. "They are my arms," he remarked with a note of scorn. "And I'd love to help, I truly would, but I'm not supposed to interfere."

"I won't offer forgiveness again," Alex said evenly. "Anyway, since when have you been afraid of bending a few rules?"

"Fine," Elias muttered, slipping back up into the rafters and disappearing through the stone wall. If looks could kill, Alex was fairly sure he'd be dead.

Alex peered through the grate as the shadow-man reappeared. There was a clatter as something fell onto the hard ground. A few unspecified noises followed quickly after, culminating in the loud scrape of the hefty table being hauled back into its previous position, before the door opened with a loud *clunk*.

"Ta-da!" Elias whooped, as he swept back into the room with a flourish.

Alex paused briefly on the threshold of the cell, an impulse making him linger a moment longer before he ran out to find his friends. With a warning in his eyes, Alex turned back toward Elias, any previous hint of softening resolve gone.

"If I hear a whisper of you having any part, however small, in Ellabell coming to harm, then we are done," he added, his voice low and threatening, rumbling gruffly from the back of his throat. "There will be no partial tolerance or potential second chances; there will be nothing. I will have nothing to do with you. Is that clear?"

For the first time, Alex thought he saw fear in the oblivion of Elias's galactic eyes, and they both knew why.

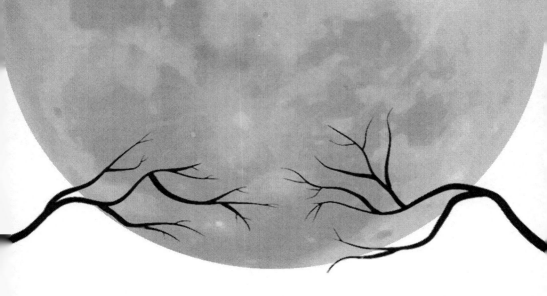

CHAPTER 25

A S ALEX SPRINTED FROM THE CELL, HE PUSHED ALL thoughts of Elias aside. He had no time for further distractions.

He ran through the hallway that led to the courtyard and stopped in the archway of the entrance. There was no sign of the guards, but Alypia was on her feet, glancing around in a disoriented manner. Alex wondered if that meant she was back to her usual self, but, as he approached, it didn't seem as if she could see him. He crept toward her, hoping to use his mind control if he could get close enough.

Alypia had other ideas, however. She suddenly lashed out with her hands, sending two vivid bolts of glowing light downward. They hit the earth, splitting the flagstones beneath Alex's feet. He stumbled, staying upright, and continued toward

her, his hands readied to reach her temples. With inhuman-
ly fast reflexes, she caught him by the throat, her elegant fingers clamping around his bones, her nails piercing his skin as
she leaned toward his face. He could feel her hot breath on his
cheek.

"I have waited a long time to put an end to your misery,
Leander Wyvern," she hissed. Alex realized she must be seeing the face of his ancestor, instead of his own. He supposed it
didn't really matter, if she strangled him regardless.

He tried to speak, but her fingers only tightened, choking
him. Black spots appeared in his vision, and he could almost
feel his eyes bulging out of his head as the pressure increased.
Although he was on the verge of blacking out, he found the
energy to lift his hands to her head. Before he could do anything, something swooped from the shadows and knocked
Alypia backward, forcing her to release her grip.

"Come here, you monster!" she shrieked, slashing blindly
at the air with her hands.

Alex ducked out of the way, hiding in a corner, and
looked up in time to see Elias disappearing into the masonry.
He wasn't sure whether to be glad or annoyed by the shadow-
man's interference, but he didn't have time to mull it over. As
much as he wanted to get Alypia into a cell there and then, he
knew he wouldn't be able to manage it alone. If he wanted to
lock her up and complete the plan, he was going to need the
others. But he had no idea where they were or if they'd even
be in any state to help. He cursed under his breath, knowing
he was going to need to rescue them, wherever they were, and
remove the fog from their brains. He just hoped they hadn't

gone far.

Alex gazed at Alypia, who was still swiping at invisible beasts. He knew he couldn't just leave her in the courtyard, in case she managed to stumble back through to Stillwater, but he also knew he wouldn't be able to trap her anywhere, not by himself. She'd have his eyes out before he even got close.

As if sensing Alex's thoughts, a manic grin spread across Alypia's face.

"I will hunt you to the ends of the earth," she whispered, her gaze resting on a spot in the courtyard ten feet away from him. "You will not escape me!"

A second later, she was hurrying past Alex and darting for the entrance to the courtyard, leaving Alex with no option but to leave his hiding place and run after her. She was fast, and as he reached the hall where he had been imprisoned, he found that she was nowhere to be seen.

Great, he thought, *now I have to keep my eye out for her trying to attack me from the depths of Kingstone, as well as for the others.* It wasn't an idea he relished. It was bad enough when he knew where she was, but the worry of her jumping out at him, catching him unawares, was one that set his nerves on edge.

He glanced around, wondering which hallway to take. There were four in total, branching off from the main room, and with the clock clanging above him, impulse made him sprint through the central one.

The prison still echoed with screams that only seemed to grow louder, the cries of the inmates masking any sound that might lead Alex in the right direction, to the place his friends had disappeared to. All around him, the walls still crackled with a menacing ripple of energy. Keeping his head as level as he could, he hoped the bristle of his angry aura wouldn't set the barrier magic off again.

A prisoner threw himself at the wooden door of one of the cells with a piercing shriek, startling Alex. Taking a moment to collect himself, Alex pressed on, though he quickly came to realize that it was only the first in a succession of escape attempts. With every door he passed, another inmate hurled themselves in his direction, gnashing their teeth at him through the grate, trying to grasp at him with dirty, scrabbling hands. It was like running a nightmarish gauntlet. Alex's heart thundered as he tried to guard himself against the fear that coursed through his veins, but it didn't matter that he was frightened—his friends were in danger, and he was the only one who could drag them out of their own personal nightmares.

Turning a corner, he breathed a small sigh of relief, though the hammering of inmates behind him still had him rattled. A short distance away, Lintz and Demeter were grappling with one another on the slick floor of the prison. Demeter seemed to have the upper hand, though Lintz had the weight advantage, as they tried to land savage punches on one another, golden magic rippling beneath their fists. Demeter roared in Lintz's face, the professor's mouth frothing with the exertion of the fight.

Alex gulped. It wasn't an altogether reassuring sight, but he knew it was a start.

Two down, if they'll let me get close enough.

Using the noise of the prison as cover, Alex inched toward

them. Demeter was on top of Lintz, grasping the professor's head in his hands as if he were about to smash it against the hard stone floor. Alex lurched forward, reaching out to grab Demeter's shoulder. He ducked as the auburn-haired man whirled on him, lashing out with a blow that would have given Alex a decent bruise if he hadn't dodged in time.

Seizing the opportunity while Demeter was off balance, Alex grasped the ex-teacher's forearm and fed his anti-magic through the freckled surface of Demeter's skin. Searching through the man's body for remnants of the fog, Alex dissipated the glistening red haze. It didn't take long for Demeter to return to normality, his paranoia eased. Like the last time, it appeared Demeter's mind-control powers were helping him to recover more swiftly than those without his skillset.

Now for Lintz.

"Help me," he said to Demeter, who was just coming back around.

Lintz lunged at Alex, grasping him by the shoulders and shoving him backward. It sent him flying against the nearby wall, his head slamming against the stone, but Alex didn't let it faze him. He dove toward the professor, forcing his hands onto the sides of Lintz's head. Despite Lintz's forceful attempts to remove him, Demeter managed to pin the old man, ensuring that Alex wouldn't be thrown off again.

Alex had only intended to calm Lintz down the way he had calmed Demeter. However, as he ran his anti-magic into the professor's temples, he found himself accidentally crossing over into the realms of mind control and spirit lines, combining the two as he searched within the professor's mind, using what he had learned from Vincent and Demeter in a strange-ly complementary fashion. It was an odd mix of skills, but it seemed to work, easing Lintz's delirious screams and violent arms. With it came an instant wave of memories and emotions. Through the sparks in Lintz's fevered brain, Alex saw flashes of the professor's life, as seen through the old man's eyes.

One fell upon a scene in which a woman of around thirty was speaking with Lintz. Glancing around, Alex realized they weren't in the familiar stone setting of Spellshadow Manor, with the recognizable hallways and Derhin as his constant shadow. It was somewhere much more clinical, the wallpaper a muted jade green, linoleum on the floor. In the center of the room was a hospital bed, and sitting at the head of it, propped up by a stack of cushions, was the woman. She looked tired but happy, and in her arms, she cradled a small, red-faced new-born who snuffled softly in the throes of slumber.

"What do you think of your baby sister?" the woman whispered.

"I love her," he heard Lintz say, in a voice much younger than the gruff old tones he was used to.

The woman smiled. "Oh, my darling, she loves you too! You will be such a good big brother to her."

Alex watched as Lintz rested his finger beneath his baby sister's outstretched hand, and felt the thrill Lintz felt as the tiny girl instinctively gripped it with surprising strength. She yawned, the sound soft and sweet, partway between a whisper and a squeal.

"Isn't she beautiful?" the woman asked.

Lintz nodded. "Kind of."

The woman laughed. "But you will protect her, won't you?"

"I'll be the best big brother," Lintz promised.

"Because you know I won't be around forever, don't you?" said the woman sadly, making Alex wonder if there was something more to the sick, tired look on her face. "And she'll need you when I'm gone. You'll need to make sure she grows up big and strong, knowing she's loved. You'll have to tell her about me, one day."

Alex could feel the sad uncertainty growing within the young Lintz, filtering through into his own emotions, and the understanding filled him with grief for the old professor, in the present day. Though he could only speculate, Alex realized that when Malachi Grey came for Lintz, that little girl must have been left alone somewhere, without her brother to look out for her, as he had promised to do. Alex imagined the prospect would have eaten away at the old man, over the years—in the same situation, Alex knew it would have eaten away at him. A similar one already was, with his mother and her illness.

Alex wondered if that was why Lintz had endeavored to become a professor at Spellshadow Manor, on the off chance his sister would have the same magical capabilities and Finder would someday bring her to the gates, giving them a long-awaited reunion—but that hadn't happened. That girl was potentially still out there somewhere, waiting for the brother who disappeared and never came home, though she would be elderly by now, Alex presumed, looking once more at the dated décor and the fifties-style pattern on the hospital chair. Lintz and his sister were just like the rest of them and their families, ever hopeful of a reunion.

Feeling like he was violating Lintz's privacy, Alex focused a few happy images into the forefront of the professor's mind. The red fog faded away, the paranoia and the demons forgotten in the wake of Alex's mental suggestions, which overtook the false images the haze had placed in the old man's head, returning him to normality. Slowly, Alex removed himself from Lintz's mind, certain that the fog had gone. Even though he felt a touch of guilt, he couldn't deny it was nice to get a few flashes of insight about the professor's much younger days, before he had ever been touched by the hands of the magical world.

Lintz blinked, suddenly aware of his surroundings.

"Goodness me, I am sorry!" he wheezed, struggling to stand. "Did I hurt you?"

Alex rose to his feet. "No harm done," he replied, eager to get moving again. There were still four people to find. "Could you look for Caius and let him know what's happened? Alypia is here, but the fog took over her, and she ran off somewhere. I need to find the others so we can try to round her up."

"Oh dear, this has all gone a bit awry, hasn't it?" Lintz said anxiously.

Alex nodded grimly. "You could say that."

"We'll find Caius, and if we come across Alypia before you do, we'll try to get her safely locked away," Demeter assured him.

"Go—find the others," Lintz agreed.

"Just watch out for traps. I don't want any more fog going off," Alex said.

"Don't worry, we'll handle it," Demeter replied.

Alex turned toward the closest corridor and broke into a

run. With the threat of Alypia fresh in his mind, he headed down a series of hallways, allowing his instincts to lead him.

You think you're hunting my kind, Alypia, but you're wrong, he thought bitterly to himself. *You are the prey, so run while you can—I am coming for you.*

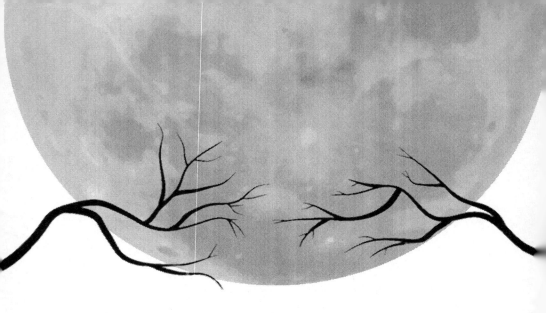

CHAPTER 26

WITH THE TAUNTS OF INMATES THUNDERING IN HIS ears, Alex raced through the labyrinthine keep, his mind focused solely on his friends. Some prisoners he found more difficult to ignore than others, especially the ones who called out things about Ellabell and Natalie, with one inmate noting how beautiful they'd be with their mouths sewn shut as he made a foul slurping sound. The rest of the comments were too repulsive to repeat, making Alex's blood boil, though he knew he couldn't stop to punish anyone, not this time.

He ran on, skidding to a halt at the entrance to the corridor that held Agatha's cell. With his heart pounding, he walked slowly down the hallway, pausing beside her door. Carefully, he reached out and checked to see if it was locked, pulling firmly on the handle. To his relief, he found that someone had been there before him and shut it tight, locking her in. He was glad of that foresight and guessed it was Vincent who had turned the key, given his concern about her relapse.

"SPELLBREAKER FILTH!" Agatha slammed her full weight against the wood, which was starting to look more than a little flimsy. The tremor sent a jolt of fear through Alex. A second jolt shot through him as her face appeared at the grate, spittle flying close to his face. "Come closer, have a taste of a mage's fury! I'll twist up your insides and turn them to mush—you'll pray for death when I'm done with you, you wretch!" she screamed, her eyes wild.

Alex quickly moved on, leaving Agatha to her slurs, hoping she'd forget about them once the haze faded.

At the next cell, he paused again. Vincent's chamber wasn't locked, the door standing slightly ajar, much to Alex's horror. He wondered if the necromancer had returned to his cell, like a bird coming back to roost. Alex braced himself for whatever he might see.

Instead of an angry changeling rushing at him, Alex was met by the sight of Vincent sitting on the floor, apparently in a calm, meditative state. The strange-faced necromancer looked up and saw Alex, waving him on with a flick of his slender wrist.

"I am fighting it, my good man. I will overcome… Do not tarry here when others require your aid," he insisted, his translucent lids sliding over the impossible black of his eyes once more.

Alex paused, uncertain, wondering if Vincent meant he

was battling a golden monster, but as he looked closer he could see that Vincent's eyes, still half-visible through the translucent lids, were clear of the misty haze of the red fog, and he was merely striving against the residual influence of paranoia.

"My thoughts are not real. My thoughts are not my own," the necromancer repeated rhythmically, letting the mantra do the work.

Satisfied, Alex hurried on. He ran down a familiar corridor and turned left into a very dark hallway he didn't altogether recognize. Where once torches had flickered on the walls, now they had sputtered out, and Alex knew it had not been caused by a chance gust of wind.

Without warning, Jari sprang from the shadows and jumped onto Alex's back. Alex cried out, grasping for Jari's arms and throwing his friend to the floor with a hefty thud. Undeterred, Jari sprang again, dragging Alex down onto the flagstones. Alex winced as a hard punch caught him square on the cheek, followed by another vicious blow to the gut that made his eyes water, but he fought back just as hard, clawing for Jari's arms. As Alex caught his friend with a lucky upper-cut to the jaw, he felt Jari go still for a moment, giving Alex the window of opportunity he had been waiting for. But Jari was quicker than that—the boy leapt straight back into the action, ducking out of Alex's range.

Frustrated, Alex fired a shield in the direction of the darkest shadows, where he could hear Jari creeping. The boy yelped as the shield found him, and Alex could hear the muffled sound of his indignation. The glowing barrier kept Jari from doing harm as Alex pushed his hands through the shield and rested them on either side of Jari's head.

As he removed the fog and paranoia with his silvery strands of anti-magic, Alex saw flashes of Jari's life that made him smile. It was like watching a slideshow of highlights from Spellshadow Manor. An image of the Christmas they had all spent together popped into the spotlight—the great tree erupting from the ground, all of them standing to watch the lights and ornaments, the fleeting joy they had felt. He saw moments between Jari and Aamir, seen through Jari's eyes, in the days before he and Natalie had arrived. They were laughing at something, stretched out on the grass, the sun beating down upon their grinning faces. Alex could almost feel the sunlight on his skin.

Among the memories of Spellshadow, there were brief glimpses of Jari's family life, his dad cracking jokes around the dinner table, an array of bright, beautiful paintings adorning the wall behind. Alex remembered something about Jari's mother being an artist, and wondered if the paintings were hers.

If they were, he thought, *she was very talented*.

Another set of images flickered into Jari's mind, showing Alex a hazy, heavily filtered montage of Helena, all the times she had looked at him with her piercing golden eyes, tossing her long silver hair. In Jari's view of her, she looked like a forties movie star, everything heightened and smoothed out, seen the way he wanted to see her. It made Alex grin; he was truly seeing things through Jari's eyes. It was tempting to Alex to search farther into his friend's mind, but he quickly recoiled, confident the paranoia had gone. He realized just how close he was to deliberately invading Jari's privacy. It wasn't what he had learned mind control for, and such intrusion was exactly what he had promised himself he wouldn't do.

Meanwhile, Jari was snapping back to reality. "Whoa—what happened?" he asked unsteadily.

"The wall thing happened again," Alex explained. "You all locked me up and ran off, thinking you were being chased by monsters. I'm in the process of trying to find everyone so I can remove the fog and we can find Alypia and get her locked up. At the moment, she's roaming free, and it's making me more than a little nervous."

Jari frowned. "Were you just in my head?"

"I had to get the fog out," Alex admitted.

"When did you learn to do that?" he asked suspiciously.

"I made Demeter teach me," said Alex.

Jari made a low noise of displeasure. "You didn't think to say something?"

Alex sighed. "I didn't think I'd have to use it on my friends."

"Well, I hope you didn't go snooping," Jari remarked, his tone wary.

Alex shook his head. "Never."

"Hang on, did I hit you? I remember hitting something, though I think I thought it was a massive lizard." Jari flashed a curious glance at Alex.

Alex nodded. "You got a few good punches in. I managed one decent one," he said, feeling for the tender skin of his cheek, where a nasty welt was slowly appearing.

"That must be why my jaw is clicking," Jari mused.

"Well, glad you're back in the land of the living, but we

need to get going," Alex said, once again pushing away the creeping weariness that slithered through his bones. There was no time for a breather with three more people to track down. "You coming?"

They set off through the darkness into the next corridor, which, thankfully, still had working torches. Alex was glad of Jari's company. At least with another person by his side, the thought of Alypia springing out wasn't quite as bad. Still terrifying, but not quite *as* terrifying.

As they headed into the deepest part of the keep, only a couple of floors above the entrance to Caius's frightening pit room, they turned down an unfamiliar hallway and stumbled upon an indoor courtyard, littered with dead plants and a fountain that no longer spewed anything but lichen. Standing at the far side, lighting up the room with a very real, magical sword, was Ellabell, fending off imaginary beasts with the fearsome golden weapon, the blade glinting sharply. She let out a sudden, blood-curdling scream, thrashing the sword around in the air before her in a frenzied manner. She looked petrified, and the sight of her in such distress tore at Alex's heart. He flashed a conspiratorial look at Jari.

"We need a pincer movement—I'll go around one side, you go around the other," Alex whispered. "Sneak up on her and hold her steady so I can put my hands on her temples."

Jari nodded. "Aye, aye, Captain!"

They skirted around the room, approaching Ellabell on both sides. Jari reached her first, almost losing his head as Ellabell swung her sword at the last moment, missing him by a hair's breadth. In a fit of panic, the softly-softly plan went out the window, Jari tackling her unceremoniously to the floor instead.

Alex ducked toward Ellabell and pressed his palms firmly against her temples, feeding his anti-magic through her skull and into her brain. He blushed as he saw himself in her memories, and felt more than a little strange watching himself through her eyes. It wasn't quite like Jari's hazy, romantically filtered movie scene, but there was a hopefulness to it that Alex felt guilty about trespassing upon. It wasn't his place to feel her feelings, and yet it pleased him to see that they were on a similar track, in terms of the way they were beginning to think about each other. He lingered a moment longer on the remembrance of his arms around her, embracing beneath the stars, before moving quickly away from such personal thoughts.

She was the one whose mind most tempted him, but he returned to the task of restoring her to her usual self. It didn't take long until all the fog and paranoia was gone, leaving Alex to recoil with reluctance.

"Get them off me, get them off me!" she screamed, throwing Jari away from her. Blinking away the last of the fog, she saw what she had done. "I'm sorry, Jari... I thought you were a demon." She gasped, turning to Alex. "What happened? Where am I?"

"Alypia's on the loose, big blast, red fog, golden monsters, intense paranoia, you wielding a great big magical sword that nearly took Jari's head off, a little mind stuff to get rid of the bad juju... I think that brings you up to speed." He forced a smile.

She frowned. "Mind stuff?"

"Yeah, he's been fishing around in our brains again!" Jari remarked, throwing Alex under the bus.

"What do you mean 'again?' I haven't fished in your brains before—I haven't been fishing in your brains!" Alex insisted, knowing how it sounded. "I just got rid of the fog, that's all."

Ellabell glanced at him warily. Alex wanted to assure her that he hadn't seen anything, and that he had never intended to use his newfound skills on any of them, but Jari cut in before he could.

"Get a good look, did you?" Jari taunted, evidently relishing Alex's discomfort.

He sighed. "I just got rid of the imaginary monsters. Speaking of which, we don't have time for this. We've still got Aamir and Natalie to find, not to mention Alypia."

The other two agreed, sharing a grim look as they followed Alex's lead. They set off into the unnerving halls of the keep's inner sanctum, moving slowly so as not to disturb the bats that slept overhead. As they walked, the cries and shouts of the inmates seemed to be dying down. Either that, or they were getting too far away to hear them anymore, edging deeper into the unknown.

Alex was so focused on keeping his eyes on the shadows and focusing on the path ahead that he almost tripped over Aamir, who was passed out in the hallway, a livid red gash rising up on his forehead. It seemed like a bizarre thing to assume, but it looked unmistakably as if he had run into the wall and knocked himself out. Concerned, Alex crouched and shook Aamir awake.

With a pained blink, the older boy came to, glancing

around with a puzzled expression, as if trying to grasp at a slippery memory. More surprisingly still, he seemed to be entirely himself, with no need for Alex's anti-magic. Whatever had knocked him out had clearly knocked the fog out too.

"What happened to you?" Alex asked.

"The last thing I remember was seeing a portal home… and trying to run into it," Aamir admitted, albeit reluctantly.

Ellabell and Jari helped Aamir to his feet. As they hurried down the hallway, Alex could taste the finish line. It was within reach now, and once they crossed it, they could get back to the task at hand—that of locking Alypia away where she belonged.

We might actually fix this mess after all, he thought anxiously.

Now, they just needed to find Natalie.

Once they reached the subterranean floor of the keep, Alex paused in front of a familiar, empty cell. He was certain Caius would have moved the cot back into place once he'd left the pit.

But there was nothing covering the staircase to the catacombs now.

With a sudden surge of panic, Alex imagined Natalie stepping through the door at the end of the hall below, falling unawares into the pit itself, driven over the edge by imaginary monsters. He could picture the misty swarm of a billion vaporous particles, snatching at her essence, wanting to tear it out of her. Of all the places in the keep, how was it that she had found the most dangerous one? He had a feeling dark magic was responsible.

He motioned for his friends to follow him down the staircase, wasting no time on an explanation. The other three shared a look, but followed anyway, and they stormed down into the catacombs.

In the narrow corridor, the torches were flickering, and Alex was slightly relieved to find the large door at the end closed—it was one of the smaller side doors that was open, light spilling out. He raced toward it. Inside, he was met by the sight of a luxurious chamber, decidedly out of place in the dank, foreboding setting of the prison around them.

The chamber was softly lit with stained-glass lanterns that pooled a multicolored luminescence onto the plush, rug-covered floor and tapestry-draped walls. The place was adorned with soft, rich furnishings, including full bookshelves and many other beautiful things—shining jewelry boxes, sleek wooden trunks with brass fittings, exquisitely carved statuary. It might once have been a charming place, but much of the furniture looked as if it hadn't been used in a long time, and a musty, mildewed scent clung to the air. Had it not been for the lack of windows, it would have been hard to tell that it was a prison cell at all.

Alex staggered backward, the others jumping in fright. Natalie was in the room, though he hadn't seen her at first. She crouched on the floor by the rotting remnants of a four-poster bed, moving unnaturally around a bottle in the center of a ruby-red rug. She was singing something quietly in an alarming, throaty whisper, her eyes entirely focused on the small, smoky black bottle that Alex recognized as a bottle of essence, though he didn't have a clue where she'd found it, nor was she in a state to tell him.

"All my friends are dead, now to kill the Head," she sang over and over, her voice low and disturbing, her eyes like saucers.

The others watched her in silent horror, but Alex's eye was caught instead by the sight of a slim, wooden door at the very far side of the room, half-tucked away behind a velvet curtain. His gaze flitted back toward Natalie, remembering what Caius had said about the harmful nature of the essence here; if the warden was right, it wasn't safe for Natalie to be so close to it. Tentatively, he walked toward her, bolstering himself with a protective layer of anti-magic as he neared.

In a split second, she turned on him, lunging up from her haunches, trying to grasp his head in her hands, her nails raking at the soft flesh of his face.

"You will pay, pay, *pay!*" Natalie screeched.

Alex managed to twist out from under her grip, some of his hair ripping away in her clenched fist. "You have to snap out of this—" he began.

Lunging again, she screamed in his face, clutching her hands to her chest as if they were burned, making Alex glad of the layer of protection around him that was keeping her slightly at arm's length.

The others edged closer, taking Alex's lead.

"Natalie, it's us—your friends," Ellabell said calmly.

"You know us, Natalie. Come on, come back to us," Aamir added, holding out his hand to her.

"Natalie, buddy, come on! There aren't any monsters. It's just us," Jari soothed.

Natalie wasn't having any of it. With each reassuring utterance, she charged toward them, leaping uncomfortably close, her face twisting into a feverish grimace, only to pull away at the very last moment. Her teeth gnashed together with a loud snap, her eyes flashing wildly, and she looked both terrified and terrifying, her hands moving quickly, creating something strange beneath her palms. Alex could feel that, whatever it was she was making, it wasn't natural. She was as far from herself as he had ever seen her. This was worse than any curse.

With a knowing look, he signaled for the others to try to distract her while he crept around the back of the room. Keeping to the walls, he moved slowly, stepping up onto the four-poster bed and moving forward, so he could try to grab her from behind.

Meanwhile, Jari broke into a dance that looked like a cross between *Saturday Night Fever* and *Riverdance*, but even the blond-haired boy's absurdity couldn't keep Natalie's eyes from flitting about the room, her limbs bent at odd angles as she crawled across the floor, rushing toward them like an angry insect. Seeing that Jari's dancing wasn't working, Aamir tried reasoning with her instead, speaking to her as if he were bargaining with a small child.

"Natalie, sweetheart, you need to calm down and come back to us. There are no demons, and nobody is dead. It is all in your imagination," he said.

This seemed to intrigue the changeling version of Natalie. With a sharp hiss that prickled the hairs on the back of Alex's neck, she scuttled half-crouched, half-upright toward Aamir. Her eyes turned white, a milky sheen sliding across them.

Behind her, standing between Alex and his quarry, wispy specters appeared from thin air, conjured by the words her mouth
was still muttering and the twist and turn of skillful hands. The
whole room went cold, everything suddenly feeling surreal.
The gaseous shapes had hollow eyes and gaping mouths, their
bodies wispy, blurry bones that bore the dangling strands of
ancient cloth. Or so Alex thought—peering closer, he saw the
scraps clinging to the translucent bones were not cloth at all,
but the final hanging strips of flesh. They stared vacantly from
skull faces, their empty mouths yawning in silent screams.

Shivers of fear shot through Alex, and he tried to get closer to her, sliding down over the musty edge of the bed and
creeping toward where she had scuttled back to, a short distance from Aamir's legs. Moving stealthily, he pushed away
the horror of the ghosts' presence, turning sideways to avoid
touching them as he slipped through a narrow gap between
two of their kind.

He was almost upon her when she whirled around, glowering at him with the milky white of her ghostly eyes. With
unexpected agility, she jumped at him, the impact almost
knocking him off his feet. Somehow, he managed to hold his
ground as she lashed out at him, her teeth coming too close to
his skin for comfort. She backed away again, preparing for a
second strike.

This time, Alex was ready for her. She leapt toward him,
but he ducked just in time, grasping her shoulders tightly as
she overshot her mark, pulling her toward him in a rough
headlock. She writhed, struggling to get free, but he managed
to hold her with enough strength that he was able to steady

her, giving him the chance to press his palms to her temples and run his anti-magic into her mind. She froze instantly in his arms.

Flashes of her history surged into his mind—all involving her loving family. The image of her little sister, in particular, served to spur him on, to complete the promise he had made to all of his friends—to get them home. If that slim doorway held what he thought it held, in a room behind it, Alex knew they might be able to meet the tight portal deadline after all.

Alex sent good thoughts to the forefront of Natalie's mind, smothering the false images the fog had created. Steadily, he worked his way through, dissipating what was left of the red haze, feeling that it had affected her more fiercely than the last time for some reason. Perhaps she had simply absorbed more of it; it was hard to say.

Eventually, he removed the strands of his anti-magic from her mind. He held Natalie tightly, watching as she blinked awake, the milky sheen gone from her eyes, revealing the glimmering dark brown beneath. Unsteadily, her knees buckled, but Alex was there to catch her before setting her gently on the ground. Cautiously, he folded up the small rug around the bottle at its center and moved it to one side, wanting to keep it out of everyone's way until he could get a better idea of what was so different, and potentially so harmful, about this essence.

The others were watching him curiously, in the wake of what he had done to dispel the demons from Natalie's mind, but he ignored them, turning back to her.

"How did you find this place?" Alex asked Natalie, his voice gentle.

She glanced up at him, her whole body shaking. "I think it was necromancy that brought me here," she whispered. "The red fog... it made me hear the voices of people crying, people screaming. Not the prisoners... other people. They were ghosts. They wanted my help... I followed them down here. Everyone was dead..." Her voice caught in her throat as she trailed off.

Alex looked at the bundled-up bottle of essence on the side and knew which ghosts she meant.

"You're safe now," he said. "The ghosts are all gone."

Natalie drew her knees up to her chin, her face a pale picture of fear. There was regret in her eyes too, and Alex had never seen her look so vulnerable. As the others fussed around her, filling her in on what had happened, Alex could detect a wariness still in their demeanor. He didn't blame them; she had been truly frightening. However, his attention was focused elsewhere.

Leaving the others to Natalie, he went to the narrow entrance, pulling back the velvet curtain, and opened the door with a shiver of trepidation. The sight that emerged from the gloom was an unmistakable one. He had seen it twice before. To Alex's delight, an antechamber stretched away into a darkened distance, the room much smaller than those he'd seen at Spellshadow and Stillwater, but still full to the brim with smoky black bottles of essence. The dim red light he knew so well, pulsing within the black glass, shone brighter here. It was a different kind of energy altogether—he could feel it, even from the mere threshold of the chamber. He still hoped that, somehow, they'd be able to use it to build the portal home.

Touching them was a challenge, however. Even with his anti-magic in full force, he found the bottles hard to handle. Vivid pulses of light forced their way into his head as he picked each one up, the memories within going off like an explosion in his brain, searing his synapses with white-hot light that felt like scorching blades in his skull. He shoved the bottles back onto the shelves—the potent pulse of each one he had touched was starting to give him a headache.

Still only marginally deterred, he picked up another bottle and plucked out the stopper. As soon as the substance within touched his palm, an explosion went off in Alex's brain. It was unbearable, voices screaming at such a pitch he thought his ears might implode, people howling, a million memories all rushing at once, pin-balling around his head. He couldn't think, worried his own mind would be lost in the fray. It was hard to extract himself from the onslaught of sound and vision, and worse than that, he could feel the burn of the essence itself against his flesh, searing it.

Forcing his eyes open, he saw that his hand was glowing, and knew it couldn't be a good thing. Thinking fast, he dove for the four-poster bed and frantically wiped his hand against the comforter. A lot of the essence came off, seeping down into the cloth with a scorching hiss, but the rest remained, as Alex battled the visions in his mind. It took all the concentration he had left to conjure strands of his anti-magic and feed them into the remaining essence, compressing it gradually until the visions began to ebb away. Over and over, he fed layers into the essence, like applying lotion to a sunburn, trying not to summon anything awful in the meantime. Slowly but surely, the last of it dissipated, though it left him feeling as if every cell in his body were on fire.

His hand was bright red, a few livid burns crisscrossing the skin. Bending his fingers, he winced. The wound was tender, to say the least. Caius had been right; this essence was no good. If he couldn't wield it, being what he was, he dreaded to think what such potent energy could do in the hands of his friends.

"Dude, are you okay?" Jari asked, walking up to Alex, concern etched on his face.

"Looks like Caius was right about the essence," he admitted grimly, lifting his burned hand.

"You shouldn't have been so—here, let me help," said Ellabell, coming forward. Twists of golden magic flowed through her hands, and she touched them to Alex's damaged palm. Instantly, snow gathered around his hand, the cool flakes soothing the seared skin beneath.

Two figures appeared in the doorway of the room, snatching Alex's attention away from the pile of snow forming in his palm. It was Lintz and Demeter, returned from their hunt.

"In all my years at Kingstone, I never knew this was here!" Demeter exclaimed, peering in. "I might've known there'd be a secret entrance or two hiding away in this place. He's probably got tons—I imagine it's how he manages to come and go as he pleases."

"How did you find us?" Alex asked, dumbfounded.

Lintz smiled. "Fortunately, you left us something of a breadcrumb trail—hallways with the torches blown out, smashed stone, blood spots on the floor. When we came down to the lower levels and saw the door of the empty cell standing open, we thought you were in there, but that's when we found the hidden stairwell. We were hoping we'd find you all in one piece."

"Any luck finding Caius?" Alex asked hopefully.

They shook their heads. "Afraid not. Looks like he's hiding again," said Demeter.

"I'm not sure what would keep the warden away, though," mused Lintz.

Alex had a feeling he might know of something important enough to keep Caius away, even with so much going on.

Did the bird flap? he wondered. He felt as if it might have, and it was a horrifying notion.

"I'll be back in a minute," he said, darting out the door and up the remainder of the hallway to the pit room at the end.

Turning the handle, he found that the door was locked. No amount of pushing or shoving could get it to budge. He knocked insistently, the sound echoing behind him, but nobody came to answer it. He tried again, in case Caius hadn't heard. Still, nobody came to the door. If Caius was in there, he wasn't receiving visitors. Pressing his ear to the thick wood, Alex listened for any sound that might give him a clue as to what was going on in the room beyond, but all he could hear was the drip of water falling from the ceiling.

If Caius was dealing with feeding time, Alex knew recruiting the warden would have to wait. He imagined the feeding of the Great Evil to be a time-consuming, energy-draining act that Caius could not simply walk away from in order to help them, and time was something they were out of; they could not risk waiting for him to finish, if that was what he was up to. Alypia was still at large, and now that he had everyone together, it was time for her takedown.

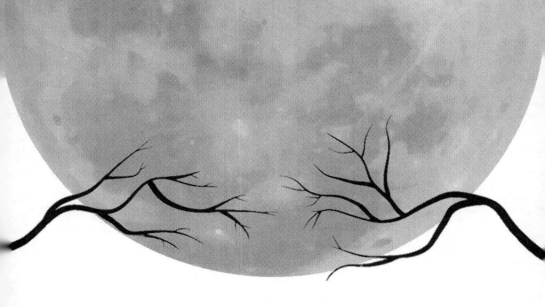

CHAPTER 27

"**W**HERE DO YOU THINK SHE MIGHT BE?" AAMIR asked.

Alex shrugged. "I don't know. We just have to keep looking."

They had been searching the prison for what seemed like hours, seeking out the elusive Alypia. Vincent and Demeter had gone to deal with the entourage that had come through with her, and Demeter had returned a short while ago to say Vincent was staying in the courtyard to stand guard beside the portal from Stillwater, to make sure she couldn't get back through, though Alex had a sinking feeling she might have already managed it.

"Looking for someone?" a voice called from the end of the hallway ahead of them. The voice was too low to belong to the person Alex wanted it to be, but he was pleased to see the familiar face of the warden, regardless.

Alex nodded. "Alypia is on the loose."

"Ah, I see," Caius murmured. "Most unfortunate… My apologies for not being around when the fog was released. I would have come to check on things sooner, but I was seeing to some duties in the core of the keep. It's hard to hear anything down there, and I was in the middle of something I simply couldn't step away from," he explained, flashing a conspiratorial look at Alex that confirmed his fears about the flapping bird and what Caius had been doing behind the locked door. "Now that I am here, I shall help you in your search. As we go, you can keep me abreast of your plans."

Jari sniggered, receiving a stern, disappointed glance from the old man. It quickly took the smile off Jari's face, his gaze trailing toward his feet with mild embarrassment.

"Do you know where she might be hiding?" Alex asked.

Caius frowned thoughtfully. "I have a few ideas."

"And you think she might still be here?"

Caius nodded. "If you're still here, then undoubtedly."

With Caius taking the lead, the group followed him dutifully, keeping their eyes peeled for any sign of their quarry. Alex couldn't get used to the fact that, everywhere Caius went, the inmates fell suddenly silent. There was an air to him that frightened them, and Alex couldn't blame them; they did not have the advantage of inside knowledge.

After half an hour of walking, Alex noticed that Caius was beginning to tire. It began with a slowing of pace, and then there was a slight jerk in his gait, and finally it flowed into an even more noticeable limp as he leaned heavily onto his cane. Now and again, he would pause to catch his breath, resting against the wall of the prison, though always out of sight of the cells. It made sense that the warden didn't want to show weakness in front of his prisoners. Still, Caius never complained as they moved from hallway to hallway, checking empty cells.

Gradually, Caius began to fall behind.

"You should seek out the eastern quarter—it's where she is mostly likely to go," he said breathlessly.

The group halted.

"Are you okay?" Alex asked, resting a hand on the old man's back.

"Fine, fine, just a little out of breath," Caius admitted. "I'll be better in a second. You go on ahead."

"We can stay with you," Alex insisted.

Caius smiled weakly. "Honestly, you go on ahead. I wouldn't want you missing her on my account."

There was no way Alex was going to leave the old man alone in the halls of the prison, even though he knew it was Caius's domain.

Alex turned to the others. "I'll stay with him and catch you up when he's feeling better," he said firmly. "If you find Alypia while I'm still here, shove her into the nearest cell and turn the key, okay?"

"Will do." Demeter grinned, jangling his keys in a self-important fashion as he beckoned for the others to follow.

For a moment, Ellabell hung back as if she might stay too, but thought better of it at the last minute and raced off after the others. When it was just the two of them left, Alex sat on the floor beside Caius, letting him rest awhile. There was a rasp in the warden's breath every time he inhaled, and it concerned Alex.

"Are you sure you're okay?" he asked.

Caius nodded insistently. "Just old age, I'm afraid. You'll find out one day," he chuckled.

Alex smiled, and the pair of them sat in companionable silence for a short while. At any moment, Alex expected Alypia to come rushing around the corner, but, as the minutes ticked on, the hallways remained empty and still. It was almost peaceful.

"Shall we?" Caius suggested finally as he began to stir, the rasp of his throat lessened.

Alex nodded, eager to be on their way. "After you," he replied, helping the old man to his feet.

"I've got an idea," Caius said suddenly, a childish look of glee on his face. "Come on, there's no time to lose!"

With that, the old man took off down the corridor at remarkable speed, even with his cane. Alex hurried after him, wondering where the warden's exhaustion had gone. Perhaps the rest truly had done him a world of good, Alex thought as he caught up, the pair of them walking along at a brisk pace, turning corner after corner. It seemed as if Caius knew precisely where he wanted to go, and all Alex could do was follow as the hallways become gradually more familiar.

Eventually, they came to rest at a room Alex recognized as the old guard room where Agatha had attacked him. Caius drew a hefty ring of keys out of his pocket, though the door appeared to already be open, resting slightly ajar. Something else fell out of the old man's pocket too, but Caius stooped quickly to snatch it up and put it back, giving Alex little chance to see what it was. As far as he could make out, it was a small silver box, though what its purpose was, he had no idea.

Suddenly, Alex felt nervous. Something wasn't quite right, and, as Caius pulled open the door and shoved Alex unceremoniously inside, he realized what it was. But it was too late.

Sitting in the armchair by the fire was Alypia, daintily holding a cup of tea in her hands. She scowled as Alex staggered into the room, skidding to a halt before he got too near her.

He whirled around to face Caius. "*Why?*"

"You will speak when you are spoken to!" Caius snapped, all trace of the kind old man gone.

Alypia sniggered. "And if you could refrain from conjuring another of your golden beasts, I'd appreciate it."

Sharply, Caius grasped Alex by the scruff of his shirt and shoved him a step closer to Alypia. "I believe this is what you're after, dear Niece?" said Caius in a low, menacing voice. "I trust you will leave us in peace now, without running to your father?"

"It is, dear Uncle," she replied, the glee evident in her words. "And I'm almost certain this is enough to keep me from saying a word about your ineptitude, though it will make me awfully sad not to see the expression on his face—I do so love it when you disappoint him." She flashed her coldest smile in Caius's direction.

With that, Caius yanked Alex backward slightly. "Then

it seems there are negotiations to be made," he stated, moving Alex farther back still. "I know the value of the boy in my hands. I want to ensure I get a good deal, seeing as your daddy behaves as if I am undeserving of reparations. I will not simply hand him over and let you have all the glory, dear Niece—so if that is what you were after, I suggest you hop on back to your false utopia and leave me to my own devices. If your pride will permit negotiation, however, then we can talk," he said, as he turned to leave the room with Alex in tow.

"Why are you doing this? I trusted you!" Alex spat, trying to wriggle free of the old man's grasp. He was shockingly strong, and held on tightly.

"SILENCE!" Caius roared, shoving Alex roughly onto a chair.

"Here, these might help," purred Alypia, throwing a set of cuffs at Caius. They were the same grim manacles Alex had seen before, the twist of gray ivy painfully familiar.

"Excellent foresight, I'll admit," Caius remarked, catching them deftly.

As Caius bent to lock Alex's wrists between the cuffs, Alex tried to head-butt him, but the old warden was too quick, ducking cleanly out of the way. When Alex writhed and struggled, Caius simply held him still with vise-like strength, before sitting in the armchair opposite Alypia.

"What will you offer me in return for Alex and the stolen bottles?" Caius asked. "I could do with something to bolster the king's opinion of me. I'm fairly certain that handing over the key to his survival would do just that, improving my standing at court immensely, but I'm open to options, if you can come up with something better to offer?" Caius remarked, a smirk upon his thin lips. "You seem to want it more."

Alypia glared. "You could certainly use a bit of collective good opinion, but I'm not sure even Alex's particular charms could clear your name, not after what you did," she sneered. "Unnatural acts aren't often forgiven, as you well know, and there is nothing more unnatural or abhorrent than that relationship you had with that *thing*. You're just lucky you never got yours with child," she spat, her face a twisted vision of abject repulsion.

Though Alypia missed the stern, icy expression on Caius's face, it had not gone unnoticed by Alex. He could feel the old man bristling beside him, color rushing into his pale cheeks.

"You think your mother was any different to me?" Caius hissed.

A look of shock lit up Alypia's face. "My mother is *nothing* like you!"

"Isn't she?" Caius taunted. "Didn't she fall in love with one of *them* too? Isn't she *exactly* like me? Isn't that why your brother is the way he is—an impossible child, forged by an impossible love?"

This seemed to rile the crown princess. "Don't you dare put my mother in the same category as you, you perverted old man. My mother was forced—my mother never asked for any of it, and it's because of *his* kind and you disgusting Spellbreaker sympathizers that it happened to her. It wasn't love, it was a foul, unwarranted attack on a pure-hearted woman. How dare you besmirch her name! How dare you try to defend what that awful creature did to her."

"If you believe that, dear Alypia, you're not nearly as smart as I gave you credit for—and I didn't think you were smart to begin with," he retorted, his own anger flaring. "Your mother loved a Spellbreaker, and you can't deal with it. Everyone knew, and they would have continued to know the truth of it if I hadn't covered it all up for her, saving her life in the process. What thanks have I ever had?" Caius snarled. "You must face the truth of the matter!"

Enraged, Alypia was in full swing now, spurred on by words she clearly didn't want to hear. Fury flashed wildly in her pale eyes, her lips drawn back in a cruel sneer.

"You know how she died, don't you—your Spellbreaker whore?" she gloated. "I saw it for myself, though I was only a child at the time. That sad, pathetic scream of her last hope being dashed, like her head upon the rock my father ended her tragic life with—after he'd torn everything from within her, naturally," she muttered coldly, a devious smile upon her lips. Alex tried to squeeze his eyes shut against the mental image, but he couldn't help but visualize the hideous scene.

"Don't speak of her," said Caius quietly, the torment clear in his golden eyes. As much as he currently wanted to dash Caius's head against a rock, Alex couldn't help but feel a twinge of pity.

"I will speak of whom I please," Alypia remarked churlishly. "It was for the best though, wouldn't you say? The world is a much better place without their sort—though, quite the last laugh, right? Needing one to end this mess we're in—a fairly surprising turn of events, though I don't doubt that monster knew exactly what he was doing, cackling in our faces the whole time, knowing what would come of it. You tell me he cared about my mother, and still went ahead and did that? I'd say you've lost whatever sanity you had in your old age, Uncle."

Alex wondered if there might be some truth to Alypia's words, but then recalled that it was unlikely Leander Wyvern even knew Venus was pregnant with what would become Virgil. The threat from Alypia's father had been geared solely toward Alex's ancestor, as far as he knew; there was no knowledge of Venus's unfortunate state. How could there have been? There hadn't been time, nor any hint of suspicion on Leander's part, seeing as it was ordinarily impossible to create a hybrid such as Virgil. In that final, split-second decision, Alex guessed that all Leander had wanted to do was destroy the mages and save his progeny, not realizing the Great Evil could be held back by a tide of unwillingly given essence. In performing the spell, Alex suspected his ancestor had thought only of the unborn child he knew about, growing in the belly of a non-magical woman—the one hope of Spellbreaker survival. The loophole of an entire race. When thinking in the moment, there was no time for the thought of future consequences. Leander had done what he had with the best intentions—of that Alex was almost certain.

"It seems we have managed to get somewhat off track, dear Niece," said Caius, an eerie calm returning to the old man's voice. "I wanted a negotiation, not a trip down memory lane. You are here for Alex, and I want something in return—a simple exchange."

Alypia smirked. "I will take him, if you are unwilling to cooperate."

"Try to remember my strength, dear Niece. I may look old, but there is fire in the old goat yet—I could destroy you and your guards before your next breath, so I wouldn't recommend trying to steal my property."

This revelation seemed to shake Alypia's resolve for a moment, her lip trembling for a fraction of second, just long enough to be seen. Shrugging off the trepidation, she launched into another offensive move, evidently smothering her fear with bravado.

"Family is family, Uncle, no matter what our differences are. I wouldn't try to steal something from you, just as I know you wouldn't try to steal from me. That boy belongs to me— he has a debt to pay, and I want him to pay it. If you don't hand him over, there will be trouble," she said, her voice dripping with malice.

Caius smirked. "Now, now, things don't need to get nasty. I am willing to negotiate—I have already told you as much— but I refuse to simply hand the boy over. I need to hear what you will offer in return, for the trouble of keeping him, if nothing else."

She shrugged languidly. "How does the glory of the mages restored to their full power sound? No more fear, no more culling of exceptional talent, no more scraping the barrel with those half-formed plebeians we fetch from the outer world. Finally, there will be no more worrying about where we're going to get our essence, though it'd be a shame not to keep a few of the lower classes around, in case we need to borrow some essence for anything major," she mused, prickling Alex's anger. "The mages will be able to get on with their lives and do as they please, with no trace of Spellbreaker left. It will finish the job my father, *your* brother, set out to achieve. It will mean justice for my mother, after what that monster did. Those are the greatest returns I can offer, for the price of this boy."

For a moment, Caius said and did nothing. Sitting in his chair, he remained perfectly still, a blank expression on his face, his eyes giving away no secrets, as he seemed to mull over what Alypia had just said. It was an unbearable wait, even though Alex had a feeling he knew what the answer would be.

Finally, Caius spoke. "That isn't good enough."

Alypia flashed him a look of disappointment, her tongue clicking in a crass *tut-tut* as she slowly shook her head in his direction. Alex could feel the tension growing even tauter between uncle and niece as they stared one another down, neither of them willing to shift the balance of their resolution. An immoveable force had met an immoveable object, and this could only end one way.

"Then you're forcing my hand, Uncle," Alypia hissed, her lips forming a petulant pout. "I came here today to give you the benefit of the doubt, hoping your time here might have changed something, but I can see you're as stubborn and disrespectful of our kind as ever. I might have known, but I am warning you, if you don't hand that boy over and give me what I want, I will send word to my father and make sure you pay a suitable price for your latest betrayal of our race. He is still your king, unless you had forgotten? You might not be so insolent toward him."

With a reluctant sigh, Caius raised his palms in surrender. "Very well. You leave me no choice," he murmured.

Alypia's pale eyes widened in gleeful delight, clearly believing she was about to get what she wanted, thanks to the threat of her father's involvement.

Caius stood, moved over to where Alex was sitting, and dragged him to his feet. "You'll have to come and help me—if you're going to get him through the portal, he'll need sedating," Caius explained.

She frowned. "What do you expect *me* to do?"

"You don't want him running off, do you? Just come over here and help me hold him still," Caius demanded.

"Fine," muttered Alypia, as she came to where Alex was being forcibly held.

Out of the corner of his eye, Alex saw Caius dip into his pocket and pull out the small silver box. The warden handed it to Alypia, who took it tentatively, eyeing the object with some suspicion.

"Open it and take out the string inside," Caius instructed.

Frowning, Alypia lifted the small silver lid. A bronze light sprang out of the tiny box, rushing at her face. It smothered her, pouring down her throat and running into her eyes. Alex leaned back instinctively, unable to look away. Alypia opened her mouth to scream, but the sound came out as more of a gurgle. Her eyes wide in horror, she sank to the floor.

Caius removed the handcuffs from Alex's wrists and slapped them onto Alypia's instead. Alex stood shakily, and, in the next instant, Caius guided him out of the room by the arm. Looking back over his shoulder, Alex could see Alypia still trembling on the ground.

Caius slammed the door shut and turned the key in the lock. There was no sound to be heard from within.

"My apologies," the warden said solemnly, putting the keys back in his pocket.

"What the hell was that all about?" Alex snapped.

"It was the only way—"

Alex shook his head. "Why did you do that? I can't believe you just did that!"

"I had to keep her here somehow," Caius said, his expression utterly calm. "She kept insisting she was going to return to Stillwater, but I promised to find you and bring you to her if she would stay put and wait. I wanted to tell you my plan, but I couldn't risk her detecting something amiss. And now she's trapped—as you planned."

"Next time you want to use me as bait, you could just *ask*!" growled Alex. "What was that thing, anyway? The silver box?"

Caius gave a small smile. "A personal barrier. It works the same as the one around the keep, and it will stay until I remove it."

Alex shuddered. "I can't believe... I can't believe you didn't say a word."

"She suspected nothing, and that is what matters."

Alex eyed Caius intently. "So you don't really want to kill me?"

"Of course not... Forgive me, my boy, I only did what I

thought was right," Caius said, leaning forward with his cane. "I hope you can forgive me for that."

Right now, Alex didn't know what to think. He just knew there was a portal open in the courtyard of the keep, and now nobody stood in its way.

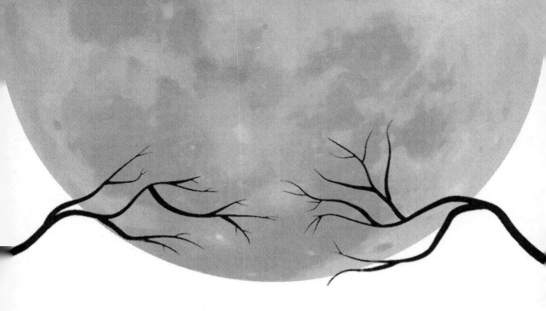

CHAPTER 28

CAIUS SEEMED TROUBLED AS THEY PARTED WAYS, insisting that Alex not tell the others what he had done. It had been for the good of all, the warden said, to successfully capture Alypia without raising any alarms or causing undue fuss. As much as Alex wanted to tell his friends about Caius's false betrayal, he agreed to keep the secret. The more Alex thought about it, the more he realized that it *had* probably been for the best. Still, it was a shock that would take some time to recover from.

Alex sat alone in the tower room, waiting for the others to return. Caius had suggested that Alex go back by himself, to seek a moment's respite, while he went to inform the others of the new development in the proceedings. At first, Alex hadn't been sure, but the earnestness in Caius's voice had won him over; it seemed the warden was eager to show Alex he wasn't all bad.

With nobody to distract him, Alex's mind wandered to Alypia. He had questions that needed answering, and she might be his best source of information. He wanted to ask what she had intended to do with him, with regards to the counter-spell and Julius. It made him antsy to think that he might return to Stillwater House without having taken the opportunity to interrogate her.

Maybe I could go back while nobody is looking, see what she has to say for herself, he thought, moving toward the entrance of the tower.

"And where do you think you're going?" a familiar voice purred.

Alex groaned as the shadows in the farthest corner above his head shifted, taking shape as the black vapors trickled down the masonry toward him. He had neither the time nor the energy to take part in a mud-slinging match with Elias, and he knew the shadow-man would be feeling particularly smug after swooping in to help him earlier.

"Not now," Alex grumbled, squeezing his eyes shut in the futile hope that the appearing creature would leave him alone. As with everything Elias did, Alex was certain these surprise visits were purely to aggravate him.

"Sorry, kiddo, you can't block me out," Elias said. "Squeeze your eyes shut as tight as you like—I can wait longer than you can resist. You know me. Patience is my middle name."

"Haven't you already bothered me enough for one day?" Alex said sharply, still refusing to give his shadow-guide the satisfaction of his full attention.

"If you wish to be treated like a child, who am I to stand in your way?" Elias replied, adopting a babyish voice that was almost more annoying than his usual one. "Would little Alex like to see what Uncle Elias has brought for him? A giftie! Ooh, isn't that exciting? Yes, it is. Isn't Uncle Elias unbelievably handsome and generous and charming and… I could go on. I will, if you don't open your eyes."

Alex opened his eyes, immediately wanting to shut them again as he saw the smug, amused expression that shifted across Elias's kaleidoscopic features.

"What do you want?" Alex frowned.

Elias tutted. "Now, now, that's no way to speak to your personal postman, is it? I've brought you information."

"About?"

"Well, if you must know, it relates to the counter-spell I told you about," the shadow-man explained. "You know, no pressure, but the one you might have to do if you choose to go ahead with the reversal of what your great-great-great-great-great-great-great—"

"I get the picture," Alex interrupted. "You have information about the spell that I may or may not decide to do."

"That's the gist of it… The spell is a complex one, not for the fainthearted or the illiterate—seriously, the thing is like a novel. It's written in a great big, dusty old book, as these ancient things usually are, which can be found within the walls of Falleaf House, under the protection of a man named Hadrian. Not my favorite royal, I have to say—not nearly enough spice for my liking. Bit of a goody two-shoes. You've got a lot in common, now that I think about it. He's just your type of person."

"Doesn't sound like a bad thing to me," Alex remarked, trying not to take the bait.

Elias scoffed. "I suppose, if you like a liberal. Me, I find dictators and despots so much more colorful. Hadrian takes a different approach to his school than the overseers of Spellshadow or Stillwater. He actually seems to care deeply about his students, if you can believe such a thing." He shuddered. "Saying that, he's the Head most likely to help *your* cause instead of the royal cause."

If Elias didn't like Hadrian, then Alex figured he might just be worth meeting—though the idea of *another* sympathetic royal, in addition to Caius, was difficult for Alex to believe. And no matter what Elias said about Falleaf House, Alex couldn't shake the image Professor Lintz had conjured of the place when recounting the tale of how he had arrived at Kingstone Keep. He had made it seem a hostile and dangerous land, rather than this pleasant utopia Elias was describing. Perhaps Elias simply wanted him to go there, in order to trick him. It didn't make sense for Lintz to lie about it… But maybe Alex wouldn't have to find out which version was the truth.

"Did you bring the book?" Alex asked.

Elias shook his head. "Afraid not, although I did try. It's tucked away somewhere safe—somewhere even my deft paws can't get at it. A veritable Fort Knox. If you want it, you'll have to go and get it yourself, I'm sad to say. Usually, I love a game of spiriting things away, but this was beyond me. I couldn't even get close."

Alex felt a twinge of disappointment, although the thought of a place that Elias couldn't access was both intriguing and concerning. More than that, he realized this information changed things slightly. Even if he didn't want to do the spell, he understood that he might need to know it, especially if he wanted to force the Head to do it. If he could learn the spell and feed it into Virgil's mind, getting him to say it and act it out with manipulated conviction, then he could escape an awful fate. He wondered what kind of protection this ancient book was under, and whether he'd even be up to the task of retrieving it, if Elias couldn't.

This fresh news gave him a renewed sense of hope, despite his qualms. Yes, it meant they might have to change their plans, with Alex traveling to Falleaf House instead of going through Alypia's portal to Stillwater, but he knew it would be better for them all in the long run, even if he had to face down unknown dangers. Surely, if Lintz had managed to sneak through Falleaf, Alex could sneak in? If he could do it, it would mean he might have found an actual, tangible way to destroy the Great Evil without having to do it himself. It would be more than a hypothesis. It would mean the ability to set everyone free from a life of pursuit and persecution.

Turning back to Elias, Alex wondered if this would be the last time he would see the shadow-man. What else could he possibly have to offer? As far as Alex could see, the wispy guide had done his job—there was surely nothing else of use that he could impart. If this was to be the last time Alex saw him, there were a few more things he wanted to know, but he knew Elias was not one for giving up secrets willingly. There was, however, one way he could try to find the answers he wanted.

Alex lunged for the shifting, shadowy creature, reaching for the galactic space where he thought Elias's mind might be. A split second later, he was feeding twisting strands of anti-magic into Elias's kaleidoscopic form. Although the shadow-man wasn't solid, Alex felt something connect on a spiritual level as memories began to race into his mind, flowing in a fast-moving torrent that Alex struggled to stop. Along the rushing tide of remembrance, however, Alex managed to pick out the scene that told him Elias was indeed responsible for what had happened to Ellabell. He watched in horror as the shadow creature swooped down upon her while she was walking innocently back to the tower room, snatching her from the corridor, apparently not so useless at controlling his faculties after all. He clutched her in grim, black claws as he staggered toward the mountain with her, pausing at the edge of the forest to rest before setting off again, soaring and stalling at sporadic intervals, his mind dead set on leaving her to the wolves and the elements. His hatred for the girl was palpable, and Alex looked on with disgust.

Anger coursed through him, tinting the silvery strands of his anti-magic with a bolt of red. The pulse of his fury threaded with the ethereal mist of Elias's strange existence, and a piece of Elias's hidden essence tore away, feeding backward through the strands of coiling anti-magic, carried along the blood that rushed through Alex's veins, seeking out the edge of his soul.

With a roar that seemed to shake the very universe, Elias threw Alex from his mind. The piece of essence went with Alex, sinking into the very core of him with a searing hot bolt of pain. He could barely speak, the agony so intense he thought he might be dying. It wasn't even clear what he had done, but he knew it couldn't be good.

Elias gasped, his shifting features distorted in a twist of angry pain. "What have you done?" he cried, a flash of rage lighting up the black of his eyes, before he disappeared in a fragmented mist of shattered shadow and glittering dust.

Alex fell to the ground, clutching his insides as they burned relentlessly. His whole body felt as if it were on fire, eating him up from the inside out. He wasn't entirely sure what had happened, but whatever he had drawn out from within Elias, it felt alien and wrong inside his own body, making him fervently wish he hadn't done it. Most of him had already known it was Elias who took Ellabell, and now he had gone and done who knew what to himself, all in the name of a foolish confirmation. It had been a mistake—he knew that much.

After a minute or two had passed, the pain began to subside, giving him hope that it was just a momentary thing, like the effects of the barrier magic or a misfired spell. He desperately wanted it to be so—he couldn't risk being in a weakened state, not when he had so much still to do.

Falleaf was calling to him, whispering promises of the book within and the hopes it might bring to so many, least of all Alex. If Lintz was correct, it was a place where Alex would need to have his wits about him.

Alex was certain now—he was going to make the Head perform the counter-spell, if it was the last thing he did. He just hoped it wouldn't be.

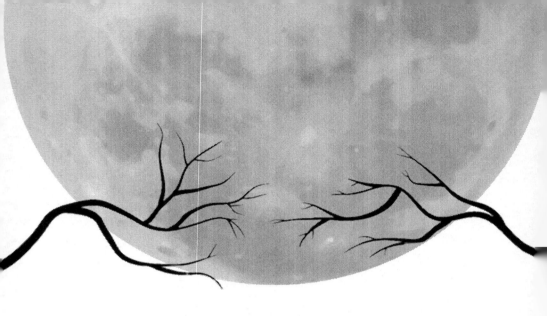

CHAPTER 29

ALEX STAGGERED BACK ONTO ONE OF THE BENCHES
that sat around the table, conscious of the cold, numb
ache that gnawed at the pit of his stomach, rising
toward his lungs, making every breath feel like the first intake
of air on a biting winter's morning.

The tower door burst open, and his friends rushed in,
their faces bearing expressions of concern. He was pleasantly surprised to see Lintz and Demeter too, knowing it would
make it easier to pass on the news of his latest revelation with
everyone in attendance.

"Are you okay? Caius told us what happened," said Aamir,
coming over to check on Alex. "I can't believe she's actually
trapped, after the gigantic mess today has been."

"I'm fine, just a bit worn out," he replied, pushing down

the sporadic bolts of pain that seared through him with the force of ten thousand volts of electricity.

"Is something the matter?" Natalie cut in, scrutinizing Alex's face.

"Elias came to me, just now, and told me about a book that contains the counter-spell," Alex said evenly, trying hard to sound like everything was fine, despite the burning sensation inside. "The only catch is, it's at Falleaf House… but I think it would be worth it for me to go and get it."

Ellabell looked at him with abject horror on her face. "You can't be serious. I thought you said you weren't going to do it," she said, her voice tight with sudden emotion.

"Don't worry. I'm still not planning on becoming a sacrifice anytime soon, not unless there's absolutely no other option. But I do think it would be good to have the book in hand, so I can take a look at the spell and see if I can find a loophole somewhere—I'm good at loopholes. I'm a walking, talking loophole of the Spellbreaker race's survival, after all," he replied, with forced brightness, wanting to soothe Ellabell's fears.

"Must have been some chat!" Jari said, but there was concern knitted upon his brow.

"And what if there isn't a loophole?" Ellabell said quietly, flashing him a look of deep worry.

"All I can say is I don't intend to do it, Ellabell," he replied, wishing she were closer so he could hold her hand. "I've got the start of an idea, which will hopefully mean I won't have to do it—there *is* an alternative to my martyrdom. I know there is; I can feel it in my bones. And something tells me I'll find answers in that book."

"So what does this mean for the plan to take control of Stillwater and Spellshadow?" Demeter asked.

Alex winced, grasping his stomach to try to hold his insides together. "Not much of a change, hopefully—more of a redirection. For me, anyway," he managed to reply, forcing the words through gritted teeth. "We still need people to take over the havens, but I'll head off to Falleaf instead of Stillwater, and then join the rest of you when I've got the book," he explained. "I'll just need a portal there... if that can be done?" He turned to Professor Lintz, who stood at the far side of the room.

"You want to build a portal to Falleaf House?" Lintz asked, his tone anxious.

Alex nodded. "You came through a portal from Falleaf House on your way here, didn't you?"

Lintz turned and nodded. "I did."

"You said you barely escaped—is it worse than here?" Alex pressed. The sharp stings of pain began to subside with each steady breath, easing slowly to a dull, manageable ache.

"I didn't get to meet anyone in charge, or even see the buildings there, but the forests all around it are teeming with soldiers and magical traps. If it's worse than here, I couldn't tell you. I saw very little, but what I did see was enough to scare me off. Though I see it will not scare you off," he added somberly.

"I *need* to fetch this book, Professor," Alex said. "Will building a portal to Falleaf House be easier than making a portal home, or will it still take forever?"

"Goodness me, it's far easier!" Lintz bellowed, twiddling his moustache. "It can certainly be achieved within a short timeframe. It requires far less essence—the essence from Stillwater should do it—and a lot less effort, not to mention the fact that there used to be a portal to Falleaf House already here. I came through it myself, though I disconnected it as soon as I did, considering the perils that lie in the woods beyond. I would never have thought to re-conjure it, but it should be simple enough to use the old network—it makes it a great deal easier when there's already a known route that the portal magic can work across, you see. It's why building portals to the outside world is so darned bothersome, because you're working blind, so to speak, forging an entirely new pathway."

This calmed Alex's nerves slightly. He wouldn't know the full extent of the dangers that lay at the unknown haven until he got there, so the only potential hurdles he could still think of rested in the hands of the havens they had already come through.

"And we can help too," said Ellabell firmly, "seeing as we'll be coming with you."

Alex shook his head, leveling his gaze at each person in turn. "Now, more than ever, it's going to be essential that we manage to take over Stillwater and Spellshadow," he said, knowing it would mean his best chance at using mind control on Virgil, without the fear of persecution or attack. "I know it might seem like a step backward, but this will offer hope to so many more than just ourselves, and I promise we will still get home after we've done this. This is why you need to go, as planned, to Stillwater... I won't ask anyone to come to Falleaf House with me, to risk their lives for a book."

With Alypia trapped here at Kingstone, Alex knew most

of the threat at Stillwater would be defused. The prison was no place for a longer stay—there were no physical resources here, no usable essence, and hardly any people they could rally to the cause. Stillwater had the resources, Spellshadow had the essence, and both had the people.

A momentary silence drifted across the room.

"Well, I think we should choose where we want to go," insisted Ellabell.

Aamir nodded. "Indeed, Alex, as noble as your sentiments are, you will require assistance too."

"Then let's take a vote," Alex said reluctantly, knowing how hard the decision was. It meant fracturing the group.

"I'll be going to Stillwater, as planned, to assist in taking control of the havens," Natalie spoke softly. "It will be sad to part from you… but I feel my presence will be needed most when the time comes to try to free Spellshadow. I am much stronger now than I was when we were students there, and I intend to be a formidable adversary. Not only that, but I will see my friend again, and get her to join us—how can we possibly fail?" She smiled, her dark eyes glittering with tears. "It is in my blood, after all—liberté, égalité, fraternité," she added with a nervous laugh. Alex felt his gut wrench. He had known it would be hard, but not this hard.

Jari nodded. "I'm going to go to Stillwater with Natalie. I want all those French things too, for Spellshadow Manor," he said firmly.

"It has nothing to do with Helena?" Natalie teased, clearly trying to bring a touch of levity to the meeting.

"I mean, obviously I'm going to jump at the chance to see

my true love again—pick up where we left off, if you know what I mean?" He grinned, blowing air kisses. "But, mainly, it's for Spellshadow, and those we left behind." It wasn't clear whether Jari was telling the truth, but the conviction in his words was unmistakable, making Alex think that, perhaps, that was indeed the main reason—it was just smothered in a goofy façade.

Both Natalie and Jari had improved by leaps and bounds since they'd left Spellshadow Manor, and Alex was certain the task of taking control of the havens would be in capable hands. Still, the fact that he would be losing them both, however temporarily, wasn't easy to take in. He would miss Natalie's strong, steady presence, and it would be too quiet without Jari to lighten the mood.

Then there was Aamir. Alex was almost entirely convinced he would go too, being Jari's best friend, which meant he would have to say goodbye to at least three of their tight-knit quintet. He waited patiently for the next person to speak, trying hard not to look at Ellabell, for fear of what decision he might see upon her face.

"I'm going with you, Alex, to Falleaf House," said Aamir solemnly. A quiet gasp ran around the room, and Alex realized he wasn't the only one who'd thought Aamir was going to choose differently. Jari gaped at his best friend in utter disbelief, rendered speechless. "It is by no means an easy decision, but I think you might need me more than Spellshadow and Stillwater do, for now. I am confident we will all return there, to join the fight, but I feel compelled to remain by your side in this."

"Are you certain?" Natalie asked, glancing between the two friends.

Aamir nodded.

A tense silence grew, all eyes on Jari and Aamir. The older boy wouldn't look at the younger, his gaze set sincerely forward. There would be time afterwards for them to talk it out, Alex knew, and he hoped they would do so before they had to part ways. He couldn't bear the thought of the two friends separating on bad terms. Fortunately, the tension was broken a moment later by Demeter's clear voice.

"I'll go to Stillwater and Spellshadow, as previously agreed. My skills can be better used in the battles yet to come. And, as they say—" the others braced for his latest botched proverb "—the mind is mightier than the sword."

"Not one I'm familiar with, old boy, but an excellent sentiment! The mind is a powerful tool indeed, and one I'm going to use right now," Lintz said. "I'm going to be coming with you too, Alex, considering you'll be in need of my, albeit limited, knowledge of Falleaf's terrain. I can also assist in the construction of a portal to Spellshadow Manor—if we decide to go that way and join in—or back here and around the long way."

"Thanks, Professor. The end goal is definitely to join the fight by meeting at Spellshadow," Alex said, trying to restrain the anxiety he felt about the fact that Ellabell still hadn't spoken. "Maybe both parties could send word to Vincent and Caius, through the portal, when havens have been taken and books have been retrieved."

"Ellabell, what are you going to do?" Natalie asked, and Alex's heart leapt into his throat. At first Ellabell had suggested they all go with him, but what would she choose now that the group was splitting up?

She sighed heavily. "I am going to come to Falleaf House, in the hopes I can stop you getting yourself killed on this… this mission of yours," she said finally, leaving a gap where Alex was certain she had wanted to say "foolish," or something worse. Clearly, she still wasn't convinced he wasn't going to get the book and just do the spell himself. Given the time, he vowed to tell her that he was halfway toward a full-fledged alternative.

Some of the tension had broken among the group, and everyone appeared to be in agreement—but realization was also dawning that this was going to be an even tougher goodbye than they'd thought. This was the group actually breaking apart, physically, for the first time in a long time. Even through arguments, curses, and secrets, they had never been far from one another, and this was different: this was a farewell with a tentative hope of reunion. There were no assurances, not anymore.

Alex's eyes rested on Ellabell. She was looking directly back.

He wasn't sure he could have said goodbye to her; there was so much still unspoken.

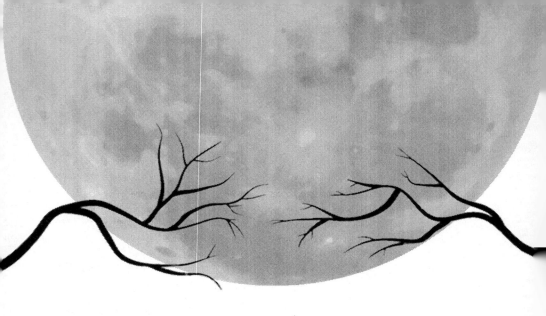

CHAPTER 30

EMETER DEPARTED TO INFORM VINCENT OF THE renewed plan, and to relieve him of his Stillwater portal guard duty. He promised to find Caius too, on the way there, to let him know there had been a slight alteration in proceedings.

"I'll see you off before you go. Remember, absence makes the heart grow bigger," Demeter had said before disappearing from the tower.

An awkward silence stretched between those who remained, and Alex understood why. Nobody wanted to be the first to say what had to be said.

"So, this means… we're all set then?" said Aamir, passing a nervous glance around the room.

"Looks like it," Jari agreed.

Seeing Ellabell sitting by herself, Alex seized the opportunity. It wouldn't be long before things got hectic, and though he knew he wasn't going to have to say goodbye to her, like Natalie and Jari, he wanted to take a calm moment with her before they left for Falleaf.

"Ellabell—will you come for a walk with me?" he asked quietly.

"Haven't you had enough of walking?" she teased.

"Not with you," he replied, hoping he sounded smooth.

She smiled. "Okay, let's walk."

With that, they made their way as inconspicuously as possible toward the door of the tower room, though it was clear all eyes were on them as they slipped out into the hall beyond.

Alex took her hand in his and pulled her toward the turret where she had stood sentinel while he went on his adventure to the gatehouse and back. Gazing back at her, he was pleased to see that she was smiling as he led her up to the top of the turret.

He was nervous in a way he had never known before. Above them, the bronze fog was ever-shifting, though Alex wished there were a sliver of sunshine. He looked into her eyes, which were the same pale blue as the sky he imagined lay beyond the fog, and he found himself suddenly tongue-tied. In the pale light, she looked perfect, her cheeks rosy, her freckles dotting her nose, her lips curved into a smile.

"I wanted to tell you something," he began, clearing his throat a little. "Though I'm sure you already know."

"I won't know unless you tell me," she murmured, brushing her thumb across his hand.

351

He rubbed the back of his neck and took a deep breath, letting the words flow out as he exhaled. "The thing is, with everything that's coming up and everything we've been through, I… I just wanted you to know how… I feel about you, while I have the chance." He paused, hardly daring to look at her. "There was a moment, back at Stillwater, when I thought none of us were going to make it, and I realized I might die having never said a word to you about… how I felt. And I'm not going to make the same mistake this time."

"You think we're going to die?" she asked, raising her eyebrows.

"That's not what I meant. I just want you to know, before we leave and things get a bit crazy, that there is one particular person in all of this who centers me, who calms me, who makes it all seem less insane. And that person is you, Ellabell," he said. "I care about you so much, and I know it's something stronger than a simple friendship. I… I'm falling for you, Ellabell. I know I'm no Romeo." He smirked, even as his heart pounded. "And it doesn't even matter if you don't feel the same. I just needed to tell you before we have to face whatever's waiting for us at Falleaf."

A moment of silence passed between them. Alex looked boldly into her eyes, and she held his gaze. No matter how hard he observed her face, he couldn't judge her reaction. There was a smile there, but was it a smile of reciprocity? There was a glitter in her eyes, but he couldn't tell if it meant she felt the same. It was torment, to stand and wait and wonder what she might say.

Finally, she spoke.

"I realized it in the prison cell, when you held me in your arms and it felt like everything was hopeless. I think I knew before then, but that was the moment I understood that the thought of losing you was unbearable," she began, dropping her gaze to the floor. "I've liked you for a long time, I think, and I've grown used to you being by my side. I want you to stay there, for as long as we both feel the way we do... I guess I'm falling for you too, Alex, and if we're both feeling this way, then we may as well fall together." She grinned widely, her whole face lighting up, making her even prettier. "I should tell you, though—I'm not exactly a roses and chocolates kind of girl."

"I would never have thought you were," he replied.

"I don't need all that. I just want something that's real—and to be with you, be beside you, and see where this takes us." She sighed nervously.

She was far more eloquent than he was, yet she didn't make him feel as if his admission had been any less powerful. There was a unity in both their confessions, a feeling of mutual affection and a place on the same page. It was a nice feeling, though the thundering of Alex's heart was not quite as pleasant.

He realized he wanted nothing more than to kiss her.

Slowly, he moved closer to her, lifting his hands to her face, brushing his thumb across the smooth skin of her cheek. She was so close to him, and all he could see and feel was her.

Tentatively, their lips met.

As his grazed hers, Alex felt overcome with emotion. Snowflakes began to fall all around them—it was his anti-magic responding to the overflowing of her own magical aura, her skin crackling with the force of it, as it glittered from within her in a flurry of beautiful golden sparks. It was everything he could have hoped for, and could never have anticipated when he walked through that gate at Spellshadow Manor.

After a few breathless moments, Ellabell pulled away, a smile upon her face. Alex grinned back, brushing the snow from Ellabell's curls.

"I hope that won't happen every time," he whispered.

"I don't mind if it does," Ellabell chuckled, and he felt like kissing her all over again.

Gazing into her eyes, however, he realized their time was trickling away. He and his friends would be parting ways at any moment, and he wanted to make sure he said goodbye to everyone before they did. He would be seeing some of them again shortly, but others... Well, he didn't know.

"Shall we get back?" Ellabell asked, as if reading his mind.

Alex nodded.

They walked back toward the tower room hand-in-hand, grinning like the besotted teenagers they were. He wondered what it would be like to have an ordinary relationship with her, out in the real world, with none of the mayhem that had shaped their current world—he hoped he'd get to find out one day.

Returning to the tower, the goodbyes began.

"I swear I'll make good on the promise I made to your sister," Alex said, hugging Natalie. "Once all of this is over, I will get you back home."

"And I will make good on the promise I made to your mother," she whispered, giving him a tight squeeze. "You will see her again, Alex. I will make sure of it—there will be no heroics that put that at risk, do you hear me?"

"Agreed," he said, pulling away from her before approaching Jari.

"Dude, you stay safe, okay? I don't want you getting any bright ideas about that book," the blond-haired boy scolded.

Alex smiled. "I won't, and don't you play the knight in shining armor either. No saving damsels, though I'm not sure you'll find many damsels around here."

"Maybe *I* can be the damsel," Jari quipped, jiggling his eyebrows.

"I'm gonna miss you," Alex muttered, pulling his friend into a hug.

"I'll miss you too, man," Jari replied, hugging back.

It was truly hard to say goodbye to friends, but the hardest goodbye wasn't even one Alex was participating in. It was the sight of Aamir parting ways with Jari. All animosity and shock at Aamir's decision to go to Falleaf forgotten, Jari leapt toward his best friend, wrapping his arms around the older boy in the tightest of bear hugs.

"I'm gonna miss you so much, man!" he cried, clutching Aamir's shoulders.

"I'm going to miss you too, Petra," said Aamir softly.

"It won't be the same without you," Jari said miserably.

"It won't be for long. We'll meet again, and we'll fight to take back our freedom, and then we'll go home. And you and I will be friends until we're old and gray, drinking tea, reminiscing about these days," Aamir whispered, tears welling in his eyes.

"And we'll cause havoc in the nursing home?" Jari grinned, brushing away defiant tears.

Aamir nodded. "Why, of course."

"Don't do anything stupid, okay?"

"Nor you."

"And if you see any nice ladies at Falleaf, you let them know where I am," the younger boy chuckled, clearly struggling to suppress his sadness.

"You'll be too busy mooning over Helena," Aamir replied, "but I'll make a mental note."

"Got to keep my options open," Jari quipped.

They drew apart, both trying to smile, but failing.

"This sucks," Jari muttered.

Alex sighed.

He was right. It really did.

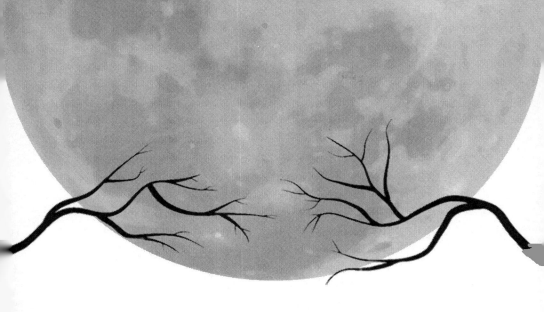

CHAPTER 31

WITH NOTHING LEFT TO SAY, ALEX GRABBED THE satchel containing the bottles of essence from Stillwater and followed those who were going through Alypia's portal, walking with them down to the courtyard. The portal gleamed enticingly, and Demeter stood beside it, ready to follow the others. If there were any guards on the other side, Demeter had already taken care of them. All they had to do now was step through, which they did, turning back for one last goodbye as Alex, Ellabell, and Aamir waved them off on their journey.

It would be up to the others to find Helena before too many people were alerted to their presence. If anyone could do it with the required level of stealth, Alex knew it was the three who had volunteered for the task. With Demeter's mind control, Natalie's ability to manipulate the magic of others, and Jari's instinctual aptitude for reading opponents, they would be okay. He hoped it with all his heart.

Now, it was their turn. They had a portal of their own to open.

"With me!" Lintz bellowed.

The others followed him, running back the way they had come until they reached a circular antechamber that sat at the very end of a long hallway Alex was only vaguely familiar with. He knew they were close to the corridor that held Alypia's new cell, but he tried not to think about that as he focused on the task at hand.

Lintz paused beside the farthest wall of the antechamber. "Here—this is where the old network is. Alex, pass me the bottles," he instructed.

Wasting no time, Alex brought forth the bulging bag of essence and handed it to Lintz, who slung it over his shoulder. He was balancing a satchel on each hip, clockwork on the right, essence on the left.

"Right, let's do this. Watch carefully—you might need to know this one day," Lintz said as he pulled the first black bottle from the bag and set to work.

He poured the contents into his hands, his eyes focused on the pulsing red strand. Golden threads of magic rippled around his fingers, feeding into the glowing essence. Alex prayed the combination didn't have the same disastrous results that he'd conjured with Alypia. However, no golden monsters surged from Lintz's palms. Instead, his mouth moved silently as his hands stretched out the strand of essence, the dim red shade stretching wider and turning a silvery white. Soon, Lintz held a long, wide ribbon of portal energy in his palms, the red tinge entirely gone from the glittering energy. He pressed it against the wall, and the thread flashed brightly before settling, the energy within seeming to undulate above the stonework.

The group braced for red fog, but none came.

"How come it hasn't set the barrier off?" Alex asked, relieved it hadn't.

Lintz smiled. "We're opening an old gateway. The barrier magic flows around the echo of the opening, allowing safe passage... Well, unless you're someone Caius doesn't like, like Alypia," he chuckled, returning to his work.

The professor moved quickly for such a stout man, weaving the portal magic in a lustrous tapestry across the wall. It was almost hypnotic, the way the threads emerged from the essence and slotted into one another. Over and under, over and under, creating a familiar oval shape. Alex watched intently, trying to figure out how he might do the same with his anti-magic.

Finally, the professor came to the end of the essence. Lintz pressed his hands into the center of the woven threads and closed his eyes. With a triumphant swell, the threads connected, the energy melding into one solid oval as the portal burst into life, appearing to shatter the very fabric of the wall with a silent explosion of vivid light that surged outwards. The silvery white light swirled from the epicenter, small at first, then growing larger, gradually filling the parameters of its former oval shape, before settling, like dropping a stone into still water.

As the luminescent ripples were subdued, now flat and

calm, a world beyond was revealed. Through the mirror-like surface, Alex could see an autumnal forest stretching away toward the horizon, the bronze and scarlet leaves falling slowly to the lush green undergrowth. There were no buildings in sight, but there were no swarms of guards either—yet. It was picturesque, the blue sky crisp and clear above the fall-hued trees as a cool breeze flowed through from the new realm, its caress feeling fresh on Alex's hot, stressed face.

"Ready yourselves, it's time to go through! Keep to the edge of the tree-line. Do *not* enter the forest. I repeat, do *not* enter the forest," said Lintz.

Aamir stepped up first, his manner decidedly tentative. There was a bit of a leap down to ground level, but it was only a short drop, not nearly as high as the one between the Head's office at Spellshadow Manor and the ground in Stillwater's realm.

"And, jump! Go, go, go!" Lintz cried, sounding like the leader of a group of paratroopers, standing by the open plane hatch and ushering his comrades out.

Aamir jumped, using his magic to soften the fall as he soared through the air with enviable grace. With barely a rustle of leaves, he landed on the dewy grass, turning back to look up at the others with a cheerful thumbs-up.

"Go, go, go!" Lintz roared again, as Ellabell stepped up.

Alex moved with her toward the edge of the portal, grasping her hand. Even as she reached the lip of it, preparing for the jump, he still held onto her. She wore a worried expression, but he knew she was much too brave to let a tiny jump bother her—there was undoubtedly something else on her mind, but whatever it was, it would have to wait. She turned back to him for a moment, flashing him her boldest smile.

With a tight squeeze of his fingers, she let go of him, leaping through the mirrored pool of the portal and landing on the grass with a light thud. The only ones left now were Alex and Professor Lintz.

Alex was preparing to jump, when a scream tore through the keep.

Immediately, he knew it had come from Alypia, and the sound of it made him step back from the edge of the portal. A million possibilities rushed through his mind.

Has she escaped? Has she wormed her way out of her restraints? Has she run into something nasty on her exodus?

He knew if he didn't go to her now, to check that she was still securely locked up, he would regret it. After so much effort to trap her, he didn't even want to think of the possibility of her running free, able to follow him once more. It wasn't a risk he was going to take again.

"Keep the doorway open for me," Alex said suddenly, turning to Lintz.

"Leave her, Alex!" the professor insisted, but Alex knew he couldn't.

"I have to be sure she hasn't gotten out. If she's free, then all of this has been for nothing," he explained quickly. "We can't risk her being on our tails—please, wait for me down there. Keep the portal open. I won't be long."

"Alex! Come back!" the professor yelled, but Alex was already halfway down the corridor, his direction clear in his mind.

He ran until he reached the familiar door of Agatha's old guard room, now Alypia's cell. However, as he neared, he saw that the door was already open. Building anti-magic beneath his palms, he burst through, ready to face what was on the other side.

The sight made Alex's eyes go wide with horror.

Caius loomed above the frozen figure of Alypia, who was kneeling on the ground, head bowed. Her mouth was moving silently, as if in prayer, though her hands were bound behind her by the ivy-wrapped manacles. In his own hands, Caius clutched the handle of a gleaming, magical sword, which shone a pure gold as he slowly raised it above her head, seeming to take a few practice swings before he dealt the final blow.

Alex rushed into the room, putting himself between Caius's blade and Alypia, threads of anti-magic still crackling along his skin.

"What are you doing?" he yelled, splaying out his hands to protect Alypia.

"Delivering justice," Caius replied bitterly, a flash of hatred in his eyes.

Alex stared at Caius in disbelief. "Not like *this*, Caius. This isn't you—this is your anger talking."

"Move, Alex. You do not understand," Caius said, his gaze cold and piercing. "She feels no remorse. My Guinevere was murdered, and they laughed. They laughed at her pain and mine. They are monsters unworthy of forgiveness."

Alex took a step closer. "She is far more useful to us alive! We can use her against Julius. We can use her to get information."

"She deserves to die." Caius lifted his sword again. "Now, move aside, my boy. I do not wish to make you."

"No." Alex met Caius's eyes and let the glitter of silver and black build in his hands. The warden frowned, his grip on the sword weakening for a moment, and Alex was almost relieved.

Almost.

In an instant, Caius's expression shifted, and he shoved Alex to the side with enough force to jar the younger man's shoulder. The impact knocked Caius off balance for a moment, no longer having his cane to lean on for support, but he rallied quickly, lifting the sword over Alypia once more in a single motion. Alex stumbled forward with a grunt as the blade came down, catching it between his palms. Gold and silver clashed in a surge of light, ice forming along the places Alex's hands gripped the sword. Caius was not letting go, and neither was he.

Alex pressed harder into the blade, though the razor-sharp edge burned his hands. As he channeled his anti-magic along its length, veins of frost began to spread from the sword's center to its point and pommel, until every trace of gold had disappeared, the weapon morphing into a solid block of ice. With one more pulse of anti-magic, the sword shattered into fragments, and Alex was left breathless and sweating, surrounded by rapidly melting shards of slush. His hands were stinging. Glancing down, he saw two dark red lines where the blade had bitten into his skin, the wounds instantly cauterized. They hurt, but he was in one piece.

Caius staggered backward and sank into a nearby chair. His mind seemed to come back to him as his eyes lost the haze of rage that had clouded them.

"I'm sorry… I do not know what came over me."

Alex breathed a sigh of relief, sidestepping Alypia to sit opposite Caius, although he was careful to remain alert. Seeing the warden in such an unstable state made Alex realize how unpredictable the man could be. It sent a shiver of fear down Alex's spine, and he was more eager than ever to leave Kingstone.

"I know what it's like to feel hatred burning you up inside, until you can't see straight," Alex said slowly. "But I hope you understand why we need to keep Alypia alive. There are other lives at stake here."

"Of course, my boy," Caius said, his face a mask of sorrow. "I was not thinking, in the moment. Anger has a way of consuming the soul."

Alex hated to ask more of the warden, given his current emotional state, but he wanted to be sure that all the necessary cogs were in place before he left. "Will you promise to keep watch over her? We just need to make sure she doesn't alert Julius to what's going on."

"Certainly. Though I am only playing a small part in your plans, I am more than happy to do so." Caius smiled weakly, an uneasiness still simmering within his eyes.

"Thank you. That's good to hear," Alex said with forced levity. It was difficult to act so congenial after what had just happened. At least Vincent would also be remaining at Kingstone, to keep an eye on things. The necromancer knew how important Alypia was to them, and Alex just hoped he would be around to prevent any future near-executions.

"You must be leaving for Stillwater shortly, I presume?" Caius asked.

"Actually, I'm headed to Falleaf House, in search of the book that contains the counter-spell you told me about," Alex said, tapping the edge of his armchair. "I'd like a moment to speak with Alypia before I go, though. The portal there is already open—the others are waiting for me."

Caius looked surprised. "Falleaf House, you say? My son is the leader there."

"Hadrian is your son?" Alex asked, equally surprised.

Caius nodded. "My beloved boy. Had I known you were going there, I would have come to find you and offered suggestions."

Alex wondered why Elias hadn't mentioned that Caius and Hadrian were related, but he knew the shadow-man well enough by now to know that he was careful to omit details that didn't work in his own favor. There was a reason Elias hadn't said anything, there always was, but it didn't seem likely Alex would be seeing the vaporous trickster again to ask him why. Regardless, Alex realized he now had an opportunity before him, to get even better insight into the realm of Falleaf House and the man who ruled there.

"I think Demeter was looking for you earlier, to tell you where we were going," said Alex, a touch guiltily. He *had* just been about to leave Kingstone without so much as a "see you later" to the old man, discarding his manners in favor of his need to get the book as quickly as possible.

"He never did find me." Caius smiled, leaning forward. "But you're here now, keeping me up to date."

"Sorry about that," Alex murmured.

"Nonsense, your head was full of adventure. Who can blame you for not pausing to tell an old man?" Caius reassured. "I have to wonder, though, what has made you decide to go after this book?"

"I'll need it for what I plan to do," Alex said, not wanting to reveal the details of his plan in front of Alypia. "There might be other spells in it, too, that could be of use to us."

"It's about time there was a bit of action in these havens," Caius murmured. "You must wish my son good tidings if you meet him at Falleaf House—though with so many soldiers around, you will have to have your wits about you, and ensure you stay on high alert, if you want to reach the sanctuary of his school."

"Why are there so many soldiers there?" Alex asked, intrigued, and wanting to get the upper hand before he set foot in the mystery realm.

"The school holds a great many secrets, that book included, which the royals would seek to protect—the royals who are unlike myself and my son. It is the most ancient haven, and Julius deems my son the only royal he can spare for the task of ruling at Falleaf, given the unfortunate circumstances of his heritage. If he were anyone else's son, he'd be the pride of court—smart, just, fair, skillful. Being my son, he has been duly hidden away. Julius likes to keep an eye on him by filling his realm with traps and guards, though I think he does it just to aggravate me."

"How will I find your son?" Alex pressed.

Caius sighed. "It won't be easy, but if your group is small, you may succeed. You must seek out a pagoda in the trees—the peak of it brushes the canopy of the forest, and there is a golden bird at the top that catches the sunlight twice a day, flashing at those times like a beacon. Find that beacon and follow it," he said solemnly. "And move slowly. Many of the magical snares can be sensed before they go off, but you have to be listening intently for them—you have to know what you're looking for. Be wary of any oddity you come across, be it a black leaf, or a tree trunk that seems oddly bent, or a glade where birds don't sing."

Alex was glad he'd asked. "Thank you, Caius. This is a huge help. If I'd known the two of you were related, I'd have come to you sooner."

Caius smiled sadly. "If you manage to get to him, you will find him a pleasant sort of man, with plenty of time for bright young things like you. A genuinely good soul, my boy. Do pass on my well wishes to him, won't you, if you make it to him?"

Alex nodded. "Of course I will. It would be my pleasure. If he's anything like you, I'm sure we'll get along just fine."

"You are too kind," said Caius. "Now, I fear I must go before I do something I regret," he added, casting a sour glance in Alypia's direction. "Do not linger too long—you should go to your friends as quickly as you can."

"I will. I just want a quick word," Alex promised.

With a hum of displeasure, Caius rose from his seat, snatching his cane from where it stood against the wall. Leaning heavily on the silver falcon's head, the warden hobbled toward the open door, casting a savage look back at his niece before disappearing out into the hallway, leaving the two of them alone. Alypia knelt on the floor, her back to him, her face hidden from view.

He had wanted his chance to speak with Alypia, and here it was.

Be careful what you wish for, he thought anxiously as the white-haired woman slowly began to turn her head in his direction.

"I suppose you think I owe you something now," Alypia said, glowering.

Alex drew closer to her. "I want to know about Julius and the counter-spell you all apparently want me for."

She smirked. "Well, help a lady up first. I'm not going to say a word while I'm stuck here on the floor, in this particularly degrading state."

Wondering if it was a trap of some sort, Alex hung back for a moment.

"Oh, come on, I'm not going to bite you or anything!" she snapped.

Her shrill voice sent a shiver up Alex's spine, but he stepped toward her regardless, grasping her by the arm as he hauled her to her feet. The manacles ensured her hands remained behind her back, her power more or less drained by the twisting gray ivy, but it didn't mean she wouldn't try something if she got the chance. Carefully, Alex helped to maneuver her back into the armchair by the fireplace, and slowly sat down opposite her.

"You're not going to undo these cumbersome chains?" she purred.

"Not a chance."

"I'd say I won't hold this against you, but I'm the kind of woman who loves to bear a grudge, and you have given me more than enough to stack against your name." She sneered, the expression looking strange on her patchwork face of beauty and ugliness.

"But you'll talk?" he asked.

She gave a casual shrug. "Seeing as you saved my life, I could be persuaded to answer a question or two, though how is it that you continue to outmaneuver me, Alex Webber?"

"Call it a bad habit."

An amused expression graced Alypia's brow. "You know, I was hoping to put you in a little gift box and hand you to my father on his birthday. And yet here I am, stuck in this foul place with my insane uncle watching over me. I must say, this wasn't quite how I'd hoped things would pan out." She laughed bitterly. "I should have just told my father about you when I had the chance. It was that wormy little brother of mine, persuading me that it would be so much better if we kept it secret until we could find you again and hand you over as planned."

"I think you underestimate me, Alypia," said Alex calmly.

"And I think you think a little too highly of yourself," she warned. "You think you can simply take over, with no consequences? You think you can run around saving all these lives, without any sort of retribution? My father will come for you, and if you think you can outmaneuver him, you are a dyed-in-the-wool idiot. You might have gotten the better of me a couple of times, but you won't have a chance with him."

"He's just a man," remarked Alex, with more confidence than he felt. "Besides, he needs me alive."

Alypia laughed coldly. "Just because he needs *you* alive doesn't mean he won't go through every person you care about in order to get to you. He is capable of anything."

"I know, I had the pleasure of seeing him in action," Alex said grimly, remembering the floppy body of the disintegrated prisoner.

"Then you should be trembling in your shoes," Alypia said with a tilt of her head. "Just because you are what you are doesn't mean you will be safe from my father. He loathes your kind—if he feels like it, he will kill you regardless of whether or not you can do the spell my brother couldn't." She gave a short laugh. "I can still hear the screams Virgil made when he failed, and Julius found out. Just think—you could be next."

"He'd kill me even if it meant the demise of mage-kind?" Alex asked dubiously. He had seen Julius kill one man without batting an eyelid, but surely the king wouldn't let *everyone* die, just to satisfy an impulse.

"Who knows?" she said, her tone disturbingly chipper. "Although, I think he'd much prefer forcing you to do it. He would relish the opportunity to get his hands on you, and make you suffer for everything your kind did to his people."

"Everything *my* kind did?" Alex spat.

She smiled coldly. "You think he cares about the indiscretions of the mages? They're his nighttime reading. Even when I was a child, he used to tell me tales about the men he'd killed, and the executions he'd attended. His greatest achievement is what he did to your race, Alex," she sighed. "You think I'm some sort of monster, but you don't know monstrous until you have seen what my father can do, and does do, on a regular basis. I am a kitten in comparison. He could blow up a man from the inside out and think no more of it than if he had squashed a fly. Mind you, he's going to be so peeved when he hears he came so close to you without knowing."

"He won't get the chance," Alex replied brazenly.

Alypia chuckled. "You have no idea what you're up against, little boy. You had just better hope that I don't find a way out of here, or find a way to get a message to my father. If I do, you will wish he knew the meaning of a quick death. He will make every one of your little friends suffer in ways you couldn't even imagine."

Alypia was making it very hard for Alex not to regret, just a little bit, that he hadn't let Caius kill her.

"We'll be long gone before he even knows there's a problem," Alex retorted.

"As I say... you'd better hope so."

Alex frowned, his heart pounding. "You sound like you worship the man. How can I look at you and not think you're a monster, when you adore a man who is capable of all those things?"

"I value power," she said simply. "And he has immeasurable power."

"And what about the way he treats your mother? Surely, you can't stand for that?" Alex asked, wanting to see how far he could push Alypia.

"My mother is weak," she whispered. "My father was right to punish her—she didn't fight back. She is my father's property, and she allowed herself to be tarnished."

Alex couldn't believe the words that were coming out of

Alypia's mouth. From such a strong, formidable woman, they sounded absurd, making him wonder if she had somehow been brainwashed along the way, to believe the vile things her father said and thought to be morally right.

"She'd be dead if it wasn't for Caius," Alex said. "You should respect Caius, not your father."

Alypia was silent for a moment. "Perhaps that would have been kinder… if she had died back then. I've often thought so."

"We're done here," said Alex suddenly. He'd heard everything he wanted to know about Julius, and the threat the king posed if he found out what the others were doing at Stillwater and Spellshadow. It made him realize he had to be quicker than ever; he had to go through the portal to Falleaf, retrieve the book, get Virgil to do the counter-spell as fast as he possibly could, and get everyone out of there.

He had just reached the door to the cell, when Alypia's sickly sweet voice called his attention back.

"You know why my uncle allowed you to stay and speak with me, don't you?" she said softly.

Alex frowned. "So I could get information from you—you heard me say it."

"Sometimes, my uncle forgets which side he is actually on. It's a personality disorder of some kind, making him believe he's a Spellbreaker when he's really one of us," she purred. "He would do absolutely anything to punish his brother. He would do anything to keep you from saving the rest of us. I wouldn't be surprised if he were already at your little portal, dismantling it as we speak. Don't get me wrong—it's the opposite of what I want, but I figured you should know… you know, in case you wanted to stop him."

Alarm rippled through Alex's body.

"*What?*"

She smiled. "Go see for yourself..." she whispered.

Pulse racing, Alex darted out of the room, slamming the door shut behind him in case she decided to make a break for it. His feet pounded hard against the flagstones as he sprinted toward the place where the portal to Falleaf was, hoping against everything that it was still there.

She has to be wrong. She has to be, he told himself as he ran, turning the corner into the hallway where the antechamber was.

Alypia's voice followed him, echoing down the corridors.

"You should have taken my offer, boy! You're doomed now!"

He skidded to a halt in front of the door to the small room. Slamming his fists against it, he pushed the door open with alarming force and peered into the darkness beyond, desperate to see the glimmer of the portal staring back.

No, no, no, no, no...

Shaking his head, his heart thudding with a sick dread, he ran toward the wall and clawed frantically at the blocks of stone, but it was no good.

The portal was gone.

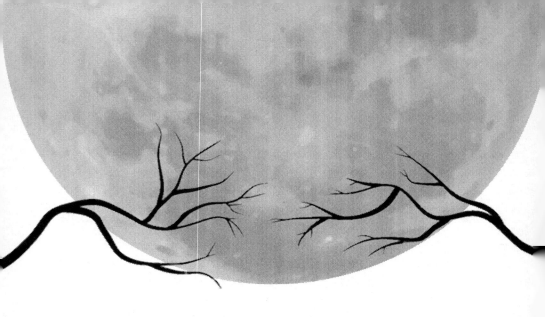

CHAPTER 32

GULPING IN GREAT, PANICKED BREATHS OF AIR, ALEX tried to rationalize the sight before him. His fingertips were raw and bleeding from attacking the stone wall in desperation, but he wasn't ready to give up yet. He had asked Lintz to keep the gateway open, and though it was gone, Alex knew there had to be a reasonable explanation for its disappearance.

Maybe it closed by accident, he thought to himself over and over, trying to calm his fractious nerves. *Alypia can't be right... Please don't let her be right.*

Just then, he became aware of the shuffle of feet behind him, and turned sharply to see Caius emerge from the darkness, his cane clicking on the stone. He was holding a half-dead Vincent by the neck with the hand not clutching the cane, dragging him along like a ragdoll. The necromancer was limp, his black eyes rolling back into his head, and there were cuts on his pale arms and bruises to his face, as if he had tried to fight the warden off.

It was more than Alex could take.

"She was right," he gasped.

"I'm sorry, Alex," Caius said softly, with a kindness in his voice that almost fooled him.

"What is this?" Alex asked, gesturing between the empty wall and the limp necromancer.

"I am so sorry for this, my boy… I thought I could let you go. I honestly believed I could, but then you spoke about the book, and the risk became too great. I realized I couldn't let you go after all, as much as I wanted to." The old man sighed heavily, dropping Vincent to the floor with a sickening thud. "I know you won't believe me, but I didn't intend it to be this way."

Alex glared. "And how was it supposed to be?" he spat.

"They have to pay, Alex. Hearing your plans to save them all… I'm sorry, but I can't allow you to walk free," said Caius, his expression infuriatingly sad.

"Why should I have to suffer for what they all did?" Alex asked, balling his hands into fists. Anger pulsed inside him, making the edges of his aura bristle with silver light. It was like being a caged animal, with nowhere left to run.

"You should blame them, not me," Caius urged, to Alex's increasing annoyance. "Your anger is misplaced."

"No, I blame you! You're the only one standing here— standing between me and what little hope I have left," Alex hissed. "Why, Caius? Make me understand, because right now I don't have a clue what you're doing this for! I trusted you... For God's sake, I *trusted* you!"

Caius had the decency to look ashamed as he spoke. "I will tell you all the answers you desire, only because you have a right to know why I have chosen this path. The simple truth is, Alex, I don't want the mages to survive—they do not deserve it. You are young, but I have had a couple hundred years to mull over my thoughts on them, to come to this conclusion. I have witnessed the horror they have inflicted upon innocents, and I have continually stood by and done nothing, because I was younger then too, and I thought as you do now. I didn't understand what had to be done." Caius closed his eyes for a moment. "Can you imagine what it is like, tearing the very essence from a person, for personal gain? It is not a means to an end—it is inhuman, and I am certain now that the Great Evil would be kinder than any of this. Who knows, when it has eaten its fill of our kind, perhaps it will leave the innocents too. We were too proud to test the theory, valuing our own lengthy lives above others we cut short," he muttered bitterly. "You heard the things Alypia said to me, and you have heard the things Julius, and all the rest of them, have done—those are their true colors."

Alex tried to calm himself with steady breaths. Surely, he could talk Caius into seeing sense. Surely, he could reason with the man who had once been an ally.

"Alypia and her father are two rotten apples in a bunch that aren't, Caius. What if your theory is wrong? What if it never stops, until there are no mages left?"

"If my theory is wrong, it is still the kinder course. The royals have learned *nothing*. They don't care even a little for what they did—give them the choice again, and they would repeat history," Caius insisted, his golden eyes glinting with angry tears. "Even nature itself wants magic gone—fewer and fewer mages are being born, even within noble magical families. Mother Nature wants to wash her hands of it, for good, as punishment for the genocide they wrought upon your kind. I am simply speeding up the inevitable."

"What would Guinevere say, if she could see you now?" Alex said desperately. "She wouldn't want innocents to burn too, would she?"

"Perhaps not, but she isn't here to stop me, because they killed her," the old man reasoned. "I have the chance to make amends for everyone who died. An eye for an eye."

"An eye for an eye makes the whole world blind, Caius."

Caius smiled. "A blind world is better than one filled with mages."

"You can't honestly believe that," said Alex, horrified. It was unimaginably awful, what Caius had been through, and he couldn't help but wonder how he might feel if it was Ellabell in a situation like that. But no matter how he dwelled upon it, he knew nothing could justify yet more death, on such an enormous scale.

Glancing around, Alex looked for any sign of a feasible exit, knowing he would need one when this talk inevitably came to blows. He understood that his chances of overcoming Caius completely were slim, but he felt he might be able to stun Caius for long enough to make a break for it. For now, he just needed to keep the warden talking, keep him distracted until he could see a viable route to take, when the time came.

There was the door to the tower room, but he knew he might not be able to get it open before Caius got up again. Then, there was the broken door leading toward the common room, but that would involve stepping over Caius. He could try magical travel too, but the thought of taking the brickwork with him and having it crush him or rip him apart prevented him from doing so. He was, for all intents and purposes, trapped.

"You won't change my mind, Alex, though I admire your spirit," Caius said, an eerie calm in his voice as he strode over Vincent's limp body.

Alex tried to take a step back, but there was only a brick wall behind him. "You don't have to kill me."

Caius grinned with odd warmth. "I tried to do this the fair way once before, with your father, but that didn't work out so well. The only option now is death."

Alex froze. "My father?"

"That vision you had, using this unnatural abomination's skillset," Caius said, nodding toward Vincent's body. "It was my man running after your father—I would have brought him here, where I could lock him up and keep him safe from those selfish savages. I even had a chamber decorated specifically for him… I believe you know the one, near the entrance to the pit." Caius smiled briefly, but all Alex could do was stare in shock. "It wouldn't have been a hard life for him. He would never have wanted for anything, and I would have come up with a tale to tell his wife, to soften the blow, but then that shadowy idiot went and killed him." He sighed woefully. "It wasn't ideal for anyone, but I suppose it did the job just as well, in the end."

Alex recalled the hooded figure in the trees, and realized it hadn't been the Head after all, but Caius, hiding in the tree-line, ensuring the task was done, waiting to have his prize brought back to him.

"My father would never have run if you hadn't had him chased. He would be alive if it weren't for you," Alex growled, not quite knowing how to process this new information.

Caius shrugged. "There are undoubtedly a number of things you could blame for what happened to your father. You could blame the ice cream man for distracting your mother's attention. You could blame the weather for encouraging your parents to go outside. You could blame your mother again, for insisting they stay in that deadwood town. You could even blame your father for not going with your mother on that day. Anyway, it makes little difference—I'm still going to have to kill you."

"You don't have to do that. You don't have to do any of this!" Alex said, feeling how fruitless his plea was. Finally, the warden's true nature was rising to the surface, and, at least to Alex, the man was at last living up to his reputation.

He realized with a sinking feeling that there had indeed been a warning sign, but he had missed it, brushing it off as pure power instead. It made sense now, the strange scarlet fog he had touched upon when he had delved into Caius's mind—it was Caius's madness, overwhelming his brain, smothering it in a red sea of accumulated rage he simply couldn't see past, always at the back of his thoughts, influencing everything he did.

"You have put it all in place for me, my boy—you have spurred me on to my purpose, and I have risen to the occasion," Caius said brightly. "Though it pained me to do it, I smashed my ill-gotten gains, letting the Kingstone essence run free, into the ground, where nobody can get their hands on it. I returned the souls of the departed to Mother Nature's loving embrace, and never have I felt so exhilarated. I imagine you felt the same when you rid Stillwater of theirs?"

"I felt sorrow and guilt," Alex whispered.

Caius sighed. "I see you take no pride in your work, my boy, but you really should. There is no essence left at Stillwater House thanks to you, and now there is none here either. I just have to destroy whatever is left at Spellshadow Manor and Falleaf House. Once it is all gone, they will have to kill more from their own ranks to replenish the supply, and when their arrogance prevents them, the Great Evil shall arise," he cackled, the cruel, mad glee glinting in his eyes.

It was clear the warden wasn't in the mood for negotiating anymore, and any plea Alex made would be useless. There was murder on the old man's mind. Right now, Alex needed to get out of Kingstone Keep. His hopes would come to nothing if he died now, in this lonely place.

It serves me right, Alex thought, *for ever trusting a royal.*

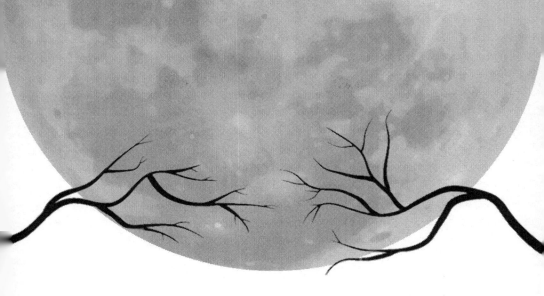

CHAPTER 33

"IF YOU HAVE ANY FINAL REMARKS, I WILL NOT DENY you them," Caius said, holding out his free hand as if in benediction. The old man, Alex realized, really believed he was showing mercy. On the floor at his feet, Vincent's hand twitched almost imperceptibly.

"I do have one last question," Alex said, conjuring threads of silvery black beneath his fingertips, fine at first, as he let the black-speckled anti-magic swell and surge all around him. The strands thickened, rippling with wave after wave of bright silver energy. His eyes burned as a spiral of glittering silver sparks began to fall all around him in a bright snowstorm of glinting light.

"Did you actually think I would die without a fight?" Alex shouted, focusing on the rage running through his every vein, brimming over the edge of his every cell. He roared as he forced it all out of his body in a vast, explosive surge that rushed forward, knocking Caius backward with a ferocious blast.

It took the warden by surprise for just long enough to give Vincent, who had come back around, the opportunity to lunge upward and force his veined hands onto the sides of Caius's head. He clamped his thin fingers around Caius's skull like two vised claws, the necromancer's mouth moving silently as he spoke incantations, while his palms conjured ghostly white lines that shimmered into Caius's temples.

Alex watched, rooted to the spot, as Caius turned a deathly shade of pale, the entirety of his eyes turning white, the gold of his irises and the black of his pupils draining away to nothing. Caius crumpled behind Vincent, his cane clattering to the ground, his body sliding down the broken surface of the door, slamming it shut as his weight fell against it.

Whatever Vincent had done, it had clearly taken a lot out of him. The veins beneath the surface of his translucent skin pulsed with a darker blue than Alex had ever seen before, the web of it more visible beneath his pale flesh, throbbing thickly in places, like tar. With a weary head, the necromancer managed to turn toward Alex, opening his mouth in a scream.

"RUN!" Vincent howled. Wispy spirits emerged from within the necromancer's body, pushing through his translucent skin. Their gaping, skeletal faces reflected the screams of their master, floating ever upward. "Get out of here, Spellbreaker! Don't look them in the eye!"

Yanking open the door, Alex dared to glance back over

his shoulder, just in time to see the necromancer turn toward his victim once more, with the clear intent of ensuring Caius couldn't hurt anyone again. It wasn't the fate Alex would have wished upon the old man, whose mind had clearly been warped by the things he had seen in his long life, but he wasn't sure there was any choice in the matter now. It no longer looked as if the necromancer were in control of the deed, as the ghoulish phantoms whirled around him, howling banshee-like wails with their cavernous mouths, the sound sending a tremor of pure terror up Alex's spine.

Alex hurried toward the nearest window and clambered up onto the ledge, hoping he still had enough focus to keep himself from falling to his death, or into the mouth of a waiting monster. Steeling himself against the nauseating drop that fell away below him, he conjured the necessary anti-magic beneath his palms and forced himself to jump from the ledge. This way, he knew, he'd have less chance of taking some of the keep with him, and getting mixed up in a mass of flesh and stone.

Alex drew his anti-magic back into himself as he plummeted through the air, folding his body in on itself just in time, everything disappearing in a rush of wind. He emerged again with a heavy thump on the grass beside the gatehouse. It was an ungainly, hard landing, and Alex was convinced he'd broken something as a jolt of pain seared through his nerves.

He got up quickly, feeling another sudden sting in his ankle, though less painful than the last. Lifting the edge of his pant leg, he saw that the flesh beneath his sock was swollen, and guessed he must have unwittingly rolled his ankle when he fell. Wincing, he turned back toward the window he had jumped from. The flash of something pale and eerie moved in the distant room. Hollow eyes and a gaping mouth appeared in the vacant frame. A scream shivered through the air toward him, pressing him on as he hurried off toward the derelict town he knew rested in the distance, offering the hope of a safe haven.

I didn't look them in the eyes, he vowed to himself as he ran. *I definitely didn't look one in the eye.*

He ran and ran, dragging his leg behind him after feeling it buckle a few times, making him wonder if he hadn't broken something after all. Emerging through the tree-line, he saw the familiar sight of the abandoned buildings up ahead, and proceeded onward, past the tumbledown tavern, past the crumbling shops and ancient houses, past Thunder Road, and up toward the mountains. Lightning cracked at the summit, a shard of bright light hurtling toward the great hunk of rock from the maelstrom of black clouds that swirled around the unseen peaks.

It didn't seem particularly welcoming, but he could make out the ancient scaffold of a structure near the peak, and knew it would be the perfect vantage point from which to survey the whole area and keep an eye out for any approaching enemies. On higher ground, he'd have a better chance of survival.

Trying to ignore the dull throb of his foot, he walked toward the entrance to the steep mountain path. At the start of it, a cracked, peeling signpost stood up from a cluster of rocks, pointing the way. Alex paused to look at it, reading the name written across the damp, warped wood.

"Tempest Mountain," it read. "Do not feed the birds."

The name seemed familiar to Alex, but he couldn't quite pinpoint why as he began the long climb upward, toward the skeleton of an outpost. He just hoped it would prove sheltered enough for him to hide in while he came up with his next plan of action, and prayed that those wispy sprites weren't going to come after him. Right now, his brain was too frazzled by recent events to even begin to function properly, but he knew he'd have to come up with something soon, unless he wanted to stay trapped in this realm.

Up in the highest reaches, the wind whipped around Alex in biting blasts of ice-cold air. His lungs burned from the exertion of the climb and the thinning oxygen, and though the view was stunning from where he stood, the wind stung his eyes every time he opened them wide enough to see it. The forest stretched away into the distance, dipping where the keep stood, distinctly medieval and looming in the center of it all. But there were other dips too, giving away the locations of settlements nearby. A river glittered on the horizon, snaking through the forest and out to sea, farther than the eye could make out. Alex wondered if the other settlements were in the same state of dereliction as the town below the mountain—a smattering of ghost towns, echoing with the memory of bygone lives.

The outpost still lay ahead, never seeming to get any closer, and desperation for its protection pushed him onward. Turning back around, Alex continued to climb, his face numb from the cold, his path reaching ever higher until the rocks he grasped for were covered in thick ice and the ground below his feet was smothered in several inches of snow. Feeling anxious about how slippery everything had become, he paused to catch his breath, holding tight to a dry ridge of stone as he heaved in as much oxygen as he could, drawing deep for the strength to push on.

A shadow darkened the snow-covered shelf of rock in front of him. Someone was standing behind him. Despair made his heart sink—he had been caught. It took all the strength he had left to turn around, expecting to see Caius standing there behind him, having somehow evaded Vincent and his spirits, or even Vincent himself, possessed by the soul of a wispy devil, intent on killing him.

To his shock, it was neither.

Perched on the ledge behind him, head cocked, stood a gigantic bird, though Alex didn't feel as if the word "bird" did the magnificent creature justice. It stood at around ten feet tall, towering over Alex with a full plumage of beautiful, glistening feathers. They began as a pale silver around its head, flowing seamlessly down through a medley of pale blues, into a darker shade of teal, and then toward the cobalt end of the blue spectrum, which bled into the gargantuan wings, though the tip of each wing was colored a regal gold.

She was like nothing he had ever seen, except in paintings and illustrations.

He didn't know how he knew she was female either; he just thought she looked decidedly female as she dipped her head toward him, making him stagger back into the ice shelf. Above his head, he noticed strands of grass and branches sticking out, nest-like, from the ledge of rock.

Alex gasped with a mixture of awe and fear as she edged closer to him, and his eyes took in the stunning creature once more, noting the deadly-looking beak that faced him, the actual curve of it seeming to be made from solid silver. As concerned as he was by the potential ferocity of the beast, he was relieved to see that the bird seemed to be more curious about Alex than she was threatened by him. Bright black eyes, shot through with a bolt of electric blue, watched him intently.

Tempest, he remembered suddenly, confident that was who the mountain was named after—the great warbird upon which Leander had driven fear into the hearts of countless warriors. Although the specimen that stood before him was likely not the same one his ancestor had ridden upon, she seemed no less fearsome than the bird of legend. Curiously, he leveled his gaze at the creature, deliberating whether she would let him ride on her back, or whether that was an accident waiting to happen.

As if sensing Alex's thoughts, the huge bird tilted her head and moved even closer to where Alex had ended up, slumped against the rock face. Getting almost too close for comfort, bending her neck toward him, she tapped close to his fingers with her beak. Alex froze, only to marvel as he realized what she was doing. Staying perfectly still, he rested his hand flat on his leg. Gently, she sought out his fingers, nudging his hand until his palm lay the other way up. Bristling her feathers in apparent delight, she made a soft cooing sound in the back of her throat that sounded almost like a purr, and lay the sharpest point of her metallic beak carefully on the soft indent of his palm.

It made no scratch or cut, she was so gentle in her actions, and though Alex wasn't sure what it meant, it gave him hope.

He wondered if, somehow, she could get him to Falleaf House, even if they took a somewhat longer route than the usual portal-to-portal one. He wasn't at all sure how he was going to navigate to the mystery realm, or if the bird would even let him on her back. But he still had one of Lintz's beetle beacons in his pocket, shoved in there when Alypia came through from Stillwater, with a sliver of magic remaining within the intricate clockwork. An idea sprang to his mind.

If he could just latch onto Lintz's magical signature, he could follow the beetle on a path toward the fourth haven.

Glancing back toward the magnificent bird, Alex realized he was getting slightly ahead of himself.

First, how to fly a Thunderbird?

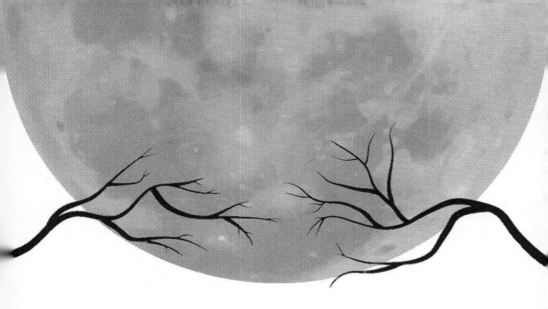

EPILOGUE

AFTER HIDING AWAY AWHILE, SEEKING OUT A SPOT where he might lick the stinging cuts of his wounded pride, Elias drifted sourly from the dank rafters of the turret room. He loathed surprises, and Alex's little stunt with the mind-trickery had been more surprise than he could stomach. It was good he didn't have a nervous system, he mused, knowing he'd be in a great deal of pain if he did happen to own something so grotesquely mortal.

He stretched languidly, glancing down to see the vaporous strands of his shadowy body trying to slip away. Rolling his galactic eyes, Elias struggled to grasp at the tendrils, trying to corral them back toward him. They had a mind of their own, and he knew precisely where they wanted to go. *But not yet*, he insisted silently, as his wispy form lunged toward a piece of torso that had almost reached the far wall.

Smugly, he thought about the overconfidence of the Spellbreaker, who was so certain he was in charge of when and how Elias came and went from his life. It never ceased to amuse him, that Alex thought he had any say in the matter. Grinning at the memory of their last encounter, Elias delighted in the delicious irony of Alex's final action, accidentally stealing a piece of Elias's soul, thus connecting them for life, whether Alex liked it or not.

And he's sure to despise it, Elias thought with utter glee. *Though it serves him right for trying to outwit the wittiest of them all.* Elias grinned to himself, relishing the idea that the young man thought he'd seen the last of the shadow-man's silver-tongued, charming, handsome self, not realizing that what he had actually done was make the opposite true.

It thrilled Elias to plot his surprise revelation, just when the young Spellbreaker least expected it. There was a stubborn desire for delayed gratification too, wanting to make Alex beg for his returned presence, to appeal for his aid with heart-breaking desperation, and perhaps an apology for the way they had parted. *That* was what Elias wanted. Whether he'd be able to hold onto the sum of his parts until then remained to be seen.

And it was all going so well, too, he pouted as he moved from the turret room and swept through the hallways, wanting to stretch out whatever counted for limbs within his unique form. It was true, Elias mused. Everything *had* been running smoothly, secrets coming out left, right, and center, tumbling into Alex's path, a veritable breadcrumb trail that even the dumbest of idiots could have followed.

But then that web-faced ghoul obeyed my instruction a lit-tle too well, and that prim do-gooder decided to bat her watery blue eyes at our weak-hearted friend, and suddenly I am the bad guy, he huffed, not sure how many more times he could say it was an accident. He was certain "sorry" was supposed to make everything better, but apparently not in this case. Besides, he mused, it was like Alex himself had said—if his father hadn't run, his father wouldn't have died. He knew he might be para-phrasing slightly, but he was pretty sure he had the gist of Alex's sentiments. And yet *he* was still the one being made to feel bad, when *he* had been the one who had tried to save the guy. It didn't sit well with Elias, not one bit. It was too real, too raw, too like a bygone Elias.

Still, the spirit lines would be an invaluable tool. Oh, yes—when the time came for Alex to force the counter-spell into Virgil's nasty head, the Spellbreaker would have memories on his side.

A memory of Alex and the girl in the turret room flashed through Elias's mind, sickeningly sweet. Perhaps he shouldn't have spirited away the love of Alex's life, however nauseated their blossoming relationship made him feel. He had known, even before he'd done it, that it would probably get him into more trouble than it was worth, and yet he hadn't been able to help himself. Like a naughty schoolboy, he'd gone against his better judgment, snatching her up from the hallway and bun-dling her out of sight, dumping her at the foot of the moun-tain, wanting her to be eaten by something particularly nasty. Alas, he sighed, it was not to be, making him wonder what a shadow-man had to do to get a wolf these days, or maybe a nest full of Thunderbird chicks to give her a peck, as a bit of an afternoon snack. If there had been any around, they'd let him down, especially thanks to Caius's foolish intervention.

That man was more messed up than any of the royals, in Elias's mind. *Well, apart from Julius*, he mused. *At least with Alypia and Virgil*—he paused to chuckle at the name—*you know what you're getting, but that old coot is a whole bundle of mixed up hurt and nonsense. By rights, they should have locked him up too. But then again, there's always a crazy uncle in the family, and I suppose royals are no exception*, he pondered, deeply pleased with himself and his judgmental musings.

With sullen disappointment, Elias realized he was going to have to shelve his devious plans for Ellabell for a while. At least now, the goody two-shoes couldn't warn Alex away from him, considering they were bound together in a way that trounced even the supposedly close bond of their vomit-inducing romance. Elias and Alex were now bound by the soul, and Elias could not have been more overjoyed, knowing the delectable misery he would inflict upon the Spellbreaker in revealing their newly forged link. Only in jest, of course. He wasn't a monster.

As he moved through the hallways, sweeping from shadow to shadow, jumping up every so often at an inmate's cell-grate, just to scare the living daylights out of whomever peered outward, his mind turned to his plump, toady accomplice.

He shuddered dramatically. *She's more goblin-amphibian hybrid than actual woman*, he sniggered to himself, though his thoughts on her were less than jovial. He had never been more furious with the old hag, who'd thought it was her place to warn him to keep out of things while she tried to "smooth things over," even though *she* was the true meddler. He was certain he could have resolved things by himself, without her acting as clumsy mediator. The painted old toad had only made things worse, as far as he was concerned.

In fact, it had been partially because of her—and partially because of the missing piece of his soul—that he'd been hiding out in the first place, away from prying eyes, in case she tried to get him to do something. He didn't need her and her lurid pink lips, not when he was perfectly capable of fixing things by himself. He'd been doing just fine, after all, until she came along and interfered, although he had to admit it was nice not to feel the weight of their curse upon them anymore. Almost everything was out in the open, and his tongue was loosened— never had anything felt more glorious.

"I might still have a whole soul left if it weren't for you, you fat oaf!" he muttered into the empty hallway, glancing around rapidly in case she suddenly appeared, having heard him, ready to give him another lecture. He could still hear the echo of her screeching voice from the last time.

He cackled as he swooped toward the cell he knew Alypia was in. Drifting down, he lounged against a cozy armchair, propping his misty head on his vaporous hand, sitting up as he realized his face kept falling through the insubstantial shadows of his palm. She was staring strangely into the fire, her arms still pinned behind her back. A great woman brought low, barely recognizable as the striking woman who had reigned supreme over Stillwater House. Had Elias been anyone else, he might have felt a little sorry for her. As it was, he didn't.

Tut, tut, bringing your father into all of this, he chided silently. *You can't always go running to daddy when things get tough.* In truth, even Elias was a little afraid of Julius, and didn't like the idea of having to deal with the top dog at any point down the road. He just hoped Alex could get himself back on track before the king decided it was time for a visit. Elias shuddered at the thought, ripples flowing through his silky form.

Bored by her relative lack of action, he swept through the hallway and up to the closed, broken door of the room where the portal to Falleaf had been, only to quickly back out of it again at the sight of hollow eyes and gaping mouths turned sharply in his direction. As amused as he was to see how things with the royals would play out, the outcome looked decidedly grim for Caius, even by Elias's standards. He didn't think he could stomach the sight of the otherworldly spirits sucking the life out of the old man, not without a bucket of popcorn and a comfier seat, anyway. It made him positively uneasy, reminding him of bad times he didn't wish to remember.

At least they can't get me, he thought to himself, hurrying from the domain of such foul acts. Conjured specters were a vicious breed, and not one Elias wanted to be anywhere near. Once he was far enough away, he breezed through the corridors until he reached the open courtyard. Whistling a silent tune through hopelessly shifting lips, he pressed his shadowy palms to the wall where the portal had been, and felt for the buzz of its magical signature. Shivering as he connected with it, he floated effortlessly through the wall and into the realm of Stillwater.

Not again, he thought grumpily as the strands of his body

decided to attempt a getaway. Regathering the parts of himself he felt were most necessary and hoping the rest wouldn't stray too far, he swept up into the darkness of the ceiling and gazed down, unseen, from the ceiling. To his surprise, he saw that the prison force had successfully slipped through the portal and closed it—*The easy part,* he mused—and were beginning to wreak havoc on the upper classes. He was delighted to see it, reveling in the sight of noble mages being taken down a peg or two.

Just as long as nobody rings any kind of alarm, we'll all get along just swell, he thought, keeping an eye on anyone he thought looked shifty.

He trailed the small group, careful to keep a good distance from Demeter in case the ginger-haired halfwit decided to have an epiphany and sense his presence. He shot upward into the darkness as the group collided with the familiar figure of Helena, who ran into them halfway down one of the grand hallways Elias had always found somewhat vulgar, the tapestries and gold adornments bordering on tacky. The silver-haired girl still left an unsavory taste in Elias's mouth, but then, he'd never been a fan of anyone with royal blood running in their pampered, privileged veins.

Eavesdropping, he was pleased to hear they were doing their duty, filling Helena in on what had happened and asking for her assistance in what was to come.

You'd do anything to screw over your old bat of a mother, wouldn't you? he mused wryly as the silver-haired girl agreed to help. *You want her place in court, no doubt.* True, he was pleased the others had her on their side, but he still couldn't bring himself to warm to any sort of princess.

Satisfied, Elias decided to return to his Spellbreaker in the hopes of watching him from afar, until he could select the right moment to strike. He knew the exact look of despair that would appear on Alex's face at the sight of his shadowy self returned, and the thought of it made him giddy with pleasure.

Since it was still daylight as Elias pushed back through to Kingstone Keep and soared toward the mountain, he wasn't sure how close he'd be able to get to his unwilling charge. But as he neared, he found he could move toward the Spellbreaker, even in broad daylight. This new skill thrilled him. Clapping his wispy hands together in soundless joy, he was pleased to see all his fronds had been restored to him too. It seemed the traitorous tendrils had been off seeking Alex.

Well, you've found him, Elias noted with a haughty flick of his shadowy hair. *Now, can we cooperate?* The remaining wisps coiled closer to him, giving him more solidity than he'd had in weeks. It felt almost strange, not to have to go chasing after the various absconding vapors of his being, but he certainly wasn't displeased at this turn of events. Another unexpected pleasure of having a piece of one's soul torn out and stolen, he mused— as well as being away from all those various pesky barriers.

Peering from the empty nest on the rocky outcrop above Alex's head, praying no chicks suddenly appeared with an appetite for shadowy half-beings, he watched as the great, exquisite bird pressed the very tip of her sharp beak into Alex's palm. Elias wondered if Alex knew how dangerous these creatures were, but it seemed the boy was more fearless than Elias had given him credit for. He saw Alex lift his hand to the side of the bird's face, stroking the soft, downy silver feathers there. With a creature as truly majestic as this, even Elias had no time for sass.

Glancing curiously at the boy he had grown attached to, like a brother or an uncle or an annoying itch it was impossible to be rid of, he pondered whether the Spellbreaker would be brave enough to walk—or in this case, fly—in the footsteps of his ancestors, and try to ride the beast. Even Elias had to admit he was impressed at Alex finding a Thunderbird, and a friendly one at that, all the way up here in these forgotten lands. It was a place where Thunderbirds had once flourished, but nobody remembered them now. They had been forgotten about, left to fall into the depths of legend, to be read about in books and seen in paintings, nothing more. He speculated upon how the beautiful bird knew what Alex was, having undoubtedly never seen a Spellbreaker in its lifetime. Perhaps it was in their blood, just as riding them was in Alex's.

Birds of a feather, he smirked.

In truth, Elias wished his friend well. To him, Alex was a friend, with views and goals paralleling his own. There was more similarity between them than there was difference, though Elias knew Alex wasn't ready to see that yet. When he was, Elias would be there. They shared the desire to make the Head pay the ultimate price, and the wish to make him do the spell, if at all possible, although Elias's motives were somewhat more personal. With everything Alex had learned, Elias's optimism had grown, despite his usual distaste for positivity.

The boy has come far, he mused, dwelling upon all the delicious dark spells the young man had been learning, and the many joyous uses for such things. They could certainly be utilized in bringing down those Elias loathed. He imagined this must be what fatherhood felt like, just without all the gross parts, and the aftercare, and most of the other parts in between.

Still, he felt true fondness for the boy. He wasn't so heartless as to believe he hadn't inflicted pain upon Alex, thanks to his role in Alexei Webber's death. He only hoped a second chance at forgiveness would come in time, when he was better able to meet the challenge, without letting his own personal pettiness get in the way... though he did so enjoy his petty side. It was one of his half-life's greatest, and in some ways only, delights.

Enough of that, he scolded himself. *No more stealing Alex's friends, no more open dislike for his little girlfriend, no more slip-ups. It has to be sweetness and light from now on.*

His hopes were too high now for any more blunders. The dream of getting his final revenge on the Head, forcing the skeletal cretin to give his life for the greater good, mirroring the way he had once tried to take Elias's life, was slowly becoming reality.

Now, if Alex could just run the gauntlet of Falleaf House and retrieve that pesky book, they might stand a chance. Elias had rarely come across a safe he couldn't crack, and the knowledge that he hadn't been able to retrieve the ancient book vexed him. He was intrigued to see if his protégée could do what he could not.

It will be your moment, Webber, to show us all your worth. He grinned, teeth flashing, as he watched Alex. *But will you fly or will you fall?*

Ready for the PENULTIMATE book in Alex's story?

Dear Reader,

Thank you for reading The Keep.

The next book is called **The Test**, and it is the penultimate book in the series as we move toward the grand finale in Book 6!

The Test releases **August 30th, 2017.**

Visit: www.bellaforrest.net for details.

I'll see you there!

Love,

Bella x

P.S. Sign up to my VIP email list and I'll send you a personal heads up when my next book releases:

www.morebellaforrest.com

(Your email will be kept 100% private and

you can unsubscribe at any time.)

P.P.S. I'd also love to hear from you—come say hi on **Instagram** or **Twitter** or **Facebook**. I do my best to respond :)

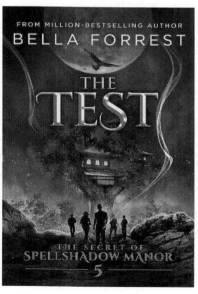

ALSO BY BELLA FORREST

THE SECRET OF SPELLSHADOW MANOR

The Secret of Spellshadow Manor (Book 1)
The Breaker (Book 2)
The Chain (Book 3)
The Keep (Book 4)
The Test (Book 5)

THE GENDER GAME (Completed series)

The Gender Game (Book 1)
The Gender Secret (Book 2)
The Gender Lie (Book 3)
The Gender War (Book 4)
The Gender Fall (Book 5)
The Gender Plan (Book 6)
The Gender End (Book 7)

A SHADE OF VAMPIRE SERIES

Series 1: Derek & Sofia's story
A Shade of Vampire (Book 1)
A Shade of Blood (Book 2)
A Castle of Sand (Book 3)
A Shadow of Light (Book 4)
A Blaze of Sun (Book 5)
A Gate of Night (Book 6)
A Break of Day (Book 7)

Series 2: Rose & Caleb's story
A Shade of Novak (Book 8)
A Bond of Blood (Book 9)
A Spell of Time (Book 10)
A Chase of Prey (Book 11)
A Shade of Doubt (Book 12)
A Turn of Tides (Book 13)
A Dawn of Strength (Book 14)
A Fall of Secrets (Book 15)
An End of Night (Book 16)

Series 3: The Shade continues with a new hero...
A Wind of Change (Book 17)
A Trail of Echoes (Book 18)
A Soldier of Shadows (Book 19)
A Hero of Realms (Book 20)
A Vial of Life (Book 21)
A Fork of Paths (Book 22)
A Flight of Souls (Book 23)
A Bridge of Stars (Book 24)

Series 4: A Clan of Novaks
A Clan of Novaks (Book 25)
A World of New (Book 26)
A Web of Lies (Book 27)
A Touch of Truth (Book 28)
An Hour of Need (Book 29)
A Game of Risk (Book 30)
A Twist of Fates (Book 31)
A Day of Glory (Book 32)

Series 5: A Dawn of Guardians
A Dawn of Guardians (Book 33)
A Sword of Chance (Book 34)
A Race of Trials (Book 35)
A King of Shadow (Book 36)
An Empire of Stones (Book 37)
A Power of Old (Book 38)
A Rip of Realms (Book 39)
A Throne of Fire (Book 40)
A Tide of War (Book 41)

Series 6: A Gift of Three
A Gift of Three (Book 42)
A House of Mysteries (Book 43)
A Tangle of Hearts (Book 44)
A Meet of Tribes (Book 45)
A Ride of Peril (Book 46)
A Passage of Threats (Book 47)

A SHADE OF DRAGON TRILOGY
A Shade of Dragon 1
A Shade of Dragon 2
A Shade of Dragon 3

A SHADE OF KIEV TRILOGY
A Shade of Kiev 1
A Shade of Kiev 2
A Shade of Kiev 3

DETECTIVE ERIN BOND (Adult thriller/mystery)
Lights, Camera, Gone
Write, Edit, Kill

BEAUTIFUL MONSTER DUOLOGY
Beautiful Monster 1
Beautiful Monster 2

For an updated list of Bella's books, please visit her website: www.bellaforrest.net

Join Bella's VIP email list and she'll personally send you an email reminder as soon as her next book is out. Sign up here: www.morebellaforrest.com

Made in the USA
Lexington, KY
20 July 2017